D1058325

LIBRARY
ST. LOUIS COMMUNITY COLLEGE
AT FLORISSANT VALLEY

If you enjoyed this book, try some of our other literature in translation:

The Missing Bureaucrat by Hans Scherfig
Translated by Frank Hugus from the Danish, $8.95 paper
Stolen Spring by Hans Scherfig
Translated by Frank Hugus from the Danish, $7.95 paper
Love & Solitude: Selected Poems 1916–1923
by Edith Södergran
Translated by Stina Katchadourian from the Swedish, $6.95 paper
Laterna Magica by William Heinesen
Translated by Tiina Nunnally from the Danish, $7.95 paper
Witness to the Future by Klaus Rifbjerg
Translated by Steve Murray from the Danish, $8.95 paper
The First Polka by Horst Bienek
Translated by Ralph Read from the German, $7.95 paper

And coming later this year:

Katinka by Herman Bang
Translated by Tiina Nunnally from the Danish, $8.95 paper
Peasants and Masters by Theodor Kallifatides
Translated by Thomas Teal from the Swedish, $8.95 paper
Niels Lyhne by Jens Peter Jacobsen
Translated by Tiina Nunnally from the Danish, $19.95 cloth
Another Metamorphosis & Other Fictions by Villy Sørensen
Translated by Tiina Nunnally & Steve Murray from the Danish,
$8.95 paper

Cloth editions of the above books are also available.
Please write for a catalog—we do American books too.

To order, send check or money order, including $1.50 postage & handling
for first book, 50¢ for each additional book, to:

Fjord Press

P.O. Box 16501, Seattle, WA 98116

PELLE THE CONQUEROR

Pelle the Conqueror

VOLUME 1: CHILDHOOD

Martin Andersen Nexø

Translated from the Danish by Steven T. Murray

(based on the 1913 translation
by Jessie Muir)

Edited and with an Afterword by
Tiina Nunnally

Fjord Press
Seattle
1989

Translation copyright © 1989 by Steven T. Murray
All rights reserved. No part of this book may be reproduced in any form, except
for the purposes of a review, without the written permission of the publisher.

Title of Danish edition: *Pelle Erobreren, Første Bog: Barndom*
Originally published in 1906 by Gyldendalske Boghandel, Nordisk Forlag,
Copenhagen

Published and distributed by:
Fjord Press
P.O. Box 16501
Seattle, Washington 98116
(206) 625-9363

Editor: Tiina Nunnally
Design & typography: Fjord Press Typography, Seattle
Cover design: Art Chantry Design, Seattle
Proofreading: Verna Murray & Julie Carter
Front cover photograph: Rolf Konow, © 1988
Frontispiece & back cover photograph: The Royal Library, Copenhagen
Printed by Malloy Lithographing, Inc., Ann Arbor

Library of Congress Cataloging in Publication Data:

Andersen Nexø, Martin, 1869–1954.
   Pelle the conqueror.

   (Fjord modern classics ; no. 1)
   Translation of: Pelle Erobreren.
   "Based on the 1913 translation by Jessie Muir."
   Contents: v. 1. Childhood.
   I. Murray, Steven T.   II. Nunnally, Tiina.
III. Title.   IV. Series.
PT8175.N4P413   1989   839.8'1372   89-7837
ISBN 0-940242-41-9 (v. 1 : alk. paper)
ISBN 0-940242-40-0 (pbk. : v. 1 : alk. paper)

Printed in the United States of America
First edition, 1989

PELLE

THE

CONQUEROR

VOLUME ONE
CHILDHOOD

I

It was the first of May, 1877, just at dawn. From the sea the mist came sweeping in, a gray trail that lay heavily on the water. There was movement in it here and there; it seemed about to lift, but closed in again, leaving only a strip of beach with two old boats lying keel uppermost upon it. The prow of a third boat and a bit of breakwater showed dimly in the fog bank a few paces off. At regular intervals a smooth gray wave would come gliding out of the mist up over the clattering pebbles of the beach, and then withdraw again; it was as if some great beast lay hidden out there in the fog, lapping at the land.

A couple of hungry crows were busy with a puffy black object down there, probably the carcass of a dog. Each time the licking wave glided in, the crows rose and hovered a few feet up in the air with their legs extended straight down toward their booty, as if invisibly attached. When the water sighed back out again, they dropped down and buried their heads in the carrion, but kept their wings spread, ready to lift off before the next lick of the wave. This was repeated with the regularity of clockwork.

A shout came vibrating in across the harbor, and a little later the heavy sound of oars creaking on the edge of a boat. The sound grew more distant and finally stopped entirely. But then a bronze bell began to ring—it must have been at the end of the jetty. Out of the distance, where the stroke of the oars had vanished, came the answering sound of a horn. They continued to answer each other every couple of minutes.

The town could not be seen, but now and then the silence up there was broken by the sound of a quarryman's iron cleats on the cobblestones. For a long time the sharp ringing could be heard, until it suddenly ceased as he turned a corner. Then a door was opened, followed by the sound of a loud morning yawn; and someone began to sweep the sidewalk. Windows were opened here and there, and various sounds floated out to greet the gray day. "You little pig, have you gone and wet the bed again?" a woman's sharp voice scolded, followed by quick, loud slaps and the crying of a child. A shoemaker began pounding leather, and as he worked fell to singing a hymn:

> But One is worthy of our hymn, O brothers:
> The Lamb on Whom the sins of all men lay.

The melody was one of Mendelssohn's "Songs Without Words."

On the bench below the church wall sat a boat's crew, staring out to sea. They were leaning forward, their hands clasped and hanging between their knees, and puffing on their pipes. All three wore earrings to ward off colds and other evils, and all sat in exactly the same position, as if each were afraid of being the slightest bit different from the others.

A traveling salesman came sauntering down from the hotel and approached the fishermen. He had his coat collar turned up around his ears, and shivered in the chill morning air. "Is anything the matter?" he asked politely, doffing his cap. His voice sounded hoarse.

One of the fishermen moved his knuckle slightly in the direction of his cap. He was the head man of the boat's crew. The others stared straight ahead, unperturbed, their gazes stony.

"I mean, since the bell's ringing and the pilot boat's out blowing her horn," the traveler went on. "Are they expecting a ship?"

"Could be. You never can tell," answered the head man distantly.

The stranger looked as if he were deeply insulted, but restrained himself. It was only their usual secretiveness, their inveterate distrust of anyone who didn't speak their dialect and look exactly like they did. They sat there inwardly uneasy in spite of their wooden exterior, stealing glances at him on the sly and wishing he would get lost. He felt tempted to tease them a little.

"Good Lord, maybe it's a secret?" he said, laughing.

"Not that I know of," replied the fisherman crustily.

"Well, of course I don't expect something for nothing. And besides, it wears out your jaw to keep opening and shutting it. How much do you generally charge?" He took out his coin purse; it was his intention to insult them now.

The other fishermen cast stolen glances at their leader. If only he didn't run them aground!

The head man took his pipe from between his teeth and turned to his companions: "No, as I was saying, there are some folks who just travel around peddling all kinds of stuff." He warned them with his eyes, and the expression on his face was unreadable. His companions nodded. They were relishing this, as the traveling salesman could see from their smirking looks.

He was furious. Here he stood, being treated as if he were air and made fun of! "Damn it, you fellows! Haven't you even learned to give a civil answer to a civil question?" he said angrily.

The fishermen looked back and forth at each other, taking mute counsel.

"No, but I'll tell you what—she'll have to come sooner or later," said the head man at last.

"What do you mean, 'she'?"

"The steamer, of course. And she generally comes about this time. There you have it!"

"Naturally—of course," jeered the traveler. "But isn't it a little unwise to talk so loud about it?"

The fishermen had turned their backs on him and sat scraping out their pipes.

"We're not quite so free with our speech here as some people, and yet we make a living," said the head man to the others. They growled their approval.

As the stranger wandered on down the hill to the harbor, the fishermen gazed after him with relief. "What a talker!" said one. "He sure wanted to show off, but you gave him something to think about for a while."

"Yeah, you can bet it got his goat, all right," replied the head man, satisfied with himself. "It's this fancy trash you have to watch out for the most."

Halfway down the harbor hill, an innkeeper stood at his door yawning. The morning stroller repeated his question to him, and received an immediate answer—the man was from Copenhagen.

"Well you see, we're expecting the steamer from Ystad today, with a big cargo of slaves—cheap Swedish laborers, that is, who live on black bread with lard and salt herrings, and do the work of three. That sort ought to be flogged on the navel with the hot end of an icicle, and those brutish farmers too. You wouldn't like a little early morning dram, I don't suppose?"

"No thank you, I don't think so—this early."

"Well, suit yourself. I can't make change for that small an order."

Down at the harbor a number of farmers' wagons were already waiting, and new ones were arriving at full gallop every moment. The newcomers guided their teams as far to the front as possible, examined their neighbors' horses with a critical eye, and settled themselves into a half-doze, slumped down with their fur collars turned up around their ears and a big, clear drop hanging under their nose. Customs men in uniform, and pilots, looking like monster penguins, wandered about restlessly, peering out to sea and listening. Every moment the bell at the end of the jetty rang, and was answered by the pilot boat's horn somewhere out there in the fog bank hanging over the sea, with a long, dreary hoot, like the howl of some suffering animal.

"What was that noise?" asked a farmer who had just arrived, catching up his reins in fright. His fear communicated itself to his horses, and they stood staring with heads raised, listening in the direction of the sea, with questioning terror in their eyes.

"It was only the sea serpent passing wind," answered a customs officer. "He always suffers from wind in this foggy weather. He's a wind-gulper, you see." The customs men put their heads together and laughed.

Merry sailors dressed in blue with white scarves around their necks went around patting the horses, or pricking their nostrils with a straw to make them rear. When the farmers woke up and scolded them, they laughed with delight and sang:

> A sailor he must go through
> A deal more bad than good, good, good!

A big pilot in an Iceland sweater and woolen mittens was rushing anxiously about with a megaphone in his hand, growling like a nervous bear. Now and then he climbed up on the breakwater, put the megaphone to his mouth, and roared out over the water: "Do—you— hear—anything?" The roar rode out on the long swells, up and down, for a long time, leaving behind an oppressive silence. Suddenly it returned from the town above, in the form of a confused babble that made people laugh.

"N-o-o!" was heard a little later in a thin and long-drawn-out cry from the depths. And again the horn was heard, a long, hoarse sound that came rocking in on the waves and burst gurgling in the splash under the wharf and on the slips.

The farmers were out of it all. They dozed a little or sat flicking their whips to pass the time. But everyone else was in suspense. A crowd had gradually gathered at the harbor—fishermen, sailors waiting to be hired, and master artisans who were too restless to stay in their workshops. They came down in their leather aprons, and breathlessly started discussing the situation; they used nautical expressions, most of them having been to sea in their youth. The coming of the steamer was always an event that brought people to the harbor; but today she had a great many people on board, and she was already an hour late. The dangerous fog kept the suspense at high pressure; but as the time passed, the excitement gave way to a mood of dull oppression. Fog is the seaman's worst enemy, and there were many unpleasant possibilities. In the best case, the ship had gone inshore too far north or south, and now lay somewhere out at sea hooting and heaving the lead, without daring to move. The captain would be storming and the sailors jumping around like cats. Stop!—Half-speed ahead!—Stop!—Half-speed astern! The first engineer would be at the engine himself, his hair gray and frizzy with nervous excitement. Down in the engine room, where they knew nothing at all, they would strain their ears painfully for any sound, and all to no purpose. But up on deck every man would be on the alert for his life; the helmsman wet with the sweat of his anxiety to watch every movement of the captain's directing hand, and the lookout on the fore-castle peering and listening into the fog until he could hear his own heart beating, while the suspense held every man on deck on tenterhooks. And the foghorn hooted its warning. But perhaps the ship already lay on the bottom of the sea.

Everyone knew all this; every man had in some way been through this overcharged suspense—as cabin boy, stoker, captain, cook—and felt something of it in his blood again now. Only the farmers were unaffected by it; they dozed, woke up with a start, and yawned audibly.

The seafarers and the peasants always had difficulty getting along; they were as different as land and sea. But today the indifferent attitude of the peasants made the seamen eye them with suppressed rage. The fat pilot had already had several altercations with them for being in his way; and when one of them laid himself open to criticism, he was on him in an instant.

It was an elderly farmer, who woke from his nap with a start as his head fell forward; he looked impatiently at his watch and said, "It's getting rather late. The captain can't seem to find his stall today."

"More likely he's dropped into an inn on the way," said the pilot, his eyes gleaming with malice.

"Why sure," answered the farmer, without thinking for a moment about the nature of the paths of the sea. The listeners laughed exultantly and passed the mistake around the harbor square. People crowded around the unfortunate man, and someone cried, "How many inns are there between here and Sweden?"

"Yes, it's too easy to get hold of liquids out there, that's the worst of it," the pilot went on. "Otherwise any porridge-eater could captain a ship. All he has to do is keep well to the right of Mads Hansen's farm, and he's got a straight road ahead of him. And it's a devil of a fine road! Telegraph wires and ditches and a row of poplars on each side—just improved by the parish council. Just wipe the porridge off your mustache, kiss the old woman, and climb up onto the bridge. Has the engine been oiled, Hans? All right then, off we go, in God's name—hand me my best whip!" He imitated the way the peasants talked. "Watch out for the inns, Papa!" he added in a shrill falsetto. There were peals of laughter, which had a malicious sound because of the oppressive mood.

The farmer sat quite calmly and accepted the deluge, only lowering his head a little. When the laughter had almost died away, he pointed at the pilot with his whip and remarked to the bystanders, "That's a hell of a head on that kid for his age! Whose father are you, my boy?" he went on, turning to the pilot.

This raised a laugh, and the thick-necked pilot swelled with rage. He seized hold of the bed of the wagon and shook it so that the farmer had a hard time keeping his seat. "You withered old clodhopper, you pig-breeder, you dung-carter!" he roared. "Do you think you can come here and call grown-up people 'boy'? And give your opinions on navigation into the bargain, eh? You lousy old money-grubber! No, if you ever felt like taking off your greasy nightcap to anybody but your deacon, then take it off to the captain who can find his harbor in a fog like this. You can give him my kind regards and tell him I said so." He let go of the wagon so suddenly that it rocked over to the other side.

"I may as well take it off to you, since the other one doesn't seem able to find us today," said the farmer with a laugh, and took off his fur cap, revealing a large bald head.

"You'd better cover up that baby rump right now, or I'll be damned if I won't give it something!" cried the pilot, blind with rage, and started to clamber up onto the cart.

All at once, as if through a telephone, there came a faint, distant croaking from the sea: "We—hear—a—steam—whistle!"

The pilot ran down to the breakwater, striking out as he passed the farmer's horses so they reared. Men made ready at the mooring posts and came dragging up gangplanks with frantic speed. Wagons that had hay in the back, as if they had come to pick up cattle, began to move without having anywhere to drive to, going round and round one spot. Everything was in motion. Labor hirers with red noses and cunning eyes came hurrying down from the sailors' tavern where they had been keeping themselves warm.

Then, as if a huge claw had come down upon the activity, everything suddenly stood still again in a strained effort to hear. The distant, vanishing hoot of a steam whistle whined newborn, somewhere a long way off. People crept together into groups and stood motionless, listening and casting angry glances at the restless wagons. Was it real, or was it a creation of the intense wishes of so many? Perhaps a warning to everyone that at that very moment the ship had gone to the bottom? The sea always sends word of its evil doings: when the breadwinner is taken his family will hear a shutter creak, or three taps on the windows facing the sea—there are so many ways.

But now it sounded again, and this time the sound came in little waves over the water, the same quivering half-whistle that gaddis ducks make when they take off; it was alive. The foghorn answered it out in the channel, and the bronze bell at the end of the jetty; then the horn once more, and the steam whistle in the distance. So it went on, a guideline of sound being spun between the land and the indefinite gray out there, back and forth. Here on solid land one could distinctly sense how they were groping their way by sound out there. The hoarse whistle slowly increased in volume, sounding now a little to the south, now to the north, but growing steadily louder. Then other sounds broke through, the heavy scraping of iron against iron, the noise of the screw when it was reversed or proceeded forward again.

The pilot boat glided slowly out of the fog, keeping to the middle of the channel, moving steadily inward and hooting incessantly. By its sound it was towing an invisible world behind it, where hundreds of voices murmured thickly amid shouting and clanging and tramping of feet—a world that floated blindly in space somewhere close by. Then a shadow began to form in the fog where no one had expected it, and the little steamer emerged—looking enormous in the first moment of surprise—in the middle of the harbor entrance.

At this the last remnants of suspense burst and scattered, and everyone had to do something to shake it off. They seized the heads of the farmers' horses and pushed them back, clapped their hands, attempted jokes, or only laughed noisily while they stamped on the cobblestones.

"Good voyage?" asked a score of voices at once.

"All right!" answered the captain cheerfully.

And now he too is relieved, and rattles off shouts of command; the backing propeller churns up the water, hawsers fly through the air, and the steam winch starts up with a ringing metallic clang. The vessel works herself broadside in toward the wharf.

In the well between the forecastle and the bridge, beneath the upper and the after decks, there is a swarm of people, a curiously stupid swarm, like sheep that get up onto each other's backs and gape. "What a cargo of cattle!" cries the fat pilot up to the captain, tramping delightedly on the breakwater with his wooden-soled boots. There are sheepskin caps, old military caps, mangy fox-red hats, and the women's winsome black kerchiefs. The faces are as different as old, wrinkled pigskin and young, ripening fruit, but want and expectancy and a certain greediness for life shine from all of them. The unfamiliarity of the moment lends a touch of stupidity to them, as they press forward, or climb to get a view over their neighbors' heads and stare open-mouthed at the land where the wages are said to be so high, and the aquavit so God-damned strong.

They see the fat, fur-clad farmers and the men who have come down to engage laborers.

They don't know what to do with themselves, and are always getting in the way. Cursing, the sailors chase them from side to side of the ship, or throw hatches and packages at their feet without warning. "Look out, you Swedish devil!" cries a sailor who has to open the iron doors. The Swede backs up in bewilderment, but his hand involuntarily flies to his pocket and nervously fingers his big folding knife.

The gangplank is down, and the two hundred and fifty passengers stream ashore—stonemasons, longshoremen, maidservants, male and female day-laborers, stablemen, herdsmen, here and there a solitary little cowherd, and elegant tailors who keep far away from the rest. There are young men straighter and better built than any born on this island, and poor old men more worn with toil and want than they ever become here in Denmark. There are also faces among them that gleam with malice—and others sparkling with energy, or disfigured by great scars.

Most of them are in work clothes and only possess what they stand in. Here and there is a man with some tool on his shoulder—a shovel or a crowbar. Those who have any luggage get it turned inside out by the customs officers: fabric is so cheap in Sweden. Now and then some girl with a tendency toward plumpness has to put up with the officers' coarse jokes. There, for instance, is pretty Sara from Simrishamn, whom everybody knows. Every fall she goes home, and comes back every spring in the most blessed circumstances. "That's contraband," say the customs officers, pointing; they say the same witticism every year, and they look forward to it. But Sara, who usually has such a quick temper and ready tongue, is staring shyly at the ground—she has fourteen yards of cloth wrapped around her under her dress.

The farmers are wide awake now. Those who dare, leave their horses and walk into the crowd; the others choose their laborers with their eyes and call them over. Each one takes his man's measure—breadth of shoulders, modest manner, wretchedness; but they're afraid of the scarred and malicious faces, and leave them to the foremen of the large farms. Offers are made and conditions fixed, and every minute one or two Swedes climb up into the hay and are driven off.

A little to one side stood an elderly, stooped man with a sack on his back, holding a boy of eight or nine by the hand; at their feet lay a green chest. They eagerly watched the proceedings, and each time a cart drove off with some of their countrymen, the boy tugged impatiently at the hand of the old man, who answered with a reassuring word. The old man examined the farmers one by one with an anxious air, moving his lips all the while—he was thinking. His red, lashless eyes kept watering with the prolonged staring, and he wiped them with the edge of the coarse, dirty sack.

"Do you see that one over there?" he suddenly asked the boy, pointing to a fat little farmer with apple cheeks. "He looks like he'd be kind to children. Shall we try him, lad?"

The boy nodded gravely, and they made straight for the farmer. But when he heard that they were to go together, he wouldn't take them; the boy was far too little to earn his keep. And so it went every time.

It was Lasse Karlsson from Tommelilla in the Ystad district, and his son Pelle.

The island was not altogether strange to Lasse, for he had been here once before, about ten years ago; but he had been younger then, in the prime of life, so to speak, and had no little boy by the hand, from whom he refused to be separated for all the world—that was the difference. It was the year that the cow had been drowned in the marl pit, and Bengta was preparing to give birth. Things looked bad, but Lasse staked it all on one card and used the couple of kroner he got for the hide of the cow to go to Bornholm. When he came back in the fall, there were three mouths to feed—but then he had a hundred kroner to get through the winter with.

At that time Lasse had been equal to the situation, and he would still straighten his bowed shoulders whenever he thought of that exploit. Afterwards, whenever there were short supplies, he would talk of selling everything and going to Bornholm for good. But Bengta's health failed after this childbirth so late in life, and nothing came of it—not until she died after eight years of suffering, this very spring. Then Lasse sold their bit of furniture at a private auction, and made nearly a hundred kroner on it; that took care of paying the expenses of the long illness. The house and land belonged to the landlord. A green chest, which had been part of Bengta's dowry, was the only thing he kept. In it he packed their belongings and a few small things of Bengta's, and sent it on in advance with a horse-dealer who was driving to the port. Some of the junk that no one would bid on he stuffed into a sack, and with it on his back and the boy's hand clasped in his, he set out to walk to Ystad, where the steamer for Rønne lay. The few coins he had would just pay their passage.

He had been so sure of himself on the way, and had talked in a loud voice to Pelle about the country where the wages were so incredibly high, and where in some places you got meat or cheese to eat with your bread, and always beer, so that the water cart at harvest time did not come around for the laborers, but only for the cattle. And—why, if you liked you could drink aquavit like water, it was so cheap; but it was so strong that it knocked you down after the third shot. They made it from real grain, not from diseased potatoes, and they drank it at every meal. And the lad would never feel cold there, for they wore wool next to their skin, not this tow-linen that the wind blew right through. And a laborer who cooked for himself could easily make his two kroner a day. That was something different from their master's lousy 80 øre!

Pelle had often heard the same thing before—from his father, from Ole and Anders, from Karna and a hundred others who had been there. In the winter, when the air was thick with frost and snow and the plight of the poor, virtually everyone talked about it in the little villages back home. And in the minds of those who had not been on the island themselves but had only heard the tales about it, the ideas produced were as fantastic as the frost tracery on the windowpanes. Pelle was perfectly well aware that even the poorest boys there always wore their best clothes, and ate bread and drippings with sugar on it as often as they liked. There money lay like dirt by the roadside, and the Bornholmers did not even take the trouble to bend over and pick it up. But Pelle meant to pick it up, so that Papa Lasse would have to empty the junk out of the sack and clear out the locked compartment in the green chest to make room for it; and even that would hardly be enough. If only they could get started soon. He tugged at his father's hand impatiently.

"Now, now," said Lasse, almost in tears. "You'll have to give it time." He looked around, at a loss. Here he was in the midst of all this splendor and couldn't even find a humble situation for himself and the boy. He couldn't understand it. Had the whole world changed since his time? He trembled all the way down to his blotchy hands when the last cart drove off. For a few minutes he stood staring helplessly after it;

then he and the boy carried the green chest over to a wall, and walked hand in hand up toward the town.

Lasse's lips moved as he walked; he was thinking. He usually thought best when he talked out loud to himself, but today all his faculties were alert, and he was content just to move his lips.

As he trudged along, his mental excuses became audible. "Damn!" he exclaimed, shifting the sack higher up his back. "It's no good taking the first thing that comes along. Lasse's responsible for two, and he knows what he wants—so there! He's been in a foreign country before today, that's for sure! And the best always comes last, you know, lad."

Pelle was not paying much attention. He already felt consoled, and his father's words—that the best was yet in store for them—were to him only a feeble expression of a great truth: that the whole world would become theirs, with all that it contained in the way of wonders. He was already busy taking possession of it, open-mouthed.

He looked as if he would like to swallow the harbor with all its ships and boats, and the great stacks of lumber that looked as though they were hollow inside. This would be a great place to play, but there were no boys! He wondered whether the boys were like those at home; he hadn't seen any yet. Maybe they had a whole different way of fighting, but he would manage all right if only they would come at him one at a time. There was a big ship right up on land, and they were skinning it. So ships have ribs too, just like cows!

At the big wooden shed in the middle of the harbor square, Lasse put down the sack. He gave the boy a piece of bread and told him to stay and mind the sack; then he went farther up the hill and disappeared. Pelle was very hungry; holding the bread in both hands he munched at it greedily.

When he had picked the last crumbs off his sweater, he set about examining his surroundings. That black stuff in that big pot was tar. He knew it quite well, but had never seen so much at once. Damn! If you fell into that while it was boiling, it would be even worse than the brimstone pit in hell. And over there lay some enormous fishhooks, just like the ones hanging on thick iron chains from the ships' nostrils. He wondered whether there were still giants alive who could fish with hooks like that. Even Strong Johan wouldn't be able to!

He satisfied himself with his own eyes that the stacks of boards were really hollow, and that he could easily get down to the bottom of them, if only he hadn't had the sack to drag along. His father had said he was to mind the sack, and he never let go of it for a moment; since it was too heavy to carry, he had to drag it behind him from place to place.

He discovered a little boat, only just big enough for a man to lie down in, and full of holes bored in the bottom and sides. He investigated the shipbuilders' big grindstone, which was nearly as tall as a man. There were curved planks lying there, with nails in them as big as the sheriff's new tether-peg at home. And the thing that boat was tethered to — wasn't it a real cannon that they had planted in the ground?

Pelle looked at everything, and examined every single object in the appropriate manner — sometimes just spitting appraisingly on it, sometimes kicking it or scratching it with his penknife. If he came across some strange wonder that his mind couldn't take in any other way, he set himself astride it.

This was a whole new world, and Pelle was busy conquering it. He wouldn't leave a shred of it behind. If he had had his friends from Tommelilla here, he would have explained it all to them. Jeez, how they would stare! But when he went home to Sweden again, he would tell them all about it, and then they would probably call him a liar, he hoped.

He was sitting astride an enormous mast that stretched along the lumberyard upon some oak trestles. He hooked his feet together under the mast, as he had heard of knights doing in the olden days under their horses, and imagined himself seizing hold of a ring and lifting himself, horse and all. He sat on horseback in the midst of his newly discovered world, bursting with the pride of conquest, slapped the horse's croup and dug his heels into its sides, while he shouted a song at the top of his voice. He had had to let go of the sack to climb up there.

> Far up in Småland there danced little devils
> With loaded pistols and rifled gun;
> All the little devils they played on the fiddle,
> But on the piano Old Satan was the one.

In the midst of his noisy joy he looked up, suddenly started howling in terror, and dropped down onto the wood shavings. On top of the shed by the place where his father had left him stood a black man and two black, gaping hellhounds; the man was leaning halfway out over the ridge of the roof, menacingly. It was an old figurehead, but Pelle thought it was the archangel Satan himself, come to punish him for his bold song, and he set off at a run up the hill. A little way up he remembered the sack and stopped. He didn't care about the sack, and he wouldn't get a thrashing if he did leave it behind, for Papa Lasse never beat him. And that horrid devil would eat him up, at the very least, if he ventured down there again; he could see clearly how red the nostrils glowed, both on the devil and on the dogs.

But Pelle still hesitated. His father was so careful of that sack, and he would certainly be sad if he lost it—he might even cry, the way he did when he lost Mama Bengta. For perhaps the first time, the boy was being subjected to one of life's serious tests, and faced—as so many before him had faced—the choice between sacrificing himself and sacrificing others. His love for his father, his boyish pride, the sense of duty that is society's gift to the poor at birth—all of these determined his decision. He stood the test, but not bravely; he howled the whole time, with his eyes fixed immovably upon the Evil One and his hellhounds, while he crept back for the sack and then dragged it behind him at a quick run up the street.

Perhaps no one is a hero until the danger is past. But even then Pelle had no opportunity of shuddering at his own courage; for as soon as he was out of reach of the black man and the terror should have let go its grip on him, it merely assumed a new form. What had become of his father? He had said he would be back right away. What if he never came back at all? Maybe he had gone away so he could get rid of his little boy, who was nothing but trouble and made it difficult for him to get a job.

In despair, Pelle felt convinced that it would come to that, as he went off with the sack, sobbing. The same thing had happened to other children he knew well. But they wound up in the gingerbread house and were quite happy, and Pelle himself would be sure to... maybe he would even go to the king and be taken in there, and have the little princes for his playmates and his own little palace to live in. But Papa Lasse wouldn't get a thing, for now Pelle was angry and vindictive, although he was still sobbing with abandon. He would let him stand knocking at the door and begging to come in for three days, and only when he started to cry pitifully—no, he would have to let him in at once, for to see Papa Lasse cry hurt him more than anything in the world. But he wouldn't get a single one of the nails Pelle had filled his pockets with down in the lumberyard; and when the king's wife brought them coffee in bed . . .

Pelle ceased both his desperate tears and his happy fantasies—out of a tavern at the top of the hill came Papa Lasse, big as life. He looked overjoyed and was holding a bottle in his hand.

"Danish aquavit, lad!" he cried, waving the bottle. "Hats off to Danish aquavit! But why have you been crying? I see, you were afraid. And why were you afraid? Isn't your father's name Lasse—Lasse Karlsson from Kungstorp? And he's not one to quarrel with; he hits hard, he does, when he's pushed. Coming and scaring good little boys, damnation! They'd better watch out! Even if the whole wide world were full of flaming devils, Lasse's here and you don't have to be afraid."

During all this fierce talk he was tenderly wiping the boy's tear-stained cheeks and nose with the back of his rough hand, and hoisted the sack onto his back again. There was something touchingly feeble about his stooping figure, as he trudged back down to the harbor, boasting and comforting the boy and holding him by the hand. He tottered along in his big waterproof boots, the tabs of which stuck out at the side and bore an astonishing resemblance to Pelle's ears; out of the gaping pockets of his old winter coat protruded on one side his red handkerchief, on the other the bottle. His knees had loosened up a little now, and the sack threatened to get the better of him at any moment, pushing him forward and forcing him to go at a trot down the hill. He looked decrepit, and perhaps his boastful words helped to produce this effect. But his eyes beamed confidently, and he smiled down at the boy running along beside him.

They drew near to the shed, and Pelle turned cold with fear—the man was still standing up there. He went around to the other side of his father and tried to pull him out in a wide curve across the harbor square. "There he is again," he whimpered.

"So that's what was after you, is it?" said Lasse, laughing heartily. "And he's made of wood, too! Well, you really are the bravest lad I ever knew. There'd be no reason not to send you out to fight a dead chicken, if you had a stick in your hand!" Lasse went on laughing, and shook the boy good-naturedly. But Pelle was ready to sink into the ground with shame.

Down by the customhouse they met a farm foreman who had come too late for the steamer and hadn't hired any laborers. He stopped his wagon and asked Lasse if he was looking for a job.

"Yes, we both want one," replied Lasse briskly. "We want to be at the same farm—as the fox said to the goose."

The foreman was a big, stocky man, and Pelle shuddered in admiration of his father, who dared to speak to him so boldly.

But the big man laughed with good humor. "Then I suppose he's to be head man?" he said, flicking at Pelle with his whip.

"Yes, he certainly will be someday," said Lasse with conviction.

"He'll probably have to eat a few bushels of salt first. Well, I could use a herdsman, and I'll give you a hundred kroner for a year—though it'll be damned hard for you to earn them from what I can see. There'll always be a crust of bread for the boy, but of course he'll have to do what little he can. You're his grandfather, I suppose?"

"I'm his father—in the sight of God and man," answered Lasse proudly.

"Oh, indeed! Then you must still be fit for something, if you've come by him honestly. But climb up, if you know what's good for you; I don't have time to wait here. You won't get an offer like this every day."

Pelle thought a hundred kroner was an awful lot of money; Lasse, on the contrary, as the older and more sensible one, had a feeling that it was far too little. But, though he was not aware of it yet, the morning's events had greatly affected his positive outlook on the future. On the other hand, the dram had put him in a reckless and generous frame of mind. "All right then," he said with an expansive wave of his hand. "But the master must understand that we don't want salt herring and porridge three times a day. We must have a proper bedroom too—and Sundays off." He lifted the sack and the boy up into the wagon, and then climbed up himself.

The foreman laughed. "I see you've been here before, old man. But I think we'll be able to manage all that. You'll have roast pork with raisins and rhubarb pudding with pepper on it, just as often as you feel like opening your mouth."

They drove down to the dock for the chest, and then rolled out toward the country. Lasse, who recognized this and that, explained it all in full to the boy. He would take a pull at the bottle once in a while, careful not to let the foreman see it. Pelle was cold and burrowed into the straw, where he snuggled up close to his father.

"You take a swig," whispered Lasse, passing the bottle to him cautiously. "But make sure he doesn't see, for he's a sly one. He's a Jute."

Pelle didn't want any liquor. "What's a Jute?" he asked in a whisper.

"A Jute? Bless me, lad, don't you know that? It was the Jutes that crucified Christ. That's why they have to wander all over the world now, selling woolens and needles and things like that; and they always cheat wherever they go. Don't you remember the one who cheated Mama Bengta out of her beautiful hair? No, that must have been before your time. That was a Jute too. He came one day when I wasn't home, and unpacked all his fine wares—combs and pins with blue glass heads, and the finest kerchiefs. Women can't resist such fancy junk; they get like the rest of us when someone holds a liquor bottle to our nose. Mama Bengta had no money, but that sly devil said he would give her the finest kerchief if she would let him cut off just the tip of her braid.

And then he went and cut it off close to her neck. By the holy cross, she
was like flint and steel when she got mad—she chased him out of the
house with a poker. But he took the braid with him, and the kerchief
was trash, as you might expect. For the Jutes are cunning devils, who
crucified . . ." Lasse began all over again.

Pelle scarcely paid attention to his father's soft murmuring. It was
something about Mama Bengta, but she was dead now and lay in the
black earth; she no longer buttoned his undershirt down the back, or
warmed his hands when he was cold. So they put raisins in the roast
pork in this country, did they? They must have money like grass. There
was none lying around in the road, and the houses and farms were not
that fine either. But the most peculiar thing was that the earth here was
the same color as back home, even though it was a foreign country. In
Tommelilla he had seen a map where each country was a different color.
So that was a lie for sure!

Lasse had long since stopped talking, and slept with his head against
the boy's back. He had forgotten to hide the bottle.

Pelle was just going to push it down into the straw when the foreman—who as a matter of fact was not a Jute from Jutland, but a
Sjællander from Sjælland instead—suddenly turned around and caught
sight of it. He told the boy to throw it into the ditch.

By midday they reached their destination. Lasse woke up as they
drove onto the cobblestones in the large courtyard, and groped mechanically in the straw. But suddenly he recollected where he was, and
sobered up in an instant. So this was their new home, the only place
where they could live and have any future on this earth. And as he
looked out over the big courtyard—where the dinner bell was just
ringing, calling servants and day-laborers out of all the doors—all his
self-confidence vanished. A despairing feeling of helplessness overwhelmed him and made his face tremble with impotent concern for his
son.

His hands shook as he clambered down from the wagon; he stood
there bewildered and at the mercy of all the inquisitive glances from the
steps down to the basement of the big house. They were talking about
him and the boy, and laughing already. In his confusion he determined
to make as favorable a first impression as possible, and began to take off
his cap and bow to each one in turn; and the boy stood beside him and
did the same. They were rather like the clowns at the marketplace, and
the people around the basement stairs laughed out loud and bowed in
imitation, and then began shouting. But the foreman came back out to
the cart, and they quickly disappeared down the steps. From the big

house itself there came a far-off, monotonous sound that never ceased, and unconsciously added to their feeling of depression.

"Don't stand there playing the fool!" snapped the foreman. "Get down there with the others and put something in your belly! You'll have plenty of time to show off your monkeyshines to them later."

At these encouraging words, the old man took the boy's hand and trudged over to the basement steps with despair in his heart, weeping inside for Tommelilla and Kungstorp. Pelle clung close to him in fear. The unknown had suddenly become an evil monster in the imagination of both of them.

Down in the basement passage the strange, persistent sound was louder, and they both realized that it was a woman weeping.

II

Stone Farm, which for the future was to be Lasse and Pelle's home, was one of the largest farms on the island. But old people knew that when their grandparents were children it was only a two-horse cottage belonging to a certain Vevest Køller, a grandson of Jens Kofoed, the liberator of Bornholm. During his time, the cottage became a farm. He worked himself to death on it, and begrudged food both to himself and others. And these two things—miserable food and land-grabbing—became hereditary in that family.

The fields in this part of the island had been stone and heather not so very many generations ago. Poor people had broken the ground and worn themselves out, one set after another, to keep it in cultivation. Surrounding Stone Farm lived only tenant farmers and two-horse families who had bought their land with sweat and hunger, and would sooner have thought of selling their parents' grave than their tiny property; they stuck to it until they died or some misfortune overtook them.

But the Stone Farm family always wanted to buy, and expand their property, and they could only buy when disaster struck. Wherever a bad harvest or sickness or bad luck with the livestock hit a man hard enough to make him reel, the Køllers bought. Thus Stone Farm grew, acquiring many buildings and much importance; it became as harsh a neighbor as the sea is, when it eats up a farmer's land field by field and there is nothing to be done to stop it. First one farm was gobbled up and then another—everyone knew that his turn would come sooner or later. No one takes the sea to court; but all the ills and discomfort that brooded over the life of the poor came from Stone Farm. The powers of darkness dwelled there, and frightened souls always pointed to it. "That's well-manured land," the people of the district would say, with a peculiar intonation that held a curse; but they ventured no further.

The Køller family was not sentimental; it thrived splendidly in the sinister light that fell upon the farm from so many frightened souls— and felt it as power. The men were hard drinkers and card players; but they never drank so much as to lose sight and feeling, and if they gambled away a horse early in the evening, they very likely would win two in the course of the night.

When Lasse and Pelle came to Stone Farm, the older tenants still remembered the master from their childhood, Janus Køller, the one who did more to get things moving than anyone else. In his youth he once fought with the devil at midnight up in the church tower, and overcame him; after that he succeeded in everything. Whatever the reason, during his time one after another of his neighbors was ruined, and Janus went around and took over their holdings. If he needed another horse, he played for and won it at three-card. It was the same with everything—the Loathsome One himself fixed it all for him. His greatest pleasure was to break in wild horses, and people who happened to have been born at the stroke of midnight on Christmas Eve could distinctly see the Evil One sitting on the box beside him and holding the reins. He came to a bad end, as might have been expected. Early one morning his horse came galloping home to the farm, and he was found lying by the roadside with his head smashed against a tree.

His son was the last master of Stone Farm from that family. He was a wild devil, but with much that was good in him. If anyone differed with him, he knocked him to the ground; but he always helped those who got in trouble. In this way no one ever was forced to leave house and home; and since he had the family fondness for adding to the farm, he bought up land among the rocks and heather. But he wisely let it lie as it was. He bound many to the farm by his magnanimity, and made them so dependent that they were always beholden to him. His tenants had to leave their own work when he sent for them, and he was never at a loss for cheap labor. The food he provided was scarcely fit for human consumption, but he always ate from the same platter himself. And the pastor was with him at the end, so there was no fault to find with his departure from this life.

He had bedded two excellent wives to death, and all he had to show for it was a daughter by the second one. And she wasn't even quite right. By the age of eleven the blood had already come over her, and she started running around and making advances to anyone she met. But no one dared so much as look at her, for they were afraid of the master's shotgun. Later on she went to the other extreme and started carrying a walking-stick just like a man, and wandered around alone out on the rocks instead of busying herself with something domestic. She let no one come near her.

Kongstrup, the present master of Stone Farm, was not a native of the island. He had come here about twenty years before, and even now no one could quite make him out. When he first came he used to wander about on the heath and do nothing, just as she did; so it wasn't so strange that he got mixed up with the old man's shotgun and had to marry her. But it was dreadful!

He was an odd fellow, but perhaps that's what people were like where he came from. He got one idea after the other, raised wages when no one had asked him to, and started stone-quarrying with contract labor. So to begin with he kept on thinking up more nonsense, and made it voluntary for his tenants to show up for work at the farm. He even went so far as to send them home in rainy weather to gather in their grain—and let his own stand and be ruined. But things went all wrong, of course, and eventually he was forced to eat all his foolish ideas.

The people of the district submitted to this state of dependence without a murmur. From father to son they were used to going in and out of the gates of Stone Farm and doing what was required of them, as dutifully as if they had been serfs. On the other hand, they focused all their craving for the tragic, all the terrors of life and gloomy mysticism, on Stone Farm. They let the devil roam about there, play three-card with the men for their souls, and ravish the women; and they doffed their caps and bowed more deeply to the master of Stone Farm than to anyone else.

All this had changed a little over the years, of course; the sharp points of the superstition had been blunted somewhat. But the bad atmosphere that hangs over large estates—over all great accumulations of what ought to belong to the many—also hung heavy over Stone Farm. It was the judgment passed by the people, their only revenge for themselves and theirs.

Lasse and Pelle were soon aware of the oppressive atmosphere and began to see with the half-frightened eyes of the others, even before they themselves had heard very much. Lasse especially thought he could never be quite happy here, because of the heaviness that continually surrounded them. And then there was that weeping that no one could explain!

All through the long, bright day, the sound of weeping had filtered out from the rooms of Stone Farm, like the refrain of some sad ballad. Now at last it had stopped. Lasse was puttering around in the lower court-yard, yet the sound was still in his ears. It was sad, so sad, with this continual sound of a woman weeping, as if a child had died, or as if she were left alone with her shame. And what could there be to cry about, when you had a farm of several hundred acres and lived in a tall stone house with twenty sets of windows?

> Riches are only a gift from the Lord,
> But poverty is in truth a reward.
> They who wealth do possess
> Never know happiness,
> While the poor man is always content!

So sang Karna over in the dairy, and indeed it was true. If Lasse only knew where he would get the money for a new shirt for the lad, he would never envy anyone on this earth. Though it might be nice to have money for tobacco and a dram now and then, if it wasn't unfair to anyone else.

Lasse was busy leveling out the dungheap. He had finished his mid-day chores in the stable and was taking his time; it was only a job he did to fill in. Now and then he glanced furtively up at the high windows and put a little more energy into his work, but weariness had the upper hand. It would have been nice to take a little afternoon nap, but he didn't dare. All was quiet on the farm. Pelle had been sent on an errand to the village dry-goods store for the kitchen help, and all the men were in the fields covering up the last spring seed. Stone Farm was late in doing this.

The agricultural trainee now came out of the stable, which he had entered from the other side so as to come up on Lasse from behind. The foreman had sent him. "Is that you, you dirty spy!" muttered Lasse when he saw him. "Someday I'm going to kill you!" But he took off his cap and bowed. The tall trainee went up the courtyard without looking at him, and began talking nonsense with the maids down in the laundry room. He wouldn't do that if the men were at home, that spook!

Kongstrup came out on the steps and stood for a while looking at the weather; then he went down to the cow stable. He sure was big—he filled the whole stable doorway. Lasse put down his pitchfork and hurried inside in case he was wanted.

"Well, how are you getting on, old man?" asked the landowner kindly. "Can you manage the work?"

"Oh, it's going all right," replied Lasse, "but that's about all. It's a lot of animals for one man."

Kongstrup stood feeling the hindquarters of a milk cow. "You've got the boy to help you, Lasse. Where is he, by the way? I don't see him."

"He's gone to the village store for the womenfolk."

"Indeed? Who told him to go?"

"I think it was the mistress herself."

"Hmm. Is it long since he left?"

"Oh yes, he ought to be back soon."

"Get hold of him when he comes, and send him up to me with the things, will you?"

Pelle was not feeling bold when he went up to the office; besides, the mistress had told him to keep the bottle well hidden under his shirt. The ceiling was very high, and on the walls hung splendid hunting rifles; and up on a shelf stood cigar boxes one on top of the other, right up to the ceiling, just as if it were a tobacco shop. But the strangest thing of all was that there was a fire in the stove, now, in the middle of May—and with the window open. They probably didn't know how to get rid of all their money. But where were the money chests?

All this and much more Pelle observed while he stood just inside the door, barefoot, not daring to raise his eyes from sheer nervousness. Then the master turned around in his chair and drew him over by the collar. "Let's see what you've got there under your shirt, my little man," he said kindly.

"It's cognac," said Pelle, pulling out the bottle. "The mistress said I wasn't to let anyone see it."

"You're a clever boy," said Kongstrup, patting him on the cheek. "You'll get on in the world one of these days. Now give me the bottle and I'll take it out to your mistress without letting anyone see." He laughed heartily.

Pelle handed him the bottle; there on the desk was a whole stack of money, thick round two-kroner pieces one on top of the other. Then why hadn't Papa Lasse gotten the money in advance that he had begged for?

Now the mistress came in, and the landowner at once went and shut the window. Pelle wanted to go, but she stopped him. "You've got some things for me, haven't you?" she said.

"I've received the *things*," said Kongstrup. "You can have them—after the boy has left."

But she remained at the door. She wanted to keep the boy there to be a witness that her husband withheld from her the things she had to use in the kitchen—everyone should know it.

Kongstrup walked up and down and said nothing. Pelle expected he would strike her, for she was calling him foul names—much worse than Mama Bengta when Lasse would come home merry from Tommelilla. But he only laughed. "Now that'll do," he said, leading her away from the door and letting the boy out.

Lasse didn't like it. He had thought the landowner was interfering to prevent them all from making use of the boy, when he needed his help so much with the cattle. And now it had taken this disgraceful turn.

"So, it was cognac," Lasse said. "Then I can understand it. But I wonder how she dares attack him like that when all the time she's the one at fault. He must be a good sort of fellow."

"But he likes to take a drink himself," said Pelle, who had heard a little about the master's doings.

"Yes, but a woman, lad, that's quite another thing. Remember, they're fine folk. Well, it's not our business to find fault with the big house; we have enough to do to take care of ourselves. But I only hope she won't send you on any more of her errands, or we may wind up like the louse between two fingernails."

Lasse went to his work. He sighed and shook his head while he dragged the fodder out. He was not at all happy.

III

All that sunshine was exhilarating; it filled the air on all sides, without the accompanying heat. The spring moisture was gone from the air, and the warm haze of summer had not yet arrived. There was only light over the green fields and the sea beyond, light that delineated the landscape clearly against the blue sky and breathed a gentle, pleasant warmth.

It was one of the first days in June—the first real summer day. And it was Sunday.

Stone Farm lay drenched in sunshine. The clear golden light penetrated everywhere; and where it could not reach, dark colors shimmered like a hot, secret breath out into the daylight. Open windows and doors looked like veiled eyes in the midst of the light, and where the roof lay in shadow it absorbed the light like velvet.

It was quiet up in the big house today; it was a day of rest from quarreling too.

The large courtyard was divided in two by a fence. The lower part consisted mainly of a large, steaming manure pit, criss-crossed by planks, and at the top a few inverted wheelbarrows. A couple of pigs lay half buried in the manure, asleep, and a busy flock of hens, wading through the liquid manure, were eagerly scattering the rectangular piles of horse dung from the last morning clearance. A large cock stood in the middle of the flock, directing the work like a foreman.

In the upper yard a flock of white doves were pecking grain off the clean cobblestones. Outside the open coach-house door, a groom was inspecting the phaeton, while inside stood another groom polishing the best harness.

The man by the phaeton was in shirtsleeves and newly polished knee-boots; his body was young and lithe, assuming graceful attitudes as he worked. He wore his cap on the back of his head, and whistled softly while he cleaned the wheels inside and out and sent stolen glances down to the laundry room. Down there, below the window, one of the maids was going through her Sunday ablutions, with shoulders and arms bare and her shift pushed down below her breasts.

The big milkmaid, Karna, went past him to the pump with two large buckets. As she returned, she splashed some water onto one of his boots, and he looked up with an oath. She took this as an invitation to stop, and put down her pails with a cautious glance up at the windows of the big house.

"You don't look like you've had enough sleep, Gustav," she teased, and laughed.

"It's not your fault, at any rate," he answered curtly. "Could you patch my work pants for me today?"

"No thanks! I won't patch where another girl's going to pat."

"Then you can go jump in the lake! There are plenty who'll mend for me besides you!" And he bent again to his work.

"I'll see if I can get time," said the big woman meekly. "But I've got to do all the work in the place by myself this afternoon; the others are all going out."

"Well, I see Bodil's washing her tits," said Gustav, spitting a squirt of tobacco juice toward the laundry window. "I suppose she's going to meeting, since she's doing it so thoroughly."

Karna got a sly look. "She asked to take time off because she wanted to go to church. Her, go to church—kiss me on a Monday! No, she's going down to the tailor's in the village, probably to meet Malmberg, from her home town. To think she isn't above getting mixed up with a married man."

"She can go on a spree with any damn man she pleases, for all I care," said Gustav, kicking the last wheel into place with his foot, while big Karna stood looking at him fondly. But then she noticed a face behind the curtains upstairs and hurried off with her buckets. Gustav spat contemptuously between his teeth after her. She was really too old for his seventeen years; she must be at least forty. He cast another long look at Bodil and went across to the coach house with his oilcan and wrench.

The tall white house that closed off the yard at its upper end was not connected to the other buildings, but stood proudly aloof, attached to them only by two short plank fences. It had gables on both sides and a daylight basement, in which were the servant's hall, the maids' bedrooms, the laundry, the ironing room, and the large storerooms. On the gable facing the yard was a clock that didn't work. Pelle called the building the Castle, and was proud of being allowed to enter the basement. The other people on the farm didn't have such nice names for it.

He was the only one whose awe of the big house had nothing sinister about it; on the others it had the effect of an enemy fortress. Everyone who crossed the pavement of the upper courtyard would glance involuntarily up at the high veiled windows, behind which an eye might secretly be kept on all that went on below. It was a little like passing a row of cannons' mouths—it made you a little unsteady on your feet; and no one crossed the clean pavement unless he had to. On the other hand they went freely about the other half of the yard, which was just as easy to see from the house.

Down there two of the servant boys were playing. One of them had grabbed the other's cap and run off with it, and a wild chase ensued, in one barn door and out another all around the yard, with panting and mischievous laughter and breathless shouts. The yard dog barked with delight and jumped around madly on its chain—it wanted to play too. Up by the fence the robber was overtaken and thrown to the ground; but he managed to toss the cap high in the air, and it floated down right in front of the high stone steps of the big house.

"You lowdown sneak!" exclaimed the owner of the cap in a voice of despairing reproach as he belabored the other with the toes of his boots. "Oh, you ugly foreman's snitch!" He suddenly stopped and measured the distance with an appraising eye. "Will you stand me half a pint if I dare go up and get the cap?" he asked in a whisper. The other nodded and sat up quickly to see how it would turn out. "You swear? You won't try and back out of it?" he asked, raising his hand to swear him to it. His companion solemnly drew his finger across his throat, and the oath was taken. The one who had lost the cap hitched up his pants and pulled himself together, his whole figure stiffening with determination. Then he grabbed the top of the fence, vaulted over, and walked with bent head and firm step across the yard, looking like someone who had staked his all on one card. After he picked up the cap and turned his back on the house, he sent a horrible grimace down the courtyard.

Bodil now came up from the basement in her best Sunday clothes, with a black silk kerchief on her head and a hymnbook in her hand. Good heavens, how pretty she was! And brave—she walked along the whole length of the house and out. But of course she could get a pat from the master any day she liked.

Outside the main yard stood a number of large and small outbuildings—the calves' stable, the pigsties, the tool shed, the cart shed, and a smithy that was no longer used. They were all like so many mysteries, with trap doors that led down to pitch-dark underground potato and sugar-beet cellars, from which, of course, you could go by secret passages to the strangest places underground, and other trap doors that led up to dark lofts where the most wonderful treasures were preserved in the form of old junk.

But Pelle unfortunately had little time to explore all this. Every day he had to help his father look after the cattle, and with so large a herd the work was almost beyond their strength. Every time he had a moment to catch his breath, someone was after him again. He had to carry water for the laundry girls, grease the agricultural trainee's boots, and run to the village store for liquor or chewing tobacco for the men. There was plenty to play with, but no one could bear to see him playing; they were always whistling for him as if he were a dog.

He tried to make up for it by turning his work into a game, and in many cases this was possible. Watering the cattle, for instance, was more fun than any real game, when his father stood out in the yard and pumped, and the boy only had to guide the water from one stall to the next. Doing this job he always felt like some great engineer. On the other hand, much of the other work was too hard to be amusing.

At this moment the boy was wandering about by the outbuildings, where there was no one to order him around. The door to the cow stable stood open, and he could hear the continual munching of the cows, interrupted now and then by a snort of contentment or the regular scraping of a chain up and down when a cow scratched its neck on the post. He felt safe when he heard his father's wooden shoes going up and down the feed alley.

Out of the open Dutch doors of the smaller outbuildings there came a steamy warmth that smelled pleasantly of calves and pigs. The pigs were hard at work. All through the long sty there was munching and smacking. One old sow slopped up the liquid through the corners of her mouth, another snuffed and bubbled with her snout along the bottom of the trough to find the rotten potatoes under the liquid. Here and there a pair of pigs would be fighting over the trough and emitting piercing squeals. The calves put their slobbering noses out the doors, gazing into the sunny air and bellowing. One little fellow, after snuffing up air from the cow stable in a peculiarly thorough way, turned up his lip in a foolish grin—it was a bull calf. He laid his chin upon the half-door and tried to jump over, but Pelle drove him back down. Then he kicked up his hind legs, looked at Pelle out of the corner of his eye, and stood with arched back, stamping up and down like a rocking horse. He was lightheaded with the sun.

Down on the pond, ducks and geese stood on their heads in the water, waving their red legs in the air. And all at once the whole flock would have an attack of giddy delight in the sunshine, and splash quacking from bank to bank, sliding the last part of the way across the water with a comical wagging of their rumps.

Pelle had promised himself a lot from this couple of hours that were entirely his own, since his father had let him take off until time for midday chores. But now he stood in bewilderment, overwhelmed by the wealth of possibilities. Would it be the most fun to sail on the pond on two tail-boards laid criss-cross? There was a manure cart lying over there waiting to be washed. Or should he go in and wrestle with the tiny calves? Or shoot with the old bellows in the smithy? If he filled the nozzle with mud and pumped hard, a pretty nice shot would come out.

Pelle gave a start and tried to make himself invisible—the master himself had come around the corner, and was now standing shading his eyes with his hand and looking down over the sloping land and the sea. When he caught sight of Pelle, he nodded without changing his expression and said: "Good day, my boy! How are you getting on?" He kept on staring, probably hardly knowing that he had said it, and patted the boy on the shoulder with the end of his walking-stick. The master of Stone Farm often walked around half asleep.

But Pelle felt it as a caress of a divine nature, and immediately ran over to the stable to tell his father what had happened. He had an elevating sensation in his shoulder as if he had been knighted, and he could still feel the walking-stick there. An intoxicating warmth spread from the spot through his little body; it made the experience go to his head and made him swell with pride. He rose and soared into the air in a vague, dizzy fantasy — something about the landowner adopting him as his son.

He soon came down again, for in the stable he ran straight into the arms of the Sunday scrubbing. The Sunday bath was the only great objection he had to life; everything else came and was then forgotten, but this was always coming back again. He detested it, especially the part dealing with the inside of his ears. But there was no use complaining; Lasse stood ready with a bucket of cold water and some green soap on a piece of broken pot, and the boy had to take off his clothes. As if the scrubbing were not enough, afterwards he had to put on a clean shirt — luckily only every other Sunday. The whole thing was nice enough to look back on afterwards — like something that was over with and wouldn't happen again for a while.

Pelle stood at the stable door with bristling hair and clean shirt-sleeves, looking important with his hands buried in his pockets. Right in the middle of his forehead his hair waved in a cowlick, said to mean good luck; and his face, all scrunched up as he turned toward the bright light, was the funniest topsy-turvy sight, with not a single feature in its proper place. Pelle stood gently rocking to and fro on his heels, imitating Gustav, who was up by the front steps where he stood holding the reins and waiting for the master and mistress.

Now the mistress came out, and the landowner too; a maid ran down in front to the carriage with a little stepladder and helped her in. The master stood at the top of the stairs until she was seated: she had difficulty walking. But what a pair of eyes she had today! Pelle hastily looked away when she turned her face down toward the yard — it was whispered among the servants that she could bring misfortune upon anyone just by looking at him, if she wanted to. Now Gustav unchained the dog, which bounded in front of the horses and barked as they drove out of the courtyard.

The sun never shone like this on a weekday. It was dazzling when the white doves flew in one flock over the yard, turning as regularly as if they were a large white sheet flapping in the sunshine. The reflection from their wings flashed over the dungheap and made the pigs lift their heads with an inquisitive grunt. Up in their rooms the men sat playing "sixty-six" or putting new soles on their wooden shoes, and Gustav started playing "Old Noah" on his concertina.

Pelle picked his way across the upper courtyard to the big doghouse, which could rotate with the wind. He sat down on the angle of the roof, and made a merry-go-round of it by pushing off with his foot every time he passed the fence. Suddenly it occurred to him that he himself was everybody's dog, and had better hide; so he dropped down, crept into the doghouse, and curled up on the straw with his head between his forepaws. He lay there for a while, staring at the fence and panting with his tongue hanging out of his mouth. Then he got an idea—it came to him as suddenly as a sneeze and made him forget all caution. The next moment he was sliding full-tilt down the railing of the front steps.

He had slid down seventeen times and was deeply engrossed in the thought of reaching fifty, when he heard a sharp whistle from the big coach-house door. The trainee stood there beckoning to him. Pelle, crestfallen, went over to him, bitterly regretting his thoughtlessness. Now he would probably have to grease boots with whale oil again, maybe for all of them.

The trainee pulled him inside the door and shoved it shut. It was dark, and the boy, coming in out of the bright daylight, could distinguish nothing; what he eventually made out assumed shapeless contours in his frightened imagination. Voices laughed and growled in his ears, and hands that seemed to him enormous tossed him back and forth. Terror seized him, and with it came crazy, disjointed images of robbery and murder, and he started screaming in fright. A big, rough hand covered his whole face, and in the silence that followed his stifled scream, he heard a voice out in the yard calling to the maids to come and see something funny.

He was too paralyzed with terror to know what was being done with him, and only wondered vaguely what could be so funny outside in the sunshine. Would he ever see the sun again?

As if in answer to his thought, the door was suddenly thrown open. The light poured in and he recognized the faces around him, and found himself standing half naked in broad daylight, his pants down around his heels and his shirt tucked up under his vest. The trainee stood at one side with a carriage whip, flicking at the boy's naked body.

"Run!" shouted a commanding voice. Pelle, wild with terror and confusion, dashed into the yard. There stood the maids, and they screamed with laughter at the sight of him, and he turned to flee back into the coach house. But the whip struck him, and he had to go back out in the daylight, leaping like a kangaroo and prompting renewed hoots of laughter. Then he stopped, stood up straight, and cried helplessly, under a shower of remarks, especially from the maids. He no longer noticed the whip, but only crouched down, trying to hide, until at last he sank in a heap upon the cobblestones, sobbing convulsively.

Karna, large of limb, came rushing up from the basement and forced her way through the crowd, crimson with rage and scolding as she went. On her freckled neck and heavy arms were brown marks left by the cows' tails at the last milking, looking like clumsy tattoos. She flung her slipper in the trainee's face, wrapped Pelle in her burlap apron, and carried him down to the basement.

When Lasse heard what had happened to the boy, he took a hammer and went off to kill the trainee. The old man had such a look in his eyes that no one wanted to get in his way. Meanwhile, the trainee had found it most expedient to disappear. When Lasse found no vent for his wrath, he fell into a fit of trembling and weeping, and became so truly ill that the men had to snap him out of it with a swig of aquavit. This broke the fever instantly, and Lasse was again himself and able to nod confidently to the frightened, sniffling Pelle.

"Never mind, lad," he said comfortingly. "Never mind. No one has ever yet escaped being punished, and Lasse will break the skull of that skinny devil so his brains spurt out of his snout, take my word for it!"

Pelle's face brightened at the prospect of such violent revenge, and he crept up into the loft to throw down the hay for the cattle's midday meal. Lasse, who was not so fond of climbing, went down the long passage between the stalls distributing the hay. He was cogitating over something, and Pelle could hear him talking to himself the whole time. When they had finished, Lasse went to the green chest and brought out a black silk kerchief that had been Bengta's Sunday best. His expression was solemn as he called Pelle.

"Run over to Karna with this and ask her to accept it. We're not so poor that we should let kindness go unrewarded. But don't let anyone see it, so the others won't feel bad. Mother Bengta in her grave won't be offended; she'd have suggested it herself, if she could have spoken. But her mouth is full of earth, poor thing!" Lasse sighed deeply.

Even then he stood for a while weighing the kerchief in his hand before handing it to Pelle. He was by no means as sure of Bengta as his words made out; but the old man liked to beautify her memory, both for himself and the boy. It could not be denied that she had generally been a little difficult in a matter of this kind, jealous as she was; and she might take it into her head to haunt them because of that kerchief. Still, she had had a heart for both him and the boy, and it was usually in the right place—they had to say that of her. So the Lord would have to judge her as kindly as He could.

During the afternoon it was quiet on the farm. Most of the men were out somewhere, either at the inn or visiting the men at the stone quarry. The master and mistress were out too; the master had ordered the carriage right after dinner and had driven to town, and half an hour later his wife set off in the pony carriage—to keep an eye on him, people said.

Old Lasse was sitting in an empty cow stall, mending Pelle's clothes, while the boy played up and down the feed alley. In the herdsman's room he had found an old bootjack, which he placed under his knee, pretending it was a wooden leg. All the while he was chattering happily to his father, but not quite so loudly as usual. The morning's experience was still fresh in his mind, and had a subduing effect; it was as if he had performed some great deed, and was now self-conscious about it. There was another circumstance, too, that made him feel solemn. The foreman had been over to say that the animals were supposed to go out the next day. Pelle was to mind the young cattle, so this would be his last free day, perhaps for the whole summer.

He paused in front of his father. "What are you going to kill him with, Papa?"

"With the hammer, I suppose."

"Are you going to kill him dead, wham—dead as a dog?"

Lasse nodded ominously. "Yes indeed!"

"But who'll read the names for us then?"

The old man shook his head pensively. "That's true enough!" he exclaimed, scratching himself first in one place and then another. The name of each cow was written in chalk above its stall, but neither Lasse nor Pelle could read. The foreman had indeed gone over the names with them once, but it was impossible to remember fifty names after hearing them just once—even for the boy, who had such a devilishly good memory. If Lasse killed the trainee, then who would help them make out the names? The foreman would never stand for it if they asked him a second time.

"I guess we'll have to be content with thrashing him," said Lasse meditatively.

The boy went on playing for a while, then came up to Lasse again. "Don't you think the Swedes can lick all the people in the world, Papa?"

The old man looked thoughtful. "Well, yes... I should think so."

"Sure, because Sweden's much bigger than the whole world, isn't it?"

"Yes, it's big," said Lasse, trying to imagine its extent. There were twenty-four provinces, of which Malmöhus was only one, and Ystad district a small part of that again; and then in one corner of Ystad district lay Tommelilla, and his holding, which he had once thought so huge with its five acres of land, was a tiny little piece of Tommelilla! Ah, yes, Sweden was big—not bigger than the whole world, of course, for that was only childish nonsense—but still bigger than all the rest of the world put together. "Yes, it's big all right! But what are you doing, lad?"

"Why, can't you see I'm a soldier who's had one leg shot off?"

"Oh, you're an invalid, eh? But you shouldn't do that, because God doesn't like things like that. You might turn into a real cripple, and that would be terrible."

"Oh, He can't see, because He's in the churches today!" answered the boy, but he was cautious enough to stop there. He stationed himself at the stable door, whistling, but suddenly came running in, all excited. "Papa, here comes the trainee! Should I go get the whip?"

"No, we'd probably better leave him alone. It might be the death of him; fine gentlemen scamps like that can't stand a licking. The fright alone might kill him." Lasse glanced uneasily at the boy.

Pelle looked very disappointed. "But what if he does it again?"

"Oh, no, we won't let him off without a good scare. I'll pick him up and hold him out at arm's length dangling in the air until he begs for dear life; then I'll put him down again just as calmly. Because Lasse doesn't like being angry. Lasse's a decent fellow."

"Then you have to pretend to let him go while you're holding him high up in the air. Then he'll scream and think he's going to die, and the others will come and laugh at him."

"No, no, don't go tempting your father. Maybe I'd feel like throwing him to the ground, and that would mean murder and prison for life! No, I'll just give him a good tongue-lashing; that's what an upper-class puppy like that will feel the most."

"Yes, and then you should call him a skinny-shanked clodhopper. That's what the foreman calls him when he's mad at him."

"No, I don't think that would do either. But I'll have a serious talk with him, and he won't be likely to forget that in a hurry."

Pelle was quite satisfied. There was nobody like his father, even when it came to bawling someone out. He had never heard him do it, and he was looking forward to it immensely as he hobbled along with the bootjack. He wasn't using it as a wooden leg anymore, for fear of tempting Providence; but he held it under his arm like a crutch, supporting it on the edge of the foundation wall because it was too short. It would be great to walk on two crutches like the parson's son back home! Then he could jump over even the widest puddles.

Light and shadow were suddenly shifting up under the roof, and when Pelle turned around he saw a strange boy standing in the doorway out to the field. He was the same height as Pelle, but his head was almost as large as a grown man's. At first sight it appeared to be bald all over, but when the boy moved in the sun, his bare head glistened as if covered with silver scales. It was covered with fine whitish hair, distributed thinly and fairly evenly over his face and everywhere else; his skin was pink, as were the whites of his eyes. His face was contorted into wrinkles in the strong sunlight, and the back of his head jutted out and looked to be much too heavy.

Pelle stuck his hands in his pockets and went up to him. "What's your name?" he said, spitting a jet through his front teeth the way Gustav did. The trick was a failure, unfortunately, and the spit just ran down his chin. The strange boy grinned.

"Rud," he said indistinctly, as if his tongue were thick and unmanageable. He was staring enviously at Pelle's pants pockets. "Is that your father?" he asked, pointing at Lasse.

"Of course," said Pelle self-importantly. "And he can thrash everybody."

"Well, my father can buy everybody, because he lives up there." Rud pointed toward the big house.

"Oh, he does, huh?" said Pelle incredulously. "Then why don't you live there with him?"

"Why, I'm a bastard child; my mother says so herself."

"The hell she does!" Pelle stole a glance at his father on account of the small oath.

"Yes, when she's annoyed—and then she beats me. But then I run away."

"Oh, you do, do you?" said a voice from outside. The boy jumped and retreated farther into the stable. A big fat woman appeared in the doorway and looked angrily around in the dim light. When she caught sight of Rud, she continued her scolding. Her accent was Swedish.

"So you run away, you cabbage-head! If you'd only run so far that you couldn't find your way back again, a body wouldn't need to wear herself out thrashing an ugly creature like you! So that's the boy's father, is it?" she said as she caught sight of Lasse.

"Yes, it is," said Lasse softly. "And surely you must be schoolmaster

Johan Pihl's Johanne from Tommelilla, who left the country nearly twenty years ago?"

"And surely you must be the smith's tomcat from Sulitjelma, the one who had twins with an old wooden shoe the year before the year before last?" retorted the big woman, mocking his tone of voice.

"All right, it doesn't matter to me who you are," said Lasse, offended. 'I'm not a police spy."

"You'd think you were from the way you're interrogating me. Do you know when the cattle are supposed to go out?"

"Tomorrow, if all goes well. Is it your little boy who's going to show Pelle the ropes? The foreman spoke of someone who could go out with him and show him the pasture."

"Yes, it's that Søren Shitkicker there—come out so we can see you properly, you calf! Oh, the boy's gone. All right. Does your boy often get a thrashing?"

"Oh yes, sometimes," answered Lasse, who was ashamed to admit that he never punished the boy.

"I don't spare mine either. It'll take a good deal to make a man out of that rubbish; beatings are half his nourishment. I'll chase the puppy up here first thing in the morning; but take care he doesn't show himself in the yard, or there'll be the devil to pay."

"The mistress can't bear to see him, I suppose?" said Lasse.

"You're right. She had nothing to do with the making of that half-crazy little terror. God knows there isn't much to be jealous about. But I could have been a farmer's wife today and had a nice husband too, if that high and mighty peacock up there hadn't seduced me. Would you believe that, you cracked old piece of shoe-leather?" she asked with a laugh, slapping him on the hip.

"I believe you could have," said Lasse. "You were the prettiest girl in town when you left home."

"Oh, you and your 'home,' " she sneered.

"Well, I can see that you prefer to wipe out your tracks behind you. And I have no trouble pretending to be a stranger, even though I held you on my lap more than once when you were a little lass—but by the way, do you know that your mother's lying on her deathbed?"

"Oh no, oh no!" she exclaimed, looking at him with a face that was growing more and more contorted.

"I went to say goodbye to her before I left home a little more than a month ago, and she was very ill. 'Goodbye, Lasse,' she said, 'and thank you for your neighborliness all these years. And if you run into Johanne

over there,' she said, 'give her my love. Things have gone terribly badly
for her, from what I've heard; but give her my love all the same. Johanne
child, little child! She was the nearest to her mother's heart, and so she
happened to tread upon it. Maybe it was our fault. You'll give her her
mother's love, won't you, Lasse?' Those were her very words—and
now she's most likely dead, so feeble as she was then."

Johanne Pihl had no command over her feelings. She was evidently
not used to weeping, for her sobs seemed to tear her to pieces. No tears
came, but her agony was like the throes of childbirth. "Little mother,
poor little mother!" she said every now and then, as she sat rocking on
the edge of the manger.

"There, there!" said Lasse, patting her on the head. "I told them
they had been too hard on you. But what did you have to crawl in
through that window for—a child of sixteen and in the middle of the
night? You can't blame them for forgetting themselves a little. Especially
since he was earning nothing but his keep and clothes, and was a bad
fellow at that, who was always losing his job."

"But I loved him," said Johanne, weeping. "He's the only one I ever
loved. And I was so stupid that I thought he loved me too, though he'd
never noticed me."

"Ah yes, you were only a child. I said so to your parents. But that
you could think of doing anything so indecent!"

"I didn't mean to do anything wrong. I only thought that the two of
us ought to be together, since we loved each other so much. No, I didn't
even think that—I just crept into his room, without thinking about it at
all. Would you believe I was so innocent in those days? And nothing
bad happened either."

"And nothing even happened?" said Lasse. "But that's terrible, the
way things turned out so sad. It was the death of your father."

The big woman began to cry helplessly. She was like a rag, Lasse
thought, and he was almost in tears himself.

"I probably should never have told you, but I thought you must
have heard about it," he said in despair. "I guess he thought that he, as
schoolmaster, had the responsibility for so many, and it cut him to the
quick that you'd thrown yourself at someone that way—and a poor
hired hand at that. It's true enough that he mixed with us poor folks as if
we'd been his equals, but the honor was there all the same; and he took
it hard when the rich folks wouldn't look at him anymore. And after all
that it was just empty talk—nothing happened? But why didn't you tell
them so?"

Johanne had stopped crying; now she sat with her eyes turned away, and her face was still quivering.

"I did tell them, but they wouldn't listen. I was found there, after all! I screamed for help when I found out he didn't even know me, but was only flattered that I came, and wanted to grab me. Then the others came running in and found me there. They laughed, and you know what they said to each other? That I'd screamed because I'd lost my innocence. I could see that my parents thought the same thing. Even they couldn't believe that nothing had happened, so what must the rabble have thought? So then they paid him to come over here, and sent me away to live with relatives."

"Yes, and then you added to their sorrow by running away."

"I went after him. I thought he'd learn to like me, if only I was near him. He'd taken a job here at Stone Farm, so I took a place here too, as a housemaid. But there was only one thing he wanted me for, and I didn't want to if he didn't love me. So he went around boasting that I'd run away from home for his sake—and the other thing too, which was a lie; so all the men thought they could grab me and make passes at me. Kongstrup was newly married then, but he was no better than the others. I got the job completely by chance, because the other housemaid had had to go away somewhere to have a baby; so I was awfully careful. He got her married off afterwards to a stonecutter at the quarry."

"So that's the sort of man he is!" exclaimed Lasse. "I had my doubts about him. But what became of the other scoundrel?"

"He went to work in the quarry when we'd been at the farm a couple of years and he'd done me all the harm he could. While he was there, he boozed and got into fights most of the time. I went to see him often, because I couldn't get him out of my head—but he was always drunk. Finally he couldn't stay there any longer, and took off, and then we heard that he was up in Nordland, raising hell among the rocks at Blåholt. He helped himself to whatever he wanted at the nearest place he could find it, and knocked people down for nothing at all. And one day they said that he'd been declared an outlaw, so that anyone who wanted to could kill him. I had great confidence in the master, who after all was the only person who wished me well; and he comforted me by saying that it would be all right: Knut would know how to take care of himself."

"Knut? Was it Knut Engström?" asked Lasse. "Well, then, I've heard about him. He was carrying on like a devil the last time I was in this country, assaulting people on the highway in broad daylight. He killed one man with a hammer, and when they caught him, he'd cut a long gash from the back of his neck right up to his eye. The other man had done that, he said; he'd only defended himself. So they couldn't do anything to him. So he was the one! But who was it he was living with, then? They said he was living in a shack in the middle of the heath that summer and had a woman with him."

"I ran away from service and made the others think I was going home. I'd heard what a wretched state he was in. They said he was gashed all over his head. So I went up and took care of him."

"Then you gave in at last," said Lasse with a roguish wink.

"He beat me every day," she answered hoarsely. "And when he couldn't have his way with me, he finally chased me away. I'd set my mind on it—he had to love me first." Her voice had grown coarse and hard again.

"Then you deserved a good whipping on your bare behind for taking a fancy to such a butcher! And you ought to be glad your mother didn't hear anything about it—she never would have survived it."

At the word "mother" Johanne gave a start. "You have to hold on to whatever you can," she said in a hard voice. "I've held on to more than Mother, and look how big and fat I've grown."

Lasse shook his head. "I guess I can't argue with you anymore. But what's happened to you since?"

"I came back to Stone Farm again in November, but the mistress wouldn't take me on again, for she would rather see my heel than my toe. But Kongstrup got his way by making me a milkmaid. He was as kind to me as ever, although I'd resisted him for nine years. But at last the magistrate got tired of having Knut running around loose; he was causing too much trouble. So they had a hunt for him up on the heath. They didn't catch him, but he must have come back to the quarry to hide when things got rough. One day when they were blasting up there, his body came out among the chunks of rock, all smashed up. They drove the pieces down here to the farm, and it made me so sick to see him come to me that way that I had to go to bed. I lay there shivering day and night, because it seemed as if he had come to me in his direst need. Kongstrup sat with me and comforted me when the others were in the fields, and he took advantage of my misery to get his way.

"There was a younger brother of the farmer on the hill who liked me. He'd been in America in his younger days and had plenty of money. He didn't give a damn what people said, and every single year he proposed to me, always on New Year's Day. He came back that year too, and now that Knut was dead, I couldn't have done better than to take him and become mistress of a farm. But I had to refuse him after all, and I can tell you it was hard when I made the discovery. Kongstrup wanted to send me away when I told him about it; but I wouldn't hear of it. I meant to stay and bear my child here on the farm where it belonged. He didn't care a bit about me any longer. The mistress put her evil eye on me every day, and nobody was kind to me. I wasn't so hard then as I am now, and it was all I could do to keep from crying all the time.

"So I got tough. When anything was the matter, I clenched my teeth so no one would ridicule me. I was working in the field the day it happened, too. I gave birth to the boy in the middle of a sugar-beet field, and I carried him back to the farm in my apron. He was deformed even then: the mistress's evil eye had done it. I said to myself, "Then they'll always have the changeling in their sight," and I refused to go away. The master couldn't quite bring himself to throw me out, so he put me in the house down by the shore."

"Then you work on the farm here in the busy seasons?" asked Lasse.

She sniffed contemptuously. "Work! You think I need to do that? Kongstrup has to pay me something for bringing up his son, and then there are some good friends who come to see me, sometimes one and sometimes another, and bring a little something with them—when they haven't spent it all on drink. You can come down and see me tonight. I'll be real good to you."

"No thanks," said Lasse gravely. "I'm a human being too, but I won't go to a woman who once sat on my knee as if she was my own child."

"Have you got any liquor, then?" she asked, giving him a poke.

Lasse didn't think there was any left, but went to see. "No, not a drop," he said, returning with the bottle. "But I've got something for you here that your mother asked me to give you as a keepsake. It was lucky I remembered it." And he handed her a package, and looked on happily while she opened it, feeling pleased on her account. It was a hymnbook. "Isn't it a beauty?" he said. "With a gold cross and a real clasp—and then, it was your mother's."

"What good is this to me?" asked Johanne. "I don't sing hymns."

"You don't?" said Lasse, hurt. "But your mother probably had no idea that you haven't kept the faith you had as a child, so you must forgive her this once."

"Is that all you've got for me?" She shoved the book off her lap.

"Yes, it is," said Lasse, his voice trembling, and he picked up the book.

"Who's going to get the rest, then?"

"Well, the house was only leased, and there weren't many things left; it's been a long time since your father died, remember. Where you should have been, strangers have taken her daughter's place. I suppose those who've looked after her will get what there is. But maybe you'd still be in time, if you took the first steamer."

"No, thank you! Go home and be stared at and pretend to be remorseful—no thanks! Let the strangers take what's left. And Mother —well, if she's lived without my help, I guess she can croak without it too. Well, I've got to be getting home. I wonder what's become of that future master of Stone Farm?" She laughed out loud.

Lasse would have sworn that she had been quite sober, and yet she walked unsteadily as she went behind the calves' stables to look for her son. It was on his lips to ask whether she wouldn't take the hymnbook with her, but he gave it up. She was in no mood for it now, and she might even blaspheme God. So he carefully wrapped up the book and put it away in the green chest.

At the far corner of the cow stable a space was divided off with boards. It had no door, and the boards were an inch apart, so that it resembled a cage. This was the herdsman's room. Most of the space was occupied by a wide bedframe made of rough boards knocked together, with nothing but the stone floor to lie on. Upon a deep layer of rye straw the bed-clothes lay in a disordered heap, and the thick striped woolen ticking was stiff with dried cow dung, to which feathers and bits of straw had stuck.

Pelle lay curled up in the middle of the bed with the down quilt up to his chin, luxuriating. Lasse sat on the edge, rummaging through the green chest and talking softly to himself.

He was in the midst of his Sunday devotions. Piece by piece he slowly took out all the little things he had brought from his broken-up home. They were all purely useful items: balls of yarn, scraps of fabric, and the like, which were to be used to keep his own and the boy's clothes in good repair. But to him each thing was a holy relic to be handled with care, and his heart bled every time one of them was used up. With each article he put down, he slowly repeated its purpose, as Bengta had told him when she lay dying and was trying to arrange everything for him and the boy as best she could: "Yarn for the boy's gray socks. Pieces to lengthen the sleeves of his Sunday jacket. Remember not to wear your socks too long before you mend them." They were the last wishes of the dying woman, and they were followed to the smallest detail. Lasse knew them by heart, in spite of his bad memory.

Then there were little things that had belonged to Bengta herself: cheap finery, each piece with its happy memory of fairs and holidays, which he recalled in his muttered reverie.

The boy liked this subdued murmur, which he didn't need to listen to or answer—and which was so pleasant to doze off to. He lay looking out sleepily at the bright sky, tired and content, and with a vague feeling that something unpleasant was over with.

He gave a start. He had heard the door of the cow stable open, and bootsteps coming down the long feed alley. It was the trainee. He recognized the hated step at once.

He thrilled with delight. Now that fellow would be made to understand that he shouldn't do anything to boys with fathers who could hold a man out at arm's length and chew him out—and much worse than the foreman. Now he'd get it! He sat up and gazed eagerly at his father.

"Lasse!" came a voice from the stable.

The old man growled sullenly, stirred uneasily, but did not rise.

"Las-se!" the voice came again, after a moment, impatiently and in a tone of command.

"Yes?" Lasse got up and went out.

"Can't you answer when you're called, you Swedish scoundrel? Are you deaf?"

"Oh, I can answer well enough," said Lasse in a trembling voice. "But Mr. Trainee shouldn't... I'm a father, let me tell you... and a father's heart—"

"You could be a midwife for all I care, but you've got to answer when you're called, or else I'll get the foreman to have a talk with you. Do you understand?"

"Yes, I see, all right... Mr. Trainee must excuse me, but I didn't hear—"

"Well, can you remember that Aspasia can't go out to pasture tomorrow?"

"Is she going to calve?"

"Yes, of course! Did you think she was going to foal?"

Lasse laughed dutifully and followed the trainee back through the stable. Now was the time—Pelle sat up, listening intently. But he only heard his father make another excuse, close the half-door, and come back with slow, tottering steps. Then Pelle burst into tears and crept far in under the quilt.

Lasse puttered about for some time, grumbling to himself about something; then he came over and gently drew the quilt down from the boy's head. But Pelle buried his face in the bedclothes, and when his father turned Pelle's face toward him, he saw a despairing, uncomprehending look that made his own eyes wander restlessly around the room.

"Yes," he said, trying to act annoyed. "It's easy for you to cry. But when you don't know what stall Aspasia's in, you've got to be civil, I'm thinking."

"I know Aspasia," sobbed the boy. "She's the third from the door here."

Lasse was going to give a peevish answer, but broke down, touched and disarmed by the boy's despair. He surrendered unconditionally, stooped down until his forehead touched the boy's, and said helplessly, "Yes, Lasse's a poor thing—old and poor! A puppy can lead him by the nose. He can't shoot off sparks in anger anymore, and there's no strength in his fist, so what's the good of clenching it. He has to put up with everything, and let himself be pushed around—and say thank you for it! That's how it is with old Lasse. But you must remember that it's for your sake he lets people spit on him. If it weren't for you, he'd shoulder his pack and go—old though he is. But you can thrive in the place where your father is moldering. And now you have to stop crying." He dried the boy's wet eyes with the quilt.

Pelle didn't understand his father's words, but they consoled him nevertheless, and he soon fell asleep. But for a long time he sniffled in his sleep.

Lasse sat still on the edge of the bed and listened to the boy sleeping. When he had quieted down, he sneaked through the stable and outside. It had been a poor Sunday, and now he wanted to go see if any of the men were home and had visitors—then there would be liquor going around. Lasse didn't have the heart to take any of his wages and buy aquavit; that money would have enough to do paying for bare necessities.

On one of the beds a man lay sleeping, fully dressed and with his boots on. He was dead drunk. All the others were out, so Lasse gave up the thought of a dram, and went across to the basement to see if it was any livelier among the maids. He had nothing against having a little fun—now that he was free and single and his own master, as he'd been in the springtime days of his youth.

Up by the dairy stood the three tenant farmers' wives who usually did the milking for the girls on Sunday evening. They were tightly wrapped, small, and bent with toil. They were all talking together about illnesses and other miseries in plaintive tones. Lasse felt a sudden desire to join them, for the subject found an echo in his being like the tune of a familiar song, and he could join in the refrain with a lifetime of experience. But he resisted the temptation, and went past them down the basement steps. "Ah yes, death will come to us all!" said one of the women, and Lasse repeated the words to himself as he went down.

Karna was sitting down there mending Gustav's moleskin pants, while Gustav lay on the bench asleep with his cap over his face. He had put his dirty feet up on Karna's lap, without so much as taking off his shoes! And she had accommodated her lap so that they wouldn't slide off.

Lasse sat down beside her and tried to make himself agreeable. He needed a little companionship. But Karna was unapproachable; that boy's dirty feet had quite turned her head. And either Lasse had forgotten how to do it, or he lacked the self-confidence—every time he tried to say something friendly, she rejected him.

"We could have such a cozy time together, we two middle-aged folks," he said hopelessly.

"Yes, and I could probably help out with what's missing," said Gustav, peeking out from under his cap. That puppy, lying there and boasting of his seventeen years! Lasse had a good mind to jump him and risk yet another trial of strength.

But he contented himself with sitting and looking at him until his red, lashless eyes grew watery. Then he got up.

"Well, well, I see you prefer youth this evening!" he said bitterly to Karna. "But you can't run away from your years either! Maybe you'll only get to lick the spoon after the others."

He went across to the cow stable and began talking to the three tenants' wives, who were still speaking of illness and misery and death, as if nothing else existed in the world. Lasse nodded and said, "Yes, yes, that's true." He could heartily endorse it all, and could add much to what they said. It brought warmth to his old body and made him feel quite comfortable—so easy in his joints.

But when he lay on his back in bed, all the sad thoughts came back, and he couldn't sleep. Generally he slept like a rock as soon as he fell into bed, but today was Sunday, and he was tormented with the thought that life had passed him by. He had promised himself so much from the island, and it was nothing but toil and trouble—and that was all.

"Lasse's old, all right!" he suddenly said aloud, and he kept on repeating the words with little variations until he fell asleep: "He's old, poor man—and played out. Ah, so old!" Those words expressed it all.

He was awakened again by singing and shouting up on the highway.

And now the boy you gave me
With the black and curly hair,
He is no longer little,
No longer, no longer,
But a fine, tall strapping youth.

It was some of the men and women from the farm on their way
home from some entertainment. When they turned in to the farm road
they fell silent.

It was just beginning to grow light. It must have been about two
o'clock.

IV

By four a.m. Lasse and Pelle were already dressed and opening the
cow-stable doors to the field. The earth was rolling out of its white
night exhalation, and the morning rose prophetically. Lasse stood in the
doorway, yawning, and figuring out the day's weather; but Pelle let the
veiled tones of the wind and the song of the lark—everything that was
rising—beat against his little heart. With open mouth and doubtful eyes
he gazed into the incomprehensible fact of each new day with all its
unimagined possibilities. "Today you have to take your coat along,
because we're going to get rain about noon," Lasse might say; Pelle
would peer into the sky to find out how his father had figured that out.
Because he was usually right.

They then set about cleaning out the dung in the cow stable. Pelle
scraped the floor under the cows and swept it up, Lasse filled the
wheelbarrow and wheeled it out. At half-past five they ate their breakfast—salt herring and porridge.

After that Pelle set out with the young cattle, his dinner basket on
his arm and his whip wound several times around his neck. His father
had made him a short, thick stick with rings on it, which he could rattle
in warning and throw at the animals; but Pelle preferred the whip,
because he was not yet strong enough to use it.

He was little, and at first he had some trouble making an impression
on the great forces he was put in charge of. He couldn't get his voice to
sound terrifying enough, and driving the cattle out to pasture was hard

work, especially up near the farm buildings, where the grain stood high on both sides of the field road. The animals were hungry in the morning, and the big steers did not feel like moving once they had their noses buried in the grain and he stood belaboring them with the short handle of the cattle whip. The twelve-foot lash, which in a practiced hand would leave little triangular holes in an animal's hide, he couldn't swing at all; and if he kicked the steer in the head with his wooden shoe, it only closed its eyes good-naturedly and kept on grazing with its back to him. Then he would collapse with a defeated howl, or have small fits of rage when he would blindly attack and try to get at the animal's eyes; but it was no use. He could always make the calves move by twisting their tails, but the steers' tails were too strong.

But he didn't cry for long when his methods didn't work. One evening he got his father to put a spike in the toe of one of his wooden shoes, and after that his kick was respected. Partly on his own, and partly from Rud, he also learned where to find the places on the animals where it hurt most. The heifers were particularly sensitive in the udder and groin, the two steers in the testicles; a well-directed blow to a horn could make even the large steers bellow in pain.

Driving them out to pasture was hard work, but the herding itself was easy. Once the cattle were quietly grazing, he felt like a general, and made his voice resound incessantly across the meadow, while his little body swelled with pride and a sense of power.

It bothered him to be away from his father. He didn't go home for dinner; even when he was playing, despair would come over him. He would imagine that something bad had happened to his father, that the big bull had gored him, or something like that. He would drop everything and start running homeward, howling, but would remember in time the foreman's whip and trudge back again. He found a remedy for his longing by stationing himself so that he could keep an eye on the fields up there and see his father when he went out to move the dairy cows.

He taught himself to whittle: boats and little farm implements and walking-sticks with patterns cut in the bark. He was good with his knife and made diligent use of it. He could also stand for hours on the top of a monolith — he thought it was a gatepost — and try to crack his whip like a pistol shot. He had to climb up there to get the lash off the ground at all.

When the animals lay down in the middle of the morning, he was often tired too. Then he would seat himself on the head of one of the big steers and hold on to the points of its horns. And while the animal lay chewing with a gentle vibration like a machine, he would sit on its head and shout at the top of his voice songs about unrequited love and horrible massacres.

Toward noon Rud came running up, famished. His mother chased him out of the house when mealtimes drew near. Pelle always shared the contents of his basket with him, but made him round up the animals a certain number of times for each piece of food. The two boys couldn't get along without each other for an entire day. They tumbled about in the meadow like two puppies, fought and made up again twenty times a day, swore the most fearful threats of vengeance to come in the shape of this or that adult, and the next moment had their arms around each other's necks.

About half a mile of sand dunes separated the Stone Farm fields from the sea. Within this belt of sand the land was stony and afforded poor grazing; but on both sides of the creek a strip of lush meadow land wedged into the dunes, which were covered with dwarf pines and lyme grass to anchor the sand. The best grazing was on this meadow land, but it was hard work minding both sides of it, since the creek ran down the middle. And it had been impressed upon the boy, with severe threats, that no animal must set foot on the dunes, since the smallest opening might cause a sand drift. Pelle took the matter quite literally, and all that summer he imagined something like an explosion that would blow everything sky high the instant an animal stepped on it. This possibility loomed like a fate behind everything when he was herding down there. When Rud came and they wanted to play, he drove the cattle up to the poor pasture where there was plenty of room for them.

When the sun was shining the boys ran around naked. They didn't dare venture down to the sea for fear of the foreman, who was surely always up in the attic of the big house watching Pelle through his telescope. But they swam in the creek—in and out of the water all day long. After a heavy rain the creek became swollen and turned quite milky from the china clay that it washed away from the banks farther upstream. The boys thought it was milk from an enormous farm far inland. At high tide the sea ran up and filled the creek with rotting seaweed that colored the water crimson. This was the blood of all the people drowned out to sea.

When they weren't swimming they lay at the foot of the dunes and let the sun lick them dry. They made a minute examination of their bodies and discussed the use and intention of the various parts. In this field Rud's knowledge was superior, and he took the part of instructor.

They often argued about which of them was the better equipped in one way or another—in other words, who had the largest. Pelle, for instance, envied Rud his disproportionately large head.

Pelle was a well-built little fellow, and had put on weight since he had come to Stone Farm. His glossy skin was stretched smoothly over his body and was a warm, suntanned color. Rud had a thin neck in proportion to his head, and his forehead was angular and covered with scars from innumerable falls. He didn't have full command of his limbs, and was always bumping and bruising himself; there were livid black-and-blue marks all over him that were slow to disappear, because his flesh didn't heal easily. But he was not as open in his envy as Pelle was. He asserted himself by inflating all his defects into achievements, so that Pelle ended up envying him everything from the bottom of his heart.

Rud didn't have Pelle's open senses to the world, but he had more instinct and on certain points a talent, almost a genius, for anticipating what Pelle only learned by experience. He was already avaricious to a certain extent, and suspicious without connecting any definite thoughts to it. He ate the lion's share of the food and had many ways of getting out of working.

Behind their play there lay, clothed in the most childish forms, a struggle for supremacy, and for the present Pelle was the one who drew the short straw. In the worst case, Rud always knew how to appeal to his good qualities and turn them to his own advantage.

And through all this they were the best friends in the world and were quite inseparable. Pelle was always looking toward "the Sow's" cottage when he was alone, and Rud would run off from home as soon as he had a chance.

It had rained hard that morning, in spite of what Lasse had predicted, and Pelle was soaked to the skin. Now the blue-black rain shower was moving out to sea, and the boats lay in the middle of it with all their red sails set, yet they were not moving. The sunlight flashed and glittered on wet surfaces, so everything looked wonderful; and Pelle hung his clothes on a dwarf pine to dry.

He was cold, so he crept up close to Per, the biggest of the steers, as he lay chewing his cud. The animal was steaming, but Pelle couldn't shake the numbness out of his hands and feet, where the cold had taken hold. His teeth were chattering too, and he was shivering.

And then one of the cows wouldn't leave him alone. Every time he had snuggled right in under the steer and started to warm up a little, the cow would stray off over the northern boundary. There was nothing but sand there, but when she was a calf there had been a patch of mixed crops, and she still remembered that.

She was one of two cows that had been turned out of the dairy herd on account of sterility. They were ill-tempered creatures, always discontented and out to do some mischief; Pelle detested them heartily. They were two regular termagants, and even a thrashing made no impression on them. One of them was a nymphomaniac cow that would suddenly start stamping and bellowing like a mad bull in the middle of her grazing; if Pelle approached her she would try to gore him. She couldn't have a calf, but she would go around trying to mount the others—and put ideas into the heads of the well-behaved steers. When she saw her chance, she would eat up Pelle's cloth dinner wrapping. The other cow was old and had twisted horns that pointed in toward her eyes, one of which had a white pupil.

It was the boisterous cow that was now up to her tricks. Pelle had to get up all the time and shout: "Hey, Blakka, you nasty brute, you come back here!" He was hoarse with anger. Finally his patience gave out, and he grabbed an enormous stick and began chasing the cow. As soon as she saw his intention she set off at a run toward the farm, and Pelle had to make a wide circle to turn her back down to the herd. Then she ran at full gallop in and out among the other animals, the herd got confused and ran all over the place, and Pelle had to give up the chase for a while until he could round them up. But as soon as he began again, indignance boiled inside him and made him bounce around like a ball, his naked body flashing in loops against the green meadow. He was only a few yards from the cow, but the distance remained the same; he couldn't catch her today.

He stopped up by the rye field, and the cow stopped almost at the same instant. She snapped at a few ears of grain and moved her head slowly to choose her direction. In two catlike leaps Pelle was there and had hold of her tail. He hit her over the snout with his cudgel so she spun out of the rye and set off at a flying pace down toward the others, as the blows rained down over her bones. Every stroke echoed back loudly from the dunes like axe blows on a tree trunk and made Pelle swell with pride. The cow tried to shake Pelle off as she ran, but she couldn't do it. She crossed the creek in long bounds, back and forth, with Pelle hanging on almost suspended in air; but the blows continued to rain down over her. She grew tired and slackened her pace, and at last she came to a standstill, coughed, and let herself be beaten.

Pelle threw himself flat on his stomach and panted. Ha, that had sure warmed him up! Now that beast would . . . All of a sudden he rolled over on his side—the foreman! But it was a strange man with a beard who stood over him, looking at him with a serious expression. The stranger went on staring at him for a long time without saying anything, and Pelle was at a total loss under his gaze. He had the sun right in his eyes too, if he tried to stare back at the man—and the cow was still standing there coughing.

"What do you think the foreman will say?" asked the man at last, quietly.

"I don't think he saw me," whispered Pelle, looking around timidly.

"But God saw you, for He sees everything. And He has led me here to stop the evil in you while there's still time. Wouldn't you like to be God's child?" The man sat down beside him and took his hand.

Pelle sat tugging at the grass and wished he had his clothes on; he nodded.

"And you must never forget that God the Father sees everything you do, even in the darkest night He sees. We are always walking in God's sight. But come now, it's not decent to run around naked!" The man took him by the hand and led him over to his clothes; then he went across to the north side and rounded up the herd while Pelle got dressed. The rambunctious cow was back over there already, and had drawn a few of the others with her. Pelle watched the man in amazement; he drove the cattle back in silence, using neither stones nor shouts. Before he got back, Blakka had once more crossed the boundary; he turned and herded her back again just as gently as before.

"That's not an easy cow to manage," he said gently when he returned, "but you've got young legs. Why don't we burn that," he asked, picking up the heavy cudgel, "and do what we have to do with our bare hands? God will always stand by you when you're in trouble. And if you want to be a true child of God, you have to tell the foreman this evening what you did—and take your punishment." He placed his hand on Pelle's head and looked at him with that intolerable gaze. Then he left, taking the stick with him.

Pelle watched him for a long time. So that was what a man looked like who was sent by God to warn you! Now he knew, and it would be some time before he chased a cow that way again. But go to the foreman and turn himself in—and get the whiplash on his bare legs? Not if he could help it! God would just have to be angry—if it was really true that He could see everything. It couldn't be worse than the foreman's whip, at least.

All that morning he was in a quiet mood. He felt the man's eyes on him in everything he did, and it robbed him of his confidence. He tried to do things silently and saw everything in a new light; it wasn't advisable to make noise if you were always walking in the sight of God the Father. He didn't crack his cattle whip anymore, but even thought a little about burning it.

But a little before noon Rud appeared, and he forgot the whole thing. Rud was smoking a bit of rattan that he had cut off his mother's stove cleaner, and Pelle traded some of his dinner for a few drags on it. First they sat astride Amor the steer, which was lying chewing its cud. It went on calmly chewing with closed eyes until Rud put the glowing cane to the root of its tail; then it got up quickly and both boys rolled over its head. They laughed and boasted to each other of the somersault they had turned, as they went up to the hedgerow to look for blackberries. From there they went to some birds' nests in the small pines, and finally they started in on their favorite game—digging up mouseholes.

Pelle knew every mousehole in the meadow, and they lay on their stomachs and examined them carefully. "Here's one that has mice in it," said Rud. "Look, here's their dunghill!"

"Yes, that smells like mice," said Pelle, sticking his nose down the hole. "And the blades of grass turn outward—so the parents are probably out."

With Pelle's knife they cut away the turf, and eagerly set to work digging with two shards of pottery. The dirt flew around their ears as they talked and laughed.

"Boy, this is going fast!"

"It sure is. Even Strøm couldn't work this fast!" Strøm was a famous farmhand who got 25 øre a day more than the other harvest workers; he was used as an example to coax the laborers to work harder.

"Pretty soon we'll be right inside the bowels of the earth."

"Sure, but it's red-hot down there."

"Come on, you're kidding." Pelle paused doubtfully in his digging.

"It is, the schoolmaster says so."

The boys hesitated and put their hands down in the hole. Yes, it was hot at the bottom—so hot that Pelle had to pull out his hand and say, "Ow, dammit!" They thought about it a while, then went on scraping out the hole as carefully as if their lives depended on it. But in a little while straw appeared in the passage, and at once the internal heat of the earth was forgotten. They quickly uncovered the nest, and laid the newborn pink mice out on the grass. They looked like half-hatched birds.

"They're ugly," said Pelle, who was a little afraid of picking them up but ashamed not to. "They're much nastier to touch than toads. I think they're poisonous."

Rud lay pinching them between his fingers.

"Poisonous? Don't be silly, they don't even have any teeth! There aren't any bones in them at all; I'm sure you could eat them."

"Ugh!" Pelle spit on the ground.

"I'm not afraid of biting into one—are you?" Rud lifted a little mouse toward his mouth.

"Afraid? Of course I'm not afraid—but..." Pelle hesitated.

"No, you *are* afraid, because you've got blue balls!"

Now this epithet really only applied to boys who were afraid of water, but Pelle quickly seized one of the little mice and held it up to his mouth, just as close to his lips as Rud was holding his. "You can see for yourself!" he exclaimed in an offended tone.

Rud went on talking, waving his arms.

"You're afraid, and it's because you're Swedish. But when you're afraid, you should just shut your eyes—like this—and open your mouth. Then you pretend to put the mouse right into your mouth, and then"—Rud had his mouth wide open, holding his hand close to it; Pelle was under his spell, imitating his movements—"and then..." Pelle received a blow that sent the little mouse down into his throat. He retched and spit it out; his hands fumbled in the grass and got hold of a rock. But by the time he was on his feet and was about to throw it, Rud was far away up the fields. "I've got to go home now!" he shouted innocently. "There's something I've got to help my mother with."

Pelle didn't care for solitude, and the prospect of a boycott made him willing to negotiate. He dropped the rock to show his serious wish for a reconciliation, and had to swear solemnly that he would not bear malice. Then at last Rud came back, giggling.

"I was going to show you something funny with the mouse," he said by way of diversion, "but you held on to it like an idiot." He didn't dare come all the way up to Pelle, but stood watching his movements.

Pelle was acquainted with the little white lie when the danger of a beating was imminent, but the lie as an attack was still unknown to him. If Rud, now that the whole thing was over, said that he only wanted to show him something funny, then it was probably true. But then why was he acting suspicious? As so often before, Pelle tried to bend his little brain around the possible devious intent of his friend, but failed.

"You might as well come all the way over here," he said bluntly. "If I wanted to, I could catch you easily."

Rud came over. "Now we'll catch some big mice," he said. "That's more fun."

They emptied Pelle's milk bottle and then found a mouse's nest that appeared to have only two exits—one up in the meadow, the other halfway down the bank of the creek. Down there they shoved in the neck of the bottle, and they widened the hole up in the meadow into a funnel; they took turns keeping an eye on the bottle and carrying water in their caps up to the other hole. It wasn't long before a mouse popped out into the bottle and they stuck in the cork.

Now what were they going to do with it? Pelle suggested that they tame it and train it to pull their little agricultural implements; but Rud got his way as usual—the mouse would go out sailing!

Down where the stream turned and had hollowed out its bed into a hole as big as a kettle, they made a slide and let the bottle slip down into the water neck first, like a ship being launched. They could follow it as it curved under the water until it popped up at an angle and stood bobbing on the water like a buoy, with its neck straight up. The mouse made the funniest leaps toward the cork to get out; the boys jumped around in the grass with delight.

"It knows the way it got in—it knows!" They imitated its unsuccessful leaps, plopped down on their stomachs again, and writhed helplessly on the grass. But after a while it got old.

"Should we take out the cork?" suggested Rud.

"Yes—oh yes!" Pelle quickly waded out after the bottle, about to set the mouse free.

"Wait a minute, you fathead!" Rud snatched the bottle from him. Holding his hand over its mouth, he put it back in the water. "Now we'll have some fun!" he cried, hurrying up the bank.

It was a little while before the mouse discovered that the path was open, but then it leaped. The jump was unsuccessful, and the bottle started to rock, so that the second leap was slanting and it bounced off the side. But then the mouse made a number of leaps like lightning, a regular bombardment; and suddenly it flew right out of the bottle and landed head first in the water.

"That was some jump!" shouted Pelle, bouncing straight up and down in the grass with his arms at his sides. "It could just squeeze its body through, just barely!" He jumped again, making himself thin.

The mouse swam to land, but Rud was there and pushed it out again with his foot. "It swims good," he said, laughing. Then it headed for the opposite bank. "Watch out!" roared Rud, and Pelle sprang forward and turned it back from the shore with a good kick. It swam helplessly back and forth in the middle of the pool, seeing the two dancing figures whenever it approached a bank, and turning and turning endlessly. It sank deeper and deeper—its fur got wet and dragged it down, until at last it was swimming completely under water. Suddenly it stretched out in a convulsion and sank to the bottom, with all four legs outspread like a wide embrace.

In an instant Pelle had understood its perplexity and helplessness—maybe he was familiar with it himself. At the animal's final twitch he burst into tears with a little scream and ran howling up over the meadow toward the pine grove. In a little while he came back. "I really thought Amor had run away," he said repeatedly, and carefully avoided looking Rud in the eye. Quietly he waded into the water and fished out the dead mouse with his foot.

They laid it on a stone in the sun so that it would come to life again. When that failed, Pelle remembered a story about some people who had drowned in a lake back home, and who came to again when cannons were fired over them. They clapped their hollowed hands over the mouse, and when that didn't work either they decided to bury it.

Rud remembered that his grandmother in Sweden was going to be buried one of these days, and this made them proceed with a certain solemnity. They made a coffin out of a matchbox and decorated it with moss; they lay on their stomachs and lowered the coffin into the grave with twine—with the utmost care so that it wouldn't stand on end. A rope might give way; that sometimes happened, and the illusion wouldn't allow them to correct the position of the coffin with their hands afterward. When this was done, Pelle looked down into his cap, while Rud prayed over the deceased and cast earth onto the coffin. Then they filled up the grave.

"I just hope it's not in a trance and going to wake up again!" exclaimed Pelle suddenly. They had both heard many unpleasant stories of such cases, and they went over all the possibilities—how they woke up and couldn't get any air, and banged on the lid, and started eating their own hands—until Pelle could distinctly hear a knocking on the lid below. They quickly dug up the coffin and examined the mouse. It hadn't eaten its forepaws, but it had definitely turned over on its side. They buried it again, putting a dead beetle in the coffin for safety's sake, and sticking a straw down into the grave to supply the mouse with air. Then they decorated the mound and set up a memorial stone.

"Now it's dead," declared Pelle gravely.

"Yes, it sure is—dead as a herring." Rud had put his ear to the straw and listened.

"Now it must be up with God in all His glory—high, high up."

Rud sniffed contemptuously. "Oh, you dope, do you think it can crawl up there?"

"Mice can too crawl!" Pelle was sullen.

"Sure, but not through the air. Only birds can do that."

Pelle felt himself beaten and wanted revenge.

"Then your grandmother isn't in heaven either!" he insisted. The incident with the baby mouse was still bothering him.

But this was more than Rud could stand. It had touched his family pride, and he gave Pelle a dig in the side with his elbow. The next moment they were rolling in the grass, holding each other by the hair, and making clumsy attempts to hit each other on the nose with their fists. They turned over and over like one lump, with one on top and then the other, wheezing hoarsely, groaning and making tremendous exertions. "I'll make you sneeze red," said Pelle bitterly as he climbed on top of his adversary. But the next moment he was down again, with Rud hanging over him and making the most fearful threats about black eyes and seeing stars. Their voices were thick with emotion.

And suddenly they were sitting facing each other on the grass, wondering whether they should start bawling. Then Rud stuck out his tongue, Pelle did the same and began to laugh, and they were once more the best of friends. They set up the memorial stone, which had been knocked over in the heat of battle, and then sat down hand in hand to rest after the storm—a little quieter than usual.

It was not that Pelle was crueler than Rud, but for him the question had taken on an importance of its own, and he just had to figure it out. A meditative expression came into his eyes, and he said thoughtfully, "Well, you told me yourself that her legs were paralyzed."

"So what?"

"Then she couldn't crawl up to heaven."

"Oh, you idiot—it's her spirit, of course!"

"Then the mouse's spirit could be up there too."

"No, it couldn't—mice haven't got any spirit."

"They don't? Then how can they breathe?"

There was a question for Rud! And the tiresome part of it was that he went to Sunday school. His fists would have come in handy again now, but his instinct told him that sooner or later Pelle would get the better of him in a fight. He had saved his grandmother, at any rate.

"Yes," he said, yielding, "sure it could breathe. Then its spirit flying up was what knocked over the stone—that's what it was!"

A distant sound reached them, and way up near the cottage they could see the figure of a fat woman, beckoning threateningly.

"The Sow's calling you," said Pelle. The two boys never called her anything else.

So Rud had to go. He was allowed to take most of the contents of the dinner basket with him, and ate as he ran. They had been too busy to eat.

Pelle sat down near the dunes and ate his dinner. As usual when Rud had been out with him, he couldn't imagine where the day had gone. The birds had stopped singing, and not one of the cattle was still lying down, so it must be at least five o'clock.

Up at the farm they were busy driving in the crop. It went at full trot—out and back, out and back. The men stood up in the carts and thrashed away at the horses with the end of the reins. The swaying loads rushed along the field roads; they looked like little bristling bugs that have been startled and are darting to shelter.

A one-horse buggy drove out from the farm and took the highway to town at a quick trot. It was the master of Stone Farm; he was driving so fast that he was evidently off to town on a spree. So something was wrong at home, and there would be crying at the farm tonight.

Yes, there was Papa Lasse driving out with the water cart, so it was half-past five. He could also tell by the pleasant evening twittering of the birds, low and scintillating like the rays of the sun.

Far inland above the stone quarry, where the cranes stood out against the sky, a cloud of smoke would rise into the air every now and then and burst into a fountain of rock shards. Long after came the sound of the explosion, broken into bits; it sounded as if someone were running along and slapping his thighs with mittens on.

The last few hours were always long—the sun was so slow going down. And time had no meaning either. Pelle himself was tired, and the tranquility of evening settled down and blocked out every loud sound. But now they were driving out for milking up there, and the cattle were starting to graze along the edge of the meadow facing the farm; so it was almost time.

At last the cowherds began to yodel over at the neighboring farms, first one, and then several joining in:

Oh, drive home, o-ho, o-o-ho!
O-ho, o-ho!
O-ho, o-ho!
Oh, drive home, o-o-ho!
O-ho!

From all sides the gentle song quivered over the sloping land; it ran out, like the sound of happy weeping, into the first glow of evening, and Pelle's cattle began to move farther after each pause to graze. But he didn't dare drive them home yet, for it only meant a box on the ear from the foreman or the trainee if he arrived too early.

He stood at the upper end of the meadow and called his homeward-drifting herd together. And when the last tones of the cowherds' call home had died away, he began to yodel it himself, and stepped to one side. The animals ran with an odd gait, their heads stretched forward. The shadows of the grass lay in long thin stripes across the ground, and the shadows of the animals were endless. Now and then the calves lowed wistfully and broke into a gallop. They were yearning for home, and Pelle was too.

From behind a clearing the sun shot long rays through the air, as if it had called all its powers home for the night and was now extending them in one great longing, from west to east. Everything pointed in long thin lines, and the yearning of the cattle seemed visible in the air behind them.

In the mind of the child there was nothing left outdoors now; everything was being taken in, and he leaned forward in an almost feverish longing for his father. And when at last he turned the corner with the herd and saw old Lasse standing there, smiling happily with his red-rimmed eyes and opening the gate to the fold, the boy burst inside and threw himself weeping into his father's arms.

"What's the matter, lad, what's the matter?" asked the old man with concern in his voice, stroking the child's face with a trembling hand. "Has someone been unkind to you? No? Well, that's good! They'd better take care, for happy children are in God's own keeping. And Lasse would be a tough customer if it came to that. So you missed me, did you? Then it's good to be in your little heart, and Lasse can only be glad. But go in now and eat, and don't cry anymore."

He wiped the boy's nose with his hard, crooked fingers, and pushed him gently along.

V

Pelle was not long in finding out all about the man who had been sent by God, the one with the grave, reproachful eyes. He proved to be nothing but a journeyman from down in the village, who spoke at the meeting house on Sundays; it was also said that his wife drank. Rud went to his Sunday school, and he was poor; so he was nothing out of the ordinary.

Besides, Gustav had gotten a cap that had three interchangeable crowns—one of blue duffle, one of waterproof oilcloth, and one of white duck for use in sunny weather. It was an exciting discovery that threw everything else into the background and roused Pelle's curiosity for days; he used this miraculous cap as a standard by which to measure everything great and desirable. Until one day he gave Gustav a beautifully carved walking-stick for permission to perform the trick of turning the crown inside out himself. That finally set his mind at ease, and the cap took its place in his everyday world along with everything else.

But what did it look like in Master Kongstrup's big rooms? Money was probably lying on the bare floor, the gold in one place and the silver in another; and in the middle of each heap stood a bushel measure. What did the word "expedient" mean, which the foreman used when he talked to the landowner? And why did the men call each other "Swede" as a term of abuse? They were all Swedes, weren't they? What was off beyond the cliffs where the stone quarry lay? On one side was the edge of the farm, of course. He hadn't been there yet, but was going with his father as soon as an opportunity arose. Quite by chance they had learned that Lasse had a brother who owned a house over there. So it was somewhat familiar territory.

Down there was the sea; he had sailed on it himself! Ships of both iron and wood sailed on it, but how could iron float when it was so heavy? The water of the sea must be strong, because in the pond, iron sank to the bottom at once. In the middle of the pond there was no bottom, so there you'd go on sinking forever! In his youth the old thatcher had had more than a hundred fathoms of rope down there with a drag, to fish up a bucket, but he never reached the bottom. And when he tried to pull up the rope again, there was something deep down that had grabbed hold of the drag and tried to pull him down, so he had to let go of the whole thing.

Our Lord God... well, He had a long white beard like the farmer at Kåse Farm; but who kept house for Him in His old age? Saint Peter was probably His foreman, of course!... How could the old dry cows have calves as young as the heifers did?

One great fact was self-evident: it was something you didn't question or even think about, because it was the very foundation of all existence— Papa Lasse. He was just there, standing like a secure wall behind everything that Pelle did. He was the real Providence, the last great refuge in good times and bad; he could do whatever he wanted to—Papa Lasse was almighty.

Then there was one natural center in the world—Pelle himself. Everything grouped itself around him, everything existed for his sake— for him to play with, to shudder at, or to put aside for a great future. Even the distant trees, houses, and rocks in the landscape, which he had never seen up close, assumed an attitude toward him, either friendly or hostile. And the relationship had to be carefully determined for every new thing that came within his sphere.

His world was small; he was just beginning to create it. Within an arm's length on all sides of him, there was more or less solid ground; beyond that drifted raw material, chaos. But Pelle already found his world immense, and was quite willing to make it infinite. He attacked everything with insatiable appetite, and his alert senses seized every-thing that came within their reach; they were like the mouth of a machine, into which matter was incessantly rushing in small, whirling particles. And in their wake came more and more—the entire universe was wandering toward him.

Pelle shaped and set aside twenty new things every second. The earth grew under him into a world that was rich in excitement and grotesque forms, terror and the most ordinary things. He moved about in it uncertainly, for there was always something that shifted and had to be evaluated or recreated; the most matter-of-fact things would change and suddenly become hair-raising miracles—or vice versa. He went around in a state of perpetual wonder, assuming an expectant attitude to even the most familiar things. For who could tell what surprises they might bring?

For instance, his whole life he had had opportunities to verify that pants buttons were made of bone and had five holes, a large one in the middle and four smaller ones around it. And then one day, one of the men comes home from town with a pair of new pants, and the buttons are made of shiny metal and are no larger than a 25-øre piece. They only have four holes, and the thread is sewn across them, not from the middle outward like on the old ones.

Or what about the great eclipse of the sun that he had been waiting for all summer; all the old people had said it would bring about the end of the world. He had looked forward to it—especially the destruction part. It would be something of an adventure, and somewhere inside him there was a scrap of faith that he would make it through all right. The solar eclipse arrived just as it was supposed to; it even became night, as if it were Judgment Day, and the birds grew so quiet, and the cattle bellowed and wanted to run home. But then it grew light again like normal, and nothing came of it all.

Then there were monstrous terrors that would all at once reveal themselves to be tiny little things—thank God! But there were also joys that would make his heart pound fast—and then turned out to be utterly boring when he got near them.

Far out in the hazy mass, invisible worlds floated by that had nothing to do with his own; a sound from the unknown would create them whole in an instant. They came into existence in the same way as this land had, on that morning when he stood on the open middle deck of the steamer and heard voices and noise through the fog: thick and mighty, with shapes that looked like giant mittens.

And inside a person there was blood and a heart and a soul. The heart Pelle had found out about himself; it was a little bird locked up in there, but the soul bored its way like a serpent to whatever part of the body desire occupied. Old thatcher Holm had once drawn the soul like a thin thread out of the thumb of a man who suffered from kleptomania. Pelle's own soul was only good; it lay in the pupils of his eyes, and reflected Papa Lasse's image whenever he looked into them.

The blood was the worst, and that's why Papa Lasse always let himself be bled whenever there was anything wrong with him—the bad humors had to be let out. Gustav thought a lot about blood, and could tell the strangest things about it; he went around cutting his fingers just to see whether his blood was ripe. One evening he came over to the cow stable and displayed a bleeding finger. The blood was totally black. "Now I'm a man," he said, and swore a mighty oath. But the maids just made fun of him: he hadn't carried his barrel of peas up to the attic yet...

Then there was hell and heaven—and the stone quarry where the men would hit each other with heavy hammers when they got drunk. The men in the stone quarry were the strongest giants on earth. One of them had once eaten ten fried eggs without getting sick. And eggs are power itself.

Down in the meadow, will-o'-the-wisps hopped about looking for something in the deep summer nights; one of them was always near the creek, standing there playing on top of a little heap of stones that lay in the middle of the lush meadow. A couple of years ago a girl gave birth to a child out here one night among the dunes, and since she didn't know what to do about a father for it, she drowned it in one of the pools that the creek makes where it turns. Decent people put up the little cairn, so that the place wouldn't be forgotten; and the child's soul used to burn over it on dark nights during the season when it was born. Pelle believed that the child itself was buried beneath the stones, and now and then he would decorate the mound with a pine bough; but he never played at that part of the creek. The girl was sent across the sea, sentenced to penal servitude for many years, and people wondered about the father. She hadn't named anyone, but everyone knew who it was all the same. He was a young, well-to-do fisherman down in the village, and the girl was very poor, so there could never have been any question of their marrying. The girl must have preferred this to begging help from him for the child—and to living in the village as a weaver with an illegitimate child, ridiculed by everyone! And they had to admit he had certainly kept a stiff upper lip, when many others would have been ashamed and gone away on a long voyage.

This summer, two years after the girl went to prison, the fisherman was going home one night along the shore toward the village with some nets on his back. He was a tough character and didn't hesitate to take the shortest way across the meadow; but when he was well into the dunes, he saw a will-o'-the-wisp following in his steps, and he grew frightened and started to run. It was gaining on him, and when he leaped across the creek to put water between himself and the spirit, it seized hold of his nets. Then he shouted the name of God, and fled like one bereft of his senses. The next morning at sunrise he and his father went to fetch the nets. They had caught on the cairn and were lying right across the creek.

Then the young man joined the Revivalists, and his father abandoned his carousing and followed him. From morning to night the young fisherman could be found at their meetings, and otherwise he went about like a criminal with his head hung down, just waiting for the girl to come home from prison, so that he could marry her.

Pelle knew all about it. The maids would shudder as they talked about it, sitting on the men's laps in the long summer evenings, and a lovesick fellow from farther inland had made up a ballad about it, which Gustav sang to his concertina. Then all the girls on the farm would weep, and even Lively Sara's eyes would fill with tears, and she would start to talk to Mons about engagement rings.

One day Pelle was lying on his stomach in the grass, singing and kicking his bare feet in the clear air, when he saw a young man standing down by the cairn and putting stones on it that he took out of his pocket; then he knelt down. Pelle went over to him.

"What are you doing?" he asked boldly, feeling that he was in his own domain. "Are you saying your prayers?"

The man didn't answer, but remained kneeling. At last he rose, spitting out tobacco juice.

"I'm praying to Him Who is to judge us all," he said, looking steadily at Pelle.

Pelle recognized that look. It was the same expression that man had the other day—the one who had been sent by God. Only there was no reproach in it.

"Don't you have any bed to sleep in?" asked Pelle. "I always say my prayers under the quilt. He hears them just as well! God knows everything."

The young man nodded, and started moving the stones on the cairn around.

"Don't touch that," said Pelle firmly. "There's a little baby buried there."

The young man gave him a strange look.

"That's not true," he said thickly. "The child lies up in the church-yard in properly consecrated ground."

"Is that so?" said Pelle, imitating his father's slow drawl. "But I know it was the parents that drowned it—and buried it here." He was too proud of his knowledge to relinquish it without a word.

The man looked as though he wanted to hit him, and Pelle backed up a little; there he stood, laughing openly. He had faith in his legs. But the man no longer seemed aware of him and stood staring dully past the cairn. So Pelle drew near again.

The man gave a start at Pelle's shadow and heaved a deep sigh. "Is that you?" he said apathetically, without looking at Pelle. "Why don't you leave me alone?"

"This is *my* field," said Pelle, "because I'm the herdsman. But you can stay here if you don't hit me. And don't touch the cairn, because there's a little baby buried there."

The young man looked gravely at Pelle. "That's not true. How dare you tell such a lie? God doesn't like lies. But you're only an innocent child, and I'll tell you how it all happened without hiding a thing—as truly as I only want to walk wholly in God's sight."

Pelle looked at him uncomprehendingly. "But I know how it all happened myself," he said, "since I know the whole song by heart. I can sing it for you, if you like; it goes like this." And Pelle began to sing, his voice a little uncertain out of shyness:

So happy are we in our childhood's first years,
  Neither sorrow nor sin is our mead;

We play, and there's nought in our path to raise fears
    That it straight into prison doth lead.

Full many there are who with voice sorrowful
    Must oft for lost happiness long.
To make the time pass in this prison so dull,
    I now will set forth my song.

I played with my father, with mother I played,
    And childhood's days came to an end;
Each day the sun shone — and I as a young maid,
    Played still, but now with my friend.

I gave him my day and I gave him my night,
    And never once he would betray;
But when I told him of my sorrowful plight,
    Then he would no longer play.

'I never have loved you,' he quickly did say;
    'Begone! I'll ne'er see you again!"
He turned on his heel and went angry away.
    'Twas then I a murderess became.

Here Pelle paused in astonishment, for the grown-up man had sunk forward and was sitting there sobbing. "Yes, it was wicked," Pelle said, "because then she killed her child and had to go to prison." He spoke with a certain amount of contempt; he didn't like men who cried. "But that's nothing for *you* to cry about," he added carelessly after a while.

"Yes it is, because she didn't do anything wrong — it was the child's father who killed it. I was the one who did the terrible deed; yes, I confess that I am a murderer. Haven't I shown my guilt openly enough?" He turned his face upward, as if he were speaking to God.

"So you were the one?" said Pelle, moving away from him a little. "Did you kill your own child? Papa Lasse could never have done that! But then why aren't you in prison? Did you tell a lie, and say that *she* did it?"

These words had a peculiar effect on the fisherman. Pelle stood watching him for a moment, and then exclaimed: "You talk so funny — 'blop, blop, blop,' like you're from another country! And why are you scratching the air with your fingers and crying? Are you going to get a beating when you get home?"

At the word "crying," the man began to sob violently. Pelle had never seen anyone cry so unrestrainedly. His face seemed all blurred.

"Do you want a sandwich?" he asked, trying to console him. "I have one with sausage on it."

The fisherman shook his head.

Pelle looked at the cairn. He was obstinate and determined not to give in.

"It *is* buried there," he said. "I've seen its soul burning on the stones at night. That's because it can't get into heaven."

A horrible sound came from the fisherman's lips, a hollow groan that made Pelle's little heart leap into his throat. He himself began to jump up and down in fright, and when he regained control and stopped, he saw the fisherman running across the meadow with his head bent low, and then he vanished among the dunes.

Pelle gazed after him in astonishment, and then moved slowly toward his dinner basket. The result of the encounter was, for the moment, disappointment. He had sung for a perfect stranger, and that was undeniably an achievement—considering how difficult it could be just to say yes or no to somebody you'd never seen before. But he never got a chance to sing most of the verses, and the extraordinary thing was that he knew the entire ballad by heart. He sang it now to himself from beginning to end, keeping count of the verses on his fingers. And he took the greatest pleasure in roaring it at the top of his lungs.

In the evening, as usual, he discussed the events of the day with his father, and then he came to understand several things that gave him an eerie feeling. Papa Lasse's voice was still the only human voice that the boy fully understood. A mere sigh or shake of the old man's head had a more convincing power than anyone else's words.

"Alas!" he said again and again. "Evil, evil everywhere; sorrow and trouble wherever you turn! He'd probably give his life to go to prison in her place—now it's too late. So he ran off when you said that to him? Well, well, it's not easy to resist the Word of God from the lips of a child when the conscience is aching. And trading in the happiness of others is a bad way to make a living. But now go see about washing your feet, lad."

There was plenty in life to grab hold of and wrestle with—and a good deal to dread. But worse than all the things that wanted to harm Pelle himself were the glimpses he occasionally had of the depths of humanity: face to face with them his child's brain was powerless. Why did the mistress cry so much and drink in secret? What was going on behind the windows in the big house? He couldn't comprehend it, and every time he puzzled his little brain over it, the eerie feeling would just glare at him from all the windowpanes, and sometimes it would envelop him in all the horror of the incomprehensible.

But the sun rode high in the heavens, the nights were light, and the darkness lay crouching under the earth and had no power. And he possessed the child's happy ability to forget instantly — and completely.

VI

Pelle had a quick pulse and a lot of energy; there was always something that he was trying to overtake in his restless striving — if nothing else, then time itself. Now the rye was under shelter, the last haystack had disappeared from the field, the shadows were growing longer every day. But one evening the darkness surprised him before his bedtime, and that made him thoughtful. He no longer tried to rush time, but tried to hold it back with small sun omens.

One day the men's midday rest came to an end. They had to harness the horses again as soon as they had finished dinner, and the chaff-cutting was put off until evening. The horse's threshing path lay on the outer side of the stable, and none of the men wanted to tramp around out there in the dark, driving the horse for the chaff-cutter — so Pelle had to do it. Lasse protested and threatened to go to the master, but it was no use; every evening Pelle had to be out there for a couple of hours. They took his best hours away from him, the hours when he and Papa Lasse puttered about in the stable, talking their way through all the day's troubles without a care and into a great future they would share — and Pelle wept. Whenever the moon chased the clouds away and he could see everything around him distinctly, he would give his tears free rein. But on the dark evenings he was quiet and held his breath. Sometimes when it rained it was so dark that the farm and everything else would disappear, and then he would see hundreds of creatures that were invisible in the light. They would appear out there in the darkness, horribly big, or come slithering up to him on their bellies. He would be rooted to the spot, and he couldn't take his eyes off them. He would seek shelter under the wall, and coax the horse from there — and one evening he ran inside. The men chased him out again, and he let them do it; when it came right down to it, he was more afraid of the men inside than the monsters outside. But one pitch-dark evening he was particularly uneasy, and when he discovered that the horse, his only comfort, was scared too, he dropped everything and ran in a second time. Their threats couldn't make him go out there again, and blows were no use either. So one of the men picked him up and carried him out. But then Pelle lost control and screamed till the building shook.

While they were wrestling with him, the landowner came out. He was very angry when he heard what was wrong, and cursed the head man up and down. Then he took Pelle by the hand and went down to the cow stable with him. "What kind of a man are you, afraid of a little dark!" he said jokingly. "You'll have to get over that. But if the men hurt you, just come to me."

The plow went up and down the fields all day long, making the earth a dark hue; the leaves turned color, and there was often sleet. The coats of the cattle grew thick, their hair grew long and stood up on their backs; Pelle had a hard time, and life as a whole became a shade more serious. His clothing didn't grow thicker and warmer with the cold weather like the cattle's coats. But he could crack his whip so that it sounded, in the best cases, like little shots; he could beat up Rud fair and square, and jump across the creek at its narrowest part. All of that lent warmth to his body.

He now kept watch all over the farmlands, wherever the cattle had been tethered; the dairy cows were indoors. Or he went inland to the marsh, where each of the farms had a piece of grassland. Here Pelle met cowherds from the other farms and got a glimpse into a completely different world that was not ruled by a foreman or a trainee or beatings, but where everyone ate at the same table, and the mistress herself sat and spun wool for the cowherds' stockings. But there he could never go, because they didn't take Swedes at the small farms—and the local people didn't want to work with them either. He felt sorry about that.

As soon as the fall plowing had started up in the fields, the boys, according to ancient custom, took down the boundary fences and let all the cattle graze together. The first few days it gave them more to do, for the animals fought until they got to know each other. They never mingled completely; they still grazed in groups, each farm's herd by itself. The dinner baskets were also combined, and each boy took his turn minding the whole herd. The other boys played robbers up among the rocks, or ran around in the woods or on the beach. When it was really cold they lit bonfires, or built fireplaces of flat stones where they roasted apples and eggs they had stolen from the farms.

It was a glorious life, and Pelle was happy. It's true that he was the smallest of them all, and he had the disadvantage of being a Swede; in the middle of their game the others would sometimes start to mimic his speech, and when he got mad they asked why he didn't pull his knife. On the other hand, he was from the biggest farm and was the only one who had steers in his herd; he was just as good as the others in physical skills, and no one could whittle the way he could. And when he grew up he intended to thrash them all.

In the meantime he had to muddle through, ingratiate himself with the older boys wherever he discovered there was a gap in the relationship, and be obliging. He had to take his turn watching the herd more often than the others did, and got the short end of the stick at mealtimes. He accepted it as something unavoidable and threw himself wholeheartedly into making the best of the situation. But he promised himself full revenge when he grew up.

Once or twice it grew too hot for him, and he left the group and kept to himself. But he soon returned to the others again. His little body was bursting with a zest for life, and it wouldn't let him shirk it; he had to take his chances—gobble his way through.

One day two new boys arrived, who herded cattle from a couple of farms on the other side of the stone quarry; they were twins, and their names were Alfred and Albinus. They were tall, thin boys, who looked as if they might have been half-starved when they were little; their skin had a bluish tinge, and they couldn't stand the cold. They were quick and agile, they could overtake the fastest calf, walk on their hands and smoke at the same time, and turn somersaults without using their hands. They weren't much good at fighting; they lacked the courage, and their physical dexterity would forsake them in a pinch.

There was something comical about the two brothers. "Here come the twins, the twelvins!" cried the whole group in greeting the first morning they showed up. "So, how many babies have you had at your house since last year?" They belonged to a family of twelve, and among them were two sets of twins, and this in itself was an inexhaustible source of jokes—they were half Swedish as well. They shared half of Pelle's disadvantage.

But nothing provoked them; they laughed at everything and exposed themselves even more. From all he saw and heard, Pelle understood that there was something ridiculous about their home in the eyes of the parish; but they didn't mind it. It was especially the fertility of their parents that was the object of derision, and the two boys quite happily exposed them to ridicule, and would tell all about the most private matters at home. One day when the group had been most persistent in shouting "Twelvins!" they told them with a grin that their mother would soon be having a thirteenth. They were invulnerable.

Every time they exposed their parents to ridicule, it hurt Pelle, for his own feelings on this point were the most sacred ones he had. Try as he might, he couldn't understand them; he had to go to his father with the matter one evening.

"So they mock and make fun of their own parents?" said Lasse. "Then they'll never prosper in this world, for you must honor your father and mother. Decent parents who have brought them into the world with pain, and have to toil hard, maybe go hungry and struggle themselves, in order to get food and clothing for them! Oh, how shameful! And you say their last name is Karlsson like ours? And they live on the heath behind the stone quarry? Then they must be brother Kalle's sons! Why, bless my soul, I believe that's it! You ask them tomorrow whether their father has a notch in his right ear. I did it myself with a piece of horseshoe when we were little boys—one day I was furious with him because he made fun of me in front of the others. He was just the same as those two; but he didn't mean anything by it, there was nothing spiteful about him."

The boys' father did have a notch in his right ear. So Pelle was their cousin. He couldn't decide whether to laugh or cry about the way the boys and their parents were ridiculed. In a way, Papa Lasse also came in for a share of the teasing, and that thought was almost intolerable.

The other boys quickly discovered Pelle's vulnerable point and used it for their own advantage; Pelle had to give in and put up with a great deal in order to keep his father out of it. He didn't always succeed, however. When they were in that mood, they would say crazy things about each other's families; they didn't really mean anything by it, but Pelle didn't understand jokes on that subject. One day one of the biggest boys said to him, "Your father got his own mother with child!" Pelle didn't understand the play on words in this coarse joke, but he could hear the laughter of the others and grew blind with rage. He flew at the bigger boy, kicking him so hard in the gut that he had to stay in bed for several days.

After that incident Pelle went around worrying. He didn't dare tell his father what had happened, since he would then have to repeat the boy's ugly accusation; so he went around in dread of the fateful consequences. The other boys had withdrawn from him, so they wouldn't share the blame if anything happened. The boy was a farmer's son—the only one in the group—and they envisioned the magistrate on the scene, and perhaps a whipping in front of the town hall. So Pelle walked alone with his cattle and had plenty of time to think about the event; as a result of his lively imagination, the consequences grew more and more severe, until at last it almost suffocated him with terror. Every wagon he saw driving along the highway sent a shiver through him; and if it turned off toward Stone Farm, he could distinctly see the policemen— three of them—with large handcuffs, just as they had come to take away Erik Erikson for mistreating his wife. He hardly dared drive the cattle home in the evening.

Then one morning the boy came herding with his cattle, and there was a grown-up man with him; from his clothes and everything else about him, Pelle judged him to be a farmer—it had to be the boy's father. They stood there for a little while, talking to the cowherds, and then came toward him, with the whole pack at their heels, the father holding his son by the hand.

Pelle broke out in a sweat; he had a great urge to run away, but he forced himself to stand his ground. The father and son moved their hands at the same time and Pelle raised both elbows to ward off a double box on the ears.

But they were only extending their hands. "I beg your pardon," said the boy, taking one of Pelle's hands; "I beg your pardon," repeated the father, clasping his other hand. Pelle stood there bewildered, looking from one to the other. At first he thought that the man was the same one sent by God; but it was only his eyes—those strange eyes. Then he suddenly burst into tears and forgot everything else, sobbing away the terrible anxiety; and the two spoke a few kind words to him, and quietly went away to let him be alone.

After this Pelle and Peter Kure became good friends, and when Pelle got to know him better, he discovered that sometimes the boy had a little of the same look in his eyes as his father, and the young fisherman, and the man who was sent by God. He thought about the strange outcome of that incident for a long time. One day a chance comparison of his experiences brought him to the discovery of the connection be- tween this mysterious expression in their eyes and their remarkable actions; the people who had looked at him with those eyes had all three acted unexpectedly. And another day it dawned on him that these peo- ple were "holy"; the boys had argued with Peter Kure that day, and had used the word as a curse against his parents.

There was one thing that was important and outweighed everything, even his victory. He had tackled a boy who was bigger and stronger than he was, and he had held his own—because for the first time in his life he had struck out recklessly. If you wanted to fight, you had to kick where it would hurt the most. If you just did that, and happened to have justice on your side too, you could take on even a farmer's son. These were two satisfying discoveries, which for the present nothing could disturb.

So he had defended his father; that was something quite new and significant in his life. He needed more space now.

At the of September the cattle were taken in, and the last of the day-laborers left. During the summer, many changes had been made among the regular servants at the farm, but now, at turnover time, there were no changes; Stone Farm was not in the habit of changing servants at regular times.

So Pelle again helped his father with the foddering indoors. Actually he should have started school, and a halfhearted inquiry to the land-owner came from the school authorities. But the boy was needed at home, since the care of the cattle was too much for one man, and nothing more was heard about the matter. Pelle was glad it was put off; he had thought a lot about school during the course of the summer, and had attached so many great and unfamiliar things to it that now he was quite afraid of it.

VII

Christmas Eve came as a great disappointment. It was the custom for the cowherds to come out and spend the whole Christmas season at the farms where they had worked during the summer, and Pelle's companions had told him about all the delights of Christmas: roast meats and sweet drinks, Christmas games and pfeffernüsse and cakes—it was an endless round of eating and drinking and playing Christmas games, from the night before Christmas Eve until "Saint Knud carried Christmas out" on Twelfth Night. That's how it was at all the small farms; the only difference was that those who were "holy" didn't play cards, but sang hymns instead. But the food was just as good.

The last few days before Christmas Pelle had to get up at two or two-thirty to help the girls pluck poultry and help old thatcher Holm heat the oven. With this his involvement in the delights of Christmas came to an end. There was dried cod and rice pudding on Christmas

Eve, and it tasted all right; but all the rest was missing. There were a couple of bottles of aquavit on the table for the men, that was all. The men were discontented and quarrelsome. They poured milk and pudding into the leg of the stocking that Karna was knitting, so that she was fuming the whole evening; then each sat with his girl on his lap and grumbled about everything. The old tenant farmers and their wives, who had been invited to partake of the Christmas fare, talked about death and all the miseries of the world.

Upstairs there was a big party. All the mistress's relations were invited, and they were hard at work on the roast goose. The courtyard was full of carriages, and the only person in good spirits was the head man, who took in all the tips. Gustav was now in a thoroughly miserable mood, because Bodil was upstairs waiting on the guests. He had brought his concertina over and was playing love songs. It was putting them into better spirits, and the bad humor faded from their eyes. One by one they started singing along, and it was just getting quite cozy down there when a message came from upstairs that they had to keep the noise down. So the group broke up, the old people went home, and the young ones dispersed two by two according to the friendships of the moment.

Lasse and Pelle went to bed.

"Why is there Christmas anyway?" asked Pelle.

Lasse scratched his hip reflectively.

"That's just the way it is," he answered hesitantly. "Well, then it's the time when the year turns around and goes upward, you see . . . And of course it's also the night when the Baby Jesus was born!" It took him quite a while to produce this last reason, but it also came with perfect assurance. "One thing goes with the other, you see."

On the day after Christmas there was going to be a party at an enterprising farmer's down by the village; it would cost 2½ kroner a couple for music, sandwiches, and liquor all night long, and coffee toward morning. Gustav and Bodil were going. Little bits of Christmas were always passing Pelle by, and he was as interested in them as if he were included himself; he gave Lasse no rest from his questions that day. So Bodil was still faithful to Gustav after all!

When they got up the next morning, they found Gustav lying on the ground by the door of the cow stable, quite helpless; his good clothes were in a sad state. Bodil wasn't with him. "So she's deceived him," said Lasse as they helped him in. "Poor boy—only seventeen and already has a broken heart! Women will be the ruin of him someday, you'll see!"

At noon, when the tenants' wives came to do the milking, Lasse's assumption was confirmed: Bodil had attached herself to a tailor's apprentice from the village and had left with him in the middle of the night. They laughed pityingly at Gustav, and for some time he had to put up with their gibes at his sad fate; but the judgment was unanimous about Bodil. She was free to come and go with whom she pleased, but as long as Gustav was paying for her amusements, she should have stayed with him. Who would protect the hens that ate their grain at home and laid their eggs at the neighbor's? Who but the neighbors?

There had still been no chance to visit Lasse's brother inland beyond the stone quarry, but they would go on the day after New Year's. Between Christmas and New Year's the men did no work after dark, and it was the custom everywhere to help the herdsman with his evening chores. There was none of that here; Lasse was too old to assert himself, and Pelle too little. They ought to feel lucky they didn't also have to do the foddering for the men who went out visiting.

But today it was serious; Gustav and Long Ole had taken on the evening chores. Pelle started looking forward to it early that morning — he was up every day by half-past three. But as Lasse said, if you sing before breakfast you'll weep before nightfall.

After dinner, Gustav and Ole were grinding the chaff-cutting knife down in the lower yard. The trough leaked, and Pelle had to pour water on the grindstone from an old kettle. He was so happy, everyone could see it on his face.

"What are you so happy about?" asked Gustav. "Your eyes are shining like cat shit in the moonlight."

Pelle told him.

"I'm afraid you won't be able to leave," said Ole, winking at Gustav. "We won't get the chaff cut in time to do the foddering. Damn this grindstone, it's so hard to turn. If only that handle-turner hadn't been broken!"

Pelle pricked up his ears. "Handle-turner? What's that?"

Gustav hopped around the grindstone, slapping his thigh with glee.

"Oh God, oh God, how stupid you are, you frog! Don't you even know what a handle-turner is? It's a device you just put on the grindstone, and it turns the whole thing by itself. They've got one, by the way, over at Kåse Farm," he said, turning to Ole — "if only it weren't so far away."

"Is it heavy?" asked Pelle in a low voice; everything depended on the answer. "Could I lift it?" His voice trembled.

"No, it's not so awfully heavy. You could probably carry it. But it's very valuable."

"I can run over and get it; I'll carry it very carefully." Pelle looked at them with a face that had to inspire confidence.

"All right then. But take a sack with you to put it in. And you'll have to be more careful than the devil himself. It's an expensive thing."

Pelle found a sack and ran off across the fields. He was as delighted as a kid goat, slapping himself and everything else as he ran, and jumping aside to frighten the crows. He was overflowing with happiness. He was saving the expedition for himself and Papa Lasse. Gustav and Ole were good men! He had to get back as quickly as possible, so that they wouldn't have to toil anymore turning the grindstone. "What, are you back already?" they would say, opening their eyes wide. "You haven't smashed that precious machine on the way, have you?" Then they would take it carefully out of the sack, and it would be safe and sound. "Well, you are a wonder of a boy! A perfect prince!"

When he got to Kåse Farm, they tried to invite him in for a Christmas snack while they were putting the machine in the sack. But Pelle said no and stuck to it: he didn't have time. So they gave him a piece of cold apple fritter out on the steps, so that he wouldn't carry Christmas away with him. They all had such kind eyes, and everyone came out when he hoisted the sack on his back and set off for home. They too advised him to be very careful, and seemed anxious—as if he could hardly realize what he had in his hands.

It was a good mile between the farms, but it was an hour and a half before Pelle reached home, and then he was ready to drop. He didn't dare put down the sack to rest, but stumbled on step by step; he only rested once by leaning against a stone fence. When he staggered into the yard at last, everyone came up to see the neighbor's new handle-turner; and Pelle was conscious of his own importance when Ole carefully lifted the sack from his back. He leaned for a moment over toward the wall before he regained his balance—the ground felt so strange to stand on now that he was rid of his burden—it pushed him away. But his face was radiant.

Gustav opened the sack, which was securely fastened, and shook out its contents onto the cobblestones. There were chunks of brick, a couple of old plowshares, and the like. Pelle stared in bewilderment and fear at the junk, looking as if he had just dropped to earth from another planet. But when laughter broke out on all sides, he understood what it all meant; he crouched down into a ball and hid his face in his hands. He refused to cry, not for the world—he wouldn't give them the satisfaction. He was sobbing deep inside, but he pressed his lips together. His blood raced with rage. Those devils—those evil Satans! Suddenly he kicked Gustav in the leg.

"Aha, so he kicks, does he?" exclaimed Gustav, lifting him up in the air. "Do you want to see old man Satan from Småland? He just had a moving party and moved his butt up to his face!" He showed off Pelle's chubby cheeks. Pelle tried to cover his face with his arms and kicked to be let down; he also made an attempt to bite. "Ow, he bites too, the little devil!" Gustav had to hold him tight to be able to handle him. He held him by the collar, pressing his knuckles against the boy's throat so he gasped, while he kept talking with derisive gentleness. "A fresh youngster, this one is! He isn't dry behind the ears yet and he already wants to fight!" Gustav went on tormenting him; he seemed to be showing off his superior strength.

"Well, now we've seen that you're the strongest," said the head man at last, "so let him go!" And when Gustav didn't respond immediately, he received a blow from a clenched fist between his shoulderblades. Then the boy was released, and he went over to the stable to Lasse, who had seen the whole thing but had not dared come near. He couldn't do anything, and his presence would only have done harm.

"Yes, but there's our outing, lad," he explained, by way of excuse, while he was comforting the boy. "I could thrash a puppy like Gustav, but if I did we wouldn't get away this evening, because he wouldn't do our work. And none of the others would either—they all stick together like burrs. But you managed it yourself! I believe you'd kick old Satan himself, right on his clubfoot! Yes, yes, it was well done, but you've got to be careful not to waste your ammunition either. It doesn't pay."

The boy wasn't so easily comforted now. It stayed deep down inside him and ached, because he had acted in such good faith; they had wounded his open, cheerful trust. What had happened had also stung his pride; he had walked into a trap, made a fool of himself for them. This incident burned into his soul and greatly influenced his subsequent development. He had already found out that a person's word was not always to be relied on, and he had made awkward attempts to see what backed it up. Now he wouldn't trust anybody blindly; and he had discovered how to reveal the secret—you just had to look at people's eyes when they said something. Both here and at Kåse Farm the people had such funny looks on their faces about that handle-turner, as if they were laughing inside. And the foreman had laughed that time when he promised them roast pork and rhubarb pudding every day; they hardly ever got anything but herring and porridge. People talked with two tongues; Papa Lasse was the only one who didn't.

Pelle began to pay attention to his own face. It was the face that spoke; that's why it went badly for him when he tried to escape a beating by telling a white lie. And today's misfortune had been the fault of his face—if you felt happy, you shouldn't show it. He had discovered the danger of letting his mind lie open; and his small body diligently set to work growing calluses over its more noble parts.

After supper they trudged off across the fields, hand in hand as usual. As a rule, Pelle chattered incessantly whenever they were by themselves, but tonight he was quieter; the events of the afternoon were still on his mind, and the impending visit filled him with a sense of solemnity.

Lasse carried a red bundle in his hand which contained a bottle of black-currant rum—they had asked Per Olsen to buy it in town the day before, when he had been in to swear himself free. It had cost 66 øre, and Pelle was turning something over in his mind but didn't know whether he should ask.

"Papa, can't I carry it for a while?" he asked at last.

"Are you crazy, boy? You must be kidding—it's expensive stuff! You might drop it."

"I wouldn't drop it—well, how about just holding it for a minute? Can I, Papa? Please, Papa?"

"Eh, what an idea! I don't know what you'll be up to next, if you aren't stopped in time. Damn, I think you must be sick, the way you're carrying on!" And Lasse walked on annoyed for a while, but then he stopped and bent down over the boy.

"Hold it then, you little rascal, but be careful! And don't budge an inch while you're holding it, I'm warning you."

Pelle hugged the bottle to his body with his arms, because he didn't trust his hands; he stuck out his stomach as far as possible to support it. Lasse stood with his hands held out under the bottle, ready to catch it if it fell.

"All right, that's enough," he said anxiously, and took the bottle.

"It's heavy!" said Pelle admiringly, and walked on contentedly, holding his father's hand.

"But why did he have to swear himself free?" he suddenly asked.

"Because he was accused by a girl of being the father of her child. Haven't you heard about it?"

Pelle nodded. "Well, isn't he? Everybody says he is."

"It's hard to believe; it would mean certain damnation for Per Olsen. But the girl says it's him and no one else. Ah, yes! Girls are dangerous playthings—you'll have to be careful when your time comes. They can drag the best of men into trouble."

"So how do you swear? Do you say 'Devil take me'?"

Lasse had to laugh. "No, that wouldn't be so good for those who swear false. No, you see, in the court all God's highest ministers are seated around a table that's just like a horseshoe, and beyond that there's an altar with the crucified Christ Himself on it. On the altar there's a big, big book that's fastened to the wall with an iron chain, so the devil can't carry it off in the night—and that's God's Holy Word. When a man swears, he places his left hand on the book, and holds up his right hand with three fingers in the air—they are God the Father, the Son, and the Holy Ghost. But if he swears false, the magistrate can tell at once, because then there are red spots of blood on the pages of the book."

"Then what?" asked Pelle, deeply interested.

"Well, then his three fingers wither away, and it goes on eating at his body. People like that suffer terribly; they completely rot away."

"Don't they go to hell, then?"

"Yes, they do. Except when they give themselves up and accept their punishment, and then they escape in the next life. But they can't escape withering away."

"Why doesn't the magistrate take them himself and punish them, when he can see in the book that they swore false?"

"Why, because then they'd escape going to hell. And there's an agreement with Satan that he'll get all those who don't give themselves up, don't you see?"

Pelle shuddered, and for a while he walked on in silence next to his father. But then he forgot all about it.

"I guess Uncle Kalle's rich, isn't he?" he asked.

"He can't be rich, but he's a landowner. That's not a small thing!" Lasse himself had never gotten any farther than renting land.

"When I grow up, I'll have a great big farm," said Pelle firmly.

"Yes, I'm sure you will," said Lasse, chuckling. Not that he didn't expect something great of the boy—if not exactly a large farm. But who could tell, maybe some farmer's daughter would fall in love with him— ladies' men ran in the family. Many of them had given proof of this: his brother, for example, who had put horns on the pastor himself. Then Pelle would have to make the most of his opportunity so that the family would be too ashamed to oppose the match. And Pelle was good enough; he had that cowlick on his forehead, fine hair at the back of his neck, and a birthmark on his thigh—it all signified good luck. Lasse went on talking to himself as he walked; he calculated the boy's future with large, round figures—and there was a little left over for himself too. Because however great Pelle's future might be, it would surely come in time to allow Lasse to share and enjoy it in his old age.

They went straight across the fields toward the quarry, following stone fences and snow-filled ditches, and working their way through the thicket of blackthorn and juniper, behind which lay the rocks and the heath. They made their way right into the depths of the quarry, and in the darkness tried to find the place where the rubble was thrown; that's where the gravel pit must be.

From up by the gravel pit came a sound of hammering, and they could see lights at several of the workplaces. Beneath a sloping straw screen where a lantern was hanging, a broad-shouldered little man sat hammering away at the rocks. He was working with peculiar vivacity: striking three blows and pushing the gravel aside, another three blows and again to the side. And while one hand pushed the shards away, the other placed a fresh rock in position on the slab—it all went as efficiently and regularly as the ticking of a clock.

"My God, if it isn't brother Kalle sitting there!" said Lasse, sounding as if this encounter were a miracle from heaven. "Good evening, Kalle Karlsson! How are you?"

The stonebreaker looked up.

"Oh, it's you, brother!" he said, rising with difficulty. The two greeted each other as if they had last been together the day before. Kalle collected his tools and placed the screen over them while they talked.

"So you break stones too? Does that bring in anything?" asked Lasse.

"Oh, not that much. We get twelve kroner a wagonload, and if I work by lantern morning till night, I can break half a wagonload in a week. It doesn't pay for beer, but we get by anyhow. But it's beastly hard work—you can't stay warm doing it, and you get so stiff in the crotch from sitting fifteen hours on the cold stone—as stiff as if you had fathered the whole world all by yourself." He walked laboriously in front of the others across the heath toward a low, hump-backed cottage.

"Look, here comes the moon, now that it's no longer needed," said Kalle, whose spirits were beginning to rise. "And jeez, what a sight the old sleepyhead is—specks of dirt in his eyes and a bad taste in his mouth. He must have been to a New Year's feast in heaven."

The wall of the house stuck out in a large round lump on one side; Pelle just had to go up and touch it. It was a total mystery what was inside—maybe a secret chamber? He tugged at his father's hand inquisitively.

"That? That's the oven where they bake their bread," said Lasse. "It's like that to make more room."

"Yes, and that's the bank where we put whatever we have left over," said Kalle, showing Pelle a little decrepit outhouse. "If you feel like making a deposit, go ahead." Lasse laughed.

"You're the same merry devil you were in the old days," said Lasse.

"Well, good spirits will soon be the only thing you can get for free. But come on inside."

Kalle stuck his head in a door that led from the kitchen to the cowshed. "Hey, Marie, you'd better put your best foot forward," he called in a low voice. "The midwife's here!"

"What in the world does she want? You're lying, you old fool!" The sound of milk squirting into a pail began again.

"So I'm lying, am I? Well then, you have to come in and go to bed; she says it's high time you did. You're staying up much too late this year. Mind what you say," he whispered into the cowshed, "because she's really here! And hurry up."

They stepped into the room, and Kalle went groping about to light a candle. Twice he picked up the matches but dropped them again to light it at the stove, but the peat was burning badly. "Oh, the hell with it!" he said, striking a match at last. "We don't get visitors every day."

"So your wife's Danish," said Lasse admiringly. "And you've got a cow too!"

"Yes, we've got plenty of room, as you can see," said Kalle with pride. "A cat is part of the crew too—with as many rats as it feels like eating."

Now his wife came in, breathless, and looked in astonishment at the visitors.

"Well, the midwife's already left," said Kalle. "She didn't have time today; we'll have to put it off till another time. But these are important strangers, so you'd better blow your nose with your fingers before you shake hands!"

"Oh, you old fool, I wasn't born yesterday. It's Lasse, I can see, and Pelle." And she held out her hand. She was short like her husband, always smiling, and had bowed arms and legs just like him. Hard work and their cheerful temperament gave them both a rotund look.

"God has certainly blessed you with children," said Lasse, looking around the room. There were three in the window seat: two little ones at one end, and a tall twelve-year-old boy at the other, his dirty feet sticking out between the little girls' heads. Other beds were made up on chairs, in an old kneading-trough, and on the floor.

"Yep, we've managed to scrape together a few," said Kalle, running around in a vain search for something for his visitors to sit on, but everything was being used as beds. "You'll have to spit on the floor and sit down on that," he said with a laugh.

But now his wife came in with a washing-bench and an empty beer keg.

"Please sit down and relax," she said, placing the seats around the table. "And you must really excuse us, but the children have to sleep somewhere."

Kalle squeezed himself in and sat down on the edge of the window seat. "Yes, we've managed to scrape together a few," he repeated. "You have to provide for your old age while you have the strength. We've made up the dozen, and started on the next. It wasn't exactly our intention, but Mother keeps on fooling us." He scratched the back of his neck and looked the picture of despair.

His wife was standing in the middle of the room with her hands resting on her belly; her skirts stuck out a good deal in front. "Let's hope it won't be twins again this time," she said, laughing.

"Why, that would be a great saving, since we have to send for the midwife anyhow," Kalle said. "People say of Mother that when she's put the children to bed she has to count them to make sure they're all there. But that's not true, because she can't count past ten."

In the alcove a baby started to cry. The mother picked it up and sat down on the edge of the window seat to nurse it. She sat facing them with her breast exposed and tickled the little girl on the nose with her nipple to make her laugh. Kalle looked lovingly at her. "Marie has always had skin as fine as a parson's daughter," he said, looking proudly at the others.

"And this is the smallest," said the mother, holding the baby out toward Lasse, who put a crooked finger down its neck.

"What a little fatty!" he said softly; he was fond of children. "What's her name?"

"She's called Dozena Endina, because when she came we thought that would be the last. And she was the twelfth too."

"Dozena Endina, that's a goddamn fine name!" exclaimed Lasse. "It sounds just like she could be a princess."

"Yes, and the one before is called Ellen—from eleven, of course. That's her in the kneading-trough," said Kalle. "The one before that is Tentius, and then Nina, and Otto. The ones before that weren't named that way, because we had no idea then that there'd be so many. But that's all Mother's fault; all she has to do is put a patch on my work pants and things start going awry."

"You ought to be ashamed of yourself, trying to get out of it like that," said his wife, shaking her finger at him. "But as far as that goes," she went on, turning to Lasse, "the others have nothing to complain about either, as far as their names are concerned: there's Albert, Anna, Alfred, Albinus, Anton, Alma, and Alvilda—let me see, yes, that's all of them. None of them can say they haven't been treated fairly. Father was all for A in those days; they all had to start with A. Poetry's always come so easy to him." She looked admiringly at her husband.

Kalle blinked his eyes in embarrassment. "No, but it's the first letter, you see, and it sounds pretty," he said modestly.

"Isn't he clever to think of a thing like that? He should have been a student. Now *my* head would never have been any good for anything of that sort. He even wanted to have the names both begin and end with A, but that wouldn't do for the boys, so he had to give that up. But then he hasn't had any book-learning either."

"No, you know what, Mother, I didn't give it up. I'd made up a name for the first boy that had A at the end too. But then the pastor and the deacon made a fuss, and I had to let it go. They objected to Dozena Endina too, but I put my foot down—for Kalle can get mad if he's badgered too long. I've always liked to have some connection and meaning in everything; and it's not a bad idea to have something for those who dig deeper to figure out. Now, has brother Lasse noticed anything special about two of these names?"

"No," replied Lasse hesitantly, "I don't know that I have. But I haven't got a head for that sort of thing either."

"Well, look here, Anna and Otto are exactly the same whether you read them forward or backward—exactly the same. Let me show you." He took down a child's slate that was hanging on the wall with a stump of slate pencil, and began laboriously writing the names. "Now, look at this, brother."

"But I can't read," said Lasse, shaking his head hopelessly. "So it goes the same both ways? Damn, that *is* remarkable!" He couldn't get over it.

"But now comes the really remarkable part," said Kalle, looking over the top of his slate at his brother with the gaze of a thinker survey-ing the universe. "Otto, which can be read from both ends, means eight, of course; but if I draw the figure 8, you can turn it upside down and it's still the same. Look here!" He wrote the figure eight.

Lasse turned the slate up and down and peered at it.

"Well, God bless my soul, it is the same, just look here, Pelle! It's like a cat that always lands on its feet, no matter how you drop it. Bless my soul, it must be nice to be able to spell. How did you learn it, brother?"

"Oh," said Kalle, in a tone of superiority, "I've sat and looked on a little when Mother's been teaching the children their ABCs. There's nothing to it if your upper story's all right."

"Pelle will be starting school soon," said Lasse reflectively. "So maybe I could too—that would really be nice. But I don't suppose I've got the head for it, do you? No, I'm sure I haven't got the head for it." He sounded quite despairing.

Kalle didn't seem inclined to contradict him, but Pelle made up his mind that someday he would teach his father to read and write—much better than Uncle Kalle could.

"But we're completely forgetting that we brought a Christmas bottle with us!" said Lasse, untying the handkerchief.

"What a brother!" exclaimed Kalle, walking delightedly around the table where the bottle stood. "You couldn't have given us anything better, brother; it'll come in handy for the christening party. 'Black Currant Rum'—and with a gold border—that looks great!" He held the label up to the light and looked around with happiness in his eyes. Then he started to open the cupboard.

"The visitors ought to taste what they brought," said his wife.

"That's just what was bothering me," said Kalle, turning around with an apologetic laugh. "They really should, of course. But once you poke a hole in it, you know how it sneaks away." He reached out slowly for the corkscrew, hanging on a nail.

But Lasse wouldn't hear of it; not on his life would he taste the drink. Was black currant rum a thing for a poor louse like him to start drinking—and on a weekday too? No indeed!

"All right, you'll be coming to the christening party anyway, you two," said Kalle, relieved, and put the bottle in the cupboard. "But we'll have a little dram, for there's a drop of liquor left from Christmas Eve, and I expect Mother will treat us to coffee."

"I've got the coffee on," answered his wife cheerfully.

"Have you ever seen the likes of such a wife? You can't even wish for something before it's already there!"

Pelle asked where his two herding companions were—Alfred and Albinus. They were away at the farms where they worked last summer, taking their share of the good Christmas fare, and wouldn't be back before Twelfth Night. "But this fellow here's no slouch either," said Kalle, pointing to the tall boy in the window seat. "Shall we take a look at him?" He pulled out a straw and tickled the boy's nose with it. "Get up, my good Anton, and harness the horses to the wheelbarrow! We're going to drive out in style."

The boy sat up abruptly and began to rub his eyes, to Kalle's great delight. At last he discovered that there were strangers present, and pulled on his clothes, which had been serving as his pillow. He and Pelle became good friends at once, and started playing. Then Kalle hit on the idea of letting the other children join in the party, and he and the two boys went around and tickled them awake, all six. His wife protested, but only faintly; she was laughing the whole time and helping them get dressed, while she kept on saying: "Oh, what foolishness, I've never seen the like! Then this one shouldn't be left out either," she added suddenly, pulling the youngest out of the alcove.

"Well, that's all eight," said Kalle, pointing to the flock. "They fill the room pretty well, don't they? Alma and Alvilda are twins, as you can see. And so are Alfred and Albinus, who are away now for Christmas. They're going to school next summer, so they'll be off my hands."

"Then where are the two eldest?" asked Lasse.

"Anna's in service in the north, and Albert's at sea, out with a whaler just now. He's a fine fellow. He sent us his picture last fall. Won't you show it to us, Marie?"

His wife hesitantly started looking for it, but couldn't find it.

"I think I know where it is, Mama," said one of the little girls over and over again. When no one heard her, she crawled up onto the bench and took down an old Bible from the shelf. The photograph was in it.

"He's a fine fellow, and no mistake!" said Lasse. "He's got quite a build. He's not like our family; he must have gotten that posture from yours, Marie."

"He's a Kongstrup," said Kalle in a low voice.

"Oh, indeed, is he?" said Lasse uncertainly, recalling Johanne Pihl's story.

"Marie was housemaid at the farm, and he sweet-talked her as he's done with so many. It was before my time, of course, and he did right by her afterwards."

His wife was standing looking from one to the other with a frozen smile, but her forehead was slightly flushed.

"There's a master's blood in that boy," said Kalle admiringly. "He holds his head different than the others. And he's good—so tremendously well-behaved." Marie came slowly over to him, put her arm around his shoulder, and looked at the picture with him. "He's good, all right, Mother," said Kalle, stroking her cheek.

"And he's so well-dressed too," said Lasse.

"Yes, he takes care of his money—he's not a boozer like his father. And he's not afraid of parting with ten kroner when he's home on a visit."

There was a rustling at the inner door, and a little, wrinkled old woman crept out onto the threshold, feeling her way with her feet, and holding her hands in front of her face to protect it. "Is anyone dead?" she asked.

"Well, there's Grandma!" said Kalle. "I thought you were in bed."

"And so I was, but then I heard there were strangers here—and I like to hear the news. Have there been any deaths in the parish?"

"No, Grandma, there haven't. People have better things to do than die. Here's someone come to court you, and that's much better. This is my mother-in-law," he said, turning to the others, "so you can guess what she's like."

"Just you come here, and I'll mother-in-law you!" said the old woman with a feeble attempt to join in the gaiety. "Well, welcome to this house then," she said, extending her hand.

Kalle stretched his out first, but as soon as she touched it she pushed it aside, saying, "Do you think I don't know you, you fool?" She felt Lasse's and Pelle's hands for a long time with her soft fingers before she let them go. "No, I don't know you!"

"It's brother Lasse and his son from down at Stone Farm," Kalle informed her at last.

"No, is it really? Well, I never! And you've come across the sea too! Well, here I am, an old woman going about all alone; and I can't see either."

"But you're not *quite* alone, Grandma," said Kalle, laughing. "There are two grownups and half a dozen children around you all day long."

"Ah yes, you can say what you like, but all those I was young with are dead now—and many others that I've watched grow up. Every week someone I know dies, and here am I still alive, only to be a burden to others."

Kalle brought in the old woman's armchair from her room and made her sit down. "What's all this nonsense?" he said reproachfully. "You pay your own way."

"Pay, oh good Lord! They get 20 kroner a year for keeping me," said the old woman to no one in particular.

The coffee was brought in, and Kalle poured aquavit into the cups of all the grownups. "Now, Grandma, you've got to cheer up!" he said, touching her cup with his. "Where the pot boils for twelve, it boils for the thirteenth as well. *Skål*, Grandma, and may you still live many years to be a burden to us, as you call it!"

"Yes, I know it so well, I know it so well," said the old woman, rocking back and forth. "You all mean so well. But with so little wish to live, it's hard for me to take the food out of others' mouths. The cow eats and the cat eats, the children eat, we all eat. And where are you, poor thing, going to get it all from?"

"Say 'poor thing' to him who has no behind, and pity him who has two," said Kalle merrily.

"How much land have you got?" asked Lasse.

"Five acres. But most of it's rock."

"Can you manage to feed the cow on it?"

"Last year it was pretty bad. We had to pull the thatched roof off the outhouse and use it for fodder last winter, and that set us back a little. But so what, it made the ceiling that much higher." Kalle laughed. "And now more and more of the children will be able to earn their keep themselves."

"Don't the grown ones lend a hand too?" asked Lasse.

"How can they? When you're young, you need what you've got for yourself. They have to take their pleasures while there's time — they didn't have many amusements when they were children, and once they're married and settled down they'll have something else to think about. Albert is good enough when he's at home on a visit; last time he gave us ten kroner and a krone to each of the children. But when they're out, you know how the money goes if they don't want to look stingy next to their friends. Anna's one of those who can spend all they get on clothes. She's willing enough to do without, but she never has an øre to spare. And she hardly has a rag to her name, no matter how much she keeps buying."

"No, she's the strangest creature," said her mother. "She never can make anything last."

They closed the window seat to make room to sit around the table, and an old deck of cards was produced. Everyone was going to play except the two smallest, who were simply too little to hold a card; though Kalle wanted them to play too, it wouldn't work. They played Starving Pig and Black Peter. Grandma's cards had to be read out loud to her. "We're playing with a blind woman!" said Kalle, shaking with glee. "That should be easy." And Grandma laughed louder at the joke than anyone.

The conversation continued among the adults.

"How do you like working for the landowner at Stone Farm?" asked Kalle.

"We don't see much of him, actually; he's almost always out, or sleeping off a hangover. But he's decent enough in other ways; and it's a house where they feed you properly."

"Well, there are places where the food's worse," said Kalle, "but there can't be many. Most of them, I must say, are better."

"Are they really?" asked Lasse in surprise. "Well, I'm not going to complain as far as the food's concerned. But there's a little too much for the two of us to do, and then it can get on your nerves hearing that woman crying nearly all the time. I wonder if he mistreats her? They say he doesn't."

"I'm sure he doesn't," said Kalle. "Even if he might feel like it—a man can understand that—he doesn't dare. He's afraid of her. She's possessed by a devil, you know."

"They say she turns into a werewolf at night," said Lasse, looking as though he expected to see a ghost in one of the corners.

"That's just stupid gossip and superstition," said Kalle. "But she is possessed by an unclean spirit, as we also know from the Bible. Ask Marie, she worked for her."

"She's a poor thing who has her own troubles," said Marie. "Every woman knows a little about that. And the master of Stone Farm isn't all kindness either, even though he doesn't beat her. His unfaithfulness affects her more than anything else would."

"Oh, you women always stick together," said Kalle, "but other people have eyes too. What do you say, Grandma? You know better than anyone else."

"Well, I know something about it at any rate," said the old woman. "I remember the time when Kongstrup came to the island as clearly as if it were yesterday. He owned nothing but the clothes he was wearing, but he was a dandy all the same, and lived in Copenhagen."

"What did he want over here?" asked Lasse.

"What did he want? To look for a young girl with money, I suppose. He wandered about on the heath here with his shotgun, but it wasn't the fox he was after. She was fooling around on the heath too, the daughter of Stone Farm, admiring the wild scenery and nonsense like that—and behaving half like a man, instead of being kept at home and taught to spin and make porridge. But she was the only daughter, and was allowed to carry on just as she liked. And then she meets this huckster from the city, and they become good friends, you can believe. He was a graduate or a pope, or some such fancy rubbish, so you can't blame the poor girl for not knowing what she was doing."

"No, indeed," said Lasse.

"There's always been something really wrong with the blood of the women in that family," the old woman continued. "They say one of them once gave herself to Satan. Since then he's had a claim on them and mistreats them whenever the moon is on the wane—whether they want to or not. He has no power over the pure, of course; but after these two had gotten to know each other, things went wrong with her too. He must have noticed it and tried to get out of the situation, because they said that the old master of Stone Farm forced him at gunpoint to take her for his wife. And he was a hard old dog, who'd have shot a man down if he had to. But he was a peasant through and through, who wore homespun clothes and wasn't afraid of working from sunup to sunset. It wasn't the way it is now, with debts and boozing and card-playing, so people had something in those days."

"Well, nowadays they'd like to thresh the grain while it's still standing, and they sell the calves in their mother's womb," said Kalle. "But look, Grandma, you're Black Peter!"

"That's because I let my tongue run on and forget to look out for myself!" said the old woman.

"Grandma has to have her face blackened!" cried the children. She begged to be spared, since she had just washed for the night. But the children blackened a cork in the stove and surrounded her, and they gave her a black streak down her nose.

Everyone laughed, both old and young. Grandma laughed with them. "It's a good thing I can't see it myself," she said. "It's an ill wind that blows nobody any good. But I'd like to have my sight again, if only for five minutes, before I die. It would be nice to see it all one more time, now that the trees and everything have grown so much, as Kalle tells me. The whole country must have changed. And I've never seen the youngest children at all."

"They say that they can cure blindness over in Copenhagen," said Kalle to his brother.

"It would cost a lot of money, wouldn't it?" asked Lasse.

"It would cost a hundred kroner at the very least," said Grandma.

Kalle looked thoughtful. "If we sold the whole works, I'd be surprised if there wasn't a hundred kroner left over. And then Grandma could get her sight back."

"God preserve us!" exclaimed the old woman. "Sell your house and home—you must be out of your mind. Throw away a lot of money on an old worn-out thing like me, who has one foot in the grave? I could never wish for anything better than what I have!" She had tears in her eyes. "God preserve me from bringing about such a misfortune in my old age."

"Oh, nonsense, we're still young," said Kalle. "We could easily start over again, Marie and I."

"Haven't any of you heard how Jacob Kristian's widow is doing?" asked the old woman to change the subject. "I've got it into my head that she'll go first, and then me. I heard the crow calling over that way last night."

"That's our nearest neighbor on the heath," explained Kalle. "So, is she failing now? There's been nothing the matter with her this winter that I know of."

"Well, you can be sure there's something to it," said the old woman firmly. "Have one of the children run over there in the morning."

"All right, if you've had an omen. Jacob Kristian gave plenty of warning himself when he went and died. But we were good friends for many years, he and I."

"Did he show himself?" asked Lasse solemnly.

"No, but one night—nasty October weather it was—I woke up when I heard knocking at the front door. That was a good three years ago. Marie heard it too, and we lay there and talked about whether I should get up. We got no further than talking, and we were just about to drop off again, when the knocking began again. So I jump up, pull on a pair of pants, and open the door a crack, but there's no one there. 'That's strange!' I say to Marie, and crawl back in bed; but before I'd gotten settled under the quilt, the knocking came a third time. Now I got mad, so I lit the lantern and went around the house; but there was nothing to be seen or heard. But in the morning word came to say that Jacob Kristian had died in the night, just at that hour."

Pelle sat listening to the conversation and snuggled up to his father in fear. But Lasse himself didn't look particularly brave. "It's not always a good idea to have anything to do with the dead," he said.

"Oh hell, if you haven't done anyone any harm and always given everybody their due, what can they do to you?" said Kalle. Grandma said nothing, but sat shaking her head very significantly.

Marie now came in and set a jar of drippings and a large loaf of rye bread on the table.

"Here's the goose," said Kalle, merrily sticking his sheath knife into the loaf. "We haven't touched it yet—it's stuffed with prunes. And that's the goose fat. Go ahead and dig in!"

After that Lasse and Pelle had to think about getting home, and started tying scarves around their necks. The others didn't want to let them go yet. They went on talking, and Kalle made jokes to keep them a little longer. But all of a sudden he was solemn—there was a sound of whimpering out in the little passage, and someone took hold of the door handle and let go of it again. "Good Lord, it's ghosts!" he cried, looking fearfully from one to the other.

The sound of crying was heard again, and Marie clapped her hands and exclaimed, "Why, it's Anna!" and quickly opened the door. Anna entered in tears. Astonished, they fell upon her from all sides with questions. She didn't answer, but just kept sobbing.

"So you got a day off to come and see us at Christmastime, and you come home crying! You're a fine one," said Kalle, laughing. "You'll have to give her something to suck on, Mother."

"I've been fired from my job," the girl finally got out between her sobs.

"You haven't, have you?" said Kalle in a different tone of voice. "But what for? Have you been stealing? Or talking back?"

"No, but the master accused me of being good friends with his son."

In a flash the mother's eyes darted from the girl's face to her figure, and she too burst into tears.

Kalle could see nothing, but he caught his wife's action and understood. "I see," he said quietly. "Is that it?" The little man was like a big child; varying expressions flickered across his good-natured face. At last his smile triumphed again. "Well then, that's fine!" he exclaimed with a laugh. "Shouldn't good children take the work off their parents' shoulders as they grow up and are able to? Take off your coat, Anna, and sit down. You're probably hungry, aren't you? And it couldn't have happened at a better time, since we've got to call the midwife anyhow!"

Lasse and Pelle pulled their scarves up over their mouths after saying goodbye to everyone in the room. Kalle circled around them, talking excitedly. "Come again soon, you two, and thanks for the visit and your present, brother Lasse. Oh yes," he said suddenly at the front door, and laughed delightedly, "it'll be a fine child—brother-in-law to the landowner in a way! Damn, Kalle Karlsson, you and I will be sticking our noses in the air now!" He went a little way along the path with them, talking all the time. It made Lasse feel quite melancholy.

Pelle knew quite well that what had happened to Anna was regarded as a great disgrace, and couldn't understand how Uncle Kalle could act so happy. "Ah, yes," said Lasse as they stumbled along through the rocks, "Kalle's just the way he's always been. He laughs where others would cry."

It was too dark to go across the fields, so they took the quarry road south to get down to the highway. At the crossroads, where the fourth path led down to the village, stood the country store, which was also a clandestine alehouse.

As they approached the alehouse, they heard a lot of noise inside. Then the door burst open and some men tumbled out, rolling the figure of a man before them along the road. "The police have probably raided them," said Lasse, pulling the boy with him out into the plowed field in order to get past without being seen. But at that moment someone placed a lamp in the window, and they were discovered.

"There's the Stone Farm herdsman!" said a voice. "Hey, Lasse, come here!" They went over and saw a man lying face down on the ground, kicking; his hands were tied behind his back, and he couldn't keep his face out of the mud.

"Why, it's Per Olsen!" cried Lasse.

"Yes, of course!" said the storekeeper. "Can't you take him home with you? He's not right in the head."

Lasse looked hesitantly at the boy. "A raving man? The two of us can't manage that."

"Oh, his hands are tied. All you've got to do is hold the end of the rope and he'll come along quietly," said one of the men. They were workers from the quarry. "You'll go with them quietly, right?" he asked, giving the man a kick in the side with the toe of his wooden shoe.

"Oh Jesus, Jesus!" groaned Per Olsen.

"What did he do?" asked Lasse. "And why did you beat him senseless?"

"We had to thrash him a little because he was going to chop off one of his thumbs. He tried it several times, the pig, and got it half off—we had to beat him to make him stop." They showed Lasse the man's thumb, which was all bloody. "What an animal—starts cutting and hacking at himself because he's drunk a pint of booze. If he wanted to fight, there were plenty of men here without doing that!"

"We'll have to tie it up or he'll bleed to death, poor fellow," said Lasse, slowly pulling out his red handkerchief. It was his Sunday handkerchief, and it had just been washed. The storekeeper came over with a bottle and poured spirits over the thumb, so that gangrene wouldn't set in. The wounded man screamed and beat his face on the ground.

"Won't one of you come with us?" asked Lasse. But no one answered; they wanted nothing to do with it, in case the authorities should hear of the matter. "Well then, the two of us will have to do it with God's help," he said in a trembling voice, turning to Pelle. "But you could help him up at least—since you knocked him down."

They lifted him up. His face was bruised and bleeding. In their eagerness to save his finger, they had handled him so roughly that he could scarcely stand.

"It's Lasse and Pelle," said the old man, trying to wipe his face. "You know us, don't you, Per Olsen? We'll take you home if you'll be good and not hurt us; the two of us will take care of you."

Per Olsen stood there gnashing his teeth, shaking all over. "Oh Jesus, oh!" was all he said. There was white foam at the corners of his mouth.

Lasse handed Pelle the end of the rope to hold. "He's grinding his teeth; the devil must be busy with him already," he whispered. "But if he tries to do any harm, just you pull on the rope with all your might. And if worse comes to worst, we'll have to jump over the ditch."

So they set off homeward. Lasse had to hold Per Olsen under the arm, because he was staggering and about to fall at any moment. He kept on muttering to himself and gnashing his teeth.

Pelle trudged behind, holding the rope. Cold shivers ran down his back, partly from fear, partly from secret satisfaction. He had finally seen someone he knew was doomed to perdition! So those who became devils in the next world looked like Per Olsen. But he wasn't evil! He was the nicest to Pelle of all the farmhands, and he had bought that bottle for them—yes, and he'd advanced the money out of his own pocket until May Day!

VIII

She was really moving! The master of Stone Farm let the gray stallion streak forward while he drove and looked steadily out over the fields, as if he had no suspicion that anyone was on his heels—but that didn't bother his wife. She whipped the bay as hard as she could and didn't care who saw her.

And it was in broad daylight that they were riding and playing around like this on the roads, instead of keeping their quarrels within four walls like decent people. It was certainly true that rich folks had no shame!

Then she screamed and stood up in the buggy and started to beat the horse—with the whip handle! Couldn't she just let him drive out to his fair mistress, whoever she was, and lay the fire for him when he came home? Good Lord, how could she keep on after twenty years of the same thing over and over—women were truly persevering creatures.

And how could *he* do it? Putting up with the everlasting quarrels at home for the sake of some hotel landlady or some other woman who couldn't be much different to deal with than his own wife. It would take a long-suffering nature to be a Don Juan in that fashion—but that must be what they call love, in a manner of speaking.

The threshing machine had come to a standstill, and the people at Stone Farm were hanging out the doors, enjoying themselves royally. It was a race, and a sight for the gods, to see the bay mare gaining on the stallion, as if he had forgotten to give her what was coming to her. It was like having two Sundays in one week! Lasse had come around the corner and was following the mad race, his hand shading his eyes—he'd never known a woman like that. Bengta was a perfect lamb compared to her. The farmer from Kåse Farm, who was standing at his gate when they dashed past, was secretly of the same opinion; and the workers in the fields dropped their tools and stared, scandalized at the sight.

At last, for the sake of decency, he had to stop and turn around. She crawled over into his carriage, and the bay followed quietly with her empty buggy. She put her arm around his shoulder and looked happy and triumphant, exactly like the district policeman when he'd made a good catch; but her husband looked like a criminal of the worst type. That's how they came driving back to the farm!

One day Kalle came to borrow ten kroner and to invite Lasse and Pelle to the christening party on the following Sunday. With some difficulty Lasse obtained the money from the foreman up in the office, but they had to say "No, thank you" to the invitation, though they didn't want to; it was quite out of the question for them to get a day off again. Another day the head man disappeared. He had left in the night, and had taken his big chest with him, so someone must have helped him. But the other men in the room swore solemnly that they hadn't noticed a thing, and the foreman, fume as he might, had to give up the attempt to solve the mystery.

A few things like this happened that made a stir for a day or two, but otherwise the winter was hard to get through. Darkness reigned for the greater part of the day, and it was never really light in the corners of the rooms. The cold, too, was hard to bear, except inside the comfortable stable; there it was always warm, and Pelle wasn't afraid to walk around in the blackest darkness. In the servants' room the men sat moping through the long evenings without anything to occupy themselves. They took very little notice of the maids, but sat playing cards for liquor—or told terrifying stories that made it a hazardous venture to run across the yard down to the stable when it was time to go to bed.

Per Olsen, on account of his good behavior, was promoted to head man when the other one ran away. Lasse and Pelle were happy about this, for he took their side whenever anyone tried to push them around. He had turned into a decent fellow in every respect, almost never touched alcohol, and kept his clothes in good repair. He was a little too quiet even for the old day-laborers of the farm and their wives, but they knew the reason for it and they liked him—because he took the part of the weak and because of the fate that hung over him. "He's going around listening," they said, and when he seemed to be listening within to the unknown, they avoided disturbing him as much as possible.

"You'll see, he'll free himself; the Evil One will have no claim on him," was the opinion of both Lasse and the laborers' wives when they discussed Per Olsen's prospects at the Sunday milking. "There are some people that even the Almighty can't find fault with."

Pelle listened to this, and tried every day to peek at the scar on Per Olsen's thumb; surely it would disappear when God lifted his punishment!

During most of the winter Pelle drove the horse for the threshing machine. All day he trudged around the horse path outside the court-yard, through slush and manure so deep it covered his wooden shoes. It was the most unbearable job that life had given him yet. He couldn't even whittle—his fingers were too cold. And he felt lonesome! As a cowherd he was his own boss, and a thousand things called to him; but here he had to walk around and around behind a bar, always in a circle. His only diversion was to keep track of the times he drove around, but that was an exhausting task and made him even more listless than the eternal walking in circles, and he couldn't quit once he started. Time held nothing of interest, and short as it was the day seemed endless.

As a rule, Pelle woke up happy, but now every morning he woke up sick of it all—that everlasting trudging around behind the bar. Grad-ually he fell into the habit of dozing off after he had been walking for about an hour. This condition would set in of its own accord, and he would long for it beforehand. It was a kind of idiocy, in which he wished for nothing and took no interest in anything, just staggered along mechanically behind the bar. The machine buzzed incessantly, and helped to maintain the condition; the dust kept pouring out of the doorway, and time passed imperceptibly. Usually dinner or evening would surprise him; sometimes it seemed to him that the horses had just been harnessed when someone came out to help him bring them in. He had entered into a condition of singing idiocy, which is life's only sign of mercy to condemned prisoners and people who spend their lives at a machine. But there was a sleepiness about him even in his free time; he wasn't very lively or eager to find out about anything. Papa Lasse missed his innumerable questions and ideas.

Now and then he was roused out of his condition for a moment by the appearance at the window of a filthy, sweaty face that swore at him because he wasn't driving evenly; then he would know that Long Ole had taken over from Per Olsen, whose job it was to feed the machine. And sometimes the lash of the whip would catch on the axle and wind around it, so that the whole thing had to be stopped and drawn backward; and that day he didn't fall into a doze again.

In March the larks appeared and brought a little life; snow still lay in the hollows, but their singing was a warm reminder of summer and grazing cattle. And one day he was awakened from his circular trudging by the sight of a starling on the roof of the house, screeching and preening its feathers in delight. On that day the sun shone brightly, and all heaviness had vanished from the air; but the sea was still a pale gray down there.

Pelle began to come alive again—it was spring, and in a couple of days the threshing would be finished too. But the main reason was his vest pocket—that was enough to put life into its owner. He trotted around behind the bar; he had to drive quickly now in order to get done, for everyone else was already in the middle of spring plowing. When he pressed his hand against his chest, he could distinctly feel the paper it was wrapped in. It was still there, wasn't it? It wouldn't do to open the paper and take a look; he had to check by squeezing it.

Pelle had become the owner of 50 øre—a perfectly genuine half-krone piece. It was the first time he had ever possessed anything more than one- or two-øre pieces, and he had earned it by his own cleverness.

It was last Sunday, when the men had had a visit from some quarry-men, and one of them came up with the idea of having some birch-fat with their dram. Pelle was supposed to run to the village store for it, and they gave him half a krone and orders to go in the back way, since it was Sunday. Pelle hadn't forgotten his experience at Christmas, and kept an eye on their faces; they were all doing their best to keep a straight face, busying themselves with one thing or another; and Gustav, who gave him the money, kept turning his face away and looking at something out in the courtyard.

When he stated his errand, the storekeeper's wife burst out laughing. "Is that the kind of fellow you are?" she exclaimed. "Weren't you the one who fetched the handle-turner too? You've found a lot of use for that, haven't you?"

Pelle turned crimson. "I thought they were making fun of me, but I didn't dare say no," he said in a low voice.

"No, sometimes you have to play the fool, even if you aren't one," said the woman.

"What is birch-fat?" asked Pelle.

"Oh, good Lord—you must have had it many a time, you little imp! It just goes to show how often you've had to swallow things you don't know the name of."

A light dawned on Pelle. "Does it mean a thrashing with a birch rod?"

"I thought you knew what it was!"

"No, I've only had it with a whip—on my legs."

"Well, well, don't worry about that—one is just as good as the other. But now sit down and have a cup of coffee while I wrap up the goods for them." She pushed a cup of coffee with brown sugar toward him, and began pouring out green soap onto a piece of paper. "Here," she said. "You give them that, it's the best birch-fat. And you can keep the money yourself."

Pelle wasn't bold enough for this arrangement.

"All right, then," she said. "I'll keep the money. They won't make fools of both of us. It's up to you. But now you'd better have your wits about you."

Pelle did have his wits about him, but he was quite nervous. The men swore at the loss of the 50 øre, and called him the biggest idiot on God's green earth; but he had the satisfaction of knowing that it was because he hadn't been stupid enough. And the half-krone was his!

A hundred times a day he touched it without wearing it out; here at last was something that didn't lose its luster by possessing it. There was no end to the purchases he made with it—now for Lasse, now for himself. He bought the most expensive things, and when he had lingered long enough over one purchase and was sated with the possession of it, he would set about buying something else. And all the while he kept the coin. Suddenly he would be seized with the fear that the money was gone; then when he touched it, he was doubly glad.

Pelle had suddenly become a capitalist—through his own cleverness—and he made the most of his capital. He had already obtained every desirable thing that he could think of—he had it all at hand, in any case. Gradually, as new things appeared in his world, he would secure an option to buy them. Lasse was the one person who knew about his wealth, and he reluctantly had to allow himself to be drawn into the wildest of speculations.

He could hear by the sound that there was something wrong with the machine; the horses heard it too, and stopped even before someone cried "Stop!" Then the shouts came one after another: "Stop! Drive on! Stop! Forward again! Stop! Pull!" And Pelle pushed the bar back, drove on, and pulled until the whole thing was whirring again. Then he knew that it was Long Ole feeding the machine while Per Olsen measured the grain—Ole was an idiot at feeding the machine.

It was going smoothly again, and Pelle was keeping an eye on the corner by the cow stable. When Lasse appeared there and patted his stomach, it meant that it was nearly dinner time.

Something stopped the bar, the horses had to pull hard, and with a jerk they cleared the invisible hindrance. There was a cry from inside the threshing barn, and the sound of many voices shouting "Stop!" The horses stopped dead, and Pelle had to grab the bar to prevent it from swinging into their legs. It was some time before anyone came to take the horses in, so Pelle could go into the barn and see what was wrong.

Long Ole was walking around, writhing over one of his hands. His shirt was wrapped around it, but the blood was dripping through the cloth onto the floor of the barn. He was doubled over and stumbling, throwing his body from side to side and talking incoherently. The girls were pale, and stood there staring at him, and the men were arguing about the best way to stop the flow of blood—one of them came sliding down from the loft with a handful of cobwebs.

Pelle went and peered into the machine to find out what was so ferocious about it. Between two of the teeth lay something like a peg, and when he moved the roller, the better part of a finger fell to the barn floor. He picked it up with some chaff and took it over to the others—it was a thumb. When Long Ole saw the thumb, he fainted; it was no wonder, since now he would be a cripple for life. But Per Olsen had to admit that he had left the machine at a lucky moment.

There was no more threshing done that day. In the afternoon Pelle played in the stable; he was free to do what he wanted. As he played, he outlined his future plans for his father; they were totally caught up in it.

"Then we'll go to America — and dig for gold!"

"Yes, that wouldn't be a bad idea, I guess. But it would take a lot more 50-øre pieces to make that trip."

"Then we could be stonemasons."

Lasse stood still in the middle of the feed alley and pondered this with head bent. He was deeply dissatisfied with their position; there were two of them toiling to earn a hundred kroner, and they couldn't make ends meet. There was no freedom either; they were no more than slaves. He himself never got past being discontented and disappointed with everything; he was too old. The mere search for a means to something new was insurmountable work, and everything seemed so hopeless. But Pelle was restless. Whenever he was dissatisfied with anything, he made scores of plans, both wild and sensible. And he pulled the old man along with him.

"We could go to the city and work too," said Lasse thoughtfully. "Over there they earn one shiny krone after another. But what's to be done with you? You're too little to handle a tool."

This stubborn fact would put a stop to Pelle's plans for the moment; but then his courage rose again. "I can go with you to the city," he said. "I can . . ." He nodded significantly.

"What can you do?" asked Lasse with interest.

"Well, maybe I'll go down to the harbor with nothing to do, and a little girl will fall into the water and I'll rescue her. But the little girl is probably a rich man's daughter, and so . . ." Pelle left the rest to Lasse's imagination.

"Then you'll have to learn to swim first," said Lasse gravely. "Or you'll just drown."

Screams came from the servants' quarters. It was Long Ole. The doctor had come and was attending to his maimed hand. "Just run over and find out what's going on," said Lasse. "Nobody will pay any attention to you at a time like this, if you don't get in the way."

A little while later Pelle came back and reported: three fingers were totally crushed and hanging in shreds, and the doctor had cut them off.

"Was it these three?" asked Lasse anxiously, holding up his thumb, forefinger, and middle finger. Actually, Pelle hadn't seen anything at all, but his imagination ran away with him.

"Yes, it was the fingers you swear an oath with," he said, nodding emphatically.

"Then Per Olsen has been set free," said Lasse, heaving a deep sigh. "What a *good* thing it was—a gift from God!"

Pelle thought so too.

The master himself drove the doctor home, and a little while later Pelle was sent for. He was to run an errand for the mistress to the village store.

IX

For Pelle it didn't matter; if he was defeated on one point, he would rise up again on two others: he was invincible. And he had a child's rich capacity for forgiveness, otherwise he would have hated all grownups except for Papa Lasse. But he was disappointed.

It was hard to say who had had the greatest expectations: the boy, whose childish imagination, unchecked, had built on all that he had heard, or the old man, who had been here once before.

But Pelle himself managed to make his life rich with meaning, and was so interested in everything that he only had time to register the disappointment in passing. His world was supersensual like that of the fakir: in the course of a few minutes a little seed could shoot up and grow into a huge tree that overshadowed everything else. In his world, cause had no connection with effect, and it was governed by a different law of gravity; events always bore him upward.

No matter how hard reality might press in on him, he would always emerge the richer from the situation somehow. And no danger could ever be overwhelmingly great as long as Papa Lasse loomed reassuringly over everything.

But Lasse had failed him at decisive moments more than once, and every time Pelle used him as a threat, he was only laughed at. The old man's omnipotence couldn't continue to coexist with his increasing decrepitude; it was crumbling away day by day. No matter how reluctantly, Pelle had to let go of his providence and seek the defensive way out within himself. He was rather young, but he viewed circumstances in his own way. Distrust he had already acquired—and shyness! Daily he made clumsy attempts to figure out what people were really saying. There was some other meaning behind everything! This often led to confusion, but sometimes the result was conspicuously good.

Some thrashings you could run away from, because in the meantime the anger would blow over, and there were other thrashings where the best solution was to shed as many tears as possible. Most people only kept hitting until the tears came, but the foreman couldn't stand a blubberer, so with him the thing was to grit your teeth and steel yourself. People went about saying you should tell the truth, but most thrashings could be avoided by telling a white lie—if it was a good one and you protected your face. If you told the truth, they hit you right away.

The beatings also took on a social significance. He could beat Rud whenever he liked, but with bigger boys it was better to have justice on his side—for instance, when his father was attacked. Then God would help him. This was a case where the boy actually shoved the Almighty aside and regarded himself as the old man's protector.

Lasse and Pelle were moving through life hand in hand, and yet each was going his own way—Lasse himself could feel this. "We've each got hold of one end," he sometimes said to himself despondently, when the difference became all too great. "He's too ambitious, that boy!"

This was most apparent in the others. In the long run they had to like the boy, they couldn't help themselves. The men would sometimes give him things, and the maids were very kind to him. He was the epitome of budding youth—they would often take him on their laps as he passed, and kiss him. They could take the very innocence of childhood in their embrace so anyone could see.

"Ah, he'll be a ladies' man, he will!" Lasse would say. "He's got that from his father." But then they would laugh.

There was always laughter when Lasse wanted to join in the grown-ups' games. Last time he was there—yes, then he had been good enough. Then it was always "Where's Lasse?" when the liquor was passed around, or tricks were being played, or demonstrations given. "Call Lasse Karlsson!" He had no need to force his way in; it was a matter of course that he was included. The girls were always on the lookout for him, married man though he was; and he had had fun with them. Within the bounds of propriety, of course, for Bengta was not easy to quarrel with if she heard anything.

But now! Sure, he was allowed to fetch liquor for the others, and do their work for them when they had a day off, without them doing anything in return. "Lasse! Where's Lasse? Can you feed the horses for me tonight? Can you take my place at the chaff-cutting tomorrow night?"

There was a difference between then and now, and Lasse had found out the reason himself—he was getting old. The very discovery brought further proof that he was right; it wrapped infirmity around him and removed the alertness from his mind and the last remnants of agility from his body. The hardest blow of all was when he discovered that he didn't count with the women anymore, had no place at all in their thoughts about men. In Lasse's world there was no word that carried more weight than the word *man*, and in the end it was the women who decided whether you were one or not. Lasse was not one—he wasn't dangerous! He was only a few poor relics of a man, a comical remnant of some bygone thing—they laughed at him when he tried to woo them.

Their laughter crushed him, and he withdrew and despondently adapted himself to his old man's world. The only thing that kept him alive was his concern for the boy, and he clung in despair to his position as Pelle's providence. There was little he could do for him, and so he would boast all the more; and when anything went against the boy, he muttered even greater threats against the world than before. He also felt that the boy was in the process of becoming independent, and he fought a desperate battle to preserve the last remains of his power.

But Pelle couldn't afford to embrace his fantasy—nor did he have the understanding to do so. He was growing fast and needed everything he possessed for himself. Now that his father no longer stood behind to shield him, he was like a little plant that has been moved out into the open and is fighting hard to comprehend the nature of its surroundings and adapt itself to them. For every root fiber that felt its way into the soil, one of the tender leaves would fall to the ground, and two strong ones would shoot forth. One after another the feelings of a child's defenselessness fell away and were replaced by the tougher feelings of an individual.

The boy was in the process of creating himself—in accordance with invisible laws. He formed an opinion about everybody around him, but he didn't imitate them. The farm hands, for instance, were not kind to the animals. They often whipped the horses just as a means of venting their own ill-humor, and the maids behaved just the same toward the smaller animals and the dairy cows. On the basis of this, Pelle taught himself sympathy. He couldn't bear cruelty to animals, and beat up Rud for the first time when he robbed a bird's nest one day.

Pelle was like a kitten that plays with everything. In his play, without suspecting it, he would take up many of the serious phenomena of his life, and romp with them in frisky leaps. He exercised his young mind the way he exercised his body: careening in and out of everything, imitating work and games and malingering, learning how to puff himself up into a devil of a fellow when the people around him would allow it, and making himself almost invisible with modesty when they were too cruel. He was training himself to be a little jack of all trades.

And it became more and more difficult to catch him unawares. The first time he had to deal with anything in earnest, he would have the knack for it right away; he was as difficult to take by surprise as a cat.

It was summer again. The heat stood still and played over the ground, shimmering, with indolent voluptuousness and soft sounds like the fish in the creek. Far inland the edge of the cliff quivered with a restless flicker of bluish white; below lay the fields beneath the baking sun, with the pollen from the rye drifting over them like the smoke of gunpowder. Up above the clover field stood the cows of Stone Farm in long rows, their heads hanging heavily and their tails swinging regularly. Lasse was moving among the ranks, looking for the mallet, and now and then he gazed anxiously down toward the meadow by the dunes and started counting the young cattle and steers. Most of them were lying down, but a few were standing with their heads close together, chewing with their eyes closed. The boys were nowhere to be seen.

Lasse stood there wondering whether he should give Pelle a warning call; there would be a real stink if the foreman showed up now. But then the sound of voices came from among the young pines on the dunes; a naked boy appeared, and then another. Their bodies were like golden flashes in the air as they raced over the lyme grass and across the meadow, each with his cap held closed in his hand.

They sat down at the edge of the creek with their feet in the water and carefully uncovered their captives—they were dragonflies. As the insects crawled one by one out of the narrow opening, the boys decapitated them and laid them in a row on the grass. They had caught nine, and nine times 35—well, that would be more than three kroner. The stupendous sum made Pelle skeptical.

"Don't you think it's all a lie?" he said, licking his shoulder where he had a mosquito bite. It was said that the pharmacist paid 35 øre apiece for dragonflies.

"A lie? Well, maybe it is," Rud said quietly. "It probably *is* a lie; something like that always is. You could give me yours too, you know!"

But Pelle wouldn't do that.

"Then give me your 50-øre piece, and I'll go to town and sell them for you. They cost 35 øre, that's what Karl says, and his mother is the cleaning lady at the pharmacy."

Pelle got up, not to get the 50 øre—he wouldn't part with that for the world—but to assure himself that it was still in his vest pocket.

When he had turned away, Rud hastily lifted a piece of turf at the edge of the stream, pushed something in under it, and jumped into the water. And when Pelle came back with slow, ominous steps, Rud climbed up the other bank and set off at a run.

Pelle ran too, in short, quick leaps. He knew he was faster, and the knowledge made him frisky. He slapped at his naked body as he ran, as if he had no joints, swaying from side to side like a balloon, prancing and stamping the ground—and then darted on again. Then the young pines closed around them; only the movement of the treetops revealed where the boys were running, farther and farther, until all was still.

In the meadow the cattle were chewing with eyes closed and ears alert. The heat played over the ground, flickering, gasping—like a fish in water. There was a heavy, stupefying hum in the air; the sound came from everywhere and nowhere.

Down across the fields came a big, stout woman. She wore a skirt, a chemise, and a kerchief on her head, and she was shading her eyes with her hand and looking around. She walked out across the meadow, found Pelle's dinner basket, took out its contents, and put them in under her chemise against her naked, sweaty breast. Then she turned in the direction of the sea.

There was a sudden break in the edge of the pine grove, and out came Rud with Pelle hanging on to his back. Rud's inordinately large head hung forward and his knees were buckling; his forehead, which receded above his eyes and jutted out just below his hairline, was full of bruises and old scars—they were quite visible now with his exertions. Both the boys had marks all over their bodies from the poison of the pine needles. Pelle dropped onto the grass and lay there on his stomach while Rud slowly went to get the 50-øre piece and handed it reluctantly to its owner. He stooped with defeat, but in his eyes lurked the thought of a new battle.

Pelle gazed lovingly at the coin. He had had it ever since April, from the time when he was sent to buy birch-fat; he had purchased everything imaginable with it, and he had lost it twice—he loved that coin. It made his fingers itch—his whole body itch; it was always egging him on to spend it, now for one thing and now for another. Roll, roll! That was probably what it was longing to do; and that was probably because it was round, said Papa Lasse. But to be rich—that meant stopping the money as it rolled! Oh, Pelle intended to be rich! And yet he was always still itching to spend it, spend it in such a way that he got everything for it—or something he could keep for his whole life.

They sat on the bank of the creek, bickering; Rud was doing his best to impress Pelle, sitting there bragging. He bent his fingers backward and wiggled his ears; he could move them forward in a listening position like a horse. All this irritated Pelle immensely.

Suddenly Rud stopped. "Won't you give me the 50 øre? I'll give you ten kroner when I grow up." Rud collected money—he was already greedy—and had a whole box full of coins that he had stolen from his mother.

Pelle thought for a moment. "No," he said. "Because you'll never grow up—you're a dwarf!" There was a trace of envy in his voice.

"That's what the Sow says too. But then I'll put myself on display for money at the fairs and on Midsummer Eve on the common. Then I'll be rich as hell."

Pelle was inwardly troubled. Should he give him the whole 50 øre for nothing at all? He had never heard of anyone doing such a thing. But maybe someday, when Rud was enormously rich, he would get half of it. "Do you want it?" he asked, regretting it instantly.

Rud put out his hand eagerly, but Pelle spit at it. "You can wait until we've eaten at least," he said, going over to the dinner basket. For a moment they stood gazing into the empty basket.

"The Sow's been here," said Rud, sticking out his tongue.

Pelle nodded. "She's a real devil."

"A thieving bitch," said Rud.

They looked at the sun's position in the sky. Rud maintained that if you could see it when you bent over and looked between your legs, then it was five o'clock. Pelle started to put on his clothes.

Rud was circling around him. "Pelle!" he said suddenly. "If you give it to me, I'll let you beat me with nettles."

"On your bare skin?" asked Pelle.

Rud nodded.

In a flash Pelle was out of his pants again and running to a patch of nettles. He pulled them up with the help of a dock leaf, as many as he could hold, and came back. Rud lay down on his stomach on a little mound, and the whipping began.

The agreement was a hundred lashes, but when Rud had received ten, he got up and refused to take any more.

"Then you won't get the money," said Pelle. "Do you want it or don't you?" He was red with excitement and exertion; the sweat was already running in beads down his slender back—he had been whipping hard. "Do you want it or don't you? Seventy-five lashes then!" Pelle's voice quivered with zeal, and he had to dilate his nostrils to get enough air; his limbs started to tremble.

"No—only sixty—you hit so hard! And you have to give me the coin first, otherwise you'll cheat."

"I don't cheat," said Pelle darkly. But Rud stood his ground.

Pelle's body writhed; he was like a weasel that has tasted blood. With a jerk he tossed the coin at Rud; growling, he pushed him down. He wept inside because he had spared him forty lashes, but he promised himself that he would hit him all the harder.

Then he struck, slowly and with all his might, while Rud burrowed his head into the grass and clasped the coin tight to keep up his strength. There was hatred in every lash that Pelle gave him, and they passed like shocks through his companion's body, but Rud never made a sound. No, there was no point in crying. The coin he held in his hand took away the pain. But around Pelle's body the air burned like fire, his arms began to give way with fatigue, and with every stroke his desire diminished—it was work, nothing but dirty work. And the money, the beautiful 50-øre piece, was slipping farther and farther away, and he would be poor again—and Rud wasn't even crying. At the forty-sixth stroke Rud turned his head and stuck out his tongue. Then Pelle burst into tears, tossed the frayed nettle stalks far away, and ran off to the pine grove.

There he sat for the rest of the day under a dune, grieving over his loss, while Rud lay under the bank of the creek, bathing his blistered body with wet clay.

X

Per Olsen was not the kind of man they thought he was, after all. Now that he had been set free in that way, it would have been proper for him to lend a helping hand to that poor fellow, Long Ole—who had fallen into misfortune because of him. But did he do it? No, he started carousing. Drinking and dissipation and fluttering petticoats for him all summer long, and now in the fall he left and took work at the quarry—so as to be more his own master. There was not enough freedom for him at Stone Farm. Whatever good was left in him that he had not yet squandered would probably find legs to stand on up there.

Long Ole could not, of course, remain at Stone Farm, crippled as he was. Through kindness on the part of the landowner, he was paid half his wages; that was more than he had any claim to—and enough at least to get him home and let him try to make a living somehow. There were many kinds of work that could be done with one hand, in a pinch, and now while he had the money he ought to get himself an iron hook; it could be strapped to the wrist, and wasn't half bad for holding tools.

But Ole had grown weak and had great difficulty in making decisions. He kept on hanging around the farm, in spite of everything the foreman did to chase him away. Finally they had to put his things outside, on the west side of the farm; and there they lay most of the summer. He himself slept among the haystacks, begging food from the workers in the fields. But this couldn't go on once the cold set in.

But then one day in the fall, his things were gone. Johanne Pihl—commonly known as the Sow—had taken him in. She probably felt the cold too, in spite of her fat, and as the proverb says: It's easier for two to keep warm than one. But whatever her reason for doing it, Long Ole could thank his Maker for her. There was always bacon hanging in her chimney.

Lasse and Pelle looked forward to the turnover day with anxiety. What kind of people would it bring this time? So much depended on that. Besides the head man, they were supposed to get a new second and third man and some new maids. They were always changing at Stone Farm when they could. Karna, poor soul, was bound to stay, since she had fixed her old mind on youth, and would stay wherever Gustav was, no matter what! Gustav stayed because Bodil stayed—he was so unnaturally fond of that girl, even though she wasn't worth it. And Bodil herself knew very well what she was doing. It couldn't be completely natural when a girl dressed the way she did, in expensive, store-bought clothes.

Lasse and Pelle just stayed, simply because there was no other place in the world for them to go. All year long they made plans for making a change, but when the time for giving notice approached, Lasse would grow quiet and let it pass.

Recently he had given quite a lot of thought to the idea of marrying again. There was something godforsaken about this solitary existence for a man of his age; you became old and worn-out before your time when you didn't have a wife and a home. On the heath near his brother Kalle's, there was a house that he could have without paying anything down. He often discussed it with Pelle, and the boy was ready for anything new.

It would have to be a woman who could look after everything and make the house comfortable; above all she had to be a hardworking woman. It wouldn't hurt if she had a little of her own, but that didn't matter so much, as long as she was good-natured. Karna would have been suitable in every respect; both Lasse and Pelle had always liked her, ever since the day she rescued Pelle from the trainee's clutches. But there was nothing to do about it as long as she had that crush on Gustav. They'd have to bide their time; maybe she would come to her senses — or something else might turn up.

"Then there will be coffee in bed on Sunday mornings!" said Pelle with delight.

"Yes, and maybe we'll get us a little horse, and take brother Kalle for a drive now and then," added Lasse solemnly.

So now it was really going to happen. In the evening Lasse and Pelle had been to the store to buy a slate and pencil, and now Pelle was standing at the stable door with a pounding heart and the slate under his arm. It was a frosty October morning, but the boy was quite hot from washing, he had on his best clothes, and his hair had been combed with water.

Lasse hovered around him, brushing him here and there with his sleeve, and was even more nervous than the boy. Pelle had been born into poor circumstances, had been christened, and had had to earn his bread from the time he was little — all exactly as Lasse had done himself. So far there was no difference to be seen; it could have been Lasse himself all over again, from the big ears and the cowlick on the forehead to the way the boy walked and wore out the cuffs of his pants. But this was something strikingly new. Neither Lasse nor any of his family had ever gone to school; this was something new that had come within the reach of his family, a miracle from heaven that had been granted to the boy and himself. It felt like a push upward; the impossible was within reach. What might not happen to a person who had book-learning! He might become a journeyman, a clerk, or maybe even a schoolmaster.

"Now take care of the slate, and see that you don't break it!" Lasse admonished. "And keep out of the way of the big boys until you can hold your own with them. But if any of them won't leave you alone, make sure you manage to strike first! That will take the wind out of most of them, especially if you hit hard; he who strikes first strikes twice, as the old proverb says. And listen well to your teacher, and keep in mind everything he says; and if anyone tries to tempt you into playing and fooling around behind his back, don't do it. And remember that you've got a handkerchief, so don't use your fingers, that isn't polite. But if no one's looking, you can save the handkerchief, of course — it'll last longer that way. And take care of your good clothes.

And if the teacher's wife invites you in for coffee, don't take more than one piece of cake, do you hear?" Lasse's hands were trembling as he talked.

"She won't do that," said Pelle, with a slightly superior air.

"All right, go now, so you won't be late—on the very first day, too. And if you need some tool or other, just say we'll get it at once—we're not total paupers." Lasse slapped his pocket, but it didn't make much of a noise, and Pelle was well aware that they didn't have any money—they had bought the slate and pencil on credit.

Lasse stood gazing after the boy as long as he could see him—and then went to his work of crushing cakes of whale oil. He put them into a vessel to soak and poured water over them, all the while talking softly to himself.

There was a knock at the outer stable door, and Lasse went to open it—it was his brother Kalle.

"Good day, brother!" he said with his cheerful smile. "Here comes the old bull from the quarry." He waddled inside on his bowlegs, and the two exchanged hearty greetings. Lasse was delighted at the visit.

"Thanks for last time!" he said, taking his brother by the hand.

"That's quite a while ago now. But you'll come over for a visit sometime soon, won't you? Grandma has always had an eye for both of you." Kalle's eyes twinkled mischievously.

"How is she, poor soul? Has she recovered yet from her eye? Pelle came home the other day and told me that the children accidentally poked a stick in her eye. I was really upset—and you even had to have the doctor, too!"

"Well, it wasn't quite like that," said Kalle. "I had moved Grandma's spinning wheel myself one morning when I was doing something in her room—and then I forgot to put it back in its place. Then when she stooped down to pick up something off the floor, the spindle went into her eye. She's used to having everything be in exactly the same place. So the honor really falls to me." He laughed heartily.

Lasse shook his head sympathetically. "So she got over it all right?"

"No, things went all wrong—she lost her sight in that eye."

Lasse looked at him with disapproval.

Kalle caught himself, apparently horrified. "Oh, what nonsense I'm talking—she lost her *blindness* in that eye, I should have said. Isn't that crazy? You poke somebody's eye out, and she starts to see! I think I'll damn well go out and cure blindness after this, there's nothing to it."

"What are you saying? She's started to—? Now you're going too far; you don't have to make jokes about everything, you know."

"Well, all kidding aside, as the prophet said when his wife thrashed him. But she really can see with that eye now."

Lasse looked at him suspiciously for a moment before he gave in. "Well, that's quite a miracle!"

"Yes, that's what the doctor said—the point of the spindle acted like a kind of operation. But it could just as easily have gone the other way. Yes, we had to call the doctor for her three times—it was no use being miserly." Kalle stood there trying to look important; he had stuck his thumbs into his vest pockets.

"It cost a lot of money, I suppose?"

"That's what I thought, too, and I wasn't very happy when I asked the doctor how much it would be. 'Twenty-five kroner,' he said, making it sound just like when the rest of us ask for a piece of bread and drippings. 'Would the doctor be so kind as to wait a few days so I can get the cow properly sold?' I asked. 'What!' he says, glaring at me over his spectacles. 'You don't mean to sell the cow in order to pay me? You can't do that; I'll wait till times are better.' 'We'll be getting off easy, even if we have to get rid of the cow,' I said. 'How so?' he asks as we walk out to the carriage—it was the farmer from Kåse Farm who was driving for me. So I told him that Marie and I had been thinking of selling everything so that Grandma could go over and get an operation. He didn't say a word, but climbed up into the carriage, and I stood there buttoning the wrap around his feet. Suddenly he grabs me by the collar and says: 'Do you know what, you little bow-legged creature?' (Kalle was imitating the doctor's city speech.) 'You're the best man I've ever met, and you don't owe me a single øre! For that matter, you were the one who performed the operation.' 'Then I should be the one getting paid for it,' I said. Then he laughed and gave me a box on the noggin with his fur cap. He's a fine man, that doctor—and damned clever. They say he has only one kind of medicine, which he cures all kinds of diseases with."

They were sitting in the herdsman's room on top of the green chest, and Lasse had brought out a drop of aquavit. "Drink, brother!" he said again and again. "It takes a little something to keep out the damp in this October drizzle."

"Thanks—but have a drink yourself! But I was going to say, you should see Grandma, she goes around peering at everything with her one eye; even if it's only a button, she keeps on staring at it. So that's what it looks like, and that. She's forgotten what everything looks like. And when she sees something, she goes over to touch it—to find out what it is, she actually says. She wouldn't have anything to do with us the first few days; when she didn't hear us talking or walking, she thought we were strangers—even though she could see us right there in front of her eyes."

"And the little ones?" asked Lasse.

"Oh yes, Anna's is chubby and plump, but our own seems to have stopped growing. It's the young pigs you ought to breed with, after all. By the way"—Kalle took out his purse—"while we're at it, don't let me forget the 10 kroner I got from you for the christenings."

Lasse pushed it away. "Never mind that," he said. "You may have rough times ahead still. How many mouths are there now? Fourteen or fifteen, I suppose?"

"Yes, but two of them nurse their mother's milk, like the parson's wife's chickens, so that's a great saving. And if things get tight, I guess I'm man enough to wring a few kroner out of my nose." He grabbed his nose and gave it a quick twist, and held out his hand—there lay a folded 10-krone note.

Lasse laughed at the trick, but wouldn't hear of taking the money; for a while they stood there passing it back and forth to each other. "Oh, all right!" said Kalle at last, keeping the money. "Thank you very much, then. And goodbye, brother. I've got to get going." Lasse went out with him, and sent many greetings to his family.

"We'll come visit you real soon," he called after his brother.

When he returned to his room a little later, the money was lying on the bed; Kalle must have seen his chance to put it there, magician that he was. Lasse put it aside to give to Kalle's wife, when an occasion presented itself.

Long ahead of time, Lasse was on the lookout for Pelle. He found the solitude wearisome, now that he was used to having the boy around from morning till night. At last he came in, out of breath from running; he had longed to get home too.

Nothing either terrible or remarkable had happened at school. Pelle had to give a detailed account, point by point. "Well, what can you do?" the teacher had asked, taking him by the ear—quite kindly, of course. "I can pull the crazy bull to the water without Papa Lasse helping at all," Pelle had answered, and then the whole class had laughed.

"That's fine, but can you read?"

No, Pelle couldn't do that. Otherwise I wouldn't be here, he was just about to add. "It's a good thing you didn't say that," said Lasse. "But what else?" Well, then Pelle was seated on the lowest bench, and the boy next to him was set to teach him his letters.

"Do you know them, then?"

No, Pelle didn't know them that day. But after a couple of weeks had passed, he knew most of them, and wrote them with chalk on the posts. He hadn't learned to write, but his hand could imitate anything he had seen, and he drew the letters just as they looked in print in the primer.

Lasse went and looked at them during his work, and had them repeated to him endlessly; but they didn't really sink in. "What's that one there?" he was perpetually asking.

Pelle replied with a superior air, "That one? Have you forgotten it already? I knew that one after I'd only seen it once! That's an M."

"Yes, of course it is! I can't imagine where my head is today. M, yes—of course it's M! Now what can you use it for, eh?"

"It's the first letter in the word 'empty,' of course," said Pelle self-importantly.

"Yes, of course. But you didn't figure that out for yourself; the teacher told you that."

"No, I figured it out by myself."

"Did you, now? Well, you're sure getting clever—just so you don't get as clever as seven fools."

Lasse was out of sorts; but soon he relented and fell into whole-hearted admiration of his son. And the instruction continued while they worked. It was lucky for Pelle that his father was so slow; for he wasn't very quick himself, after he had mastered all that could be picked up spontaneously by a sharp mind. The boy who had to teach him—the Slob, he was called—was the dunce of the class and had always been at the bottom until Pelle came to take his place.

Two weeks of school had greatly changed Pelle's ideas on the subject. On the first few days he arrived in a state of anxious anticipation, and all his courage left him as he crossed the threshold of the school; for the first time in his life he felt that he was good for nothing. Trembling with awe, he opened himself to this new and unfamiliar thing that would unveil for him all the mysteries of the world, if only he kept his greedy ears open; and he did. But there was no awe-inspiring man, who looked at them affectionately through gold-rimmed spectacles—while he told them about the sun and the moon and all the wonders of the world. Up and down the middle aisle walked a man in a dirty canvas coat, with gray bristles sticking out of his nose; as he walked he swung the cane and smoked his pipe, or he sat at the desk and read a newspaper. The children were noisy and restless, and when the noise broke out into an open fight, the man would jump down from his desk and

lash out indiscriminately with his cane. And Pelle himself was bound—
for good, it seemed—to a filthy boy, covered with oozing sores, who
pinched his arm every time he read his "b-a—ba, b-e—be" correctly.
The only variety was an hour's daily exam on the tedious observations
of the textbook, and then the repetition of unwieldy hymns on Saturdays.

For a time Pelle swallowed everything whole and passed it on faithfully to his father, but at last he grew tired of it. It wasn't his nature to
remain passive to his surroundings for long, and one fine day he cast
aside all admonitions and good intentions and dived into having fun.

After that he had less information to impart, but on the other hand
there were the thousands of roguish tricks to tell about. And Papa Lasse
would shake his head, not comprehending a thing; but he couldn't help
laughing.

XI

A mighty Fortress is our God,
A bulwark never failing;
A Helper He amid the flood
Of mortal ills prevailing.
  For still our ancient foe
  Doth seek to work us woe;
  His craft and power are great;
  And, armed with cruel hate,
On earth is not his equal.

The whole school sat swaying back and forth, grinding out hymns in
endless succession. Schoolmaster Fris was walking up and down the
center aisle, smoking his pipe; he was getting some exercise after an
hour's reading of the paper. The cane was beating the air like a metro-
nome; now and then it would fall on the back of an offender, but always
at the end of a line—as a kind of exclamation point. Fris couldn't bear
to have the rhythm broken. The children who didn't know the hymn
were carried along by the crowd, some of them content to move their
lips, while others made up words of their own. When the words got to
be too awful, their neighbors would laugh, and then the cane would fall.

When one verse came to an end, Fris quickly started the next—for the mill was hard to set in motion again once it had come to a standstill. "Did we in . . ." and the fifty children continued:

> Did we in our own strength confide,
> Our striving would be losing . . .

Then Fris had another breathing space; he could enjoy his pipe and be lulled by this noise that spoke of great and industrious activity. When things were like that, his indignation would fall away for a while, and he could smile at his thoughts as he paced up and down—and, old though he was, look on the bright side of life. People passing by would stop to rejoice over the diligence displayed, and Fris would beat more briskly with the cane and feel a long-forgotten ideal stirring within him: he had this whole flock of children to educate for life; he was engaged in creating the next generation.

When that hymn came to an end, without a pause he got them started on "Who puts his trust in God alone," and then on to "We all, we all have faith in God." They had had all three of them all winter long, and now finally, after tremendous labor, he had brought them so far that they could sing them more or less in unison.

The hymnbook was the preoccupation of Fris's life, and his forty years as deacon of the parish had resulted in his knowing the whole thing by heart. He had a natural gift for it! From childhood on, Fris had been destined for the ministry, and his studies as a young man were in accordance with that intent. God's Word fell with effect from his lips, and he had a promising future, when an evil bird came all the way from the Faroe Islands to bring trouble upon him. Fris fell down two flights of stairs from spiritual guide to parish deacon and child-whipper. He regarded this occupation as an almost too transparent punishment from heaven, and arranged his school like a miniature parish.

The whole village bore traces of his work; there was not much knowledge of reading and writing, but when it came to hymns and Scripture, these fishermen and craftsmen were hard to beat. Fris gave himself credit for the fairly good circumstances of the adults, and the receipt of proper wages by the young people. He followed each of them with something of a father's eye, and found them all to be a success. And he was on friendly terms with them once they had left school; then they would come to the old bachelor and have a chat, and relieve their minds of some difficulty or other.

But it was always quite another matter with the accursed brood that sat wearing out the school benches at the moment; they resisted learning with both hands and feet, and Fris predicted no good for them in the future.

Fris hated the children. But he loved those stolid hymns, which seemed to wear out the whole class, while he himself could sing them without taxing a muscle. And when it went the way it was going today, he could almost forget that there were such things as children, and surrender himself to the endless procession in which column after column filed past him—in the footsteps of the rhythm. They weren't hymns, either; they formed a mighty parade of all the forces of life; in it all the things that Fris had missed in life extended in one endless tone. That's why he was nodding so happily, and why the loud tramp of feet rose around him like the acclamations of armies, a salute to Cæsar.

He was sitting with the third section of the newspaper in front of him, but he wasn't reading; his eyes were closed, and his head bobbed gently to the rhythm.

The children babbled on incessantly, almost without stopping for breath; they were hypnotized by the monotonous flow of words. They were like the geese that had been given permission by the fox to say a prayer before being eaten, and now went on praying and praying forever. When they came to the end of the three hymns, they began all over of their own accord. The mill kept getting louder, they kept time with their feet, and it was like the stroke of a mighty piston, a roar! Fris nodded along, and a long tuft of hair flapped in his face; he fell into a rapture, carried away so he couldn't sit still in his chair.

> And though this world, with devils filled,
> Should threaten to undo us,
> We will not fear, for God hath willed
> His truth to triumph through us.

It sounded like a stamping mill; some were beating their slates on the tables, others were thumping with their elbows. Fris didn't hear it; he heard only the mighty tramp—of advancing hosts.

> The prince of darkness grim,
> We tremble not for him . . .

"Pee-yew! Pee-yew!" Suddenly the whole school stopped and sat there holding their noses. "Ugh! Ugh!"

Fris was brought to earth again with a shock. He opened his eyes and realized bitterly that he had once again allowed himself to be taken by surprise. "You spawn of Satan! You brats from hell!" He stood roaring in their midst with his cane. "Who did it? Who did it?" he asked excitedly. "Was it you, Morten?"

Morten started to cry with great success, muttering something about not putting up with such treatment and having his father talk to the teacher.

"Peter, Marta!" hissed Fris. A boy and a girl stood up and began to walk down the rows, sniffing at the backs of the children to find the guilty party. Now the whole school was in a tumult; fights broke out all around. The girls were the worst, screeching and accusing each other. Fris struck out indiscriminately.

He tried to bring them back to the rote-work. "Who puts his trust in God alone!" he shouted in a deafening voice; but they didn't bite—the little devils! Then he struck out at random; he knew quite well that one was just as good as the next, and he wasn't particular about where the blows fell. He grabbed the long-haired ones by the hair and dragged them to the table, thrashing them until the cane splintered. The boys had been waiting for this moment; they had rubbed onion into the cane that morning, and the most defiant of them had on several pair of pants for the occasion.

When the hollow, cracked sound proclaimed that the cane was disintegrating, the whole school burst into deafening cheers. Fris gave up and let them rage. He walked up and down the center aisle like a sick animal, and the gall burned in his throat. "You little devils!" he hissed; "You infernal brats! Sit down, children!" This last plea was so ridiculously touching in the midst of all the rest that it had to be imitated.

Pelle sat farthest away, in the corner; he was fairly new at this sort of thing, but he did his best. Suddenly he jumped up on the table and danced there in his stocking feet. Fris stared at him so strangely, Pelle thought. He looked like Papa Lasse when everything was going wrong for him—and he slid down, ashamed. Nobody had noticed his behavior anyway; it was far too common.

It was all a deafening uproar, and occasionally some mean remark would be hurled out of the seething tumult. It was difficult to say where they came from, but each one of them struck Fris to the quick and made him jump. Errors of his youth made on the other side of the water fifty years ago were brought up again here on the lips of these ignorant children, as well as some of his best deeds, which had been so altruistic that the district regarded them in the worst light. And if that were not enough—but hush! He was sobbing.

"Shh—shh!" It was Henrik Bødker, the biggest boy in school, and he was standing on a bench and shushing them threateningly. The girls adored him and quieted down at once, but some of the boys wouldn't obey. But when Henrik held his clenched fist up to one eye, they too fell silent.

Fris walked up and down the center aisle like a pardoned offender; he didn't dare raise his eyes, but everyone could see that he was crying. "It's a shame!" said a low voice. All eyes turned to him, and it was dead silent in the room. "Recess!" commanded a boy's voice—it was Nilen. Fris nodded feebly, and they rushed out.

Fris stayed behind to collect himself. He walked up and down with his hands behind his back, swallowing hard. He was going to send in his resignation. Every time things went really bad, Fris sent in his resignation, but after he had collected himself, he would put it off until the spring exams were over. He didn't want to leave like this, as a kind of failure. This very winter he had worked harder than ever so that his resignation would have something of a bombshell effect, and so they would really feel the loss when he left. When the exam was held, he would use the hymnbook for recitation in unison—right from the beginning. Some of the children would quickly drop out, but into some of them he had gradually managed to hammer most of its contents. Long before they had finished, the clergyman would lift his hand to stop them, saying, "That's enough, my dear deacon! That's enough!" and thank him, greatly moved—while the school commission and the parents would put their heads together, whispering, and cross themselves in admiration.

That would be the time to resign!

The school lay on the outskirts of the fishing village, and the playground was the beach. When the boys were let out after a few hours' lessons, they were like young cattle out for the first time after the long winter. They darted like flitting swallows in all directions, threw themselves on the fresh rampart of kelp and beat each other about the ears with the wet, salty weeds. Pelle was not fond of this game; the sharp weeds stung, and sometimes there were rocks hanging on to them. But he didn't dare keep out of it, for that would attract attention at once. The trick was to join in and yet not be part of it all, to make himself little or big according to the moment, so that sometimes he was invisible and sometimes he was fierce. He was busy twisting and turning, slipping in and out.

The girls would always gather over by the outhouses—that's where they always were. They stood and gossiped and ate their lunch, but the boys criss-crossed the area like swallows in aimless flight. One big boy was crouching close to the climbing bars, with his sleeve hiding his face, and chewing. They whirled around him excitedly, one after the other, making the circle tighter and tighter. Per Kofod—"Blubbering Per"—looked as if the world were collapsing under him; he clung to the climbing bars and hid his face. When they got right up to him, they let out with a roar from behind, and the boy screamed in terror, turning up his face and breaking into a lengthy howl. Afterwards he was given all the food that the others didn't feel like eating.

Blubbering Per was always eating and always howling. He was a pauper child and an orphan; he was big for his age, but with a strangely blue, frozen tinge to him. His frightened eyes seemed to pop out of his head, and under them the flesh was swollen and puffy from crying. He would jump at the slightest sound, and he always looked like he was scared. The boys never really did him any harm, but they screamed and crouched down whenever they passed him—they just couldn't resist. Then he would scream too, and cower in fear. Sometimes the girls would run up and tap him on the back, and then he screamed himself silly, and they knew he would wet his pants in fright. Afterwards all the children gave him some of their food. He would eat everything, howling, and be as famished as ever.

No one could understand what was wrong with him. Twice he had tried to hang himself, and nobody could figure out why—including himself. And yet he wasn't totally stupid. Lasse believed that he was psychic, and saw things that other people couldn't see, so the very fact of living and breathing scared him. But whatever the reason, Pelle should never do anything to hurt him, not for all the world.

The crowd of boys had retreated to the beach, and there they suddenly threw themselves at Henrik Bødker, with little Nilen in the lead. He was knocked down and buried under the swarm, which sprawled in a heap on top of him, pounding with their fists wherever there was an opening. But then a pair of fists started pushing upward, pchoo, pchoo, like steam pistons; the boys rolled off on all sides with their hands to their faces, and Henrik Bødker shot straight out of the heap, kicking at random. Nilen was still hanging like a leech to the back of his neck, and Henrik had to tear his shirt to fling him off. Pelle thought he grew enormous as he stood there, just breathing a little hard—and now the girls came over and pinned his shirt together and gave him candy. By way of thanking them he grabbed their pigtails and tied them together, four or five of them, so they couldn't get away from each other. They stood still and bore it patiently, just gazing at him with devotion in their eyes.

Pelle had ventured into the battle and had received a kick. But he held no grudge. If he had any candy he would have given it to Henrik Bødker like the girls, and would have put up with mistreatment too. He worshiped him. But he measured himself by Nilen—little bloodthirsty Nilen, who knew no fear and attacked so recklessly that the others got out of his way! He was always in the middle of the crowd, jumping right into the worst of it all and emerging unscathed. Pelle examined himself critically to find similarities, and found them—in his defense of Papa Lasse that first summer, when he had kicked a big boy and gave him a hernia, and in his relationship with the crazy bull that didn't scare him a bit. But in other areas he failed—he was afraid of the dark, and he couldn't stand a thrashing! Nilen could take a beating with his hands in his pockets. This was Pelle's first attempt at taking a real look at himself.

Fris had gone inland, probably over to the church, so recess would last for several hours. The boys began to look around for some more time-consuming games. The "bulls" went into the schoolroom and started playing around on the tables and benches, but the "eels" stayed on the beach. "Bulls" and "eels" were the land and the sea at war; the division came naturally on any more or less solemn occasion, and sometimes gave rise to actual battles.

Pelle stayed with the shore boys—Henrik Bødker and Nilen were among them—and they were something new! They didn't care about animals and the land, but the sea, which scared him, was like a cradle to them. They romped around in the water as if it were their mother's parlor, and they had much of its easy movement in them. They were quicker than Pelle, but not as persevering, and they had a freer manner and were less conscious of the place where they belonged. They talked about England in the most everyday terms and brought things to school that their fathers and brothers had brought home from the other side of the world, from Africa and China. They spent nights on the sea in an open boat, and when they played hooky it was always to go fishing. The cleverest of them had their own fishing tackle and little flat-bottomed boats that they had built themselves and caulked with oakum; they fished for themselves and caught pike, eels, and carp, which they sold to the wealthier people in the district.

Pelle thought he knew the creek well, but now he saw it from a new angle. Here were boys who in March and April—during the holidays— were up at three in the morning, wading barefoot at the mouth of the creek to catch the pike and perch that swam up into the fresh water to spawn. And nobody told the boys to do it; they did it because they thought it was fun!

They had strange games. Now they were standing "before the sea" — in a long, exhilarated row. They followed the receding wave to the larger rocks out in the water, and then stood on the rocks and jumped when the water came in again, like a flock of sea birds. The trick was to keep your shoes dry, and yet it was the quickest boys who got the wettest. There was, of course, a limit to how long you could stay perched there. When wave followed wave in rapid succession, you had to land right in the middle of it, and then sometimes the water went over your head. Or an unusually large wave would come and catch all their legs as they were drawn up in the middle of the jump — then the whole row turned beautifully and fell splash into the water. And with a deafening noise they would go up to the schoolroom to chase the "bulls" away from the tile stove.

Farther along the shore, there were usually some boys sitting with a hammer and a large spike, boring holes in stones there. They were sons of stonemasons from the quarry. Pelle's cousin Anton was one of them. When the holes were deep enough, gunpowder was packed into them, and the whole school witnessed the explosion.

In the morning, when they were waiting for the schoolmaster, the big boys would stand along the school wall with their hands in their pockets, discussing the set of the sails and the home ports of vessels passing far out at sea. Pelle listened to them open-mouthed — they were always talking about the sea and what belonged to the sea, and most of it he didn't understand. All these boys wanted only one thing after they were confirmed — to go to sea. But Pelle had had enough of it on the trip over from Sweden — he couldn't figure them out.

How carefully he had always shut his eyes and put his fingers in his ears, so his head wouldn't fill up with water when he dived into the creek. But these boys swam underwater like real fish, and from what they said, he gathered that they could dive down in deep water and pick up rocks from the bottom.

"Can you see down there?" he asked, amazed.

"Sure! How else would the fish be able to keep out of the nets? Whenever there's moonlight, they swim right around, the whole school of them."

"And the water doesn't run into your head when you take your fingers out of your ears?"

"Take our fingers out of our ears?"

"Yes, to pick up the rock."

A burst of scornful laughter greeted this remark, and they began to question him cunningly. He was priceless—a regular country bumpkin! He had the funniest ideas about everything, and soon it came out that he had never swum in the sea. He was afraid of the water—a "blue-balls"; the creek didn't count.

After that he was called Blue-balls, even though one day he took the cattle whip to school with him and showed them how he could cut triangular holes in a pair of pants with the long lash, hit a pebble so that it vanished into thin air, and make those loud cracks with the whip. That was all wonderful, but the name stuck all the same; and this seared his little soul.

During the winter, some strong young men came home to the fishing village in blue uniforms and white neck-cloths. They had "put into shore," as it was called, and some of them drew wages all winter long without doing anything. They always came over to the school to see the schoolteacher. They would arrive in the middle of lessons, but it didn't matter; Fris would be joy personified. They would always bring something for him—a cigar of such fine quality that it was enclosed in glass, or some other remarkable thing. And they talked to Fris as they would to a comrade, told him what they had been through, so that the listening youngsters shivered with delight. They quite nonchalantly smoked their clay pipes in class—with the bowl turned neatly downward without losing its tobacco. They had been engaged as cook's boys and deck-hands on the Spanish main and in the Mediterranean and many other wonderful places. One of them had ridden up a fire-spewing mountain on a donkey. And they brought matches home with them that were almost as big as Pomeranian logs—and you lit them with your teeth.

The boys worshiped them and talked about nothing else; it was a great honor to be seen in the company of such a man. For Pelle it was unimaginable.

Later on, the village was waiting for the return of a boy like this, but he did not arrive. And one day word came that such and such a ship had sunk with all hands on board. It was the winter storms, said the boys, spitting like grown men. For a week the brothers and sisters were kept home from school, and when they came back Pelle eyed them with curiosity—it must be strange to have a brother lying at the bottom of the sea in the flower of his youth. "Now you don't want to go to sea, do you?" he asked them. Oh yes, they wanted to go to sea too!

One day Fris came back in a bad mood after an unusually long recess. He kept blowing his nose hard, drying his eyes behind his glasses now and then; the boys nudged each other. He cleared his throat loudly, but couldn't make himself heard, and then hit his desk a few times with his cane.

"Have you heard the news, children?" he asked, when they had quieted down somewhat.

"No! Yes! What?" they cried all at once. "The sun's fallen into the sea and set it on fire!" said one of them.

The teacher quietly picked up his hymnbook. "Shall we sing 'How blessed are they'?" he said. Then they knew something must have happened, and solemnly sang the hymn with him.

But at the fifth verse Fris stopped; he couldn't go on any longer. "Peter Funk has drowned," he said, in a voice that broke on the last word. A horrified whisper passed through the class, and they looked at each other with uncomprehending eyes. Peter Funk was the most energetic boy in the village, the best swimmer, and the greatest scamp the school had ever known—and he had drowned.

Fris walked up and down, struggling to control himself. The children dropped into softly whispered conversation about Peter Funk, and all their faces had grown old with someberness. "Where did it happen?" asked one of the big boys.

Fris came to with a sigh—he had been thinking about that boy, who had shirked everything and had then become the best sailor in the village; about all the thrashings he had given him, and the pleasant hours they had spent together on winter evenings when the lad was home from a voyage and had looked in to see his old teacher. There had been many wrongs to right, matters of grave importance that Fris had had to patch up for the lad in all secrecy, so that they wouldn't ruin his whole life, and . . .

"It was in the North Sea," he said. "I think they'd been to England."

"To Spain with dried fish," said a boy. "And from there they went to England with oranges, and were bringing home a cargo of coal."

"Yes, I think that's right," said Fris. "They were in the North Sea and were surprised by a storm, and Peter probably had to go aloft."

"Yes, because the *Trokkadej* is such an old hulk. As soon as there's a little wind, they have to go aloft and take in sail," said another boy.

"Then he fell," Fris went on, "and struck the railing—and dropped into the sea. There were marks from his sea-boots on the railing. They hove to—or whatever it's called—and managed to turn around; but it took them half an hour to get back to the spot. And just as they got there, he sank before their eyes. He had been struggling in the icy water for half an hour—with sea-boots and oilskins on—and yet..."

A long sigh passed through the class. "He was the best swimmer on the whole coast!" said Henrik. "He dived backward off the gunwale of a ship that was anchored offshore here, taking in water, and came up on the other side of the vessel. He got ten pieces of hardtack from the captain for that."

"He must have suffered terribly," said Fris. "It would almost have been better for him if he hadn't been able to swim."

"That's what my father says," said a little boy. "He can't swim, because he says it's better for a sailor not to know how; it only tortures you longer."

"My father can't swim either," said another. "Mine either," said a third. "He could learn easy enough, but he won't." And they went on like this, holding up their hands. They could all swim themselves, but it turned out that hardly any of their fathers could—they were superstitious about it. "Father says you shouldn't tempt Providence if your ship sinks," one boy added.

"But then you wouldn't be doing your best!" objected a faltering voice. Fris turned quickly toward the corner where Pelle sat blushing to the tips of his inquisitive ears.

"Look at that little man!" said Fris, impressed. "Isn't he right and all the rest of us wrong? God helps those who help themselves!"

"Maybe," said a voice. It was Henrik Bødker.

"Well, yes, I know He didn't help in this case—nevertheless, we should always do what we can in any situation in life. Peter Funk did his best—and he was the sharpest boy I ever had."

The children smiled at each other, remembering various incidents. Peter Funk had once gone so far as to wrestle with the schoolteacher himself—but they didn't have the heart to bring it up. But one of the bigger boys said, half-teasingly, "He never got any farther than the twenty-seventh hymn!"

"Is that so?" snarled Fris. "Is that so? So maybe you think you're smarter? Let's see if you've gotten any farther!" And he grabbed the hymnbook with a trembling hand; he couldn't stand hearing anything said against the boys who had left.

The name Blue-balls continued to bother Pelle; nothing had ever stung him as much as that name. There was no chance of getting rid of it before summer came, and that was a long way off.

One day the fisher boys ran out onto the breakwater during recess. A boat had just come in through the pack ice with a gruesome cargo—

five frozen men, one of whom was dead and lay in the engine house; the other four had been taken into various cottages, where they were being rubbed with ice to draw the frost out of them. The farmer boys were not allowed to share in all the excitement, for the fisher boys, who went in and out and saw everything, chased them away if they came too near— and sold scanty information at exorbitant prices.

The boat had met a Finnish schooner drifting in the sea, completely covered with ice, its rudder frozen. She was too heavily laden, so that the waves went right over her and froze; the ice had made her sink even deeper. When they found her, the deck was just level with the water; ropes as thick as a finger had become as thick as an arm with ice, and the men who were lashed to the rigging were shapeless masses of ice. They looked like knights in armor with closed visors when they were taken down, and their clothes had to be hacked off their bodies. Three boats had gone out now to try and save the vessel; there would be a large sum of money to divide if they were successful.

Pelle was determined not to be left out, even if he got his shins kicked, so he stayed close and listened. The boys were talking gravely and looked gloomy—what those men had been through! And maybe their hands or feet would get gangrene and have to be cut off. Each boy acted as if he were bearing his share of their sufferings, and they talked in a manly way, in gruff voices. "Get lost, bull!" they shouted at Pelle— they didn't care for Blue-balls at the moment.

Tears came to Pelle's eyes, but he wouldn't give up, so he wandered away along the wharf.

"Get lost!" they shouted again, picking up rocks menacingly. "Go join the other bumpkins!" They came over and shoved him. "What are you standing there staring into the water for? You might get dizzy and fall in head first! Go up to the other yokels, Blue-balls!"

Pelle was actually dizzy, because a decision had seized his little brain so vigorously. "I'm no more a blue-balls than you are!" he said. "You wouldn't even dare jump in the water!"

"Just listen to him. He thinks you jump in the water for fun in the middle of winter—and get cramps!"

Pelle just managed to hear their scornful laughter before he sprang off the breakwater; the water, thick with ground-up ice, closed over him. The top of his head appeared again, he paddled two or three times like a dog—and sank.

The boys ran up and down in confusion and shouted, and one of them got hold of a boat-hook. Then Henrik Bødker came running up, sprang in head first, and vanished; a cake of ice that he had struck with his forehead skipped across the water. Twice his head appeared above the ice-filled water to snatch a breath of air, and then he came up with Pelle. They hoisted him up onto the breakwater, and Henrik set about giving him a good thrashing.

Pelle had passed out, but the beating had an invigorating effect. He suddenly opened his eyes, was on his feet in a flash, and darted off like a sandpiper.

"Run home!" the boys roared after him. "Run as hard as you can, or you'll be sick! Just tell your father you fell in!" And Pelle ran. He needed no convincing. When he reached Stone Farm, his clothes were frozen stiff, and his pants could stand on their own when he took them off. But he himself was as warm as toast.

He didn't want to lie to his father, so he told him exactly what had happened. Lasse was angry, angrier than the boy had ever seen him before. The old man knew how to treat a horse to keep it from catching cold, and he began to rub Pelle's naked body with a wisp of straw, while the boy lay on the bed, tossing about under the rough handling.

Lasse paid no attention to his groans, but scolded him. "You crazy devil, jumping straight into the sea in the middle of winter like a love-sick woman—you little devil! You ought to have a whipping, that's what you ought to have—a good sound whipping! But I'll let you off this time if you'll go to sleep and sweat so we can get that nasty salt water out of your system. I wonder whether it wouldn't be a good idea to bleed you."

Pelle didn't want to be bled; he was quite comfortable lying there, after he had thrown up. But his thoughts were very serious. "What if I'd drowned?" he said solemnly.

"Then I would have thrashed you to within an inch of your life," said Lasse hotly.

Pelle laughed.

"Go ahead and laugh, you word-twister!" snapped Lasse. "But it's no joke being father to a disrespectful puppy like you!" Then he went angrily out into the stable. But every minute he listened, and kept on going over to peek in and see whether fever or any other deviltry had come of it.

But Pelle was sleeping soundly with his head underneath the quilt. He dreamed that he was none other than Henrik Bødker himself.

Pelle didn't learn to read much that winter, but he learned twenty-odd hymns by heart just by using his ears, and he had the name Blue-balls removed. He had gained ground and strengthened his position with several bold strokes—the school began to count him as a brave boy. And Henrik, who generally didn't care for anyone, many times took him under his wing.

Once in a while he had a guilty conscience, especially when his father in his newly awakened thirst for knowledge would come to him for the solution to some problem. Then he would stand there at a loss for an answer.

"But you're the one who's supposed to have the learning," Lasse would say reproachfully.

As winter drew to an end, and the examination approached, Pelle grew nervous. Numerous horrible rumors about the severity of the exam circulated among the boys—about flunking out and complete expulsion from the school.

Pelle was unlucky enough not to be asked to recite a single hymn. He had to give an account of the Fall. The theft of the apple was easy to get through, but the curse! "And God said unto the serpent: Upon thy belly shalt thou go, upon thy belly shalt thou go, upon thy belly shalt thou go!" He couldn't get any farther.

"And does it still do that?" asked the clergyman kindly.

"Yes—because it has no limbs."

"And can you explain to me what a limb is?" The pastor was known to be the best examiner on the island; he could start in the gutter and end up in heaven, people said.

"A limb is . . . is a hand."

"Yes, that's one of them. But can't you tell me something that distinguishes all limbs from other parts of the body? A limb is—well? —a what?—a part of the body that can move by itself, for instance?"

"The ears!" said Pelle, maybe because his own were burning.

"Oh? Can you wiggle your ears?"

"Yes." With great perseverance, Pelle had acquired that art during the previous summer, so as not to be outdone by Rud.

"I would certainly like to see that!" exclaimed the clergyman.

So Pelle wiggled his ears earnestly back and forth, and the pastor and the school committee and the parents all laughed. Pelle got an A in religion.

"So it was your ears that saved you after all," said Lasse, amused. "Didn't I tell you to use your ears well? Highest marks in religion just for wiggling your ears—you could probably be a pastor if you wanted to!"

And he went on like that for a long time. Wasn't he the devil of a lad to be able to answer like that!

XII

"Come on, come on! Come on, you silly hen, there's nothing to be scared of!" Pelle was enticing his favorite calf with a wisp of green grain, but it didn't really trust him today. It had gotten a beating for bad behavior.

Pelle felt like a father whose child causes him grief and forces him to take stern measures. And now this misunderstanding—the calf would have nothing to do with him, even though he had beaten it for its own good! But it couldn't be helped; as long as Pelle was the cowherd, he had to be obeyed.

Finally the calf let him come up close so he could pet it. It stood still for a moment, sulking, but gave in at last, ate the green fodder and snuffled his face to thank him.

"Are you going to be good now?" said Pelle, shaking the calf by its horn stumps. "Are you?" It tossed its head mischievously. "Well, then you won't get to carry my sweater today."

The strange thing about this calf was that the first day it was let out, it wouldn't budge, and at last the boy left it behind for Lasse to take back in. But as soon as Pelle left it behind, it followed of its own accord—with its forehead close to his back. After that it always walked behind him when they went out and came home, and it carried his heavy sweater on its back when there was a threat of rain.

Pelle's years were few in number, but to his animals he was a grown man. In the past he had only been able to make them respect him enough to obey him at close range. But this year he could hit a cow at a hundred paces with a rock, and that gave him power over the animals at a distance—especially when he figured out that he should shout the animal's name as he hit it. In this way they realized that the pain came from him, and learned to obey the shout alone.

For punishment to be effective, it had to follow the offense at once. He would no longer lay in wait for an animal that had done something wrong, and then come up behind it later on when it was grazing peacefully; that only caused confusion. To run an animal ragged, hanging onto its tail and beating it all over the meadow just to take revenge, was stupid too; it made the whole herd restless and hard to manage for the rest of the day. Pelle weighed the end and the means against each other; he learned to quench his thirst for revenge, for sound practical reasons.

Pelle was a boy, and he wasn't lazy! All day long, from five in the morning until nine at night, he was busy with something, often the most useless things. For hours he practiced walking on his hands, turning somersaults, and jumping across the creek—he was always in motion. Hour after hour he would run tirelessly around in a circle in the meadow—like a tethered foal—leaning inward as he ran so that his hand skimmed the grass, kicking up behind, and neighing and snorting. He poured out energy from morning till night with a profusion of joy.

But minding the cattle was *work*, and there he rationed his energy. Every step that could be saved was like capital acquired, and Pelle took careful note of everything and was always improving his methods. He learned that punishment worked best when it just hung as a threat—too many beatings made an animal obstinate. He also learned when it was absolutely necessary to intervene. If this couldn't be done when the situation occurred, he would control himself and, based on the strength of his experience, try to bring about exactly the same situation again— and then be prepared. The little fellow, unknown to himself, was always engaged in adding inches to his stature.

He had obtained good results. Driving the cattle out and home again no longer gave him any difficulty; for a whole week he had succeeded in driving the herd along a narrow field road, with grain growing on both sides, without any animal biting off a single blade. And the even greater trick of keeping them under control on a hot, muggy day—to hem them in at a full gallop, so that they stopped in the middle of the meadow stamping, tails uplifted in fear of the gadflies. And if he wanted to, he could stampede them home to the stable in wild flight, with their tails in the air, on the coldest October day—just by lying down in the grass and imitating the hum of gadflies. But that was a big secret that even Papa Lasse knew nothing about.

The funny thing about the buzzing was that calves that were out to pasture the first year, and had never seen a gadfly, would stick their tails in the air at once and run when they heard its angry buzz.

Pelle had a remote dream—to lie on some high place and direct the whole herd with nothing but his voice, with no need to resort to beatings. Papa Lasse never beat him either, no matter how wrong things went!

Days passed—well, what did become of them? Before he knew it, it was time to drive the cattle home. Other days were long enough, but seemed to sing themselves away, in the ring of scythes, the lowing of cattle, and people's shouts from far away. Then the day itself went singing over the earth, and Pelle had to stop every so often and listen.

Listen, there was music! And he would run up onto the dunes and gaze out across the sea. But it wasn't coming from there, and inland there was no party that he knew of, and there were no migrating birds flying overhead at this time of year. But listen, there was the music again! Real music, far off in the distance—the kind of music where you can't make out the melody or tell which instruments are playing. Could it be the sun itself?

Then light and life would flow through him, singing as though he were a spring, and he would walk around in a dreamy half-doze of melody and joy.

When the rain poured down he would hang his coat over a briar and lie sheltered beneath it, whittling or drawing with a lead button on paper—horses, and reclining bulls. But most often ships, ships that sailed across the sea on their own soft melody, far away to foreign lands—to Africa and China for rare objects. And when he was in the right mood, he would take out a broken knife and a piece of shale from a secret hiding place and set to work. There was a picture scratched on the stone, and now he was busy carving it in relief—he had been working on it off and on all summer. Now it was beginning to materialize: it was a ship in full sail, sailing over rippling water. To Spain—yes, it was going to Spain, for grapes and oranges! And all the other wonderful things Pelle had never tasted yet!

On rainy days it was work to keep track of the time; it required the utmost exertion. On other days it was easy enough, and Pelle could tell by instinct. There were certain signs at home on the farm that told him the time at specific moments of the day, and the cattle told him the time by their habits. At nine the first one lay down to chew the morning cud, and then all of them gradually lay down one by one. There was always a moment at about ten when they all lay there chewing. By eleven the last of them was on its feet again. It was the same in the afternoon between three and five.

Noon was easy to determine when the sun was out. Pelle could always feel when it turned in its path. And there were a hundred things in nature that gave him a connection with the times of day: the habits of the birds, for instance, and something about the pine trees. And many other things that he couldn't put his finger on and identify, because it was just a feeling he had. The time to drive home was indicated by the cattle themselves. As it drew near, they would graze, slowly turning around until their heads were pointing toward the farm. There was a visible tension in their bodies—they yearned for home!

Rud hadn't shown himself all week long; no sooner had he turned up today than Pelle had to give him a scolding for some dirty trick. Then he ran home, but Pelle lay down at the edge of the pine grove and sang, on his stomach with his feet in the air. All around him there were marks of his knife on the tree trunks. On the oldest ships you could see the keel, and the deck had wound up perpendicular to the hull; those had been carved the first summer. There was also a collection of tiny fields on the edge of the meadow, properly plowed, harrowed, and sown. Each field was about two feet square.

But now Pelle was resting after the exertion with Rud—making the air rock with his jubilant howling. Up at the farm a man came out and went along the road with a bundle under his arm; it was Erik, who had to appear in court for brawling. Then the master drove out at a good clip toward town, so he was evidently off on a spree. Why couldn't the man ride with him, since they were both going the same way? How fast he drove, although she never followed him anymore—she consoled herself at home instead! Could it be true that he had boozed away 500 kroner in one night?

> The war is raging, the red blood streams,
> Among the mountains ring shouts and screams!
> The Turk advances with cruel rage,
> And sparing neither youth nor age.
> They go—

"Ho!" Pelle sprang to his feet and stared across the clover field. For the last quarter of an hour the dairy cows over there had kept glancing up at the farm all the time, and now Aspasia was lowing, so his father must be coming down soon to move them. Here he came, sauntering around the corner of the farm. It wasn't far to the nearest cows; when his father had reached them Pelle could take the opportunity to run over and say hello to him.

He gathered his animals closer together and drove them slowly over to the other fence and up across the fields. Lasse had moved the upper half, and was now crossing over to the bull, which stood a little apart from the others. The bull snorted and pawed up the dirt; its tongue was hanging out of the side of its mouth, and it kept snapping one horn into the air—it was angry. Then it advanced with short steps and a lot of hocus-pocus—and how it kicked! Pelle felt like kicking it in the nose the way he had often done before; it had no business bellowing at Lasse, even if it didn't mean anything by it.

Papa Lasse paid no attention to it either. He stood hammering away at the big tether-peg to loosen it. "Hello!" shouted Pelle. Lasse turned his head and nodded, then bent down and hammered the peg into the ground. The bull was right behind him, stamping rapidly, with open mouth and tongue hanging out; it looked like it was throwing up, and it sounded like it too. Pelle laughed as he slackened his pace. He was almost there.

But suddenly Papa Lasse turned a somersault, fell, and was in the air again—and then fell a little way off. The bull was about to toss him again, but Pelle was at its head; he didn't have his wooden shoes on, but he kicked it with his bare feet until he was dizzy. The bull knew him and tried to go around, but Pelle sprang at its head, shouting and kicking; almost beside himself, he grabbed it by the horns. Then the bull flung him gently aside and moved toward Lasse, who was lying nearby; the bull was snorting along the ground so that the grass waved.

It took Lasse by the shirt and shook him a little, and then tried to get both its horns under him to toss him into the air. But Pelle was on his feet again, and as quick as lightning he drew his knife and plunged it in between the bull's hind legs. The bull uttered a brief roar, turned Lasse over on one side, and dashed off over the fields at a gallop, goring the air and bellowing as it ran. Down by the creek it started to tear up the bank, and the air was thick with dirt and turf.

Lasse lay groaning with his eyes closed, and Pelle stood pulling at his arm in a vain attempt to help him up, crying, "Papa, little Papa Lasse!" At last Lasse sat up.

"Who's that singing?" he asked. "Oh, it's you, lad—and you're crying! Has somebody hurt you? Ah yes, of course, it was the bull. It was just about to play fandango with me. But what did you do to it to make the devil take hold of it so fast? You probably saved your father's life, little though you are. Goddamn, I think I'm going to be sick." Lasse threw up. "Oh well," he said, wiping the sweat from his brow. "If only I had a dram. Oh yes, he knew me, that fellow, otherwise I wouldn't have gotten off so easy. He just wanted to play with me a little, you know—he was a little mad at me for driving him away from a cow this morning, I knew that well enough. But who'd have thought he'd turn on me? And he wouldn't have done it, either, if I hadn't been dumb enough to wear someone else's clothes. This is Mons' shirt; I borrowed it from him while I was washing mine. And the rascal couldn't stand the strange smell on me. Well, we'll see what Mons will say about this rip—he probably won't be too happy."

Lasse went on rambling for quite a while until he tried to get up, and managed to stand with Pelle's help. He stood leaning on the boy's shoulder, swaying back and forth. "I almost feel like I'm drunk, if it weren't for the pain!" he said, laughing feebly. "Well, I have to thank God for you, lad. You always make me happy, and now you've saved my life too."

Then Lasse stumbled homeward, and Pelle moved the rest of the cows on the road down to his own. He was both proud and shaken, but mostly proud. He had saved Papa Lasse's life—and from the big, furious bull that no one else on the farm dared to have anything to do with. Next time Henrik Bødker came out to see him, he would hear all about it.

It bothered him a little that he had pulled his knife; here everyone looked down on that, and said it was a Swedish thing to do. It wouldn't have been necessary either, if there had been time—or if only he had been wearing his wooden shoes to kick the bull in the eye with. He had often gone after it with the toes of his wooden shoes, when it had to be driven back into its stall after servicing a cow; and it was always careful not to do anything to him. Maybe he would poke his finger in the bull's eye and blind it, or take it by the horns and twist its head around, just like in the story, until he wrung its neck.

Pelle kept growing and swelling up until he overshadowed everything; there was no limit to his energy as he ran around gathering his animals back together. He stormed over everything, flung Strong Erik and the foreman around, and lifted—yes, he could lift the whole of Stone Farm merely by putting his hand under the roof-beam. It was a regular Viking berserker fit!

In the midst of it all, it occurred to him how terrible it would be if the foreman found out the bull was running loose. It might mean a beating for both himself and Lasse. He had to go out and look for it; for safety's sake he took along his whip and put on his wooden shoes.

The bull had made an awful mess down on the bank of the creek; a good piece of the meadow was plowed up. There were bloody tracks along the bed of the stream and across the fields. Pelle followed them out toward the hedgerow, where he found the bull. The huge animal had gone right into the thicket and was standing there licking its wound. When it heard Pelle's voice, it came out. "Turn around!" he cried, flicking its nose with the whip. It put its head to the ground, bellowed, and moved heavily backward; Pelle kept on flicking it on the nose as he approached step by step, shouting firmly: "Turn around! Come on, turn around!" At last the bull turned and set off at a run, and Pelle grabbed the tether-peg and ran behind. He kept at it with the whip, so that it wouldn't have time to think up anything wicked.

When that was over, he collapsed with fatigue. He lay curled up at the edge of the pine grove, thinking sadly about Papa Lasse, who must be going around up there feeling sick, and there was no one to lend a helping hand with his work. At last the situation became unbearable: he had to go home.

"Zzzz! Zzzz!" Pelle crawled on his stomach through the grass, imitating the maddening buzz of the gadfly. He forced the sound out between his teeth, rising and falling, as if it were flying here and there over the grass; the cattle stopped grazing and stood stock still with ears alert. Then they started to get nervous, kicking up their legs under their bodies, turning their heads from side to side, and twitching; their tails went up! He made the sound more persistently angry, and the whole herd whirled around; they infected each other and started stamping around in wild panic. Two calves broke out of the tumult and made a beeline for the farm, and the whole herd followed, over any obstacle. Now it was just a matter of running after them, making a lot of commotion—slyly keeping up the buzzing so the mood would last until they reached home.

The foreman himself came running out and opened the gate to the enclosure; he helped chase the animals inside. Pelle expected a box on the ears and stood waiting, but the foreman merely looked at him with a peculiar smile. "They're beginning to get the upper hand over you," he said, looking Pelle straight in the eye. "Well, that's all right, as long as you can handle the bull!" He was teasing him, and Pelle blushed to the roots of his hair.

Papa Lasse had crept into bed. "What a good thing you came," he said. "I was just lying here wondering how I was going to get the cows moved. I can hardly move at all, much less get up."

It took a week before Lasse was on his feet again; during that time the field cattle remained in the enclosure, and Pelle stayed home and did his father's work. He ate with the others and took his midday nap in the barn with them.

Around noon one day, the Sow came into the courtyard, drunk. She took her stand in the upper yard, where she was forbidden to go, and stood there shouting for Kongstrup. The master was home, but didn't come out, and not a soul could be seen behind the high windows. "Kongstrup! Kongstrup! Come out here for a minute!" she called, with her eyes on the pavement, because she couldn't lift her head. The foreman wasn't around, and the men hid in the barn, hoping to see some fun. "Kongstrup, come out for a minute, I want to talk to you!" said the Sow thickly. Then she went up the steps and tried the door. She hammered on it a few times, and stood there talking with her face close to the door; when nobody came, she reeled down the steps and went away, muttering to herself and looking straight ahead.

A little while later the long, wailing sobs started in up there, and just as the men were going out to the fields, the master came rushing out and gave orders to have the horse harnessed to the buggy. Meanwhile, he walked about nervously, and then set off at full speed. As he turned the corner of the house, a window was thrown open and a voice called to him imploringly: "Kongstrup, Kongstrup!" But he drove quickly on. The window closed, and the weeping began anew.

In the afternoon Pelle was busy in the lower yard when Karna came to him and told him to go up to the mistress. Pelle went up reluctantly. He didn't feel safe with her, and all the men were out in the fields.

Mrs. Kongstrup was lying on the sofa in her husband's study; she always lay there, day or night, whenever her husband was out. She had a damp towel across her forehead, and her whole face was red from crying.

"Come here," she said in a dull voice. "You aren't afraid of me, are you?"

Pelle had to go over to her and sit on the chair beside her; he didn't know what to do with his eyes. His nose began to run from the tension, and he didn't have a handkerchief.

"Are you afraid of me?" she asked again, and a bitter smile crossed her lips.

He had to look at her to show that he wasn't afraid; to tell the truth, she didn't look like a witch, just a person who was crying and unhappy.

"Come here," she said, and she wiped his nose with her own fine handkerchief and stroked his hair. "You don't even have a mother, poor thing." She smoothed down his clumsily mended shirt.

"It's three years ago that Mama Bengta died; she's buried in the west corner of the churchyard."

"Do you miss her a lot?"

"Well, Papa Lasse mends my clothes."

"I suppose she wasn't very good to you."

"Oh, yes!" said Pelle, nodding earnestly. "But she was so grumpy all the time. She was always sickly, so it's better that she went. But we're going to get married again soon, when Papa Lasse finds somebody who'll do."

"And then I suppose you'll go away from here? You don't like it here much, do you?"

Pelle had found his tongue, but now he was afraid of a trap and clammed up. He merely nodded—nobody was going to come and accuse him afterwards of complaining.

"No, you don't like it here," she said in a plaintive voice. "No one likes it at Stone Farm. Everything turns into misfortune here."

"It's probably an old curse!" said Pelle.

"Is that what they say? Yes, yes, I know they do. And they say that I'm a devil—just because I love only one man—and can't accept being trampled on." She wept and pressed his hand to her quivering face.

"I've got to go out and move the cows," said Pelle, wriggling uneasily, trying to get away.

"Now you're afraid of me again!" she said and tried to smile. It was like a gleam of sunshine outdoors after the rain.

"No, but I've got to go out and move the cows."

"There's still a whole hour before that! But why aren't you herding today? Is your father ill?"

Then Pelle had to tell her about the bull.

"You're a good boy!" said the mistress, patting his head. "If I had a son, I would like him to be just like you! But now you shall have some jam, and then you must run over to the store for a bottle of black-currant rum, so we can make a hot drink for your father. If you hurry, you can be back before it's time to move the cows."

Lasse got his hot drink, even before the boy returned; and every day while he lay sick he received something invigorating—though there was no black-currant rum in it.

During this time Pelle went up to the mistress nearly every day—Kongstrup must have gone to Copenhagen on business. She was kind to him and gave him sweets; while he devoured them she would talk incessantly about Kongstrup, or ask Pelle what people thought about her. Pelle had to tell her, and then she would be upset and start to cry. There was no end to her talk about the master, but she kept contradicting herself, and Pelle gave up trying to make sense out of it. Besides, the treats she gave him were enough to keep him busy.

Down in their room he repeated everything word for word, and Lasse lay and listened, amazed at this boy who had the run of high places and was in the mistress's confidence. Yet he didn't really like it.

"... She could hardly stand; she had to hold on to the table when she was going to get me the zwieback, she was so sick. It was all because he'd treated her badly, she said. She hates him, Papa, and would like to kill him, she says. And yet she says he's the handsomest man in the world, and asks me if I ever saw anyone handsomer in all of Sweden. And then she cries and goes into hysterics."

"Is that so?" said Lasse thoughtfully. "She probably doesn't know what she's saying—or else she has her own reasons for it. But all the same, it's not true that he beats her! I'm sure she's lying."

"Why should she lie?"

"Because she wants to hurt him, I suppose. But it's true he's a fine man—and cares for everybody but her; and that's the whole trouble. I don't like it that you spend so much time with her; just so you don't come to any harm."

"How could I? She's so kind to me."

"How's a poor devil to know? No, she's not kind—her eyes aren't kind, at least. She's brought trouble to more than one person just by looking at them. But I guess there's nothing to be done about it; a poor man has to risk everything."

Lasse was silent, and stumbled around for a moment. Then he came over to Pelle.

"Now look at this! Here's a piece of steel I found, and you must always remember to keep it with you—especially when you go up *there*! And then—yes, then we'll have to leave the rest in God's hand. He's the only one who might look after poor little boys."

Lasse was up for a short while that day. Thank God he was making progress rapidly; in two days they could be back to their old routines again. And by winter they would have to try to get away from all this!

On the last day that Pelle stayed home, he went up to the mistress and ran her errand for her. And that day he saw something spooky that made him glad that this was over—she took her teeth, palate and all, out of her mouth and laid them on the table in front of her!

So she *was* a witch!

XIII

Pelle was coming home with his young cattle. As he came down near the farm he shouted his commands so that his father would hear. "Hey, Spasianna, you old hag, where are you going? Dannebrog, you confounded old ram, turn around!" But Lasse didn't come out to open the gate of the enclosure.

When Pelle got the animals inside, he ran into the cow stable. His father wasn't there or in their room either, and his Sunday clogs and his woolen cap were gone. Then Pelle remembered that it was Saturday—the old man had probably gone to the store to get liquor for the men.

Pelle went down to the servants' room to get his supper. The men had come home late and were sitting at the table, which was covered with spilt milk and potato peels. They were in the middle of a wager—Erik would eat twenty salt herrings with potatoes after he had already finished his meal. The stakes were a bottle of aquavit, and the others would peel the potatoes for him.

Pelle took out his pocket knife and peeled himself a heap of potatoes. He left the skin on the herring, but scraped it carefully and cut off the head and tail; then he cut it into pieces and ate it, bones and all, with the potatoes and gravy. Meanwhile, he looked at Erik—the giant Erik, who was so incredibly strong and wasn't afraid of anything in heaven or earth. Erik had children everywhere! Erik could put his finger into the barrel of a shotgun and hold the gun straight out at arm's length! Erik could drink as much as three other men!

And now Erik was sitting there eating twenty salt herrings, even though he was already full. He took the herring by the head, drew it once between his legs, and then ate it as it was. And he ate potatoes too, just as fast as the others could peel them. In between bites he swore because the foreman had refused to let him have the evening off. Not on your life—trying to keep Erik home when he wanted to go out!

Pelle quickly downed his herring and porridge, and took off again to meet his father; he was longing greatly to see him. Out by the pump the girls were busy scouring the milk pails and kitchen pans; Gustav was standing in the lower yard with his arms on the fence, entertaining them. He was actually watching Bodil, whose eyes were always following the new trainee, who was strutting back and forth, showing off his long boots with the patent leather tops.

Pelle was stopped as he ran past and set to pumping water. Now the men came up and went across to the barn, maybe to try their strength. Since Erik had arrived they were always testing their strength in their free time. Pelle thought there was nothing as exciting as trials of strength, and he was rushing to finish so he could go over there.

But Gustav, who was generally the most eager, continued to stand there, venting his bad humor on the trainee. "Look, he shines like cat shit in the moonlight!" he said loudly.

"There must be money there!" said Bodil thoughtfully.

"Yes, you ought to try him; maybe you could become a landowner's wife. The foreman won't, for sure. And the master—well, you saw the Sow the other day. It must be nice to have prospects like that."

"Who told you the foreman won't?" replied Bodil sharply. "Don't think we need you to hold the candle for us! Little children shouldn't be allowed to see everything anyway."

Gustav turned red. "Oh, shut up, you old bag!" he muttered, and sauntered down to the barn.

Oh, Jesus, my poor old mother
Who's up on deck and stumbling!

sang Mons from the stable door, where he was standing hammering on a cracked wooden shoe. Pelle and the maids were arguing, and up in the loft the foreman could be heard walking back and forth; he was busy fixing the pipes. Every now and then a long-drawn-out sound would come from the big house, like the distant howl of some animal, making the servants shudder with dread.

A man slipped out of the door from the men's quarters. He was wearing his Sunday clothes and had a bundle under his arm. It was Erik—he crept along by the building in the lower yard.

"Hey you! Where the devil are you going?" thundered a voice from the foreman's window. The man ducked his head a little and pretended not to hear. "Do you hear, you damned scoundrel! *Erik!*" This time Erik turned and darted in through a barn door.

Right after that the foreman came down and strode across the yard. In the chaff-cutting barn the men were standing laughing at Erik's bad luck. "He's a devil for keeping an eye out," said Gustav. "You have to get up pretty early to fool him."

"Oh, I'll manage to trick him," said Erik. "I wasn't born yesterday either. And if he gets too nosy, he'll get one in the gums."

Suddenly they fell silent when they heard the foreman's familiar step outside on the cobblestones. Erik sneaked away.

The figure of the foreman filled the entire doorway. "Who sent Lasse for liquor?" he asked harshly.

They looked at each other blankly. "Is Lasse out?" asked Mons, with the most innocent expression in the world.

"Yes, the old man does like his liquor," said Anders in explanation.

"Oh, yes, fine fellows you are," said the foreman. "First you send off the old man, and then you leave him in the lurch. You deserve a thrashing, all of you."

"No, we don't deserve a thrashing, and won't submit to one either," said the head man, taking a step forward. "Let me tell you—"

"Hold your tongue, man!" shouted the foreman right in his face, and Karl Johan stepped back. "Where's Erik?"

"He must be in his room."

The foreman went in through the horse stable; something about his posture showed that he was not totally unprepared for an attack from behind. Erik was in bed, with the quilt pulled up over his nose.

"What's the meaning of this? Are you sick?" asked the foreman.

"Yes, I think I've caught cold—I'm shivering so bad." He tried to make his teeth chatter.

"It isn't mumps, is it?" asked the foreman sympathetically. "Let's have a look at you, poor fellow." He whipped off the quilt with a jerk. "Oho, so you're in bed with your Sunday clothes on—and top-boots! Your funeral clothes, maybe? And I guess you were just going out to order a pauper's grave for yourself, weren't you? It's about time we put you underground too; seems to me you're starting to smell already!" He sniffed at him a couple of times.

But Erik leapt out of bed like a coiled spring, and stood erect right next to him. "I'm not dead yet, and I don't smell any more than some other people!" he said. His eyes flashed, and darted about the room like lightning, looking for a weapon.

The foreman felt his hot breath on his face—it wouldn't be advisable to retreat. He planted his fist in the man's stomach, so that Erik fell back onto the bed, gasping for air; then he clutched his chest and held him down. He was burning to do more—to drive a heavy fist into the face of this rascal, who grumbled whenever his back was turned and had to be driven to every little task. Here he had in his grip at last all the servant trouble that gave his life that bitter taste: dissatisfaction with the food, cantankerousness at work, threats of leaving when things were at their busiest—trouble without end. Here was the chance to strike out for years of annoyance and insults. All the foreman needed was the slightest pretext—just one shove from this big oaf who never used his strength for work, but only to take the lead as a rabble-rouser.

But Erik lay perfectly still, looking at his enemy with watchful eyes. "Go ahead and hit me. I guess there's such a thing as a magistrate in this country," he said with irritating calm.

The foreman's muscles burned, but he had to let him go for fear of being arrested. "Next time remember not to be so disobedient," he said, releasing his grip, "or I'll show you that there's a magistrate, all right."

"When Lasse gets here, send him up to me with the liquor!" he said to the men as he passed through the barn.

"The hell we will," said Mons under his breath.

Pelle had gone to meet his father. The old man had sampled the wares and was in good spirits. "There were seven men in the boat, and

they were all named Ole except one, and he was named Ole Olsen," he
said solemnly when he saw the boy. "Yes, wasn't it a strange thing, little
Pelle, that they would all be named Ole—except the one, of course. His
name was Ole Olsen." Then he laughed, and nudged the boy mysteriously. Pelle laughed too; he liked to see his father in good spirits.

The men came toward them and took the bottles from the herdsman.
"He's been tasting it!" said Anders, holding the bottles up to the light.
"Look at the old drunk! He's had a taste of the goods."

"No, the bottles have a leak in the bottom," said Lasse, emboldened
by the aquavit. "I haven't done anything but sniff at them. You have to
make sure you're getting the genuine article and not just water."

They moved on past the enclosure; Gustav walked in front, playing
his concertina. A kind of tense merriment reigned over the group. First
one and then another would leap into the air as they walked; they
uttered short howls and shouted disconnected oaths at random. The
awareness of the full bottles, Saturday night with the day of rest ahead
of them, and above all the war with the foreman, had roused their
spirits.

They settled down below the cow stable in the grass close to the
pond. The sun had gone down long ago, but the evening sky was bright.
When their faces turned toward the west, it was as if a flaming light
passed over them, and the white farms inland were dazzling in the
twilight.

Now the maids came sauntering through the grass. They walked
with their hands under their aprons, looking like silhouettes against the
brilliant sky; they were humming a tender folk song, and they sank
down onto the grass next to the men. The evening twilight was in their
hearts and made their figures and voices as soft as a caress. But the men
were not in a gentle mood; they preferred the bottle.

Gustav walked around improvising on his concertina. He was looking for a place to sit down, and at last threw himself into Karna's lap and
began to play a dance tune. Erik was the first one on his feet. He led off
on account of his quarrel with the foreman, and pulled Bengta up from
the grass with a yank. They danced a polka, and at a certain spot in the
melody he would toss her up in the air with a shout. She shrieked every
time, and her heavy skirts stood out around her like the tail of a tom
turkey, so that everyone could see all the way to Sunday.

In the middle of a whirl he let go of her so she stumbled across the
grass and fell. The foreman's window was visible from where they sat,
and a light patch had appeared at it. "He's staring at us! Lord in heaven,
how he's staring! Hey, can you see this?" Erik shouted, holding up an

aquavit bottle. Then he took a drink. "*Skål!* Old man Satan's *skål*! He stinks, the pig! Pee-yew!" The others laughed, and the face at the window disappeared.

In between the dances they played, drank, and wrestled. Their actions grew wilder and wilder: they yelled suddenly and made the girls scream, they threw themselves flat on the ground in the middle of a dance, groaned as if they were dying, jumped up again waving their arms, and tripped those closest to them. A couple of times the foreman sent the trainee down to tell them to be quiet, but that only made the noise worse. "Tell him to do his own dirty work!" Erik shouted after the trainee.

Lasse nudged Pelle and they gradually moved farther and farther away. "We'd better go to bed now," Lasse said, when they had slipped away unnoticed. "You never know what this might lead to. All of them are seeing red; pretty soon they'll start dancing the dance of blood. Oh, if only I were young, I wouldn't have snuck away like a thief, but stayed and taken whatever might come. There was a time when Lasse could put both hands on the ground and kick his man in the face with his boot-heels so he went down like a blade of grass. But that time is gone, and it's best to look out for yourself. This could end with the police and a lot worse. Not to mention the foreman. They've been riding him all summer with that Erik in the lead; but if they ever make him really mad, Erik might as well give up."

Pelle wanted to stay up for a while and watch them. "If I crawl along behind the fence and lie down—oh please, Papa!" he begged.

"Eh, what a dumb idea! They might rough you up if they catch you—the worst in them has come out. Well, it's up to you—and for goodness' sake make sure they don't see you!"

Then Lasse went to bed, but Pelle crawled on his stomach behind the fence until he got up close to them and could see everything.

Gustav was still sitting on Karna's lap and playing, and she was holding him tight in her arms. But Anders had put his arm around Bodil's waist. Gustav discovered this, and with an oath he flung his concertina so it rolled across the grass, and sprang up. The others threw themselves down in a circle on the grass, breathing hard. They were expecting something.

Gustav was like a savage dancing a war dance. His mouth was open and his eyes shone. He was the only man standing, and he bounced up and down like a ball, hopped on his heels, and kicked up his legs one after the other as high as his head; with each kick he uttered a shrill cry. Then he shot up in the air, spun around, came down on one heel, and went on spinning like a top. As he spun he made himself smaller and smaller as if he was going to spin down into the earth, and then exploded in a leap and landed in Bodil's lap; she threw her arms around him in delight.

In a flash Anders had both hands on his shoulders from behind, set his feet against his back, and sent him somersaulting over the grass. It all happened so fast, and Gustav got dizzy from rolling across the grass, jolting along like a lumpy ball. But suddenly he stopped and rose to his feet with a bound; he stared straight ahead, turned around with a jerk, and moved slowly toward Anders. Anders got up quickly, cocked his cap to one side, clicked his tongue, and advanced. Bodil settled herself more comfortably on the ground and looked exultantly around the circle, greedily taking in the envy of the others.

The two opponents stood face to face, feeling their way for a good grip. They stroked each other affectionately, pinched each other in the side, and made little joking remarks.

"By Jesus, you sure are fat, brother!" said Anders.

"And what a superstructure you've got! You could be a woman," replied Gustav, feeling Anders' chest. "Eeh, you sure are soft!" Their faces gleamed with scorn. But their eyes alertly followed the least movement of their opponent, each of them expecting a sudden attack from the other.

The others lay stretched out around them on the grass. "Can't you get it over with?" they yelled impatiently.

The two men continued to stand there, playing as if they were afraid to really get going—maybe they were dragging it out to enjoy it even more. But all of a sudden Gustav grabbed Anders by the collar, threw himself backward, and flipped Anders over his head. It happened so fast that Anders couldn't get a hold on Gustav, but as he flipped he hooked his fingers into Gustav's hair, and they both fell—on their backs, with their heads together and their bodies stretched in opposite directions.

Anders had fallen hard, and lay half dazed, but didn't release his hold on Gustav's hair. Gustav twisted around and tried to get to his feet, but couldn't free his hair. Then he wriggled back into the same position as quick as a cat, turned a backward somersault over his opponent, and fell onto him, face to face. Anders tried to raise his feet to intercept him, but he was too late.

Anders threw himself from side to side with violent jerks, lay still and then tensed his body again with sudden strength, trying to throw Gustav off, but Gustav was tough. He flung himself heavily on his adversary and stuck out his arms and legs to brace himself against the ground, raised himself suddenly and sat down on Anders' belly, knocking the wind out of him. The whole time both of them were thinking about pulling out their knives. Anders, who had now fully recovered his senses, remembered distinctly that he didn't have his with him. "Oh no!" he said aloud. "What a fool I am!"

"So you're whining, eh?" said Gustav, bending his face over him. "Do you want to say uncle?"

At that moment Anders felt Gustav's knife pressing against his thigh, and in a flash had his hand down there and wrenched it free. Gustav tried to take it away from him, but gave up for fear of being thrown off; then he confined himself to pinning one of his hands so that he couldn't open the knife, and began thumping his body against Anders' stomach.

Anders lay in half surrender, and bore the blows without trying to defend himself—a gasp escaped him with each one. But his left hand was working hard to open the knife against the ground, and suddenly he plunged it into Gustav just as he lifted his body to land another blow.

Gustav seized Anders by the wrist, his face contorted. "What the hell are you after, you pig?" he said, spitting in Anders' face. "He's trying to sneak out the back door, the poor sap!" Gustav looked around the circle, frowning like a young bull.

They fought furiously for the knife, using hands and teeth and foreheads. When Gustav couldn't grab the weapon, he tried to guide Anders' hand so he would plunge it into his own body. He succeeded, but the stab wasn't straight; the blade closed on Anders' fingers so that he tossed it away with a curse.

Meanwhile Erik sat there getting angry because he was no longer the hero of the evening. "Aren't you finished yet, you two bantams, or can I get a little taste too?" he said, trying to separate them. They took a firm grip on each other, but then Erik got mad and did something that was talked about for a long time afterwards. He grabbed hold of them and planted them both on their feet.

Gustav looked as though he wanted to jump into the fray again, and a sullen expression spread across his face. But then he started to sway like a tree chopped at the roots, and sank straight to the ground. Bodil was the first to come to his aid; with a cry she ran over and threw her arms around him.

He was carried in and laid on his bed; Karl Johan poured aquavit into the deep cut to clean it, and held it together while Bodil stitched it up with needle and thread from one of the men's lockers. Then they dispersed, in pairs, as friendship dictated. But Bodil stayed with Gustav —she was true to him after all.

That's the way things were that summer: war and friction with the foreman, but they still didn't dare do anything, when it came right down to it. Then the hatred would strike inward, and they turned on each other. "It has to come out somewhere," said Lasse, who didn't like this state of affairs, and vowed they would leave as soon as another offer came up—even if they had to run away without their wages and their clothes and everything.

"They're unhappy with their pay, their work hours are too long, and the food isn't good enough. They throw it around so it makes you sick to watch them—it's still God's gift, even if it could be better. And Erik's at the bottom of it all! He's always boasting and bragging and stirring up the others all day long. But as soon as the foreman gets after him, he doesn't dare do anything either. Then they all creep into a mousehole, every one of them. Papa Lasse isn't such a coward as some of them, old as he is.

"A good conscience is the best foundation, I suppose. If you have a good conscience and do your duty, you can look both the foreman and the master—and God the Father too—in the eye. You must always remember, lad, not to fight against those who are placed above you. Some of us have to be servants and others masters; how would it all work out if those of us who work didn't do our duty? You can't expect the rich folks to scrape up the manure in the cow stable and clean the outhouses."

All this Lasse expounded after they had gone to bed. But Pelle had something better to do than listen to this. He was sound asleep and dreaming that he was Erik himself, and was thrashing the foreman with a big stick.

XIV

In Pelle's day, salt herring was the Bornholmer's most important food. It was the regular breakfast dish in all classes of society, and in the lower classes it predominated at the supper table too—and sometimes appeared at dinner in a slightly altered form. "It's a bad place for food," people would say derisively of such and such a farm. "All you get there is herring twenty-one times a week."

When the elder was in flower, people of regular habits would take out their saltboxes, according to old custom, and stand looking out to sea; that's when the herring is fattest. From the sloping land, which nearly everywhere has a glimpse of the sea, people would gaze out in the early summer mornings for the boats coming home. The weather and the way the boats lay in the water gave omens regarding the winter provisions. Then the rumors would come wandering up across the island, of large hauls and good bargains. The farmers drove to the town or the fishing village with their largest wagons, and the herring man worked his way up through the countryside from cottage to cottage with his nag, which was so wretched that anyone would have been justified in putting a bullet through its head.

In the morning, when Pelle opened the stable doors to the field, the mist lay in every hollow like a pale gray lake; on the high ground, where the smoke rose briskly from houses and farms, he saw men and women coming around the gable-ends, half-dressed or only in their night-clothes, gazing out to sea. He too ran around the outbuildings and peered out toward the sea, which lay as shiny as silver and took its colors from the day. The red sails were hanging motionless, resembling splashes of blood in the glare of day; the boats lay deep in the water and were struggling slowly homeward to the stroke of the oars, dragging themselves along like cows that are all too pregnant.

But all this had nothing to do with him. Stone Farm, like the poor of the parish, didn't buy its herring until after harvest time, when it was as dry as sticks and cost almost nothing. At that time of year, herring was generally plentiful, and eighty fish would sell for 15 to 20 øre as long as the demand continued. After that it was sold by the cartload as food for the pigs, or thrown on the dungheap.

One Sunday morning in late fall, a messenger came running from town to Stone Farm to say that there was herring to be had. The fore-man came down to the servants' room while they were at breakfast and gave orders for all the working teams to be harnessed up. "Then you'll have to come too," said Karl Johan to the two quarry drivers, who were married and lived up near the quarry, but came down for meals.

"No, we won't take our horses out of the stable for that," said the drivers. "We drive only stone and nothing else." They sat for a little while and indulged in sarcasms at the expense of certain people who didn't even have Sunday to themselves. One of them stretched in a

damnably irritating way and said: "Well, I think I'll go home and take a
nap. It feels good to be your own man once a week, at least." So they
went home to wife and children to observe the Sabbath.

For a while the hired hands went around grumbling; that was normal. Actually they had nothing against the trip; there was bound to be
a little fun involved. There were plenty of taverns in town, and they
would make sure to arrange the matter with the herring so that they
wouldn't get home much before evening. If worse came to worst, Erik
might crack up his wagon, and then they would have to stay in town
while it was being fixed.

They stood out in the stable and turned their coin purses inside
out—big, hefty leather purses with steel locks that could only be
opened by pressure on a secret mechanism; but they were empty.

"Damn it all!" said Mons, peering with disappointment into his
purse. "Not so much as the smell of a one-øre! There must be a leak in
it." He examined the seams, held it up close to his eyes, and finally put
his ear to it. "The devil only knows why, but I think I hear a 2-krone
talking to itself. It must be haunted!" He sighed and stuck his purse in
his pocket.

"You poor louse," said Anders. "Have you ever talked to a 2-krone?
No, I'm the man for you!" He hauled out a large purse. "I've still got
the 10-krone that the foreman cheated me out of on May Day, but I
haven't the heart to spend it. I'm going to keep it until I get old." He
stuck his hand into the empty purse and pretended to take something
out and hold it up. The others laughed and joked, and they were all in
good spirits at the thought of the trip to town.

"But Erik's sure to have some money at the bottom of his chest!"
said one. "He works for good wages and has a rich aunt in hell."

"Oh, no you don't," whined Erik. "I have to pay for a dozen young
brats who can't lay claim to any other father. But Karl Johan should go
get it, or what's the good of being head man?"

"That's no use," said Karl Johan dubiously. "If I ask the foreman for
an advance now, when we're going to town, he'll just say no. God
knows, maybe the girls have some money lying around."

The milkmaids were just coming up from the cow stable with their
pails.

"Listen, girls," Erik called out to them, "can't one of you lend us
ten kroner? You'll get double for it next Easter."

"You and your promises!" said Bengta and stopped; they all set
down their milk pails and talked it over.

"You think Bodil's got it?" said Karna.

"No," said Marie. "She sent the ten kroner she'd saved up to her mother the other day."

Mons slapped his cap on the floor and jumped. "I'll go up to Old Man Satan himself," he said.

"Then you'll come down the stairs headfirst for sure!"

"The hell I will, when my old mother's lying deathly ill in town with no money for doctor or medicine. I'm no worse a child than Bodil is." He headed toward the stone steps. They stood and watched him from the stable door, until the foreman came and they had to get busy with the wagons. Gustav walked around in his Sunday best with a bundle of clothes under his arm, watching them.

"Why don't you get to work?" said the foreman. "Get your horses hitched up."

"The foreman himself gave me the day off," said Gustav, making a face. He was going out with Bodil.

"Ah, so I did. But that'll be one less wagon. You'll have to take off another day instead."

"I can't do that."

"What the hell—and why not, if I might ask?"

"Well, because you gave me today off."

"But damn it, man, when I tell you you can take another day off instead!"

"No, I can't do that."

"But why not, man? Is there something urgent you have to do?"

"No, but I've been given the day off." It looked as if Gustav was grinning slyly, but he was just turning the quid of tobacco in his mouth. The foreman stamped in anger.

"But I could just as well leave for good if the foreman doesn't like looking at me," said Gustav softly.

The foreman no doubt heard him, but turned away quickly. Long experience had taught him to be deaf to that sort of offer in the busy season. He looked up at his window as if he had suddenly thought of something, and ran up the stairs. They had him in a bind when they played on that string. But his turn would come in the winter, and then they would have to keep their mouths shut and put up with things— just to have a roof over their heads during the slack time.

Gustav kept on strutting about with his bundle, without lending a hand with anything. The others laughed encouragingly to him.

The foreman came back down and went over to him. "Then hitch up the horses before you go," he said curtly, "and I'll drive your team."

An angry growl passed from man to man. "We're going to have the dog with us," they muttered to each other, and then, so that the foreman could hear: "Where's the dog? We're going to take the dog along."

Matters were not improved when Mons came down the steps with a wonderfully pious expression on his face, holding a 10-krone bill in front of his stomach. "It doesn't matter now, because we've got to take the dog along!" Mons' face changed all of a sudden, and he started swearing fiercely. They fiddled with the wagons without getting anything done, and their eyes shone with malice.

The foreman came out on the steps with his overcoat on. "Look sharp and get those horses hitched!" he thundered.

The men of Stone Farm were just as strict about their pecking order as the native inhabitants of the island, and it was just as complicated. The head man sat at the head of the table and helped himself first, he went first during the reaping, and had the first girl to lay the load when the hay was taken in; he was the first man up, and led the way when they set out for the fields, and no one could throw down his tools before he did. After him came the second man, the third, and so on, and finally the day-laborers. When no great personal preference interfered, the head man was as a matter of course the sweetheart of the first girl, and so on down the line; if one of them left, his successor took over the relationship—it was a question of equilibrium. Here the pecking order was often broken, but never when it came to the horses. Gustav's horses were the poorest, and no power in the world could have induced the head man or Erik to drive them—let alone the landowner himself.

The foreman knew this, and saw how the men were enjoying themselves when Gustav's nags were hitched up. He concealed his irritation; but when they exultantly placed Gustav's wagon last in line, it was too much for him. He ordered them to move it ahead of the others.

"My horses aren't used to going behind the rump-dragger's!" said Karl Johan, throwing down his reins; that was the nickname for the last man in line. The others stood trying not to smile, and the foreman was about to blow his top.

"If you're so bent on being first, go ahead," he said with restraint. "I can drive behind you."

"No, my horses come after the head man's, not after the rump-dragger's," said Erik.

This was really a term of abuse, the way they all used it, one after the other, with sly looks. If he had to put up with this from the whole line, his position on the farm would be untenable.

"Yes, and my team comes after Erik's," Anders now began, "not after . . . after Gustav's," he corrected himself quickly, for the foreman had fixed his eye on him and had taken a step forward to knock him down.

The foreman stood silent for a moment as if listening—the muscles of his arms quivered. Then he sprang into the wagon. "You're all out of your minds today," he said. "But now I'm going to drive first, and the man who dares to say a word against it will get one between the eyes that will send him five days into next week!" He swung out of line, and Erik's horses, which wanted to turn, received a lash from his whip that made them rear. Erik raged at the animals.

The men went about crestfallen, giving the foreman time to get well ahead. "Well, I suppose we'd better get going now," said Karl Johan at last, getting into his wagon. The foreman was already way ahead; Gustav's nags were doing their best today—they seemed to like being in front. But Karl Johan's horses were unhappy, and hurried on; they didn't approve of the new arrangement.

At the village store they made a stop, and that lifted their spirits a bit. When they started off again, Karl Johan's horses were unruly, and he had to rein them in.

The report of the catch had spread through the countryside, and wagons from other farms caught up with them or passed them by on their way to the fishing villages. Those who lived nearer to town were already on their way home with swaying loads. "Shall we meet in town for a drink?" one man shouted to Karl Johan as he went by. "I'm coming in for another load."

"No, we're driving for the master today," replied the head man, pointing to the foreman up ahead.

"Yes, I see him—he's driving a fine pair today. I thought it was King Lazarus!"

One of Karl Johan's acquaintances came toward them with a swaying load of herring. He was the only hired hand on one of the small farms. "So you've been to town too for winter provisions," said Karl Johan, reining in his horse.

"Yes, for the pigs!" replied the other man. "We got supplies for the rest of us at the end of the summer. This isn't people food!" And he picked up a herring in both hands and pretended to break it in half.

"No, I guess not for such fine gentlemen," answered Karl Johan caustically. "Of course, you've got such a high position that you eat at the same table as your master and mistress, I've heard."

"Yes, that's the custom at our place," said the other man. "We don't know anything about masters and dogs."

"Then it's probably true that you sleep with the mistress every other night, isn't it?" said Karl Johan venomously. The others laughed; the stranger didn't reply but drove on. The words rankled in Karl Johan's mind—he couldn't help drawing comparisons.

They had caught up with the foreman, and now the horses went stark raving mad; they kept trying to pass and seized every unexpected opportunity to push forward, so that Karl Johan nearly drove his team into the back of the foreman's wagon. At last he got tired of holding them in, and gave them their head; they raced along the edge of the ditch and on past Gustav's team, danced about a little on the highway, and then settled down. Now it was Erik's horses that were mad.

At the farm all the tenants' wives had been called in for the afternoon, the young cattle were in the enclosure, and Pelle ran from cottage to cottage with the message. He was going to help the women, along with Lasse, and was delighted at this break in the daily routine; it was like a holiday for him.

Around noon the men came home with their heavy loads of herring, which were dumped out onto the cobblestones around the pump in the upper yard. There had been no chance for them to cut loose in town, and they were in a bad temper. Only Mons, that joker, went around grinning all over his face. He had been up to visit his sick mother with money for the doctor and medicine, and came back at the last minute with a bundle under his arm, in the best of spirits. "That was some medicine!" he repeated over and over, smacking his lips. "Mighty strong medicine."

It had been an uphill battle for him to get permission from the foreman to run the errand. The foreman was a suspicious man, but it was difficult to hold out against Mons' trembling voice when he talked about it being too cruel on a poor man to deny him the right to help his sick mother. "Besides, she lives close by here, and maybe I won't ever see her again in this life," said Mons mournfully. "And then there's the money that the master advanced me. Maybe I should go and throw it away on drink, while she's lying there with barely enough to buy bread."

"Well, how was your mother?" asked the foreman, when Mons came hurrying up at the last moment.

"Oh, she can't last much longer," said Mons, with a quiver in his voice. But his face was beaming all over.

The others threw him angry glances as they unloaded the herring; they could have thrashed him for his infernal good luck. But they got over it when he undid the bundle in his room. "This is for all of you from my sick mother," he said, pulling out a whole keg of liquor. "And I'm supposed to give you her greetings, and thank you for being so good to her little son."

"Where did you go?" asked Erik.

"I sat in the tavern on the harbor hill the whole time, so I could keep an eye on you. I couldn't resist watching you, you looked so incredibly thirsty. It's a wonder you didn't lie down on your stomachs and drink out of the sea, every last one of you."

In the afternoon the tenants' wives and the maids sat around the great heaps of herring by the pump and cleaned the fish. Lasse and Pelle pumped water for rinsing them and cleaned out the big salt barrels that the men rolled up from the cellar. Two of the older women were entrusted with the task of mixing the herring. The foreman walked back and forth in front of the steps, smoking his pipe.

Pickling the herring was generally considered pleasant work, but today the whole line was in a bad mood. The women chattered away as they worked, but their talk was not innocuous. It was all carefully aimed; the men had made them malicious. When they laughed, there was a hidden meaning in their laughter. The men had to be called out and given orders for every single thing that had to be done; they worked sullenly, and then withdrew at once to their quarters. But in there they were all the merrier, singing and having fun.

"They're really going at it," said Lasse with a sigh to Pelle. "They've got a whole keg of liquor that Mons had hidden in his load of herring. It's supposed to be extra specially good." Lasse hadn't tasted it himself.

Lasse and Pelle kept out of the wrangling—they felt themselves too weak. The women had not had the courage to refuse the extra Sunday work, but they weren't afraid of making small gibes and giggling at nothing, so the foreman would think they were laughing at him. They kept on asking loudly what time it was, or stopped working to listen to the ever-increasing merriment in the men's quarters. Once in a while a man would be thrown out into the yard; he would shuffle inside again, shamefaced and grinning.

Eventually the men came sauntering out; they had their caps on the back of their heads now, and their eyes were glazed. They took up a position in the lower yard—hanging over the fence—and watched the women. Every now and then they would burst out laughing and then stop abruptly, with an apprehensive glance at the foreman.

The foreman was pacing back and forth by the steps. He had laid aside his pipe and calmed down. When the men came out, he was cracking a whip and exercising his self-control. "If I wanted to I could bend him until both ends met!" he heard Erik say loudly in the middle of a conversation. The foreman sincerely wished that Erik would try it; his muscles were burning with the ungratified compulsion to let himself go. But his brain was already reveling in battle; he was grappling with the whole bunch of them and going over all the details of the fight. He had lived through these battles so often, especially lately. He thought out all the difficult situations, and there wasn't a place in all of Stone Farm where he didn't know what could be used as a weapon.

"What's the time?" shouted one of the women for at least the twentieth time.

"A little longer than your chemise," replied Erik swiftly.

The women laughed. "Oh, come on, tell us what it really is!" exclaimed another.

"Forty-five minutes on the miller's daughter," said Anders.

"Oh, what fools you are—can't you give a straight answer? How about you, Karl Johan?"

"The time is short," said Karl Johan gravely.

"No, seriously, now I'll tell you what it is," said Mons innocently, pulling a huge "stem-winder" out of his pocket. "It's..." he looked carefully at the watch and moved his lips as if calculating. "Well, I'll be damned!" he exclaimed, slapping his hand on the fence in amazement. "It's exactly the same time as it was this time yesterday." It was an old joke, but the women shrieked with laughter—because Mons was telling it.

"Never mind about the time," said the foreman, coming over. "Just try and get done with your work."

"No, time is for tailors and shoemakers—not for honest folks," said Anders under his breath.

The foreman turns toward him quick as a cat, and Anders throws his arm up around his face as if to ward off a blow. Then the foreman just spits with a scornful smile, and starts to pace again, and Anders stands there, bright red, not knowing what to do with his eyes. He scratches the back of his head a couple of times, but that can't explain away that strange movement of his arm. The others are laughing at him; something bold has to be done to save his honor. So he hitches up his pants and lets loose a loud fart as he saunters down toward the men's quarters in order to be upwind. The women howl, and the men put their heads down on the fence and shake with laughter.

That's how the day passed, with endless mean jokes and teasing. In the evening the men wandered out to play around on the highway and harass the passersby. Lasse and Pelle were tired and went to bed early.

"Thank God this day is over," said Lasse when he was under the quilt. "It's been a real bad day. It's a miracle that no blood was shed; there was a time when the foreman looked like he was capable of anything. But Erik must know how far he can go."

The next morning everything seemed to be forgotten. The men attended to the horses as usual, and at six o'clock they went out into the field with their scythes to cut a third growth of clover. They looked bleary-eyed, listless, and out of sorts. The tin keg lay empty outside the stable door, and as they went past they gave it a kick.

Pelle helped with the herring today too, but he no longer thought it was fun. He was already longing to be out in the open with his cattle; here, he was at everybody's beck and call. As often as he dared, he found some excuse to leave the courtyard, for that helped make the time pass.

Close to noon, as the men were mowing the thin clover, Erik flung down his scythe so that it bounced with a ringing sound across the cut swaths. The others stopped working.

"What's the matter with you, Erik?" asked Karl Johan. "Have you got flies in your head?"

Erik stood with his knife in his hand, feeling its edge, neither hearing nor seeing. Then he turned his face upward and scowled at the sky; his eyes seemed to have sunk into his head, blind, and his lips puffed out thickly. He muttered a few inarticulate sounds and set off toward the farm.

The others stood still for a moment, following him with piercing eyes; then one after another they threw down their scythes and started moving. Only Karl Johan stayed where he was.

Pelle had just come out to the enclosure to see that none of the young cattle had broken out. When he saw the men come rushing up toward the farm, spread out like a herd of cattle on the move, he suspected something was wrong and ran inside.

"The men are coming up here fast, Papa," he whispered.

"Surely they're not going to do it?" said Lasse, starting to shake.

The foreman was carrying things from his room down to the pony wagon; he was going to drive into town. He had his arms full when Erik came striding through the big, open gate below, his face contorted and a large, broad-bladed knife in his hand. "Where the devil is he?" he shouted, turning around once with head bent; he looked like an angry bull. Then he walked up past the fence, straight toward the foreman.

The foreman gave a start when he saw him—and through the gate the others were coming up full speed behind him. He measured the distance to the steps, but changed his mind and advanced toward Erik; he kept behind the wagon, watching every movement that Erik made, while he tried to find a weapon. Erik followed him around the wagon; he was gnashing his teeth and glaring straight up.

The foreman went around and around the wagon, making half-hearted gestures; he couldn't decide what to do. But then the others came up from below and blocked his way. His face turned white with terror, and he tore a crossbar from the wagon traces; with a shove he sent the wagon rolling into the thick of them so that they rushed to get out of the way. This made an opening between him and Erik, and Erik leapt like a coiled spring over the harnesses with his knife ready to strike. But as he jumped, the crossbar fell on his head. The knife thrust toward the foreman's shoulder, but it glanced off, and the knife just grazed his side as Erik sank to the ground. The others stood staring in bewilderment.

"Carry him down to the ironing room in the basement!" cried the foreman in a tone of command; the men dropped their knives and obeyed.

Pelle was standing over by the pump, jumping up and down. The battle had stirred his blood into a terrible uproar. Lasse had to take a firm grip on him, because it looked as though he wanted to throw himself into the fight. Then when big strong Erik sank to the ground insensible from a blow to the head, he began to jump as if he had St. Vitus's dance. He jumped into the air with head drooping and let himself drop heavily, uttering incessant, shrill bursts of laughter. Lasse spoke to him angrily, because he thought this was inappropriate and foolish behavior. Then he held him firmly in his arms while the little fellow trembled all over and struggled to get free so he could continue his jumping.

"He's got the fits," said Lasse tearfully to the tenants' wives. "Dear Jesus, what can an old man do?" He carried him over to their room in a sad state of mind because the moon was waxing—now the fits would never go away!

Down in the ironing room they were busy with Erik, pouring liquor in his mouth and bathing his head with vinegar. Kongstrup was not home, but the mistress herself was down there, wringing her hands and cursing Stone Farm—her own childhood home! Stone Farm had become a hell with its murder and debauchery! she said, not caring that they were all standing around her and heard every word.

The foreman had raced off in the pony wagon to get a doctor and to report what he had done in self-defense. The women stood around the pump and gossiped, while the men and maids wandered around in confusion; there was no one to give orders. But then the mistress came out onto the steps and glared at them for a moment, and they all found something to do. Those eyes were piercing! The old women shuddered and went back to their work—it reminded them so pleasantly of the old days, when the master of Stone Farm from their youth would rush up with anger in his eyes when they were idling.

Over in their room, Lasse sat watching Pelle, who lay talking and laughing in delirium; his father hardly knew whether to laugh or cry.

XV

"She must have had right on her side, since he never once raised his voice when she started in with her complaints and reproaches—you could hear them right through the walls and down in the servants' room and all over the farm. But it was stupid of her all the same, because she only drove him distracted and chased him away. And how will a farm survive in the long run, when the master spends all his time driving around on the highways because he can't stay at home? It's a poor sort of love that drives a man away from his home."

Lasse was standing in the stable on Sunday evening talking to the women about it while they milked. Pelle was there too, busy with his own chores, but still listening.

"But she wasn't completely stupid either," said thatcher Holm's wife. "For instance when she took in Fair Marie to do housemaid's work, so that he would have a pretty face to look at here at home. She knew that if you have food in the house you don't go out for it. But of course it all came to nothing, since she couldn't stop scaring him away from the farm with her crying and her drinking."

"I'm sure he drinks too!" said Pelle.

"Sure, he probably gets drunk once in a while," said Lasse in a reproving tone. "But he's a man, you see, and may have his reasons besides. But it looks bad when a woman takes to drink." Lasse was annoyed. The boy was starting to have opinions of his own about pretty near everything, and was always breaking into the conversation when grown people were talking.

"I maintain," Lasse went on, turning again to the women, "that he'd be a good husband if only he wasn't tormented by all this crying and a guilty conscience. Things are going fine now that she's away. He's home pretty much every day and looks after things himself, so that the foreman's quite upset, because *he* likes to be king of the castle. To the rest of us, the master acts like one of our equals; he's even forgotten the grudge he had against Gustav."

"There can't be very much to begrudge him, unless it's the fact that he's getting a wife with money. They say Bodil's saved up more than a hundred kroner from her two or three months' work as housemaid. Some people can do it—they get paid for what the rest of us have always had to do for nothing." It was one of the old women speaking.

"Well, let's just see whether he ever gets her for a wife," said Lasse. "I doubt it. You shouldn't say anything bad about your fellow servant, but Bodil's not a faithful girl. That business with the master has to be accepted for what it was—as I once told Gustav when he was raging about it, the master comes before his men! Bengta was a good wife to me in every way, but she too had a hard time fending off the landlord back home. The greatest take first—that's the way of the world. But Bodil is fickle; now she's fooling around with the trainee, though he isn't even sixteen yet, and accepting presents from him. Gustav ought to get out of it in time—it always leads to trouble when love gets into a person. We've got an example of that here at the farm."

"I was talking to someone today who thought that the mistress hadn't gone to Copenhagen at all, but was staying with relatives on the south side of the island. She's run away from him, you'll see."

"That would be just fine," said Lasse, "if she'd only stay away! Things are much better the way they are."

A whole different atmosphere had come over Stone Farm. The dismal feeling was gone; no wailing tones floated down through the air and settled upon them like horse flies and black sorrow. The change was most apparent in the master of Stone Farm; he looked ten or twenty years younger, and joked good-humoredly like someone freed from chains and fetters. He took an interest in the farm work, drove to the quarry two or three times a day in his buggy, showed up whenever a new piece of work was started, and would often throw off his coat and lend a hand. Fair Marie laid his table and made his bed, and he wasn't afraid to show that he was good to her. How many others would want to be seen with a humble girl like that in broad daylight? His good humor was infectious and made everything more pleasant.

But it couldn't be denied that Lasse had his own burden to bear. His desire to get married grew greater with the arrival of an early hard frost at the beginning of December; he longed to put his feet under his own table and have a woman who would be everything to him. He had not entirely given up thoughts of Karna yet, but he had promised thatcher Holm's wife ten shiny kroner if she could find someone who would suit him.

Actually he had put the whole matter out of his mind as an impossibility and had surrendered himself to the land of old age. But what was the use of shutting yourself in, when you were constantly looking for doors to slip out of again? Lasse took one more look outside, and as usual it was Pelle who brought life and joy to the family.

Down on the outskirts of the fishing village there lived a woman whose husband had gone to sea and hadn't been heard from for several years. Two or three times on his way to and from school, Pelle had sought shelter from the weather in her entryway, and they had gradually become good friends; he would do little chores for her and receive a cup of hot coffee in return. When the cold was really bitter, she always called him in; then she would tell him about the sea and about her good-for-nothing husband, who ran off and left her to toil for her living by mending nets for the fishermen. In return Pelle felt bound to tell her about Papa Lasse, and Mama Bengta who lay in the churchyard back home in Tommelilla. The talk never got any further, because she would always come back to her husband who had gone away and left her a widow.

"He probably drowned," Pelle would say.

"No, he didn't, because I haven't received any omen," she would reply firmly, always with the same words.

Pelle repeated it all to his father, who was very interested. "Well, did you visit Madam Olsen today?" was the first thing he would say when the boy came home from school. Then Pelle had to tell him every detail several times over; Lasse couldn't hear enough about it.

"I suppose you've told her that Mother Bengta is dead? Yes, of course you have! Well, what did she ask you about me today? Does she know about the inheritance?" (Lasse had recently had 25 kroner left to him by an uncle.) "You might mention it, so she doesn't think we're total paupers."

Pelle was the bearer of secret messages back and forth. From Lasse came little things in gratitude for her kindness to Pelle, such as embroidered handkerchiefs and a fine silk scarf—the last remnants of Mama Bengta's personal effects. It would be hard to lose them if this new chance failed; then there would be no memories to fall back on! But Lasse was staking everything on one card.

One day Pelle brought word that an omen had appeared to Madam Olsen. She had been awakened in the night by a big black dog that stood panting at the head of her bed. Its eyes shone in the dark, and she heard the water dripping from its fur. She understood that it must be the ship's dog with a message for her, so she went to the window. Out in the moonlight on the sea she saw a ship sailing with full sails. The ship was riding high in the water, and she could see the sea and sky right through it. Over the bulwarks hung her husband and the others; they were transparent, and the salt water was dripping from their hair and beards and running down the side of the ship.

That evening Lasse put on his best clothes.

"Are we going out tonight?" asked Pelle, pleasantly surprised.

"No—well, that is, *I* am, just a little errand. If anyone asks for me, tell them I've gone to the smithy to get a new nose ring for the bull."

"Can't I go with you?" asked Pelle on the verge of tears.

"No, you have to be good and stay home this time." Lasse patted him on the head.

"Where are you going?"

"I'm going . . ." Lasse was about to make up a story, but he didn't have the heart. "Don't ask me!"

"Will you tell me some other time . . . even if I don't ask?"

"Yes, I will—absolutely."

Lasse went out, but came right back. Pelle was sitting on the edge of the bed, crying—it was the first time Papa Lasse was going somewhere without him.

"Now you must be sensible and go to bed," he said gravely. "Or else I'll stay home with you; but then it may spoil things for us both."

So Pelle pulled himself together and began to undress. And finally Lasse could leave.

When Lasse reached Madam Olsen's house, it was shut up and dark. He recognized it easily from Pelle's description, and walked around it a couple of times to see how the walls were. Both timber and plaster looked good, and there was a fair-sized piece of land that belonged to it—just big enough to take care of on Sundays, so you could work for a daily wage on weekdays.

Lasse knocked at the door, and a moment later a white figure appeared at the window. "Who is it?"

"It's Pelle's father, Lasse Karlsson," said Lasse, stepping out into the moonlight.

The door was unbolted and a soft voice said, "Come inside. Don't stand out there in the cold!" and Lasse stepped across the threshold.

There was a smell of sleep in the room. Lasse could sense where the sleeping alcove was, but couldn't see a thing. He heard puffing, as though a plump woman were pulling on stockings. Then she struck a match and lit the lamp.

They shook hands and looked each other over. She wore a skirt of striped bed-ticking, which held her nightshirt closed, and had a blue nightcap on her head. She had strong-looking limbs and a good bust; her face made a good impression too. She was the kind of woman who wouldn't hurt a fly if she wasn't overtaxed—but she wasn't a hard worker, she was too soft for that.

"So this is Pelle's father!" she said. "It's a young son you've got. But do sit down."

Lasse blinked his eyes a little. He had been afraid that she would think he was old.

"Yes, he's what you'd call a latecomer, but I can still do a man's work—in more ways than one."

She laughed while she busied herself setting the table—cold pork belly and sausage, aquavit, bread, and a clay crock of drippings. "Now eat—please eat!" she said. "That's how you can tell a man. And you've come a long way."

It only now occurred to Lasse that he would have to give some excuse for his visit. "I really ought to be going again right away. I only wanted to come down and thank you for your kindness to the boy." He even stood up as if to leave.

"Oh, what kind of nonsense is that!" she exclaimed, pushing him back down into his chair. "It's nothing special, but please go ahead and have a bite." She pressed a knife and fork into his hands and eagerly pushed the food in front of him. She radiated warmth and kind-heartedness all over as she stood close to him and attended to his wants. And Lasse enjoyed it all.

"You must have been a good wife to your husband," he said.

"Yes, that's true enough," she said as she sat down and looked frankly at him. "He got all that he could want, and more, when he was ashore. He'd stay in bed until noon, and I'd look after him like a little child. But he never lent me a hand in return—eventually you get tired of that."

"That wasn't right of him," said Lasse, "for one good turn deserves another. I don't think Bengta would have anything like that to say about me if she was asked."

"Well, there's certainly plenty to do around the house, when there's a man who's willing to help out. I only have one cow, of course, because that's all I can manage. But there's room for two, and there's no mortgage on the place."

"I'm only a poor devil compared to you," said Lasse despondently. "All told I've got 50 kroner, and we both have decent clothes to wear; but beyond that I've only got a pair of good hands."

"Well, that's worth a good deal. And I imagine you're not afraid of fetching a pail of water or that sort of thing, are you?"

"No, I'm not. And I'm not afraid of a cup of coffee in bed on Sunday morning either."

She laughed. "Then I suppose I ought to have a kiss!"

"Yes, I suppose you should," said Lasse delighted, and kissed her. "And now we must hope for happiness and good fortune for all three of us. I know you're fond of the lad."

There still remained several things to discuss, there was coffee to drink, and Lasse had to see the cow and the rest of the house. In the meantime it had grown late.

"You'd better stay here for the night!" said Madam Olsen.

Lasse stood there wavering—there was the boy sleeping alone, and he had to be at the farm by four o'clock. But it was cold outside, and here it was so warm and comfortable in every way.

"Yes, maybe I'd better," he said, taking off his hat and coat again.

At about four o'clock when he crept into the cow stable from the back, the lantern was still burning in the herdsman's room. Lasse thought he was discovered, and started to tremble; it was a criminal and unjustifiable act to be away from the herd a whole night. But it was only Pelle, who lay huddled on the chest asleep, fully clothed. His face was dirty and swollen from crying.

All that day there was something reserved, almost hostile, about Pelle's behavior. Lasse suffered under it. There was nothing else to do; he had to speak up.

"It's all settled now, Pelle," he said at last. "We're going to have a house and home, and a pretty mother into the bargain. It's Madam Olsen. Are you satisfied now?"

Pelle had nothing against it. "Then can I come with you next time?" he asked, still a little sulky.

"Yes, next time you can go with me—probably on Sunday. We'll ask permission to go out early, and pay her a visit." Lasse said this with a peculiar flourish—he had drawn himself up erect.

Pelle went with him on Sunday; they were free from the middle of the afternoon. After that it wouldn't have done to ask to get off early again very soon, but Pelle saw his future mother nearly every day. It was more difficult for Lasse. When the longing to see his sweetheart came over him too strongly, he would fuss over Pelle until the boy fell asleep, then change his clothes and steal away.

After one of these sleepless nights he wasn't much good at his work, and he went around stumbling over his own feet. But his eyes shone with a youthful light, as if he had made a secret treaty with life's most powerful forces.

XVI

Erik was standing near the front steps, with stooping shoulders and his face half turned to the wall; he stationed himself there every morning at about four and waited for the foreman to come down. It was now six, and it had just started to grow light.

Lasse and Pelle had finished mucking out the cow stable and distributing the first feed, and now they were hungry. They were standing at the stable door, waiting for the breakfast bell to ring; at the doors to the horse stable, the men were doing the same. At a quarter past the hour they headed toward the basement, with Karl Johan in the lead, and Lasse and Pelle stepped out and hurried to the servants' room, with every sign of a good appetite.

"All right, Erik, we're going down to breakfast now!" shouted Karl Johan as they passed. Erik came out of his corner by the steps and shuffled along after them. There was nothing wrong with his stomach, at any rate.

They ate their herring in silence—the food muffled their mouths completely. When they were finished, the head man knocked on the table with the handle of his knife, and Karna came in with two dishes of porridge and a pile of bread and drippings.

"Where's Bodil today?" asked Gustav.

"How should I know? Her bed wasn't slept in this morning," replied Karna exultantly.

"That's a filthy lie coming out of your fat face!" cried Gustav, slamming his spoon down on the table.

"You can go to her room and see for yourself—you know the way!" said Karna tartly.

"And what's become of the trainee today? He hasn't rung yet," said Karl Johan. "Have any of you girls seen him?"

"No, I expect he's overslept," called Bengta from the laundry room. "But leave him alone—I don't feel like running up and shaking life into him every morning."

"Don't you think you'd better go up and wake him, Gustav?" said Anders with a wink. "You might see something funny." The others chuckled.

"If I wake him up, it'll be with this mouse-castrator," replied Gustav, displaying a large knife. "Because then I think I'll relieve him of his equipment."

Then the master himself entered, holding a piece of paper in his hand and looking elated. "Have you heard the latest news, good people? In the dead of night Hans Peter has run off with Bodil!"

"What the devil, are babies getting into the act now too?" exclaimed Lasse cockily. "I'll have to keep an eye on Pelle there, and see that he doesn't run off with Karna—she has a thing about young men." Lasse felt in control of the situation, and wasn't afraid to tell a good one on anybody.

"Hans Peter is fifteen," said Kongstrup reprovingly, "and passion rages in his heart." He said this with such comical solemnity that they all burst out laughing. Only Gustav didn't laugh; he sat there blinking his eyes and nodding his head like a drunken man.

"Listen to what he says—this was lying on his bed." Kongstrup held out the paper and read:

> When the master reads this, I will be gone forever. Bodil and I have agreed to run away together tonight. My stern father will never give his consent to our union, therefore we will enjoy the happiness of our love in a secret place where no one can find us. It would be a great wrong to search for us, for we are determined to die together rather than fall into the wicked hands of our enemies. I wet this paper with Bodil's and my own tears. But the master must not condemn me for my last desperate step, since there is nothing else I can do for the sake of my great love.
>
> *Hans Peter*

"That fellow must read storybooks," said Karl Johan. "He'll do great things someday."

"Yes, he knows exactly what's required for an elopement," replied Kongstrup, amused. "Even right down to a ladder, which he dragged up to the girl's window—even though it's level with the ground. If only he were half as thorough in his agricultural work."

"What now? I suppose we have to search for them?" asked the head man.

"Well, I don't know—it's almost a shame to disturb their young happiness. They'll probably come back on their own when they get hungry. What do you think, Gustav? Should we organize a hunt for them?"

Gustav didn't answer; he rose abruptly and went across to the men's quarters. When the others followed him, they found him in bed.

All day long he lay there and never uttered a syllable when anyone came in to see him. Meanwhile the work suffered, and the foreman was angry. In general he didn't like the new ways Kongstrup was introducing—with freedom for everyone to say and do exactly as they pleased.

"Go in and pull Gustav out of bed!" he said in the afternoon, when they were in the barn winnowing grain. "And if he won't put his clothes on, dress him by force."

But Kongstrup, who was there himself writing down the weights, intervened. "No, if he's sick he must be allowed to stay in bed. But it's our duty to do something to cure him."

"How about a mustard plaster?" suggested Mons, with a defiant glance at the foreman.

Kongstrup rubbed his hands with delight. "Yes, that's just the thing! Mons, you go over and get the girls to make a mustard plaster that we can put over his heart—that's where the pain is."

When Mons came back with the plaster, they walked over in a procession to deliver it, the master himself in the lead. Kongstrup was well aware of the foreman's angry looks, which plainly said: More wasted time for the sake of a foolish prank! But he felt like having a little fun, and the work would get done somehow.

Gustav had probably smelled a rat, because when they arrived he was dressed. For the rest of the day he did his work, but nothing could coax a smile out of him. He was like a man moonstruck.

A few days later a wagon drove up to Stone Farm. In the driver's seat sat a broad-shouldered farmer in a fur coat, and beside him, wrapped from head to foot, sat Hans Peter; at the back, on the floor of the wagon, lay the beautiful Bodil on some straw, shivering with cold. It was the trainee's father who was bringing back the two fugitives; he had found them at an inn down in town.

Up in the office Hans Peter received a thrashing that was clearly audible. Then he was let out into the courtyard, where he wandered about crying and ashamed, until he started playing with Pelle behind the cow stable.

Bodil was treated more severely. It must have been the strange farmer who demanded that she be instantly dismissed; otherwise Kongstrup was not usually a harsh man. She had to pack her things, and after dinner she was driven away. She looked nice and gentle as she always did; you would have thought she was a perfect angel—if you didn't know any better.

Next morning Gustav's bed was empty. He had vanished completely—with chest, wooden shoes, and everything.

Lasse regarded it all with a man's indulgent smile—child's play! All they needed now was for Karna to squeeze her fat body through the basement window one night, and to disappear like smoke too—chasing after Gustav.

This didn't happen, though. But she grew kindly toward Lasse again, looked after his and Pelle's clothes, and tried to make them comfortable.

Lasse wasn't blind: he saw very well which way the wind was blowing, and enjoyed the consciousness of his power. Now there were two that he could have whenever he pleased; he only had to stretch out his hand, and the womenfolk snatched at it. He went about all day in a state of joyful intoxication, and there were days when he was so high up that there was a whisper within him to seize his opportunity. All his life he had trod his path through the world so sedately, done his duty, and lived his life with such unwavering decency! Why shouldn't he take a chance for once—and try to leap through the fiery hoops too? There was an enticing feeling of power in the thought.

But the honorable side of his nature won out. He had always kept to one woman, as the Scriptures commanded, and he would continue to do so. The other way was only for the great—Abraham, whom Pelle had begun to tell him about, and Kongstrup. And Pelle must never have occasion to say anything against his father on that point; he must be pure in the mind of his child, and be able to look him in the eye without flinching. And then—yes, the thought of how the two women would take it if they found out could make Lasse blink his red eyes and hang his head.

Toward the middle of March, Mrs. Kongstrup came back unexpectedly. The master was getting along very comfortably without her, and her return must have taken him by surprise. Fair Marie was instantly turned out and sent down to the laundry room; the reason she wasn't sent away altogether was because there was a shortage of maids at the farm now that Bodil had left. The mistress had brought a young relative with her, who was to keep her company and help her in the house.

They seemed to get on very well together. Kongstrup stayed at home and behaved sedately. The three took drives together, and the mistress was always hanging on his arm when they were out showing the farm to the young lady. It was easy to see why she had come back—she couldn't live without him!

But Kongstrup was not nearly as pleased about it; he had put away his high spirits and retreated into his shell once more. When he wandered about like that, he often looked as though there was something invisible lying in ambush for him and he was afraid of being caught unawares.

This invisible something reached out for the others too. Mrs. Kongstrup never interfered unkindly in anything, either directly or indirectly, and yet everything became stricter. People no longer moved freely about the courtyard, but glanced up at the tall windows and hurried past. The atmosphere was once again oppressive; it made people feel recalcitrant and obstinate and put them in a bad mood.

Mystery once again hung heavy over the roof of Stone Farm. For generations the farm had meant earthly prosperity or misfortune for so many—this was its foundation, and the thoughts of most people continued to gravitate toward the farm. Dark things—horror, dread, vague intimations of malevolent powers—sought it out, like a graveyard.

And now it all gathered around this woman, whose shadow was so heavy that everything brightened whenever she went away. Her interminable wailing protest against the wrongs done to her spread darkness everywhere and attracted everything gloomy. She hadn't returned with the idea of submitting to the inevitable—but to continue on, with renewed strength. She couldn't live without him, but she couldn't offer him anything good either; she was like those beings who can only live and breathe in the fire, yet still complain about it. She writhed in the flames, yet she herself kept them burning—Fair Marie was her own doing, and now she had brought this new relative into the house. She met him halfway so that she could shake the house over his head with her lamentations.

Love like this was not the Lord's work; powers of evil resided within her.

XVII

How cold it was! Pelle was on his way to school at a trot, leaning into the wind. Near the big thicket Rud stood waiting for him; he fell in, and they ran side by side like two worn-out nags, panting and with heads low. Their jacket collars were turned up around their ears, and their hands were stuffed into the tops of their pants to share the warmth of their bodies; the sleeves of Pelle's jacket were too short, and his wrists were blue with cold.

They said little, just ran; the storm snatched the words from their mouths and filled them with hail. It was hard to get enough breath to run, or to keep an eye open. They kept having to stop and turn their backs to the wind while they filled their lungs and blew warm air up over their numb faces. But the worst part was the transition, before they really got up against the wind and fell into step again.

The three miles came to an end, and the boys turned into the fishing village. Down here by the shore it was almost sheltered; the rough sea broke the force of the wind. Not much of the sea was visible; what did appear here and there through the rain squalls came like a moving wall and broke with a roar into greenish-white foam. The wind ripped the tops off the waves in spiteful snatches and carried salty rain in over the land.

The schoolmaster had not yet arrived. Up at his desk stood Nilen, busily picking its lock to get at a pipe that Fris had confiscated during class. "Here's your knife!" he cried, tossing a sheath knife over to Pelle, who quickly pocketed it. Some peasant boys were pouring coal into the tile stove, which was already red-hot; over by the windows sat a crowd of girls, reciting hymns to each other. Outside, the waves kept crashing and collapsing; when their roar subsided for a moment, the wild voices of boys filled the air. All the village boys were out there on the beach, running in and out under the breakers, which looked as if they would crush them, and hauling driftwood ashore.

Pelle had barely thawed out when Nilen made him go outside with him; most of the boys were soaked through, but they were laughing and steaming with excitement. One of them had brought in the name-plank from a ship — *The Simplicity,* it said. They stood around it and argued about what kind of vessel it was and what home port it came from.

"Then the ship's gone down," said Pelle gravely. The others didn't reply; it was all too obvious.

"Well," said a boy hesitantly, "the name-plank could have been torn off by the waves; it was only nailed on." They examined it carefully again—Pelle couldn't find anything special about it.

"I think the crew must have torn it off and thrown it into the sea—one of the nails has been pulled out," said Nilen, nodding mysteriously.

"But why would they do that?" asked Pelle incredulously.

"Because they killed the captain and took over the command themselves, you lunkhead! Now all they have to do is rechristen the ship and sail on as pirates." The other boys confirmed this with eyes that shone with the spirit of adventure; this one's father had told him about it, and that one's had even played a part in it. He didn't want to, of course, but then he was tied to the mast while the mutiny proceeded.

On a day like this Pelle felt small in every way. The raging of the sea oppressed him and made him feel uneasy, but the others were in their element. They took possession of all the horrors of the sea, and let them reappear in exaggerated form in their imaginations. In their play they heaped up all the terrors of the sea on the beach: ships went to the bottom with all hands on board or broke up on the rocks; corpses lay rolling in the surf, and drowned men in sea-boots and sou'westers came up out of the sea at midnight and walked right into the little cottages in the village to bring omens of their departure. The boys dwelled upon them with a seriousness that shone with inner joy—as though they were singing hymns of praise to the mighty ocean. But Pelle stood outside all this, and felt cowardly when listening to their tales. He stayed behind the others, wishing he could bring down the big bull and let it loose among them. Then they would come running to him for protection.

The boys had orders from their parents to take care of themselves— Marta, the old skipper's widow, for three nights in a row had heard the sea demand corpses with a short bark. They talked about that too, and about when the fishermen would venture out again, as they ran around on the beach. "A bottle, a bottle!" cried one of them suddenly, dashing off along the shore; he was quite sure he had seen a bottle bob up out of the surf a little way off, and vanish again. The whole crowd stood for a long time gazing eagerly out into the seething foam. Nilen and another boy had thrown off their jackets to be ready to jump in when it appeared again.

The bottle didn't appear again, but it had spurred their imagination, and every boy had his own solemn knowledge about these things. Just now, during the equinoctial storms, many bottles were probably thrown over a ship's side with a last message to those on shore. Strictly speaking, that was why you learned to write—so you could write your messages when your time came. Then maybe the bottle would be swallowed by a shark, or maybe it would be fished up by stupid peasants who took it home with them to their wives to put liquor in—this was a good-natured gibe at Pelle. But sometimes it would also drift ashore at the very place it was meant for; or else it was the finder's job to take it to the nearest authorities, if he didn't want to lose his right hand.

Out in the harbor the waves crashed over the jetty; the fishermen had pulled their boats up on shore. They couldn't rest indoors in their warm cottages; the sea and the bad weather kept them on the beach night and day. They stood in the shelter of their boats, yawning heavily and gazing out to sea, where now and then a sail fluttered past like a storm-tossed bird.

"Inside, inside!" cried the girls from the schoolhouse door, and the boys sauntered slowly back. Fris was pacing back and forth in front of his desk, smoking his pipe with the picture of the king on it, and with the newspaper sticking out of his pocket. "Take your places!" he shouted, striking his desk with the cane.

"Is there any news?" asked a boy after they had taken their seats. Fris sometimes read the shipping news aloud to them.

"I don't know," answered Fris, annoyed. "You can get out your slates and arithmetic books."

"Oh, we're going to do arithmetic, oh, what fun!" The whole class was gloating as they took out their things.

Fris didn't share the children's delight in arithmetic—his talents, he was accustomed to saying, were of a purely historical nature. But he accommodated himself to their needs, because long experience had taught him that pandemonium might easily break out on a stormy day like this; the weather had a strange influence on the children. His own knowledge extended only as far as Christian Hansen's Part I; but there were two peasant boys who had worked their way into Part III, and they helped the others.

The children were absorbed in their work and kept at it industriously, their long, regular breathing rising and falling in the room like a deep sleep. There was continual traffic back and forth to the two math experts. Their industry was only seldom interrupted by some little bit of mischief that came over one of the children like a reminder, but they soon fell into line again.

At the back of the class there was a sound of sniffling, growing more and more distinct. Fris put down his newspaper impatiently.

"Peter's crying," said those closest to him.

"Is that so?" said Fris, peering over his spectacles. "What's the matter now?"

"He says he can't remember what two times two is."

Fris snorted and seized the cane—but thought better of it. "Two times two is five!" he said calmly. Then they laughed at Peter's expense, and set to work again.

For some time they worked diligently, and then Nilen stood up. Fris saw him, but went on reading.

"Which is lighter, a pound of feathers or a pound of lead? I can't find it in the answers."

Fris's hands trembled as he held the paper up close to his face to look at something more closely. It was his mediocrity as an arithmetic teacher that the little devils were always making fun of; but he refused to be drawn into a discussion with them. Nilen repeated his question, while the others giggled, but Fris paid no attention—he was too deep in his paper. So the whole thing was dropped.

Fris looked at his watch; soon he could let them take recess—a good long recess. Then there would only be an hour of torment left, and that school day could be laid aside as one more ordeal survived.

Pelle stood up in his place in the middle of the class. He had some trouble keeping a straight face, and had to pretend that his neighbors were bothering him. At last he got out what he wanted to say, but his ears were a little red at the tips. "If a pound of flour costs 12 øre, what will a bushel of coal cost?"

Fris sat for a moment and looked irresolutely at Pelle. It always hurt him more when Pelle was naughty than when it was one of the others— he had a liking for the boy. "Very well!" he said bitterly, coming slowly down the aisle with the thick cane in his hand. "Very well!"

"Watch out," whispered the boys, preparing to obstruct Fris's approach. But Pelle did one of those things that was in direct opposition to all accepted rules, and yet it gained him respect. Instead of shielding himself from the beating, he stepped forward and held out both hands, palms up; his face was crimson.

Fris looked at him in surprise, and the last thing he wanted to do was hit him—the look in Pelle's eyes warmed his heart. He didn't understand boys as a category, but with regard to human beings his perceptions were sensitive, and there was something human here—it wouldn't be right not to take it seriously. He gave Pelle a sharp lash across his palms and threw down the cane. "Recess!" he shouted abruptly, and then turned away.

The spray was coming right up to the school wall. A little way out there was a vessel, looking very battered and at the mercy of the storm; she moved quickly forward a ways, and then stood still and staggered for a while before moving on again, like a drunken man. She was moving in the direction of the southern reef.

The boys had gathered behind the school to eat their lunch in shelter, but suddenly there was the hollow thudding sound of wooden-soled boots over on the shore; the coastmaster and a couple of fishermen rushed out. Then they came rolling the life-saving equipment at top speed, the horses' manes flying in the wind. There was something mesmerizing about that pace, and the boys just had to fling everything aside and follow.

The vessel was now right down by the point. She lay tugging at her anchor, with her stern toward the reef and the waves washing over her. She looked like an old nag kicking viciously at some obstacle with its hind legs. The anchor couldn't hold her, and she was drifting backward onto the reef.

There was a crowd of people on the shore, both from the coast and from inland—the country people must have come down to see whether the water was wet! The vessel had run aground and lay rolling on the reef; the men on board had maneuvered her like swine, said the fishermen—and by the way, she wasn't a Russian, but a Lapp vessel. The waves went right over her, washing over the whole cadaver; the crew had climbed into the rigging, where they hung motioning with their arms. They must have been shouting something, but the noise of the waves drowned it out.

Pelle's eyes and ears were taking in all the preparations; he was quivering with excitement, and had to fight back his fits, which returned whenever anything stirred his blood. The men on the beach were busy; they drove stakes into the sand to anchor the equipment, and arranged ropes and hawsers so that everything would go smoothly. Special care was bestowed on the long, fine line that the rocket was to carry out to the vessel; changes were made in it at least twenty times.

The foreman of the rescue party stood and took aim with the rocket launcher—his glance was like a claw, darting out and back again to measure the distance.

"Ready!" said the others, moving to one side.

"Ready!" he answered gravely. For a moment all was still, while he moved it to another position and then back again.

Whoo-o-o-o-sh! The thin line hung like a quivering snake in the air, with its runaway head drilling through the thick fog above the sea; its body flew shrieking from the drum, riding out with deep humming tones to cut its way far out through the storm. The rocket had cleared the distance perfectly; it was a good way beyond the wreck, but too far to leeward. It had run out of steam and now stood wavering in the air like the restless head of a snake as it fell.

"It's going afore her," said one fisherman. The others were silent, but from their looks it was clear that they thought the same.

"It can still make it," said the foreman. The rocket had struck the water a good way to the north, but the line still stood in an arc in the air, held up by the tension. It dropped in long undulations toward the south, made a couple of folds in the wind, and dropped dully across the bow of the ship.

"That's it! It made it, all right!" shouted the boys, jumping up and down in the sand. The fishermen stamped about with delight, tipped their heads toward the foreman, and nodded appreciatively at each other. Out on the vessel a man crawled around in the rigging until he got hold of the line, and then crept back down into the shrouds to the others. Their strength must be almost gone, since otherwise they didn't move.

On shore there was a lot of activity. The roller was fastened more firmly into the ground and the rescue cradle was made ready; the thin line was knotted to a three-quarter-inch rope, which in turn would pull the heavy hawser aboard—it was important that everything would hold. To the hawser was attached a pulley as big as a man's head for the hauling ropes to run through; it was impossible to know what equipment they would have on board such an old tub. For safety's sake a board was attached to the line, which said in English that they should haul on it until a hawser of such-and-such a thickness came aboard; this was unnecessary for ordinary people, but you never knew how stupid those Finnish Lapps could be.

"They can start hauling on it now, so we can get this over with," said the foreman, beating his hands together.

"Maybe they're too exhausted—they must have been through a lot!" said a young fisherman.

"Surely they can haul in a three-quarter-inch rope. Fasten an extra line to the rope, so we can give them a hand getting the hawser on board—when they get that far."

This was done. But out on the wreck they hung stupidly in the rigging without moving—what in the world was wrong with them? The line still lay motionless on the sand. It wasn't stuck on the sea bottom, because it moved when it was tightened by the sea; it had to be attached to the rigging.

"They've made it fast, the blockheads," said the foreman. "I guess they're waiting for us to haul the ship up on land for them—with that scrap of thread!" He laughed in despair.

"I suppose they don't know any better, poor things," said the Mormon.

No one spoke or moved. They were paralyzed by the incomprehensible; their eyes moved in dreadful suspense from the wreck down to the motionless line and back again. The dull horror that ensues when men have done their utmost, and are beaten back by stupidity itself, crept over them. The only thing the shipwrecked men did was to wave their arms. They must have thought the men on shore could work miracles— in spite of them.

"In an hour it'll be all over for them," said the foreman heavily. "It's hard to just stand here and watch."

A young fisherman stepped forward. Pelle knew him well; he had met him occasionally by the cairn where the baby's soul burned in the summer nights. "If one of you will go with me, I'll try to go out to them," said Niels Køller quietly.

"That's certain death, Niels!" said the foreman, laying his hand on the young man's shoulder. "You know that, don't you? I'm not one to be afraid, but I won't throw my life away. Now you know what I think."

The others held the same view. It would be impossible to get a boat out of the harbor in this weather—a boat would be dashed to pieces against the jetties—let alone work your way to the wreck with wind and waves athwart. It could be that the sea was making a demand on the village. No one would try to shirk his destiny, but this was sheer madness. With Niels Køller himself it was another matter. His position was a peculiar one—with the murder of a child practically on his conscience and his sweetheart in prison! He had his own account to settle with the Almighty—no one ought to dissuade him.

"So none of you will go?" asked Niels, staring down at the ground. "Well, then I'll have to try it alone." He plodded up the beach. How he was going to set about it no one knew, not even he himself—but the spirit was clearly with him.

They stood and watched him go. "I suppose I'd better go with him and take one oar," said a young fisherman slowly. "He can't do anything by himself." That was Nilen's brother.

"It wouldn't sound right if I tried to stop you, my son," said the Mormon. "But can two of you do more than one?"

"Niels and I went to school together and have always been friends," answered the young man, looking at his father for a moment. Then he left, and a little farther off he started running to catch up with Niels.

The fishermen gazed after them in silence. "Youth and madness!" one of them said. "It's a blessing that they'll never be able to get the boat out of the harbor."

"If I know Karl, they'll get the boat out," said the Mormon gloomily.

It seemed like a long time. Then a boat appeared on the south side of the harbor, where there was a little shelter—they must have dragged it in overland with the women's help. The harbor jutted out a little, and the boat escaped the worst of the surf before emerging from its shelter. They were working their way out; it was all they could do to keep the boat up against the wind, and they were hardly moving. Every other moment the whole inside of the boat was visible, as if it would take nothing to overturn it. But there was one advantage: the water they took on ran right out again.

It was obvious that they intended to work their way out so far that they could make use of the high sea and scud down onto the wreck—a desperate plan. But the whole thing was such pigheaded madness, you wouldn't think they had been born and raised by the sea. After half an hour of rowing, it seemed as if they couldn't go any farther, and they were only a couple of cable-lengths out from the harbor. They lay still, one of them keeping the boat heading into the waves with the oars, while the other was wrestling with something—a piece of sail as big as a sack. Yes, yes, of course! Now if they took in the oars and surrendered themselves to the mercy of the weather—with wind and waves abaft the beam—then they would fill with water at once!

But they didn't take in the oars. One of them sat and kept a frenzied lookout while they ran before the wind; it looked very awkward, but it was clear that it gave greater control of the boat. Then they suddenly dropped the sail and rowed the boat hard up against the wind—when a wave was about to break. None of the fishermen could recall ever seeing navigation like that before; it was young blood, and they knew what they were doing! Every moment they felt it would be "Now!" But the boat was like a living thing that understood how to face everything—it always rose above every caprice. The sight made their blood race, so for a moment they forgot it was sailing toward death. Even if they managed to get down to the wreck, what then? They were certain to be dashed against the side of the ship!

Old Ole Køller, Niels's father, came down over the sand dunes. "Who's that out there throwing away their lives?" he asked. The question brutally broke through the silence and suspense. No one looked at him—Ole was quite a talker. He glanced around the crowd, as though he were looking for someone in particular. "Niels—have any of you seen Niels?" he asked softly. One man nodded toward the sea. Ole fell silent and his shoulders drooped.

The waves must have broken their oars or carried them away; they dropped the piece of sail, the boat drifted aimlessly with its prow, and settled down lazily with its broadside to the wind. Then a great wave took them and carried them in one long sweep toward the wreck, and they disappeared in the breaking swells.

When the water fell again, the boat was lying keel up, rolling in the lee of the ship.

A man was working his way from the deck up into the rigging. "Isn't that Niels?" said Ole, staring so hard his eyes watered. "Don't you think that's Niels?"

"No, it's my brother Karl," said Nilen.

"Then Niels is gone," said Ole plaintively. "Then Niels is gone." The others didn't know what to say; it had been a given that Niels would be lost.

Ole stood there for a moment, hunched up, as if expecting someone to say it was Niels. He dried his watery eyes and tried to stare out there himself, but his eyes filled with water again. "Your eyes are young," he said to Pelle, his head trembling. "Can't you see that it's Niels?"

"No, it's Karl," said Pelle softly. Then Ole walked through the crowd with head bowed, not looking at anyone or noticing anything. He moved as though he were alone in the world, walking slowly out along the south shore—he was going to receive the corpse.

There was no time to think. The line came to life, gliding out into the sea and pulling the rope after it. Yard after yard it unrolled and slipped slowly into the sea like a sea creature awakened, and the thick hawser began to move.

Karl fastened it high up on the mast, and it took all the men—and boys too—to haul it taut. Even then it hung in a heavy arc from its own weight, and the rescue cradle dragged through the crests of the waves when it went out empty. It was more under than above the water as they pulled it back again with the first of the crew, a funny little swarthy man dressed in mangy gray pelts. He was practically choked in the crossing, but after they had emptied the water out of him there was nothing wrong with him, and he chattered away in a ridiculous language that nobody understood. Five little fur-clad creatures, one by one, were brought over by the rescue cradle, and last of all came Karl with a little squealing pig in his arms.

"What a poor bunch of sailors!" said Karl, in between vomiting up water. "God help me, they didn't understand a thing. They tied the rocket line to the shrouds and put the loose end around the captain's waist! And you should have seen the mess on board." He talked loudly, but his glance seemed to veil something.

Then the men went home to the village with the shipwrecked sailors; the vessel looked as if it would withstand the water for a while.

Just as the schoolchildren were about to go home, Ole came staggering along with his dead son's body on his back. His knees buckled as he walked, bending low and moaning under his burden. Fris stopped him and helped him lay out the dead body in the schoolhouse. There was a deep wound in Niels's forehead. When Pelle saw the dead body with its dirty, gaping wound, he started jumping up and down; he jumped up quickly, and let himself drop like a dead bird. The girls drew away from him, screaming; Fris bent over him, looking at him sorrowfully.

"He's not acting up," said the other boys. "It's his fits; he gets like that sometimes. It happened to him once when he saw a man knocked silly." And they carried him off to the pump to bring him to his senses again.

Fris and Ole busied themselves over the body, placed something under the head, and washed off the sand that had been ground into the face. "He was my best boy," said Fris, stroking the dead man's head with a trembling hand. "Look at him well, children, and never forget him—he was my best boy."

Then he stood silently, staring straight ahead, with spectacles fogged and his hands hanging loosely. Ole was crying; he had suddenly grown pitifully old, utterly decrepit. "I suppose I ought to get him home?" he whimpered, trying to lift his son's shoulders; but his strength was gone.

"Just let him be!" said Fris. "He's had a hard day, and he's resting now."

"Yes, he's had a hard day," said Ole, raising his son's hand to his mouth to breathe on it. "And look how he used the oar—the blood has burst out of his fingertips!" Ole laughed through his tears. "He was a good lad. He was my food, and my light and heat too. An unkind word never crossed his lips toward me, who was such a burden to him. And now I have no son, Fris—I am childless now! And I'm not worth anything anymore!"

"You'll have enough to live on, Ole," said Fris.

"Without going on relief? I wouldn't want to go on relief."

"Yes, without going on relief, Ole."

"If only he'll have peace now; he had so little peace here on earth these last few years. There's a song about his misfortune, Fris; every time he heard it he was like a newborn lamb in the cold. The children sing it too." Ole looked around at them imploringly. "It was only youthful folly, and now he's taken his punishment."

"Your son hasn't had any punishment, Ole, and hasn't deserved any either," said Fris, putting his arm around his shoulders. "But he's given a great gift as he lies there unable to speak. He gave five men their lives and gave up his own in return for the one offense that he committed out of thoughtlessness. That was a generous son you had, Ole." Fris looked at him with a bright smile.

"Yes," said Ole animatedly, "he saved five people—of course he did—yes, he did!" He hadn't thought about that before—it would probably never have occurred to him. But now someone else had given it form, and he clung to it. "He saved five lives, even if they were only Finnish Lapps. So maybe God won't disown him after all."

Fris nodded so his gray hair fell over his eyes. "Never forget him, children!" he said. "Now go home quietly." The children silently picked up their things and left; at that moment they would have done anything Fris told them to do—he had complete power over them.

Ole stood staring absently, and then took Fris by the sleeve and drew him over to the body. "He rowed well," he said. "The blood came out of his fingertips, look!" And he raised his son's hands to the light. "And there's a wrist for you, Fris! He could pick up an old man like me and carry me like a little child." Ole laughed feebly. "But I carried him; all the way from the south reef I carried him on my back. 'I'm too heavy for you, father!' I could hear him say, because he was a good son. But I carried him—and now I can't do any more. If only they notice that!"— he was looking again at the blood-stained fingers. "He did his best. If only God Himself would discharge him."

"Yes," said Fris. "God will discharge him Himself—and he sees everything, you know, Ole."

Some fishermen entered the room. They took off their caps, and one by one came quietly over and shook hands with Ole. Then each of them passed his hand over his face and turned questioningly to the school-master—Fris nodded. They lifted the dead body between them and walked with heavy, cautious steps out through the entryway and on toward the village. Ole followed behind them, bent over and moaning.

XVIII

One day in his first year at school, when Pelle was being questioned in Religion, Fris asked him whether he could name the three greatest holidays of the year. Pelle amused everyone by answering, "Midsummer Eve, Harvest Day, and... and..." There was a third too, but when it came right down to it, he was too shy to mention it—his birthday! In certain ways it was the greatest holiday of them all, even though no one but Papa Lasse knew about it. And the people who wrote the almanac, of course—they knew about everything.

It fell on the 26th of June and was called Pelagius in the calendar. In the morning his father would kiss him and say, "Happy birthday, and God bless you, lad!" and then there was always some small thing in Pelle's pocket when he pulled on his pants. His father was just as excited as he was, and stood next to him while he got dressed, waiting to share in the surprise. But Pelle liked to drag things out when something nice was going to happen—it made the pleasure all the greater. He purposely passed over the interesting pocket, while Papa Lasse stood fidgeting and unable to contain himself.

"Hey, what's the matter with that pocket? It looks so fat to me! You haven't been out stealing hens' eggs in the night, have you?"

Then Pelle had to take it out—a large bundle of paper—and unwrap it, layer after layer. And Lasse would be thunderstruck.

"Ha, it's nothing but paper! What junk to go and fill your pockets with!" But way inside there was a pocket knife with two blades.

"Thank you," whispered Pelle then, with tears in his eyes.

"Oh, what the devil, it's a poor enough present!" said Lasse, blinking his red, lashless eyelids.

Other than this the boy didn't encounter anything better on that day than usual, but still he had a solemn feeling all day long. The sun never failed to shine—it was even unusually bright; and the animals gazed meaningfully at him while they lay chewing. "It's my birthday today!" he said, putting his arms around the steer Nero's neck. "Can you say 'happy birthday'?" And Nero breathed warm air down his back, along with green juice from his cud. Then Pelle wandered around happily, stealing green grain for him and for his favorite calf, holding the new knife—or whatever the present might be—in his hand all day long, and dwelt in an oddly solemn way on everything he did. He could make the whole long day swell with a festive mood, and when he went to bed he tried to fight off sleep in order to make the day even longer.

But Midsummer Eve was in a way an even greater holiday—at any rate it had the air of the unattainable about it. On that day anything that could crawl or walk went up to the Common; there was not a servant on the whole island so wretched that he would submit to being denied a holiday on that day—none but Lasse and Pelle.

Each year they had seen the day come and go without sharing in its joy. "Someone has to stay home, damn it!" the foreman always said. "Or maybe you think I can do all the work for you?" They were too powerless to assert themselves. Lasse helped pack delicious food and beverages into the wagons and saw the others off—only to wander about despondently at home, one man to do all the work. From the field Pelle watched their merry departure and the pale stripe of dust far away beyond the rocks. And for six months afterwards, at mealtimes, they would listen to reminiscences of drinking and fighting and lovemaking —the whole celebration.

But now this was over. Lasse was not the man to continue letting himself be trampled on; he had the affection of a woman—and a house in his future. He could give notice any day he liked. The authorities were presumably busy with the prescribed advertising for Madam Olsen's husband, and as soon as the legal waiting period had passed, they would get married.

Lasse no longer sought to avoid the risk of dismissal. Even last winter he had put his foot down with the foreman, and only agreed to stay on the express condition that they both could go on the Midsummer Eve outing; he had witnesses to this. On the Common, where all lovers held a rendezvous that day, she and Lasse were to meet too, but Pelle knew nothing of this.

"Today we can say the day after tomorrow, and tomorrow we can say tomorrow," Pelle went about repeating to his father two evenings before the day; he had been keeping track of the days ever since the first of May, by making strokes for all the days on the inside of the lid of the chest, and crossing them off one by one.

"Yes, and the day after tomorrow we'll say today," said Lasse, kicking up his feet spryly.

Then they opened their eyes on an incomprehensibly brilliant world, not remembering at first that this was the day. Lasse had borrowed five kroner against his wages and had found an old tenant-farmer to do their chores—for half a krone and his meals. "It's not a big wage," said the man, "but if I give you a hand, maybe the Almighty will give me one in return."

"Yes, we don't have anyone but Him to hold on to, we poor souls," answered Lasse. "But I will thank you even in my grave."

The tenant arrived by four o'clock, so Lasse could start his holiday in the morning. Every time he was about to lend a hand in the work, the other man would say, "No, leave it alone! I'm sure you don't often get a holiday."

"No, this is the first real holiday since I came to the farm," said Lasse, drawing himself up with a lordly air.

Pelle was in his best clothes from first thing in the morning; he went about smiling in his shirtsleeves, his hair slicked down with water. He couldn't put on his best cap and jacket until they started off. When the sun fell on his face, it sparkled like dewy grass. There was nothing to worry about. The animals were in the enclosure. The foreman himself was going to look after them.

He kept near his father, who had brought this about. Papa Lasse was fantastic! "It's a good thing you threatened to leave!" he kept on saying.

And Lasse gave the same answer every time: "Yes, you have to have a forceful hand if you want to achieve anything in this world," and nodded with a consciousness of power.

They were supposed to leave at eight o'clock, but the girls couldn't get the provisions ready in time. There were jars of stewed gooseberries, huge piles of pancakes, one hard-boiled egg apiece, cold veal, and an endless supply of bread and butter. The wagon boxes couldn't possibly hold it all, so large baskets were pushed in under the seats. In the front was placed a small cask of beer, covered with green oats to keep the sun off it; there was a whole keg of aquavit and three bottles of cold punch. Almost the entire bottom of the big spring-wagon was covered, so it was going to be difficult to find room for their feet.

Mrs. Kongstrup could be inclined kindly toward her servants when she wanted to be; she went about like a nice mistress and saw that everything was well packed and that nothing was missing. She wasn't like Kongstrup, who always had to have a foreman between him and the others. She even joked and did her best; it was obvious that she wanted them to have a happy day—whatever else might be said about her. The fact that her face was a little sad was no surprise, since the master had driven out that morning with her young relative.

At last the girls were ready, and everyone climbed in—in high spirits. The men inadvertently sat down on the girls' laps and jumped up in alarm. "Ouch! I must have gotten too near a stove!" cried the rogue Mons, rubbing his behind. Even the mistress had to laugh.

"Isn't Erik going with us?" asked his old sweetheart Bengta, who still had a warm spot in her heart for him.

The foreman whistled shrilly twice, and Erik came slinking slowly out of the barn, where he had been standing and keeping watch on his master.

"Don't you want to go with them to the woods today, Erik?" asked the foreman kindly. Erik stood twisting his big body and mumbled something that no one could understand, twitching involuntarily with one shoulder.

"You'd better go with them," said the foreman, pretending he was going to take him and put him in the wagon. "Then I'll have to see whether I can get over the loss." The people in the wagon laughed. But Erik shuffled off down across the yard, with his hangdog look unflinchingly directed backward at the foreman's feet. He stationed himself at the corner of the stable, where he stood watching; he was holding his cap behind his back, the way a boy does when he snatches another boy's cap.

"He's a wily bird," said Mons. Then Karl Johan guided the horses carefully through the gate, and they set off with a crack of the whip.

Along all the roads, vehicles were making their way toward the highest part of the island, filled to overflowing with merrymakers, sitting on each other's laps and hanging all the way over the sides. The dust rose behind the wagons and hung white in the air; it revealed in mile-long stripes where the roads lay, like spokes in a wheel all pointing toward the middle of the island. The air hummed with merry voices and the strains of concertinas; they missed Gustav's playing now. Yes, and Bodil's pretty face too, which used to shine so blessedly bright on a day like this.

Pelle had years' worth of appetite for the great world, and devoured everything with his eyes. "Look over there, Papa! Just look!" Nothing escaped him. The others looked at him happily, he was so rosy and cute. He was wearing a newly washed blue shirt under his vest, which showed at the neck and wrists and doubled as a collar and cuffs. But Fair Marie leaned back from the box seat, where she was sitting alone with Karl Johan, and tied a bright white scarf around his neck. Karna, who wanted to be motherly to him, wiped his face with a corner of her handkerchief, which she moistened with her tongue. She was rather overdoing it, but then it was conceivable that the boy might have gotten dirty again since his thorough morning wash.

The side roads continued to pour their contents out onto the highway, and soon there was a whole river of vehicles. There were wagons as far as the eye could see in both directions—it was hard to believe that there were so many vehicles in the entire world. Karl Johan was a good driver, always pointing with his whip and telling them something; he knew all about every single house. They had passed the farms and plowed fields by now, but on the heath, where self-sown birch and aspen trees stood fluttering restlessly in the summer breeze, there stood desolate new houses with bare plastered walls, and not so much as a henbane in the window or a scrap of curtain. The fields around them were as stony as a newly laid road, and the crops were crying pitifully to heaven; the grain was only two or three inches high, and already ripe. The people there were all Swedish servants who had saved a little and had now become landowners. Karl Johan knew quite a few of them.

"It looks pretty miserable," said Lasse, comparing in his own mind the rocks here with Madam Olsen's rich land.

"Oh well," replied the head man, "it's not the best, of course; but the land yields something, anyhow." And he pointed to the fine large heaps of road stones and hewn rock surrounding every cottage. "Even if it isn't exactly grain, it gives them something to live on. And then it's probably the only land that poor people can afford." He and Fair Marie were thinking of settling down here themselves. Kongstrup had promised to help them get a farm with two horses when they got married.

In the woods the birds were in the midst of their morning song—it seemed they were later with it here than in the grove by the dunes. The air sparkled so festively, and something invisible seemed to rise from the undergrowth—it was like being in a church when the sun shone down through tall windows and the organ was playing. They drove around the foot of a steep cliff with overhanging trees on top, and into the woods.

It was almost impossible to thread their way through the crowd of unharnessed horses and vehicles; you had to have all your wits about you to keep from damaging your own and other people's equipment. Karl Johan sat watching both front wheels and inched his way forward step by step; he looked like a cat in a thunderstorm, he was so wary. "Shut up!" he said sharply when anyone in the wagon opened their mouth. At last they found room enough to unharness; a rope was tied from tree to tree to form a square, and the horses were tethered inside. Then they got out the curry combs—jeez, how dusty it had been! And finally—well, no one said anything, but they all stood there expectantly, half turned toward the head man.

"Well, I suppose we ought to take a walk in the woods and look at the view," he said.

They gave it some thought as they wandered aimlessly around the wagon, furtively eyeing the provisions.

"If only it'll keep," said Anders, lifting a basket.

"I don't know why—I have the funniest feeling in my stomach today," Mons began. "It couldn't be consumption, could it?"

"Maybe we ought to sample the food first, then?" said Karl Johan.

Yes—oh yes—there it was at last!

Last year they had eaten their dinner on the grass—it was Bodil who had thought of that; she was always thinking up new ideas. This year nobody wanted to be the one to make such a suggestion. They looked at each other expectantly; then they climbed up into the wagon and settled down there like other decent people. After all, the food was just the same.

The pancakes were as big and thick as a saucepan lid—it reminded them of Erik, who had eaten ten of them last year. "It's a shame he's not here this year," said Karl Johan. "He was a merry devil."

"He's doing all right," said Mons. "Gets his food and clothes for free, and doesn't do a thing but follow at the foreman's heels and imitate him. And he's always happy now—I wouldn't mind trading places with him one bit."

"And run around like a dog with its nose to the ground, sniffing at its master's footsteps? Hell no!"

"Whatever you say, remember that it's the Almighty Himself who's taken his wits into safekeeping," Lasse admonished. For a moment they were quite somber at the thought.

But then solemnity had claimed its due. Anders wanted to scratch his leg, but made a mistake and caught hold of Lively Sara's and made her scream; this flustered his hand so much that it couldn't find its way up, but fumbled around down there making more mistakes. Mons stood up and asked whether anyone wanted to play the church and the steeple? They laughed and joked merrily.

Karl Johan didn't take part much in the hilarity; he looked as though he were pondering something. Suddenly he snapped out of it and pulled out his coin purse. "What the hell," he said boldly, "I'll buy a round! Bavarian beer, of course. Who'll go and get it?"

Mons leapt quickly from the wagon. "How many?"

"Four." Karl Johan's eye swept across the wagon, calculating. "No, bring five, will you? That'll be a schooner for everybody!" he said easily. "But make sure it's real Bavarian beer they give you."

A "schooner"—so it was called a schooner? There was really no end to the things Karl Johan knew about. And he said the name "Bavarian beer" just as easily as other people turned over a quid in their mouth. Of course he was a trusted man on the farm now, and often drove on errands into town.

They were in good spirits and very curious, since most of them had never tasted Bavarian beer before. Lasse and Pelle openly admitted their inexperience, but Anders pretended he had gotten drunk on it more than once, though everyone knew it was a lie.

Mons returned, moving cautiously, with the beer in his arms—it was a precious commodity. The beer was poured into the large dram glasses that were meant for the punch—in town they drank beer out of huge mugs, of course, but Karl Johan thought that was just boozing like a pig. The girls refused to drink at first, but did eventually and were delighted. "They're always like that," said Mons, "when you offer them something really good." They grew flushed with the excitement of the occasion, and thought they were drunk. Lasse rinsed his beer down with a dram; it didn't taste of anything to him. "I'm too old," he said in excuse.

The food was packed up again, and they set out in a group to see the view. They had to make their way through a whole fortress of wagons to reach the pavilion. Everywhere horses were neighing and kicking up their hind legs so that the bark flew off the trees; men flung themselves at them and yanked at their muzzles until they quieted down again. The women screamed and ran around like frightened hens, with their skirts lifted.

From the top they could assess the swarms of people, on the sides of the hill and in the woods beyond the roads—everywhere there were crowds of wagons. And down at the triangle where the two wide highways met, new loads of people were constantly turning in. "There must be more than a thousand pair of horses in the woods today," said Karl Johan. Yes, far more! There were a million, if not more, thought Pelle. He was determined to get as much as possible out of everything today.

There stood the Brogård wagon, and there came the people from Hammersholm, all the way out at the extreme north of the island. Here were crowds of people from the shore farms at Dueodde, and people from Rønne and Neksø—the whole island was there. But there was no time now to fall in with acquaintances. "We'll see you this afternoon!" was shouted everywhere.

Karl Johan led the expedition—it was one of a head man's duties to know his way around the Common. Fair Marie kept faithfully by his side, and everyone could see how proud she was of him. Mons walked hand in hand with Lively Sara, and they went strolling along like a couple of happy children. Bengta and Anders had some trouble agreeing, and they kept arguing but didn't mean anything by it. And Karna made herself agreeable.

They went down to a marsh and then up again by a steep path where the huge trees stood with their toes in each other's necks. Pelle leapt about all over the place like a kid goat. Underneath the pines there were anthills as big as haystacks; the ants had trampled down broad paths that ran like footpaths off among the trees, on and on endlessly; a multitude of armies passed back and forth upon those roads. Under some small pine trees a hedgehog was busy attacking a wasps' nest; it poked its nose into the nest, drew it back quickly, and sneezed. It looked ridiculous, but Pelle had to go on—after the others. And soon he was far ahead of them, lying on his stomach in a ditch where he had smelled wild strawberries.

Lasse couldn't keep pace with the younger people up the hill, and it was no better for Karna. "We're getting old, we two, " she said as they toiled upward, panting.

"Oh, we are?" replied Lasse, who felt quite young in spirit—it was only breath that he was short of!

"I expect you feel the same way I do; when you've worked for others for so many years, you feel you want something of your own."

"Yes, that could be," said Lasse evasively.

"One wouldn't come quite empty-handed either—if it should come to that."

"Is that so?"

Karna kept on in this way, but Lasse was sparing with his words until they reached the Rocking Stone, where the others stood waiting. That was some boulder! Fifty tons they said it weighed. But Mons and Anders could rock it by putting a stick under one end.

"And now we ought to go see the Robbers' Castle," said Karl Johan, and they trudged on—constantly up and down. Lasse forged ahead to keep up with the others; he didn't feel very brave about being alone with Karna. What an ungodly number of trees there were, and not all one kind, as in other parts of the world. There were birches and pines, beech and larch and mountain ash all mixed together—and lots of cherry trees. The head man led them across a small, dark pond that lay at the foot of the rock, staring up like an evil eye. "It was here that Little Anna drowned her baby—she's the one whose master got her in the family way," he said pensively. They all knew the story, and stood silently next to the water; the girls had tears in their eyes.

As they stood there in silence, thinking solemnly of Little Anna's
sad fate, an unspeakably soft tone rose up to them, followed by a long,
heartrending sob. They moved closer to each other. "Jesus!" whispered
Fair Marie, shivering. "That's the baby's soul crying." Pelle stiffened as
he listened, and cold shivers ran down his back.

"Why, that's a nightingale," said Karl Johan. "Don't you even know
that? There are hundreds of them here in these woods, and they sing in
the middle of the day." This was a relief to the older people, but Pelle
couldn't let go of his horror so easily. He had gazed into the depths of
the other world, and every explanation bounced off him.

But then the Robbers' Castle came as a great disappointment. He
had imagined it peopled with robbers, but it was only ruins, granite
boulders on top of a little hill in the middle of a marsh. He went by
himself all around the bottom of it to see if there wasn't a secret underground passage leading down to the water. If there was, he would
quietly get hold of his father, and they could make their way in and
search for the chests of money — otherwise there would be too many to
share it. But this idea vanished as a peculiar scent arrested his attention.
He tumbled down into a clearing in the woods that was lushly green
with lilies-of-the-valley still faintly in bloom — and with wild strawberries. There were so many that he had to go and call the others.

But he forgot this too as he made his way through the underbrush to
get up the hill. He had lost the path and gotten lost in the damp, chilly
darkness under the cliff. Vines and thorns wove themselves in among
the overhanging branches to make a thick, low roof; he couldn't see an
opening anywhere, but a strange green light filtered through the inter-
twining branches. The ground was slippery with moisture and decaying
vermin; from the cliff hung quivering fern fronds with their tips drooping, and water dripped from them like wet hair. Huge tree roots lay
stretched across the rocks, looking like the naked bodies of black
goblins writhing to get free. A little farther on, the sun cut through the
darkness like burning fire, and beyond rose a bluish vapor, and a sound
like a threshing machine far away.

Pelle stood still, his terror growing so his knees trembled. Then he
set off running as if possessed. All of a sudden a thousand shadowy
hands reached out for him; he scrambled through briars and vines,
sobbing faintly. Daylight struck him like a blow, and behind him something had a firm grasp on his clothes; he had to shout for Papa Lasse
with all his might before it let him go.

And there he stood in the middle of the marsh, and high up over his
head the others were sitting on a rock jutting out from among the trees.

From up there it looked as if the world were nothing but treetops, rising and falling endlessly; there was foliage far down beneath your feet and out as far as the eye could see. You were almost tempted to cast yourself into the depths, it looked so invitingly soft. As a warning to the others, Karl Johan had to tell them about the tailor's apprentice who jumped off a projecting rock here—because the foliage looked so temptingly soft. Strangely enough, he escaped with his life, but the tall tree he fell through stripped him entirely of his clothing.

Mons had been teasing Sara by saying that he was going to jump off, but now he drew back cautiously. "I don't want to risk my confirmation clothes," he said, trying to look jovial.

The most remarkable thing of all turned out to be Cavalryman's Hill with the King's Monument. The tower alone — not a scrap of wood had been used in it, only granite; you went around and around it endlessly. "I hope you're counting the steps," admonished Karl Johan. Oh yes, they were all counting to themselves.

The weather was clear, and the island lay spread out beneath them in all its lushness. The first thing the men wanted to do was to try spitting off the tower, but the girls were dizzy and stood together in a cluster in the middle of the platform. The church spires were counted under Karl Johan's able guidance, and all the well-known places were pointed out. "There's Stone Farm too," said Anders, pointing at something far off near the sea. It wasn't Stone Farm, but Karl Johan could say precisely which hill it ought to lie behind, and they did recognize the quarries.

Lasse took no part in this. He stood alone, quite still, and gazed at the coast of Sweden—a blue line far away beyond the shining water. The sight of his native land made him feel weak and old; he would probably never go home again, although he would have dearly loved to see Bengta's grave once more. Ah yes, and the best that could befall him would be to be allowed to rest by her side, when everything else was over. At that moment he regretted that he had gone into exile in his old age—he wondered what Kungstorp looked like now, whether the new people kept the land cultivated at all. And all the old memories rose up so strongly in him that for a time he forgot Madam Olsen and everything about her. He let himself be lulled by past memories, and wept in his heart like a little child. Ah, it was desolate to live away from your native land and everything in your old age. But if it proved a blessing for the lad in some way, then it would all be worth it.

"I suppose that's the King's Copenhagen we see over there?" asked Anders.

"That is Sweden," said Lasse softly.

"Sweden, is it? But it was on the other side last year, if I remember rightly."

"Yes, of course. Why else should the world go around?" said Mons.

Anders was just about to believe him when he caught a grimace that Mons made to the others. "Oh, you ugly monkey!" he cried, and sprang at Mons, who dashed down the stone stairs; the sound of their footsteps rumbled hollowly behind them like the sound of a huge cask. The girls stood leaning against each other, rocking gently and gazing silently at the shining water that far away wrapped itself around the island. The dizziness had relaxed their bodies.

"You're all standing there with dreams in your eyes," said Karl Johan, trying to gather them all into his arms. "Aren't you coming down with us?"

They were all very tired now. No one said a word, for Karl Johan was leading, of course; but the girls had a tendency to sit down.

"Now all that's left is the Echo Valley," he said encouragingly, "and that's on our way back. We have to see it; it's unbelievable! You'll hear an echo there that even burning hell can't equal."

They moved slowly, because their feet were tender from the leather boots and much aimless walking. But when they had come down the steep cliff into the valley and had drunk from the spring, they perked up. Karl Johan positioned himself with legs straddled and called across to the cliff: "What is Karl Johan's greatest treat?" And the echo answered right away: "Eat!" It was extremely funny, and they all had to try it with their own names—even Pelle. When that was exhausted, Mons made up a question that made the echo give a vulgar reply.

"You shouldn't teach it stuff like that," said Lasse. "What if some fine ladies came up here, and he started calling that after them?" They just about died laughing at the old man's joke, and he was so delighted at the applause that he kept on repeating it to himself all the way back. Ho, ho—he wasn't quite ready to be thrown to the rats after all.

When they got back to the wagon they were ravenously hungry and settled down to another meal. "You have to have something to keep you going when you're wandering around like this," said Mons.

"Now then," said Karl Johan when they had finished, "everyone can do what they like. But at nine sharp we meet back here. Then we'll drive home."

Up by the clearing, Lasse gave Pelle a secret nudge, and they started haggling with a cake-seller until the others had gotten well ahead. "It's no fun being third wheel on a buggy," said Lasse. "Now the two of us will go around by ourselves for a while."

Lasse was craning his neck. "Are you looking for someone?" asked Pelle.

"No, no one in particular; but I was wondering where all these people come from. There are people from all over the country, but I haven't seen anyone from the village yet."

"Don't you think Madam Olsen will be here today?"

"God knows," said Lasse, "but it would be nice to see her. I'd like to have a few words with her too. Your eyes are young—can't you keep a lookout for her?"

Pelle was given 50 øre to spend on whatever he liked. Around the grounds sat the poor women from the heath in little stalls, selling colored candy sticks, gingerbread, and 2-øre cigars. For the time being he went from one woman to another and spent one or two øre at each stall.

Over beneath the trees stood Blind Høyer, who had come straight from Copenhagen with new songs; there was a crowd around him. He played the tune on his concertina as his little shriveled-up wife sang along, and the whole crowd sang cautiously along with her. Those who had learned the tunes went away singing, and others pushed forward to take their place and put down their 5-øre piece.

Lasse and Pelle stood at the edge of the crowd listening. There was no use paying money before you knew what you were getting; anyway, the songs would be all over the island by tomorrow, and passing free from mouth to mouth. " 'A Man of Eighty'—a jolly new song about what happens when a decrepit old man takes a young wife!" shouted Høyer hoarsely before the song began. Lasse didn't care much for that song. But then came a terribly sad one about the sailor George Semon, who bid such a tender farewell to his sweetheart:

> And said, 'When here once more I stand,
> We to the church will go hand in hand.'

But he never did come back, for the storm fell upon them for forty-five days, provisions gave out, and the girl's lover sank into the depths of madness. He drew his knife on the captain and demanded to be taken home to his bride; the captain shot him down. Then the others threw themselves on the corpse, carried it to the galley, and made soup out of it.

> The girl still waits for her own true love,
> Away from the shore she will not move.
> Poor maid, she's hoping she still may wed,
> And does not know that her lad is dead.

"That's beautiful," said Lasse, rummaging in his coin purse for a 5-øre. "You must try to learn that one—you've got an ear for that sort of thing." They pushed through the crowd right up to the musician, and began cautiously singing along, while the girls all around were sniffling.

They wandered up and down among the tents, and Lasse was rather fidgety. There was a whole long street of dance booths, tents with conjurers and magic-lantern men, and refreshment stalls. The hawkers were sweating, the tavern keepers were pacing up and down in front of their tents like greedy birds of prey. Things were not yet in full swing; most of the people were still out looking at the sights, or amusing themselves in all propriety—tackling tests of strength or slipping in and out of the conjurers' tents. There was not a man unaccompanied by a woman. By the refreshment tents many a man would stop, but his woman would drag him on; then he would yawn and allow himself to be dragged onto a carousel or into a magic-lantern tent, where the most wonderful pictures were shown of the way that cancer and other miseries wreak havoc in people's insides.

"This is really something for the women," said Lasse, heaving a sigh for Madam Olsen.

High up on a horse on Madvig's carousel sat Gustav with his arm around Bodil's waist. "Hey, old man!" he cried as he whizzed past, and flapped Lasse on the ear with his cap, which had the white side out today. They were as radiant as the day and the sun, those two.

Pelle wanted to have a ride on the carousel. "Then by God I'm going to have something too that makes things go around!" said Lasse, and went in and had a "cuckoo"—coffee with aquavit in it. "There are some people," he said when he came back out, "who can go from one tavern to the next without their purses getting any lighter. It would be nice to try—just for a year. Shh!" Over by Max Alexander's "Green House" stood Karna, quite alone and looking around wistfully. Lasse pulled Pelle away in a wide circle.

"There's Madam Olsen with a strange man," said Pelle suddenly.

"Where?" Lasse gave a start. Yes, there she stood, and she had a man with her! And she was talking so excitedly. They went past her without stopping—she could choose for herself, then.

"Hey, wait a minute!" cried Madam Olsen, running after them so that her petticoats crackled around her. She was plump and kind as usual, and bursting with many layers of good home-woven material— there was no scrimping anywhere.

They walked on together, talking about irrelevant things; now and then they exchanged glances above the boy's head, who was in their

way. They had to walk so sedately without daring to touch each other—
he couldn't stand the slightest nonsense.

It was black with people now up at the pavilion, and you could
hardly take a step without meeting someone you knew. "It's even worse
than a swarm of bees," said Lasse. "It's not worth trying to get in
there." At one spot the crowd was moving outward, and by following
them they found themselves in a valley, where a man stood shouting and
beating his fists on a podium. It was a revival meeting; the audience was
encamped in small groups, far up the slopes, and a man in long black
clothes went quietly from group to group, selling leaflets. His face was
pale, and he had a very long, thin red beard.

"Do you see that man?" whispered Lasse, giving Pelle a nudge.
"God bless my soul if it isn't Long Ole—and with a glove on his
crippled hand. He was the one who had to take the sin upon himself for
Per Olsen's false witness!" explained Lasse, turning to Madam Olsen.
"He was standing at the machine when Per Olsen was supposed to pay
the penalty with his three fingers, and so his were cut off instead. Now
he can be glad of the mistake after all; they say he's become a big shot
among the holy folks. And his complexion's as fine as a young lady's—
a lot different than when he was carting manure at Stone Farm. It'll be
fun to say good day to him again."

Lasse was quite proud of having served together with this man, and
stationed himself in front of the others, intending to make an impression
on his woman friend by saying a hearty "Good day, Ole!" Long Ole
was at the neighboring group, and now he moved on to them and was
about to hold out his tracts. But a glance at Lasse made him drop both
his hand and his eyes; with a deep sigh he passed on with bowed head to
the next group.

"Did you see how he rolled his eyes?" said Lasse derisively. "When
trash get promoted they don't know how to act! He's got a watch in his
pocket too, and long clothes; and before he didn't even have a shirt on
his back. And an ungodly devil he was too! But the devil looks after his
own, as the saying goes; I expect he's the one who helped him by
exchanging places at the machine. The way they've cheated the Almighty is enough to make Him weep."

Madam Olsen tried to shush Lasse, but the "cuckoo" drink rose up
in him along with his wrath, and he continued: "So *he* doesn't want to
be seen with decent people who come by what they have honorably and
not by trickery! They say he even makes love to all the farmers' wives
wherever he goes; but there was a time when he had to make do with the
Sow."

People were starting to look at them, and Madam Olsen took Lasse by the arm and drew him away.

The sun was now low in the sky. Up in the clearing the crowds were tramping around and around as if on a treadmill; now and then a drunken man would reel by, making a broad path for himself through the crowd. The noise came seething up from the tents—barrel organs each grinding out a different tune, hawkers, the bands at the various dance booths, and the steady beat of a schottische or polka. The women wandered up and down in clusters, casting long glances into the refreshment tents where their men were sitting; some of them would stop at the tent door, beckoning.

Under the trees stood a dead-drunk man, pawing at a tree trunk, and beside him stood a girl, crying with her black damask apron to her eyes. Pelle watched them for a long time. The man's clothes were in disarray, and he lurched against the girl with a foolish grin when she, crying, tried to straighten his clothes. When Pelle turned away, Lasse and Madam Olsen had vanished into the crowd.

They must have gone ahead a ways, and he walked down to the very end of the street. Then he turned despondently and walked back up, burrowing his way in and out of the stream of people and looking everywhere. "Have you seen Papa Lasse?" he asked pathetically when he met anyone he knew.

In the thickest part of the crowd, a large man was swaggering along, declaiming blissfully. He was a head taller than anyone else, and very broad; but he beamed with kindness and wanted to embrace everybody. People ran screaming out of his way, so that a broad path formed wherever he went. Pelle kept behind him and managed to get through the thickest crowds; there policemen and foresters had stationed themselves, leaning on their thick cudgels. Their eyes and ears were on the alert, but they didn't interfere with anything. It was said that they had handcuffs in their back pockets.

Pelle had reached the road in his desperate search. Wagon after wagon was cautiously working its way out through the gloom beneath the trees, then rolling out into the dazzling evening light and onto the highway with much cracking of whips. It was the holy people driving home.

He happened to think about the time, and asked a man how late it was. Nine! Pelle had to run so he wouldn't miss the wagon. Karl Johan and Fair Marie were sitting in the wagon, eating, "Come on up and have something to eat!" they said. Pelle was ravenous, and he forgot everything while he ate. But then Karl Johan asked about Lasse, and his anguish returned.

Karl Johan was annoyed; not a single person had returned to the wagon, even though it was the appointed time. "You'd better keep close to us now," he said as they walked back up, "otherwise you might get beaten to a pulp."

Up at the edge of the woods they met Gustav running. "Haven't any of you seen Bodil?" he asked, gasping. His clothes were torn and there was blood on the front of his shirt. He ran on, groaning, and disappeared under the trees. In there it was quite dark, but the clearing lay bathed in a strange light that came from nowhere, but seemed to have been left behind by the day as it fled. Faces loomed out there in the light, ghostly pale—or stood black like holes only to burst forth suddenly, crimson with the heat of blood.

People cavorted around in reeling groups, shouting and shrieking. Passionate couples forgot themselves in the midst of the tumult; two men came along with arms around each other's necks, and the next moment lay rolling on the ground in a fight. Others joined in and took sides without bothering to ask what it was all about—it turned into one large, thrashing heap. Then the police arrived and started flailing their sticks; those who didn't run away were handcuffed and tossed into an empty stable.

Pelle felt quite sick, and kept close to Karl Johan; he jumped every time a crowd approached. "Where's Papa Lasse?" he whimpered. "Let's go find him."

"Oh, shut up!" yelled the head man, who was standing there trying to catch sight of his fellow servants. He was furious at their negligence. "Don't stand there blubbering! Run down to the wagon instead and see whether anyone's showed up yet."

Pelle had to go, no matter how much he disliked venturing in beneath the trees. The branches hung silently listening, but the noise from the clearing came down in bursts, and in the darkness under the bushes life was rustling, with voices of joy or weeping. Suddenly a scream rang through the woods, and it made his knees buckle.

Karna was sitting in the back of the wagon asleep, and Bengta stood leaning against the front seat, crying. "They've locked Anders up," she sobbed. "He got wild, so they put him in handcuffs and locked him up." She followed Pelle back.

Lasse was with Karl Johan and Fair Marie; he looked defiantly at Pelle, and in his squinty eyes there was a little mutinous gleam.

"So now there's only Mons and Lively Sara," said Karl Johan as he ran his eye over them.

"But what about Anders? You wouldn't drive off without Anders, would you?" sobbed Bengta.

"There's nothing we can do about Anders!" said the head man. "He'll come of his own accord when he gets out."

They found out that Mons and Lively Sara were down in one of the dance booths, and went down there. "Now you stay here," said Karl Johan sternly, and went in to look over the dancers. In there the blood was burning like dancing suns; faces looked like balls of fire, making red circles in the blue mist of sweat, heat, and dust. Thump! Thump! Thump! The beat fell booming like fists of doom; in the middle of the floor stood a man wringing out his jacket so the water splashed.

Out of one of the dance tents stumbled a big fellow with two girls. He had his arms around their necks, and they had linked arms firmly behind his back. His cap was on the back of his head, and he was about to take off, totally out of control, but he felt himself too pleasantly encumbered to express himself by leaping around; so he opened his mouth wide and shouted joyfully, so it echoed: "The devil take me! The devil take me! Seven hundred devils take me!" and disappeared into the trees with his girls.

"That was Per Olsen himself," said Lasse, gazing after him. "That's what I call a man! He certainly doesn't look like he's carrying any debt of sin to the Almighty."

"His time may still come," said Karl Johan.

Quite by chance they found Mons and Lively Sara sitting asleep in each other's arms on a bench beneath the trees. "Well now, I suppose we should see about getting home?" said Karl Johan slowly; he had been going around feeling righteous for so long that his throat was dry. "I don't suppose any of you would give a farewell glass?"

"I will," said Mons, "if you'll go up to the pavilion with me and drink it." Mons had missed something by falling asleep and wanted to go once around the grounds again. Every time a yell reached them he would give a leap as he walked beside Lively Sara, and answer with a long howl. He tried to get away, but she clung to his arm; so he swung the heavy end of his weighted stick and shouted defiantly. Lasse kicked up his old legs and imitated Mons's shouts, for he too was in favor of anything besides going home. But Karl Johan put his foot down—they were going now! And he had the support of Pelle and the women.

Out in the clearing a roar made them stop, and each of the women got behind her man. A man came running bareheaded, with blood running from a large gash in his temple down over his face and collar, his features contorted in fear. Behind him came a second man, also bareheaded — with his knife drawn. A forester tried to block his way, but was stabbed in the shoulder and fell; the pursuer ran on. As he passed them, Mons uttered a short yell and jumped straight up in the air, bringing down his weighted stick on the back of the man's neck; the man sank to the ground with a sigh. Mons slipped into the crowd and disappeared; the others found him waiting for them at the edge of the woods. He wasn't answering any more yells.

Karl Johan had to lead the horses until they got out onto the road, and then they all got in. Behind them the noise had vanished; only a single cry for help rang through the air and fell again.

Down by a little lake, some abandoned girls had gathered in the meadow and were playing by themselves. The white mist lay over the grass like a shining lake, and only the upper part of the girls' bodies rose above it. They were walking around in a circle, singing the midsummer's night song. Pure and clear rose the merry song, and yet was so strangely sad to listen to — because those who were singing it had been left in the lurch by drunkards and brawlers.

> We'll dance upon hill and mountain,
> Wear out our shoes and stockings.
> Heigh ho, my little heartthrob,
> We'll dance till the sun comes up.
>   Heigh ho, my queen!
> Now we've danced upon the green.

The music sounded so sweet in the ear and in the mind; memories and thoughts were purified of all that was ugly; let the day itself take its due as the holiday it was. It had been an incomparable day for Lasse and for Pelle — making up for many years of neglect. Too bad that it was over instead of just beginning.

In the wagon they were exhausted now, some nodding off and others sitting silently. Lasse sat fumbling in his pocket with one hand. He was trying to get an idea of how much money he had left. It was expensive to have a sweetheart if you didn't want to be outdone by the young men in any way. Pelle was asleep, and was slipping farther and farther down until Bengta took his head in her lap; she herself was weeping her brave tears over Anders.

The daylight was dawning bright as they rolled in to Stone Farm.

XIX

The master and mistress of Stone Farm were almost always the subject of gossip, never quite out of the thoughts of the people. There was as much said and thought about Kongstrup and his wife as about all the rest of the parish put together; they meant bread for so many people and were their providence in both good times and bad. Nothing they did could ever be irrelevant.

No one ever thought of measuring them by the same standards they used for others; they were something unique, creatures endowed with great possessions, and they could do and act as they liked—disregarding all considerations and indulging all passions. What came from Stone Farm was too great for ordinary mortals to sit in judgment on; it was difficult enough to figure out what was going on, even at such close quarters to it all as Lasse and Pelle were. For them as for the others, the Stone Farm people were beings apart, who lived their life in higher circumstances—halfway between the human and the supernatural, as it were—in a world where such things as unquenchable concupiscence and deranged love wrought havoc.

So what happened at Stone Farm supplied a different excitement from the other events of the parish. People listened with open-mouthed interest to the smallest utterance from the big house and, when the outbursts came, trembled and went about oppressed by fear. No matter how clearly Lasse, in the calm periods, might think he understood it all, life up there would suddenly shift off the track of everyday comprehension again, and wrap itself around his and the boy's world like a misty sphere where capricious powers warred—right over their heads.

It was now Miss Køller's second year at the farm, in spite of all the evil prophecies; indeed, things had turned out so that everyone had to admit that they had been wrong. She grew more and more fond of driving with Kongstrup to town instead of staying home to cheer up Mrs. Kongstrup in her abandonment—but such is youth. Otherwise she behaved properly enough, and it was well known that the landowner had returned to his old hotel-romancing in town. Mrs. Kongstrup herself displayed no mistrust toward her young relative—if she had ever felt that way. She was as kind to her as if she had been her own daughter,

and often it was she who persuaded Miss Køller to go along in the
carriage and look after her husband.

Otherwise the days passed as usual. Mrs. Kongstrup regularly suc-
cumbed to little drinking bouts and to grief. In her bad periods she
would weep over her wasted life, and if he was home she would harangue
him with her accusations from room to room, until he would hitch up
the buggy and take flight—in the middle of the night. The walls were so
saturated with her voice that it penetrated through everything like a
melancholy droning. Those who happened to be up at night to look
after the animals or the like, could hear the heavy sound of her words
stumbling along incessantly up there, even when she was alone.

But then Miss Køller began to talk about going away; she suddenly
got the idea that she wanted to go to Copenhagen to learn something, so
she could earn her own living. It sounded odd, since there seemed every
likelihood that she would inherit the master's property someday. Mrs.
Kongstrup was quite upset at the thought of losing her; she forgot all
about her other troubles and continually tried to dissuade her. Even
when everything was settled, and they were standing in the ironing
room with the maids, getting Miss Køller's things ready for her journey,
she still kept on—but it was no use. She could never let go of anything
once she had gotten hold of it—like everyone in the Stone Farm family!

There was something strange about Miss Køller's stubbornness; she
wasn't even quite sure herself what she was going to do over there. "I
suppose she's going over there to learn to cook," said one of the maids
with a sly smile. The milkmaids made up errands to the big house with
their milk pails so they could interrogate the housemaids about Miss
Køller's laundry: there were marks here and marks there!

The mistress herself had no suspicions. She, who was always suspecting something, either with or without reason, seemed to be struck
blind in this case. It must have been because she had complete trust in
her niece and thought so highly of her! She didn't even have time to
sigh, she was so busy putting everything in order. There was a lot to be
done, too; Miss Køller must have had her head full of quite different
things, judging from the condition of her clothes.

"I'm glad Kongstrup's going over there with her," said the mistress
to Fair Marie one evening when they were sitting around the big darning
basket, mending the young lady's stockings after the wash. "They say
Copenhagen's a bad town for inexperienced young people. But Sine will
get by all right; she has the good stock of the Køllers in her." She said
this with such childish simplicity; you could tramp in and out of her
heart with big wooden shoes on, suspicious though she was. "Perhaps

we'll come over to see you at Christmas, Sine," she added out of the kindness of her heart.

Miss Køller opened her mouth and gasped in terror, but did not reply. She stayed bent over her work and didn't look at anyone the whole evening. She never looked directly at anyone anymore. "She's ashamed of her deceitfulness," they said. The judgment would fall upon her; she should have known what she was doing, and not gone between the bark and the wood, especially here where one of them trusted her implicitly.

In the upper yard the new man Pær was busy getting the closed carriage ready. Erik stood idly beside him. He looked unhappy and troubled, poor fellow—the way he always did when he wasn't near the foreman. Each time a wheel had to be put on or taken off, he had to put his giant's back under the heavy carriage and lift it. Every now and then Lasse came to the stable door to keep an eye on what was going on; Pelle was at school, since it was the first day of the new semester.

So today she was leaving—the deceitful wretch who had let herself be lured into betraying the one who had been like a mother to her! Mrs. Kongstrup was probably going with them all the way down to the steamer, since the closed carriage was being readied.

Lasse went into the bedroom to take care of a few things so he could slip out tonight without Pelle noticing. He had given Pelle a little paper full of candy for Madam Olsen. On the paper he had drawn a cross with a lead button, and the cross meant, in all secrecy, that he would visit her that night.

As he took out his best clothes and hid them under some hay close to the outer door, he hummed:

> Love's longing so strong
> It helped me along,
> And the way was made short
> With the nightingale's song.

He was looking forward to the evening immensely; he had not been alone with her now for nearly three months. He was also proud of availing himself of writing—a handwriting that Pelle, quick reader though he was, would probably not be able to decipher.

While the others were taking their after-dinner nap, Lasse went out and leveled out the dungheap. The carriage was standing up there with one large trunk strapped on behind, and another standing on end on the box. Lasse wondered what a girl like that would do when she was alone out in the wide world and had to pay the price of her sin. There must

be places where they took in such girls in return for good payment—
everything existed over there!

Johanne Pihl came waddling in through the gate up there. Lasse gave
a start when he saw her—she was never up to any good. When she
boldly stationed herself up here, she was always drunk, and then she
would stop at nothing. It was a shame to see how low misfortune could
drag a person—Lasse couldn't help thinking what a pretty girl she had
been in her youth. And now she was only out to extort money from her
disgrace! He cautiously withdrew into the stable, so he wouldn't be an
eyewitness to anything. He stood inside and kept watch.

The Sow walked up and down in front of the windows, shouting in a
thick voice, which wouldn't quite obey her: "Kongstrup, Kongstrup!
Come out and let me talk to you! You've got to let me have some
money—your son and I haven't had any food for three days."

"That's a damned lie!" said Lasse to himself indignantly. "She has a
good livelihood. But she squanders God's gifts—and now she's out to
do some harm." He had a great urge to take the pitchfork and chase her
out the gate; but it wasn't good to expose yourself to her venomous
tongue.

She had her foot on the stairs, but didn't dare go up. Something kept
her in check, bleary though she was. She stood there groping at the
handrail and turning over some idea in her mind. Once in a while she
would lift her fat face and shout for Kongstrup.

Miss Køller came unawares up from the basement and went toward
the steps. Her eyes were on the ground, and she didn't see the Sow
before it was too late. Then she turned around quickly. Johanne Pihl
stood there laughing.

"Come here, miss, and let me wish you good day!" she cried. "So
you're too grand, are you? But the one may be just as pure as the other!
Maybe it's because you can drive away in a carriage and have yours on
the other side of the sea, while I had mine in a sugar-beet field. But is
that anything to be proud of? We both fell for the same short-horn,
didn't we? Go up and tell my fine gentleman that his eldest is starving. I
don't dare go myself because of the evil eye."

Long before this Miss Køller had disappeared into the basement
again; but Johanne Pihl continued to stand there going over and over the
same thing, until the foreman came rushing toward her. Then she retreated from the yard, scolding the whole time.

The men had been awakened early by her screeching and stood
drowsily peering out from the barn doors. Lasse kept a tense watch

from the stable, and the maids had gathered in the laundry room. What would happen now? They all expected some terrible outburst.

But nothing happened. Now, when Mrs. Kongstrup would have been entitled to shake heaven and earth—so faithlessly had they treated her—now she was silent. The farm was as peaceful as during the days when they had reached some sort of understanding and Kongstrup behaved himself. Mrs. Kongstrup walked by the windows up there, and looked just like anybody else—nothing happened!

Words must have been said, however, for the young lady had a very tear-stained face when they got into the carriage, and Kongstrup had that dazed look about him. Then Karl Johan drove off with the two; the mistress did not appear. She was probably ashamed for the sake of the others.

Nothing had happened to relieve the tension, and it lay oppressively on everyone. She must have accepted her unhappy lot and given up defending her rights—now, just when everyone would have supported her! This tranquility was so unnatural, so unreasonable, that it made them melancholy and depressed. It was as if other people were suffering on her behalf, and she herself had no heart!

But then the dam burst; the sound of weeping began to seep out over the farm, quiet and regular like the flow of blood from the heart. All evening long it flowed; the weeping had never sounded so inconsolable —it cut right to their marrow. She had taken in the poor child and treated her as her own, and the poor child had deceived her—everyone understood how much she must be suffering.

During the night the weeping rose to screams so heartrending that they even woke up Pelle—wet with sweat. "It sounds like someone in terrible agony!" said Lasse, hastily pulling on his pants; his hands were shaking and wouldn't obey him. "Surely she hasn't laid blasphemous hands on herself?" He lit the lantern and went out in the stable. Pelle followed him, naked.

Abruptly the screams ceased, as suddenly as if the sound had been chopped off with an axe; the silence that fell sounded so dead that it would last forever. The farm sank into the dark of night like an extinguished world. "Now our mistress is dead," said Lasse, shivering and passing his fingers over his lips. "May God receive her kindly!" They crept frightened into bed.

But when they got up in the morning, the farm looked the way it always did; the maids were chattering and making as much noise as usual in the laundry room. A little while later, the mistress's voice was heard up there, giving instructions about the work. "I don't understand it," said Lasse, shaking his head. "Nothing but death can stop anything so suddenly. She must have an accursed amount of power over herself."

It now became apparent what a capable woman she was. She hadn't wasted a thing during the long period of idleness; the maids became brisker and the food better. And one day she showed up in the cow stable to see that the milking was being done cleanly. She treated everyone fairly too. One day the men came from the quarry and complained that they hadn't been paid in three weeks. There wasn't enough cash on the farm. "Then we'll have to get some," said the mistress, and they had to set about threshing at once. And one day when Karna made too much of a fuss she got a sharp box on the ear.

"She's had a change of heart," said Lasse.

But the old laborers recognized several things from their younger days. "It's her family's nature," they said. "She's a real Køller."

Time passed like that without any change; she was as constant in her tranquility as she had been constant in her misery before. The Køllers were not in the habit of changing their minds once they had decided about something. Then Kongstrup came home from his trip; she didn't drive out to meet him, but was on the steps to greet him, gentle and kind. Everybody could see how pleased and surprised he was—he had probably expected a quite different reception.

But during the night, when they were all sound asleep, Karna came and knocked at the men's window. "Get up and go for the doctor!" she cried, "and hurry up!" It sounded like a matter of life or death, and they rushed out headlong. Lasse, who was in the habit of sleeping with one eye open, like the hens, was the first man on the spot, and had already gotten the horses out of the stable; in a few minutes Karl Johan's wagon was driving out the gate. He had a man with him to hold the lantern. It was pitch dark, but they could hear the carriage tearing along until the sound became unfathomably thin. For a moment the sound changed— the vehicle had turned onto the asphalt road a couple of miles off—then it died out altogether.

In the courtyard they walked around shuddering, unable to stand still, then wandered in and out of their rooms and gazed up at the tall windows where people were running back and forth with lights. What had happened? It had something to do with the master, for now and then the commanding voice of the mistress could be heard down in the kitchen—but what was it? The laundry room and the servants' room were dark and locked.

Toward morning, when the doctor had come and had taken control of things, a greater calm fell over them all, and the maids took the opportunity to slip out into the yard. At first they wouldn't say what was going on, just stood there evading each other's glance and laughing in such an oddly stupid way. At last they managed to spit it out by taking turns talking, first one and then another, in bits and pieces: in a fit of insanity Kongstrup had done violence to himself—he must have been drunk. Their faces were contorted with a mixture of horror and giggles; and when Karl Johan gravely said to Fair Marie, "You're not lying, are you?" she burst into tears. There she stood alternately laughing and crying, and it made no difference how Karl Johan scolded her.

But it was true—although it sounded like the craziest tall tale that a man would do such a thing to himself. It was a truth that robbed everyone of speech!

It was some time before they had collected themselves enough to think it over seriously; there were one or two things about it that seemed slightly unreasonable. It couldn't have happened during a bout of drunkenness, since the master never drank at home; he didn't drink at all, as far as anyone knew, except for an occasional glass in good company. It was more likely to have been remorse and contrition; considering the life he had led, this was not impossible—although it seemed strange that a man of his character would resort to such a desperate act.

But that was not satisfactory! And little by little, with no origin discernible, all thoughts turned toward her. She had changed lately; the Køller blood had burst forth in her! And in that family they had never let themselves be stepped on unavenged.

XX

Out in the shelter of the gable wall of the big house sat Kongstrup, well bundled up, staring straight ahead with expressionless eyes. The feeble winter sun shone full upon him, luring forth signs of spring, and the sparrows were hopping about him gaily in the sunshine. His wife went back and forth, fussing over him; she wrapped his feet up better, and brought a shawl to put around his shoulders. She touched him warmly with her breasts and arms as she spread the shawl over him from behind, and he slowly raised his head and slid his hand down over hers. She stood there for a while with her breast leaning on his shoulder, looking down at him like a mother, with eyes that were tranquil with the joy of possession.

Pelle came bounding across the yard, licking his lips. He had taken advantage of his mistress's preoccupation to sneak down to the dairy and get a drink of buttermilk from the girls, and tease them a little. He was bursting with health, and sauntered along in happy nonchalance as if he owned the whole world.

It was quite outrageous the way he grew and wore out his things; it was almost impossible to keep clothes on his body! His arms and legs stuck far out of every piece of clothing he put on, and he wore things out as fast as Lasse could get them. New clothes were continually acquired for him, and before you could turn around, his arms and legs were sticking out of those too. He was as strong as an oak; for lifting or anything that didn't require perseverance, Lasse had to let him get the better of him.

The boy had acquired independence too, and every day it became more difficult for the old man to assert his paternal authority. That would come, though, as soon as Lasse was master of his own house and could pound his fist on his own table. But when would that be? As matters now stood, it almost looked as if the authorities didn't want him and Madam Olsen to be decently married. Bosun Olsen had sent a clear omen of his demise, and Lasse thought there was nothing to do but put up the banns. But the authorities continued to raise difficulties and weasel about in true lawyers' fashion. First there was one question that had to be investigated, then another; there were time limits, and summonses to be issued to the dead man to make his appearance by such and such a date—and the devil and his great-grandmother! It was all a put-up job, so that the pettifoggers could take their cut out of it.

He was thoroughly tired of being at Stone Farm. Every day he made the same complaint to Pelle: "It's nothing but backbreaking work from morning till night—one day just like the next all year round, as if you were in slavery! And the wages are hardly enough to keep your behind decently covered. You can't put anything aside, and one day when you're worn out and no good anymore, you can go on relief."

The worst thing, however, was the desire to work once more for himself. This sat like a sigh in Lasse's flesh, and his hands would grow sick with longing for the feeling of taking hold of his own. Lately he had been thinking a lot about cutting the matter short and moving in with his sweetheart, without regard for the law. She was quite willing, he

knew—she badly needed a man's hand around the house. And they
were being gossiped about anyway; it wouldn't make much difference if
he and the boy pretended they were her lodgers, especially if they
worked at different places.

But the boy could not be persuaded; he was too jealous of their
honor. Whenever Lasse brought up the subject he became strangely
sullen. Lasse pretended it was Madam Olsen's idea, and not his.

"I'm not particularly in favor of it either," he said. "People are sure
to believe the worst at once. But we can't go on here wearing out every
thread on our bodies for nothing. And a man can't take a free breath on
this farm—he's always bound."

Pelle made no answer to this; he was not good at giving reasons, but
knew what he wanted.

"If I ran away from here one night, I guess you'd come trotting after
me."

Pelle was stubbornly silent.

"I think I'll do it—I can't stand this anymore. Now you've got to
have new pants for school, and where are they going to come from?"

"Well then, do it! Go ahead and do what you say."

"It's easy for you to let things go up in smoke," said Lasse deject-
edly, "because you've got time and years ahead of you! But I'm starting
to get old, and I have no one to take care of me."

"Don't I help you with everything?" asked Pelle reproachfully.

"Yes—yes, of course you do your best to make things easier for me,
no one could say you didn't. But you see—there are certain things you
don't... there's something..." Lasse came to a standstill. What was
the use of explaining the longings of a man to a boy? "You shouldn't be
so stubborn, you know." And Lasse stroked the boy's arm imploringly.

But Pelle *was* stubborn. He had already put up with plenty of sar-
castic remarks from his classmates, and fought a good many battles since
it had gotten around that his father and Madam Olsen were sweethearts.
If they started living together openly, it would be quite unbearable.
Pelle wasn't afraid of a fight, but he needed to have right on his side if he
was going to kick out properly.

"Move down to her place, then, and I'll run away!"

"Where will you go?"

"Out into the world and get rich!"

Lasse raised his head, like an old war horse that hears a signal; but
then it dropped again.

"Out into the world and get rich—I see," he said slowly. "That's
what I thought too, when I was your age. But things don't happen that

way—if you aren't born with a caul." Lasse fell silent, thoughtfully kicking at the straw bedding under a cow; he wasn't altogether sure that the boy hadn't been born with a caul, after all. He was a latecomer— they were always meant for either the worst or the best in life. And then he had that cowlick on his forehead, which meant good fortune. He was merry and full of song—and clever at everything; and he won over everyone by virtue of his character. It was quite possible that good fortune lay waiting for him somewhere out there.

"But what you need first and foremost is to be properly confirmed. You'd better take your books and learn your lesson for the pastor, so you won't be turned away. I'll finish the foddering."

Pelle took his books and sat down in the feed alley right in front of the big bull; he read in an undertone. Lasse walked back and forth, busy with his work. For some time each was preoccupied, but then Lasse came over—drawn by the new lesson books Pelle had gotten for his confirmation classes.

"Is that Bible history, that one there?"

"Yes."

"Does it talk about the man who drank himself silly in there?"

Lasse had long ago given up learning to read—he didn't have the head for it. But he was always interested in what the boy was doing; the books held a peculiar enchantment for him. "Now I wonder what that stands for?" he would say with astonishment, pointing at something in print; or "What wonderful thing do you have in your lesson today?" Pelle had to keep him informed from day to day. And the same questions were often repeated; Lasse didn't have a very good memory.

"You know—the one whose sons pulled off his pants and shamed their own father?" Lasse went on, when Pelle didn't answer.

"Oh, Noah!"

"Yes, that's right, old man Noah—the one Gustav used to play a song about. I wonder what he got drunk on . . . that old man?"

"Wine."

"Was it wine?" Lasse raised his eyebrows. "Then that Noah must have been a fine gentleman. The owner of the estate back home drank wine too, on grand occasions. I've heard that it takes a lot to put a man under—and it's expensive stuff. Does it tell about *him* too, the one who cheated so mercilessly? What was his name again?"

"Laban, maybe?"

"Laban, yes of course! To think that I could forget it, too, because he was a regular rascal, so the name suits him just right. He was the one who let his son-in-law have both his daughters, and work off their price at his daily wage too! If they'd been alive nowadays, they'd have been thrown in prison at hard labor, both him and his son-in-law, but in those days the police probably didn't look so closely at people's papers. It would be nice to know whether a wife was allowed to have two husbands in those days. Does the book say anything about that?" Lasse stood there, rocking inquisitively.

"No, I don't think it does," replied Pelle absentmindedly.

"Oh well, I shouldn't disturb you," said Lasse, going back to his work. But it wasn't long before he was back again. "Those two names have accidentally slipped my mind; I can't understand where my head was at that moment. But I know the great prophets well enough—if you'd like to hear me."

"Say them, then!" said Pelle, without raising his eyes from his book.

"But you have to stop reading while I say them," said Lasse, "or you might get lost." He didn't like it when Pelle wanted to treat it like child's play.

"Well, I don't think I'd get lost with the four great ones," said Pelle with an air of superiority, shutting the book anyway.

Lasse took the quid out from his lower lip with his finger and threw it on the ground in order to have his mouth clear; he hitched up his pants and stood for a while with closed eyes as he moved his lips in inward recital.

"Are they coming soon?" asked Pelle.

"First I have to make sure that they're there," answered Lasse, annoyed at the interruption, going over them again. "Isaiah, Jeremiah, Ezekiel, and Daniel!" he said, dashing them off hastily so that none of them would escape along the way.

"Shall we take Jacob's twelve sons too?"

"No, not today. It might be too much for me all at once. At my age you have to go gently; I'm not as young as you are, you know. But you could go through the twelve lesser prophets with me."

Pelle went through them slowly, and Lasse repeated them one by one. "What devils of names they thought up in those days!" he exclaimed, panting. "You can hardly get your tongue around them. But I'll get hold of them eventually."

"What do you want to know them for, Papa?" asked Pelle suddenly.

"What do I want to know them for?" Lasse scratched one ear. "Well, of course I ... er ... that's a hell of a dumb question! What do *you* want to know them for? Learning's good enough for one as for the other—and since all those wondrous things were kept from me when I was young ... Maybe you want to keep it all for yourself?"

"No, because I couldn't care less about all this prophet stuff—if I didn't *have* to."

Lasse was about to fall over.

"Then you're the most ungodly little cub I ever knew, and don't deserve to be born into this world! Is that all the respect you have for learning? You ought to be glad you were born in an age when the poor man's child can take part in everything just like the rich. It wasn't like that in my day—or else, who knows, maybe I wouldn't be going around here mucking out the stables if I'd learned something when I was young. Take care you don't take pride in your own shame!"

Pelle half regretted what he had said. "I'm at the head of the class now!" he said to clear himself.

"Yes, I know that well enough, but that's no reason to put your hands in your pockets—while you're catching your breath, the others will be eating the porridge. I hope you haven't forgotten anything over the long Christmas holidays?"

"Oh no, I'm sure I haven't!" said Pelle confidently.

Lasse didn't doubt it either, but only pretended he did to tease the boy. He could think of nothing more splendid than to listen to a rushing torrent of learning, but it was getting harder and harder to make the lad exert himself. "How can you be sure? Don't you think you'd better have a look? It would be such a comfort to know that you hadn't forgotten anything—you must have so much inside your head."

Pelle felt flattered and yielded. He stretched out both legs, closed his eyes, and began to rock mechanically back and forth. And God's Ten Commandments from the mountain, the Patriarchs, the Judges, Joseph and his brothers, the four major and the twelve minor prophets—all the wisdom of the world spilled from his lips in one long breath. For Lasse it was as if the universe itself were whirling around the countenance of God the Father with his mighty white beard. He had to bow his head and cross himself—so much could be stored behind that boy's childlike forehead.

"I wonder what it costs to be a student?" said Lasse, when he once again could feel the earth beneath his feet.

"It's probably expensive—a thousand kroner at least!" Pelle guessed. Neither of them connected anything definite with this figure—it simply meant something insurmountably great.

"I wonder if it would be so impossibly expensive," said Lasse. "I've been thinking that when we have something of our own—it has to work out someday—you might go to Fris and learn the trade from him for a reasonable fee, and take your meals at home. Then we could probably manage it."

Pelle didn't answer—he felt no desire to be apprenticed to the deacon. He had taken out his knife and was carving something on one of the stall posts. It was a picture of the big bull with its head down to the ground, and its tongue hanging out of one corner of its mouth. One hoof all the way up next to its muzzle indicated that the animal was pawing the ground in anger. Lasse had to stop, for now it was beginning to look like something. "That's supposed to be one of the cattle, isn't it?" he said—he had been wondering about it every day, as it gradually took shape.

"It's Volmer, that time he picked you up on his horns," said Pelle.

Lasse could see at once what it was supposed to be, now that he had been told. "It's really very lifelike," he said, "but he wasn't so snorting mad as you've made him! Well, we'd better see about getting back to work; a man can't make a living doing that." Lasse didn't care for this weakness in the boy—making drawings with chalk or his pocket knife all over the place; soon there wouldn't be a single beam or wall in the place that didn't bear his mark. It was useless nonsense, and the master would probably be angry if he came into the stable and happened to see them. Lasse regularly had to throw cow manure over the most conspicuous drawings, so they wouldn't catch the eye of people who shouldn't see them.

Up at the house, Kongstrup was just going in, leaning on his wife's arm; he looked pale but in good condition. "He's still limping a little," said Lasse, peering out, "but it probably won't be long before we have him down here—so it's not a good idea for you to destroy the post completely."

Pelle went on chipping out pieces of wood.

"If you don't stop that tomfoolery right now, I'll throw cow dung over it!" said Lasse angrily.

"Then I'll draw you and Madam Olsen on the big gate!" replied Pelle roguishly.

"You—you just try it! I ought to banish you from my sight, and get the pastor to send you away—if not something worse!" Lasse was completely beside himself; he rushed off to the other end of the cow stable and started the afternoon mucking, thrashing and banging around with his tools. Then he was stuck—in his anger he had loaded a wheelbarrow too full and couldn't move it backwards or forwards.

Pelle came over with the kindest expression on his face. "Could I roll the wheelbarrow out? Your wooden shoes aren't so good on the cobblestones."

Lasse growled some reply and let him take it. He sulked for a little while, but it was no good — that boy could be damned cheerful when he felt like it.

XXI

Pelle had been to confirmation class, and now he was sitting in the servants' room eating his dinner — boiled herring and porridge. It was Saturday, and the foreman had driven into town; that's why Erik was sitting and moping by the stove. He never said a word of his own accord, just sat and stared; his eyes followed Pelle's movements back and forth from his mouth to his plate. He always kept his eyebrows raised, as if everything were new to him — they had almost lost their shape completely. In front of him stood a mug of beer in a large pool, for he drank constantly and spilled some every time.

Fair Marie was washing dishes, and kept looking in to see if Pelle was finished yet. When he licked his horn spoon clean and tossed it in the drawer, she came in with something on a plate — they had had pork rib roast for dinner upstairs.

"Here's a little treat for you," she said. "I expect you're still hungry. What'll you give me for it?" She held the plate in her hand and leered at him.

Pelle was still very hungry — ravenous, in fact; he looked at the delicious tidbit until his mouth watered. Then he dutifully put up his lips and Marie kissed him. She glanced involuntarily at Erik, and a hint of something passed over his doltish face — like a distant memory.

"Here he sits, that great big oaf, slobbering!" she said, scolding as she snatched the beer mug away from him. She held it under the edge of the table and swept the spilled beer into it with her hand.

Pelle gnawed away at the pork, not caring about anything else. But when she had gone out, he spit carefully on the floor between his legs and wiped off his mouth with his shirtsleeve.

Afterwards he went into the stable and cleaned out the mangers, while Lasse curried the cows — things ought to look nice for Sunday. As they worked, Pelle gave a full account of the day's events, and repeated everything the pastor had said. Lasse listened attentively and made occasional exclamations: "Is that so?" — "I'll be damned!" — "So David was such a buck, yet he walked in the sight of God all the same! Yes, God's forbearance is great — there's no mistake about that!"

There was a knock at the outer door. It was one of Kalle's children with a message that Grandma wanted to bid them farewell before she passed on.

"Then she must not have long to live," said Lasse. "It will be a great loss for Kalle's family to be without her, they've been so happy together. But there will be a little more food for the others, of course."

They agreed to wait to go up there until they were finished — and then steal away. If they asked to be let off early, they would never get permission to go to the funeral. "And that will be an all-day feast, with plenty of food and drink, if I know brother Kalle!" said Lasse.

When they had finished their work and eaten, they sneaked out the outer door to the field. Lasse had bunched up the quilt and placed an old wooly cap so that it stuck out on the pillow; at a glance it could easily be mistaken for the hair of someone asleep, if anyone came to investigate. When they had gone a short way, Lasse had to go back once more and check to see that the lanterns were extinguished.

It was snowing gently and silently; the ground was frozen, so they could walk straight across everything. Now that they knew the way, it didn't seem far at all; before they knew it, the plowed fields came to an end and the rocks began.

There was light in the cottage. Kalle was sitting up waiting for them. "The end is near for Grandma," he said, more serious than Lasse ever remembered seeing him before.

Kalle opened the door to Grandma's room and whispered something; his wife answered softly from the darkness.

"Oh, I'm awake," said the old woman in a slow monotone. "Go ahead and speak up, I'm awake."

Lasse and Pelle took off their leather shoes and stepped in in their stocking feet. "Good evening, Grandma!" they both said solemnly. "And God be with you!" Lasse added.

"Well, here I lie," said the old woman, feebly patting the quilt. She had big mittens on. "I took the liberty of sending for you since I don't have long now. How are things in the parish? Have there been any deaths?"

"No, not that I know of," replied Lasse. "But how are you, you look so healthy — so plump and rosy! We'll see you on your feet again in two or three days."

"Oh, go on!" said the old woman, smiling indulgently. "I suppose I look like a young bride after her first baby, eh? But thank you for coming—you're like my own family. Well, now I've been sent for, and I will leave in peace. I've had a good time here on earth, there's nothing to complain about. I had a good husband and a good daughter—not to mention Kalle there. And I got my sight back, so I got to see the world one more time."

"But you only saw it with one eye—like the birds, Grandma," said Kalle, trying to laugh.

"Well yes, but that was good enough; there were so many new things since I lost my sight. The woods had gotten bigger, and a whole family had grown up without my realizing it. Ah yes, it has been wonderful in my old age to have them all around me—Kalle and Marie and the children. And everybody my own age has gone before me; it's been wonderful to live to see what became of each one of them."

"How old are you now, Grandma?" asked Lasse.

"Kalle looked it up in the church book, and from that I ought to be almost eighty. But that can't be right."

"Yes, it's right enough," said Kalle. "The pastor himself looked it up for me."

"All right, then—the time has gone so quickly, and I wouldn't mind at all living a little longer, if it was God's will. But now the grave is calling; I can feel it on my eyelids." The old woman had a little trouble breathing, but her mouth wouldn't stop.

"You're talking way too much, Mother!" said Marie.

"Yes, you need to rest and get some sleep," said Lasse. "Maybe we'd better say goodbye to you."

"No, now I have to be allowed to talk; this will probably be the last time I see you, and I'll have plenty of time to rest. My eyes feel so light—God be praised; there's no sand in them."

"I don't think Grandma has slept in a whole week," said Kalle thoughtfully.

"And why should I sleep away my last hours, when I'll have plenty of time for that later? At night when the rest of you are asleep, I lie here and listen to all of you breathing—and rejoice in your good health. Or else I look at the heather-broom, and think about Anders and all the fun we had together."

Grandma lay silent for a moment, catching her breath, as she gazed at a withered bouquet of heather hanging from a beam.

"He tied that broom for me the first time he made our bed in the flowering heather. He was so unreasonably fond of the heather, Anders was, and every year he would wake me up and lead me out there when it bloomed—right up until he was called away. I was always as new for him as on that first day—that's why happiness and joy took up residence in my heart. I breathed so happily that no clothes could cover my breast, and he ripped the ties off my apron in his joy over me."

"Now, Mother, you ought to be quiet and not talk so much about things like that," said Marie, shyly smoothing the old woman's pillow.

But Grandma would not be silenced, though her thoughts shifted a little.

"Yes, my teeth were hard to get and hard to lose, I brought my children into the world with pain, and laid them in the grave with sorrow—one after the other. But otherwise I've never been sick, and I had a good man. He had an eye for God's creations, and we got up with the birds on summer mornings. Then we'd go out onto the heath and watch the sun rise magnificently out of the sea before we went to our day's work."

Grandma's ponderous voice died away, as if a song ceased to resound in their ears. They sat up and took a deep breath. "Ah yes, the voice of memory is beautiful!" said Lasse.

"What about you, Lasse?" said the old woman suddenly. "I hear you're looking around for a wife."

"Am I?" exclaimed Lasse in alarm. Pelle saw Kalle wink at Marie. So they knew about it too.

"Aren't you coming over soon to show us your sweetheart?" asked Kalle. "I hear it's a good match."

"I don't know what you're talking about," said Lasse, quite flustered.

"Well, all right, but what you're up to isn't so bad," said Grandma. "She's good enough—as far as I know. I hope you'll suit each other perfectly like Anders and me. It was a beautiful time—during the days when we each went around and took care of things the best we could, and during the nights when the wind shook everything. Then it was good to be two and keep each other warm."

"You've been so happy with everything, Grandma," said Lasse.

"Yes, and I'm leaving in peace and can lie quietly in my grave; I've never been treated unfairly in any way, and I've got nothing to haunt anyone about. Just so Kalle makes sure that I'm carried out feet first, I don't expect to bother you."

"Just come and visit us once in a while if you like. We won't be afraid to welcome you—we've been so happy together here," said Kalle.

"No, no one knows how they might be in the next life. You have to promise to have me carried out feet first; I don't want to disturb your sleep at night, as hard as you two have to work all day. And besides, you've had to put up with me long enough; it'll be nice for you to have things to yourselves for once. And there'll be a bit more food for the rest of you after this."

Marie started to cry.

"Now look here!" Kalle burst out hotly. "I don't want to hear any more of that talk; none of us has had to do without because of you. If you don't behave, I'll throw a big shindig afterwards to celebrate your departure."

"No you won't!" said Grandma sharply. "I won't hear of a three-day wake! Promise me now, Marie, that you won't go and ruin yourselves to make a fuss over poor old trash like me. But you have to ask the neighbors over in the afternoon—along with Lasse and Pelle, of course. And if you asked Hans Henrik, maybe he'd bring his concertina with him, and you could have a dance in the barn."

Kalle scratched the back of his neck. "Then you'd damn well better wait until I've finished the threshing—I'm not too anxious to clear off the floor now. Couldn't we borrow Jens Kure's horse and take a little drive across the heath in the afternoon?"

"You could do that too, but the children must have a share in whatever you decide to do. It'll be a comfort knowing that they'll have a happy day out of it—they don't get too many holidays! And there's money for it, you know."

"Yes, would you believe, Lasse—Grandma has spun together 50 kroner that none of us knew anything about—to put toward her funeral party."

"I've been putting it by for twenty years now; I'd like to leave the world in a decent way—and without pulling the clothes off my relatives' backs. My funeral clothes are all ready too. I've got my wedding shift waiting, which was only used once, and I don't plan to wear anything other than that and my nightcap."

"But that's so bare," objected Marie. "What will the neighbors say if we don't dress Mother properly?"

"I don't care!" answered Grandma firmly. "That's the way Anders liked me best, and it's all I've worn to bed the past sixty years. So there!" She turned her face to the wall.

"It will all be just the way you want it, Mother," said Marie.

The old woman turned around again and felt for her daughter's hand on the quilt. "And you'll have to make a soft pillow for my old head, because it's gotten so grumpy it'll be hard to find rest."

"We could take one of the babies' pillows and cover it in white."

"Thank you. And then I think you should send word to Jakob Kristian's for the carpenter tomorrow—he'll be up near here anyway—and have him measure me for the coffin. Then I could have my say about the way it should be—Kalle's so free at throwing his money around."

Grandma closed her eyes. She had worn herself out after all.

"Now I think we ought to tiptoe out into the other room and let her get some rest," whispered Kalle, getting up. But then she opened her eyes.

"Are you going already?" she asked.

"We thought you were asleep, Grandma," said Lasse.

"No, I don't think I'll sleep anymore in this life—my eyes are so light, so light. Well, goodbye to you, Lasse and Pelle—may you be very, very happy, as happy as it was given me to be. Marie was the only one spared the grave, but she's been a good daughter to me; and Kalle has been as good and kind to me as if I'd been his childhood sweetheart. I had a good man too, who chopped firewood for me on Sundays and got up in the night to look after the little ones when I was confined after childbirth. We were quite well off: lead weights in the clock and plenty of fuel for the stove. And he promised me a trip to the King's Copenhagen. I churned my first butter in a bottle, since we didn't have a churn in the beginning; I had to break the bottle to get it out. Then he laughed; he always laughed when I did something wrong. And how glad he was when each baby was born! Many a morning he would wake me up and we would go out naked to watch the sun come up out of the sea. 'Come and see, Anna, the heather has bloomed in the night,' he would say, putting his arm around me. But it was only the sun that shed its red glow over it. It was more than two miles to our nearest neighbor, but he didn't care—as long as he had me. I could give him the greatest pleasure, poor as I was. The animals were fond of me too; everything went well for us in a small way."

Grandma lay moving her head from side to side, tears running down her cheeks. She no longer had trouble breathing; words called up other words in her, gliding like one long tone from her lips. She probably didn't know what she was saying anymore, but was still under the power of words. She started at the beginning and repeated the words, evenly, in a sing-song—like someone who is carried away and *must* speak.

"Mother," said Marie anxiously, putting her hands on her mother's thrashing head, "pull yourself together, Mother!"

Then the old woman stopped and looked at her in amazement. "Ah yes, the memories came over me so fast. I almost think I could sleep a little now."

Lasse rose and went over to the bed. "Goodbye, Grandma, and a pleasant journey, in case we don't meet again." Pelle followed him and repeated his words. Grandma looked at them inquiringly but did not move. Then Lasse gently took her hand, Pelle did too, and then they tiptoed out into the other room.

"Her flame is burning so remarkably clear right to the end," said Lasse when the door was shut. Pelle noticed how free the sound of their voices was again.

"Yes, she'll be herself right to the very end; she's made of extra good timber. The people around here don't like it that we aren't getting the doctor for her. What do you think? Should we go to the expense?"

"I don't think there's anything wrong with her except that she can't live any longer," said Lasse thoughtfully.

"No, and she won't hear of it either. Even if he could keep life in her a little while longer."

"Yes, times are hard," said Lasse, and went around to look at the children. They were all asleep; the room seemed heavy with their breathing. "The flock's getting a lot smaller."

"Yes, one or two fly away from the nest almost every year," said Kalle, "and now I don't suppose we'll have any more. It's an unlucky number we've stopped at—a damned awful number. But Marie has turned deaf in that ear, and I can't do anything by myself." Kalle had that roguish look in his eye again.

"I'm sure we'll do just fine with what we've got," said Marie. "When we count Anna's too, that makes fourteen."

"Oh yes, count the others too—you'll get off all the easier!" Kalle teased her.

Lasse was looking at Anna's child, which lay next to Kalle's thirteenth. "She looks healthier than her aunt," he said. "You'd hardly think they were the same age. She's so pink and the other one's so pale."

"Yes, there is a difference," Kalle admitted, looking affectionately at the babies. "It must be because Anna's is a product of youth—*our* blood is starting to get old. And of course the ones who show up at random always turn out the best—like our Albert, for instance. He has a completely different bearing than the others. Did you know, by the way, that he's going to have a ship of his own next spring?"

"No, are you kidding? Is he really going to be a captain?" said Lasse, practically falling over.

"It's Kongstrup who's behind it all—just between us, of course."

"Does the father of Anna's child still pay what he's supposed to?" asked Lasse.

"Yes, he's honest enough. We get our five kroner a month for taking care of the child—that helps a lot toward expenses."

Marie had placed aquavit, bread, and a crock of drippings on the table. "Sit down and have a bite to eat."

"You're holding out a long time at Stone Farm," said Kalle when they were seated. "Are you going to say there the rest of your life?" he asked with a mischievous wink.

"It's not such a simple matter to strike out into the unknown," replied Lasse evasively.

"Oh, we'll soon be hearing some news from you, won't we?" asked Marie.

Lasse didn't answer; he was working away at a crust of bread.

"Just cut off the crust if it's too much for your teeth," said Marie. Every now and then she listened at her mother's door. "She's dropped off after all, poor old thing."

Kalle pretended that he had just discovered the bottle. "What, we've got aquavit on the table too—to think not one of us could smell it!" He filled their glasses for the third time. Then Marie corked the bottle. "Do you even begrudge us our food?" he said, looking at her wide-eyed— what a devil he was!

Marie stared back at him with eyes that were just as big and said, "Bah, so you want to fight, eh?" It warmed Lasse's heart to see their happiness.

"How's it going with the landowner at Stone Farm? He must be over the worst of it by now," said Kalle.

"Well, I suppose he's as much of a man as he'll ever be; something like that leaves its mark on a man," answered Lasse. Marie stood there smiling; as soon as they looked at her, she glanced away.

"Go ahead and laugh," said Lasse, "but I think it's sad." Then Marie couldn't stand it anymore; she had to go out to the kitchen to have a laugh.

"That's what all the women do at the mere mention of his name," said Kalle. "It's a sad change—today red, tomorrow dead. Well, she's got her own way now; she gets to keep him for herself—in a way. But to think that he could live with her after that."

"They seem more fond of each other than I've ever seen them before —he can't do without her for a single minute. But of course . . . he could never find anyone else to love him now. What a strange sort of deviltry love is! But we'd better see about getting home."

"Well, I'll send word when she's to be buried," said Kalle when they were standing outside.

"Yes, do that. And if you need a 10-krone toward the funeral, let me know. Goodbye now!"

XXII

Grandma's funeral still seemed like a bright light behind everything that they thought and did, the way certain kinds of food leave a pleasant taste in the mouth long after they have been eaten. Kalle had certainly done everything to make it a festive day; there was an abundance of food and drink, and no end to his comical tricks. And like the sly dog that he was, he had found an excuse for inviting Madam Olsen—it was a nice way of announcing the relationship.

Lasse and Pelle had enough to talk about for a whole month; after the subject was quite talked out and set aside for other matters, it remained in the background as a sense of well-being, and no one really knew where it came from.

But now spring was approaching, and with it came troubles; not everyday trifles, which could be bad enough, but great troubles that darkened everything, even when you weren't thinking about them. Pelle was going to be confirmed at Easter, and Lasse was at his wits' end over how he was going to get him all that he would need—new clothes, new cap, new shoes! The boy often talked about it; he was probably afraid of being put to shame in front of the others that day in church.

"It'll be all right," said Lasse. But he too could see no solution. On all the farms where the good old customs prevailed, the master and mistress provided everything; but here everything was so damned new-fangled, with hard cash that slipped right through your fingers. A hundred kroner a year in wages seemed like a tremendous amount when you thought of it as a lump sum; but the money was used up gradually, øre by øre, and you couldn't put your finger on anything and say: There you got a good round sum! "Yes, yes, it'll be all right," said Lasse aloud when he had gotten himself entangled in the despairing speculations; Pelle had to be satisfied with that. There was only one way out— borrow the money from Madam Olsen—and Lasse would have to do it, no matter how much he didn't want to. But Pelle was not to know anything about it.

Lasse refrained as long as he possibly could, hoping that something would turn up to free him from the ignominy of borrowing from his sweetheart. But nothing happened, and time was passing. One morning he broke down; Pelle was just setting out for school. "Will you run over to Madam Olsen's and give her this?" he said, handing the boy a package. "It's something she promised to mend for us." Inside on the paper was the large cross that announced Lasse's arrival in the evening.

From the hills Pelle saw that the ice had broken up in the night. It had filled the bay for almost a month with a rough, compact mass, where you could play around as safely as on dry land. This was a new side of the sea's character, and Pelle had cautiously felt his way forward with the toes of his wooden shoes, to the great amusement of the others. Later he learned to walk about freely on the ice without constantly shuddering at the thought that the great fish of the sea were passing right underneath his wooden shoes, and maybe were just waiting for him to fall in. Every day he went out to the high rampart of pack ice that formed the boundary about a mile out, where the open sea churned around in the sunshine like a green eye. He went out there because he didn't want to be left out, but he never felt safe on the sea.

Now it was all broken up; the bay was full of heaving ice floes that rubbed against one another with a rattling sound. The pieces farthest out, carrying bits of the rampart, were already on their way out to sea. Pelle had performed many exploits out there, but he was actually pleased that it was now packing up and getting ready to leave—so that it would once again be honorable to stay on dry land.

Old Fris was sitting at his place; he never left it now during a lesson, no matter how badly things might go down in the classroom, but was content to beat on the desk with his cane. He was little more than a shadow of his former self; his head trembled constantly, and his hands often miscalculated their grip. He still brought the newspaper with him and opened it at the beginning of the lesson, but he didn't read it. He would doze off sitting bolt upright, with his hands on the desk and his back against the wall. Then the children could be as noisy as they liked; he didn't move. Only a slight change in the expression of his eyes showed that he was alive at all.

It was quieter in school now—it wasn't worth the effort to tease the schoolmaster, since he scarcely noticed it. So the fun lost most of its attraction. A kind of self-rule had gradually developed among the bigger boys, who decided the order of the school lessons; disobedience and disputes as to authority were settled on the playground—with fists and the toes of wooden shoes. The instruction was carried out the same way as before—the smarter ones taught what they knew to the others. There was more arithmetic and reading than in Fris's day; on the other hand, the hymns suffered.

Sometimes Fris would actually wake up and interfere with the instruction. "Hymns!" he would cry in his feeble voice and strike the desk from old habit. Then the children would put aside what they were doing to please the old man, and start reciting some hymn or other; they took their revenge by going through the same verse over and over for a whole hour. It was the only real trick they played on the old man, and the joke was all on their side—Fris didn't notice a thing.

Fris had so often talked of resigning his post, but now he didn't even think about it. He shuffled to and from school at the regular times— probably without even knowing he did it. The authorities didn't have the heart to dismiss him. Except for the hymns, which got the short end of the stick, there was nothing to say against him as a teacher; no one had ever left his school without being able to write his own name and read a printed book—as long as it was in the old Germanic typeface. The new kind of printing using Roman letters Fris did not teach, although he had studied Latin in his youth.

Fris himself probably didn't feel the change, for he had ceased to feel, for himself or for others. No one brought their human sorrows to him now, to find comfort in a sympathetic soul—his soul was not there to consult. It floated outside him, half detached, like a bird that is unwilling to leave its old nest to set out on a flight into the unknown; it must have been the fluttering soul that his eyes were always following when they gazed dully into space. But the young men who came home to spend the winter in the village, and sought out Fris as an old friend, felt the change. For them there was now an empty place at home. They missed the old growler who had hated every single one of them in school—only later to love them all, both good and bad, and who was always ready with his ridiculous "He was my best boy!" about each of them.

The children took their recess early, and rushed out before Pelle had given the signal; Fris trotted off as usual into the village, where he would stay the customary two hours. The girls gathered in a flock near the outhouses to eat their lunches, and the boys circled around the playground like birds let loose from a cage.

Pelle was quite angry at the insubordination, and wondered how he could make himself respected—today he had had the other boys against him. He dashed across the playground like a circling gull, his body tilted and his arms stretched out like a pair of wings. Most of them made room for him, and those who didn't move willingly were shoved aside just the same. His position was threatened, and he kept in constant motion—as if to keep the question hovering until a chance to strike presented itself.

This went on for some time; he knocked some over and struck out at others in his flight, while his offended sense of power grew—he wanted to make enemies of them all. They began to gather like rats over by the climbing bars, and suddenly he had the whole pack on top of him. He tried to get up and shake them off, flinging them in every direction— but he couldn't; down through the heap came their remorseless knuckles, making him grimace in pain. He worked away doggedly, but it had no effect until he got wild and resorted to less refined tactics—poking his fingers into eyes, noses, throats, or wherever he could. That thinned them out, and he was able to get up and toss one last little fellow across the playground.

Pelle was well bruised and quite out of breath—but happy. The whole pack stood there gaping and let him brush himself off—he was the victor. He went over to the girls with his torn shirt, and they fastened it with pins and gave him candy. In return he tied two of them together by their pigtails; they screamed and let him pull them around without getting mad—it was all just the way it should be.

But he was not completely confident in his victory. He could not— like Henrik Bødker in his day—walk right through the whole flock with his hands in his pockets right after a battle, pretending that they didn't exist. He had to keep stealing glances at them as he sauntered down to the beach, trying with all his might to calm his breathing; next to crying, being out of breath was the greatest disgrace that could befall you.

Pelle walked along the beach, regretting that he hadn't leapt on them again right away while the flush of victory was still upon him—it was too late now. Then they might have said about him too that he could lick the whole class at once; now he would have to be content with being the strongest boy in the school.

A wild war-whoop from the school gave him a start; the whole swarm of boys was coming around the end of the house with sticks and pieces of wood in their hands. Pelle knew what was at stake if he retreated, so he forced himself to stand quietly waiting even though his legs twitched. But suddenly they made a wild rush at him, and with a leap he turned to flee. There lay the sea barring his way, closely packed with heaving ice. He ran out onto an ice floe, jumped over to the next one, which wasn't big enough to bear him—had to keep going.

The idea of flight possessed him and made the fear of what was pursuing him enormously great. The blocks of ice gave way beneath him; he had to leap from piece to piece. His feet moved as fast as fingers over the keys of a piano—he noticed just enough to head for the harbor breakwater. The others stood gaping on the beach as Pelle danced across the water like a rock skipping over the sea. The pieces of ice bobbed under as soon as he touched them, or turned up on edge; but Pelle slipped and slid past with the barest touch on them, flinging himself to one side with lightning speed, shifting direction in the middle of a leap like a cat. It was like a dance on red-hot iron, he picked up his feet so quickly, leaping to a new spot and then leaping again. The water spurted up from the pieces of ice he touched, and behind him stretched a crooked trail of disturbed ice and water all the way back to the place where the boys stood, holding their breath. There was nobody like Pelle—not one of them could do what he was doing out there! When with a final leap he dived onto the breakwater on his stomach, they yelled hurray. Pelle had triumphed in his flight!

He lay on the breakwater, exhausted and gasping for breath, and gazed dully at a brig that had cast anchor near the village. A boat was rowing in—perhaps with a sick man who had to be quarantined. The seedy look of the vessel told that she had been out on a winter voyage, in ice and heavy seas.

Fishermen came down from the cottages and sauntered out to the spot where the boat would come in, and all the schoolchildren followed. In the stern of the boat sat an elderly, weatherbeaten man with a fringe of beard around his face; he was dressed in blue, and in front of him stood a sea chest. "Hey, that's Bosun Olsen!" Pelle heard one fisherman say. Then the man stepped ashore and shook hands with all of them. The fishermen and the schoolchildren closed around him in a tight circle.

Pelle made his way up—he sneaked along behind boats and sheds; as soon as he was hidden by the schoolhouse, he took off running straight across the fields to Stone Farm. His grief burned bitterly in his throat; a feeling of shame made him stay far away from houses and people. The package that he hadn't had the chance to deliver in the morning was like an obvious witness to everyone of his shame, and he threw it away into a marl pit as he ran.

He didn't want to go through the courtyard, but pounded on the outside door to the stable. "Are you home already?" exclaimed Lasse, pleased.

"Now—now Madam Olsen's husband has come home!" panted Pelle and went past his father without looking at him.

For Lasse it was as if the world exploded and the pieces bored into his flesh. Everything forsook him; he moved around shaking and picked up everything the wrong way. He couldn't talk; everything in him had come to a standstill. He had picked up a caulking tool and was walking back and forth, staring upward.

Then Pelle went over to him. "What are you going to do with that?" he asked harshly.

Lasse dropped the tool and began to lament about the sadness and poverty of existence. One feather fell off here, and another there; finally you stood there trampling in the mud like a featherless bird—old and worn out and robbed of any hope of a happy old age. He went on complaining like this under his breath, and the complaining comforted him.

Pelle did not respond. He only thought of the disgrace and the shame that had befallen them, and he found no solace.

Next morning he took his lunch and went off as usual, but when he was halfway to school he lay down under a thicket. There he lay, fuming and half-frozen, until it was about time for school to be over; then he went home. He repeated this for several days. Toward his father he was silent, almost mean. Lasse went around complaining, and Pelle had enough of his own troubles. Each of them moved in his own world, and there was no bridge in between; neither of them had a kind word to say to the other.

But one day when Pelle came sneaking home this way, Lasse met him with a radiant face and weak knees. "Why the devil should you go around worrying?" he said, squinting and turning his blinking eyes on Pelle—for the first time since the bad news had arrived. "Look here at the new sweetheart I've found—give her a kiss, lad!" Lasse pulled a bottle of aquavit out of the straw and held it out to him.

Pelle pushed it angrily away.

"So you're too grand, are you?" said Lasse. "All right, it would be a sin and a shame to waste good on bad." He put the bottle to his lips and sailed over backwards.

"Papa, stop that!" yelled Pelle, bursting into tears and shaking his father's arm so the liquor sloshed out.

"Hey hey!" said Lasse in astonishment, wiping his mouth with the back of his hand. "She's certainly lively, hey hey!" He gripped the bottle with both hands and held it steady, as if it had tried to get away from him. "So you're being naughty, are you?" Then his eye fell on Pelle. "And you're crying! Has someone hurt you? Don't you know that your father's name is Lasse—Lasse Karlsson from Kungstorp? Don't be afraid, for Lasse's here! And he'll make the whole wide world answer for it."

Pelle saw that his father was rapidly becoming more befuddled, and ought to be put to bed so that no one would come and find him lying on the floor. "Come on, Papa," he begged.

"All right, I'll go now. I'll make him pay for it, if it's old Beelzebub from Småland himself—don't cry!" Lasse was heading for the yard.

Pelle blocked his way. "Now you have to come with me, Papa. There's no one for you to settle accounts with for anything."

"Isn't there? But you're crying! That goddamned landowner will have to answer to me for all these years!"

This made Pelle scared. "But Papa, Papa!" he cried. "Don't go up there! He'll be furious, he'll turn us out! Remember, you're drunk!"

"Sure, of course I'm drunk, but I'm not malicious." He stood fumbling with the hook that fastened the lower half of the door.

It was wrong to lay a hand on your own father, but now Pelle was compelled to put aside all such scruples. He took a firm grip on the old man's collar. "Now you come with me!" he said, dragging him toward their room.

Lasse laughed and hiccuped and struggled; he clutched hold of anything he could—the posts and the animals' tails—as Pelle dragged him along. He had hold of him from behind and was half carrying him; in the doorway they stuck fast, as the old man held on with both hands. Pelle had to let go of him and knock his arms away so that he fell; then he dragged him over to the bed.

Lasse laughed foolishly the whole time, as if it were a game, behaving wickedly whenever he could. Once or twice when Pelle's back was turned, he tried to get up; his eyes had almost disappeared, but there was a sly expression around his mouth—he was like a naughty child. Suddenly he fell back in a heavy sleep.

The next day was a school holiday, so there was no need for Pelle to hide. Lasse was ashamed and slunk around humbly. He must have had a very clear idea of what had happened the day before, for suddenly he touched Pelle's arm. "You're like Noah's good son, who covered up his father's shame," he said. "But Lasse is a beast. It's been a hard blow for me, believe me! But I know quite well that it doesn't help matters to drink yourself silly; it's a poorly buried sorrow that is rooted out by liquor. What's hidden in the snow comes up in the thaw, as the saying goes."

Pelle did not answer.

"How are people taking it?" asked Lasse cautiously. He had now reached the point of thinking about the shameful side of the matter. "I don't think they know about it yet here at the farm; but what are they saying outside?"

"How should I know?" answered Pelle sullenly.

"Then you haven't heard anything?"

"Do you think I would go to school to be jeered at by all of them?" Pelle was almost in tears again.

"So you've been wandering around and letting your father believe that you'd gone to school? That wasn't right of you. But I won't find fault with you, considering all the disgrace I've brought on your self-respecting soul. But what if you get in trouble for playing hooky, even if you don't deserve it? Misfortunes go hand in hand, and evils multiply like lice in a fur coat. We have to think what we should do, we two—so that things won't go too badly for us."

Lasse walked briskly into their room and returned with the bottle, took out the cork, and let the liquor run slowly out onto the floor. Pelle looked at him in amazement. "God forgive me for abusing his gifts," said Lasse, "but it's a bad temptation to have on hand when you have an aching heart. And now if I give you my word that you will never again see me the way I was yesterday, won't you have a try at school again tomorrow—and try to get over it gradually? We might get in trouble with the authorities themselves if you keep on staying away; there's probably a heavy punishment for that sort of thing in this country."

Pelle promised and kept his word. But he was prepared for the worst, and secretly slipped a knuckleduster into his pocket that Erik had used in his prime when he went to open-air dances and other places where a man might have to strike a blow for his girl. There was no need for it, however; the boys were totally preoccupied with a ship that had to be run aground to prevent her from sinking, and now lay discharging her cargo of wheat into the boats of the village. In the harbor the wheat was already lying in great heaps, wet and swollen with the salt water.

And a few days later, when this had grown stale, something happened that put a stop to Pelle's school days forever. The children were busy at arithmetic with a constant murmur, and clattering with their slates. Fris was sitting as usual in his place, with his head against the wall and his hands resting on the desk; his glazed eyes were somewhere out in space, and not a movement betrayed that he was alive. It was his usual position, and he had been sitting that way ever since recess.

The children grew restless; it was nearly time for them to go home. A farmer's son who had a watch held it up so that Pelle could see it, and said "Two" out loud. They noisily put away their slates and began to fight. Fris generally woke up at this noise of departure, but he didn't move. Then they tramped out; in passing, one of the girls out of mischief stroked the schoolmaster's hand. She jumped back in fright. "He's completely cold!" she said, shuddering and drawing back behind the others.

They stood in a semicircle around the desk and tried to see into Fris's half-closed eyes, then Pelle went up the two steps and laid his hand on his teacher's shoulder. "We're going home," he said in an unnatural voice. Fris's arm dropped stiffly from the desk, and Pelle had to hold up his body. "He's dead!" The words passed like a shiver over the children's lips.

Fris was dead—dead at his post, as the honest folks of the parish expressed it. Pelle had finished his schooling for good and could breathe freely.

He helped his father at home, and they were happy together and drew closer now that there was no third person to stand between them. The gibes from the others on the farm were not worth paying attention to; Lasse had been on the farm a long time, and knew too much about each of them, so he could bite back. He basked in Pelle's gentle, childlike nature and kept the talk flowing incessantly. He kept on coming back to the same thing. "I'm glad I had you, because if you hadn't held back that time when I was bent on moving down to Madam Olsen's, we would have been in big trouble. I think he might have killed us in his rage. You were my guardian angel, the way you've always been."

For Pelle, Lasse's words were as pleasant as caresses; he was happy, and more of a child than his years let on.

But one Saturday he came home from the pastor's completely changed; he drooped like a dead herring, did not go over and eat dinner, but came straight in through the outer door and threw himself onto a pile of hay.

"What's the matter now?" asked Lasse, coming over to him. "Has someone been mean to you?"

Pelle didn't answer, but lay plucking at the hay. Lasse was going to turn his face up to him, but Pelle buried it in the hay. "Can't you even trust your own father? You know I don't want anything on earth except your happiness." Lasse's voice was sad.

"I'm going to be thrown out," Pelle managed to say before he burrowed into the hay to hold back his tears.

"No, you can't be serious?" Lasse started to tremble. "But what have you done?"

"I've beaten the pastor's son to a pulp."

"Oh no, that's about the worst thing you could have done—lay hands on the pastor's son! I'm sure he must have deserved it, but ... you still shouldn't have done it. Unless he accused you of stealing; no honest man has to put up with that from anyone, not even the king himself."

"He ... he called you Madam Olsen's concubine." Pelle had trouble getting this out.

Lasse's mouth grew hard and he clenched his fists. "Oh, he did, did he! If I had him here I'd kick his guts out, the little monkey! You gave him something he'll remember for a long time, I hope?"

"Oh no, it wasn't much, because he wouldn't stand up to me—he threw himself down and screamed. And then the pastor came!"

For a while Lasse's face was contorted with rage, and every so often he muttered a threat. Then he turned to Pelle. "So they threw you out, too?—Just because you stood up for your old father? I'm always getting you into trouble, though I'm only thinking of your welfare. But what are we going to do now?"

"I won't stay here any longer," said Pelle firmly.

"No, let's get away from here; nothing has ever grown on this farm for us but wormwood. Maybe there are new, happy days waiting for us out there. And there are probably pastors everywhere. If the two of us work together at some good job out there, we'll make money like grass. Then someday we'll go up to a pastor and throw down 50 kroner right before his eyes, and it wouldn't surprise me if he didn't confirm you on the spot—and maybe let himself be kicked in the butt too. Those kinds of people are very fond of money."

Lasse had drawn himself up in his anger, and had a sharp look in his eyes. He walked quickly along the feed alley, flinging things around carelessly; Pelle's adventurous proposal had infected him with youth. While they were working they gathered all their things together and packed the green chest. "There will be some wide eyes here on the farm tomorrow morning when they come and find the nest empty," said Pelle cheerfully. Lasse chuckled.

Their plan was to take shelter with Kalle for a day or two, while they surveyed what the world might offer. When everything was done in the evening, they picked up the green chest between them and sneaked out through the outside door into the field. The chest was heavy, and the darkness didn't make walking any easier. They moved on with little jolts, changed hands, and rested. "We've got the night ahead of us!" said Lasse cheerfully.

He was quite animated; while they sat resting on the chest he talked about everything that was in store for them. When he came to a stand-still Pelle would start in. Neither of them had made any definite plans for their future; they simply expected a regular fairy tale, with its inconceivable surprises. All the specific possibilities that they were capable of imagining fell so far short of what *must* come that they didn't bother, but abandoned themselves to the profusion of them.

Lasse was not sure-footed in the dark, and more and more often he had to set down his burden. He grew weary and out of breath, and the cheerful words faded from his lips. "Oh, it's so heavy," he sighed. "What a lot of junk you scrape together over the years." Then he sat down on the chest, gasping for breath—he couldn't go on. "If only we had something to pick us up a little," he said faintly. "It's so dark and gloomy tonight."

"Help me get it onto my back," said Pelle, "and I'll carry it a little way."

Lasse wouldn't at first, but then gave in, and they moved on again; he ran on in front to give warning of ditches and walls. "What if brother Kalle can't take us in?" he said all of a sudden.

"I'm sure he can—there's Grandma's bed; that's big enough for two."

"But what if we don't find anything to do, then we'll be a burden on him."

"Oh, we'll find something all right. There's a shortage of laborers everywhere."

"Yes, they'll be glad to take you on, but I'm really too old to offer myself for hire." Lasse had lost all hope, and he was undermining Pelle's too.

"I can't go on anymore," said Pelle, letting the chest drop. They stood with their arms hanging and stared into the blackness at nothing in particular; Lasse showed no desire to take hold again, and Pelle was too worn out. The night lay dark around them and made everything seem so forsaken, as if the two of them were floating all alone in space.

"Well, we ought to be getting on," said Pelle, taking a handle of the chest; when Lasse didn't move, he dropped it and sat down. They sat back to back, and neither could find the right words to say—the distance between them seemed to grow greater and greater.

Lasse shivered with the night cold. "If only we were home in our good bed," he sighed.

Pelle was almost wishing he had been alone, then he would have gone on to the end. The old man was just as heavy to drag along as the chest.

"I think I'll go back again," said Lasse at last, crestfallen. "I guess I'm no good at traveling the open road. And you'll never be confirmed if we go on like this! Suppose we go back and get Kongstrup to put in a good word for us with the pastor." Lasse stood there holding on to one handle of the chest.

Pelle sat there for a moment as if he hadn't heard a thing. Then he silently took hold, and they trudged on homeward in a laborious journey across the fields. Every other minute Pelle got tired and had to rest; now that they were going home, Lasse had the most stamina. "I think I could carry it a little way by myself—if you'd help me get it onto my back," he said. But Pelle wouldn't hear of it.

"Whew!" sighed Lasse with pleasure when they once again stood in the warmth of the cow stable and heard the animals breathing in lazy well-being—"it's comfortable here. It's almost like coming into your childhood home. I think I would know this stable by the air, if they led me into it blindfolded anywhere in the world."

And now that they were home again, Pelle too couldn't help thinking that it really was nice.

XXIII

On Sunday morning, between the watering and the midday feeding, Lasse and Pelle walked up the high stone steps. They took off their wooden shoes in the corridor, and stood and shook themselves outside the door of the office—their gray socks were full of chaff and dirt. Lasse raised his hand to knock, but drew it back. "Have you blown your nose properly?" he whispered, with a look of anxiety on his face. Pelle sniffed one more time, then wiped his nose on his shirtsleeve.

Lasse raised his hand again; he looked greatly oppressed. "You might at least keep quiet!" he said irritably to Pelle, who was standing as still as a mouse. Lasse's knuckles were poised in the air two or three times before they fell upon the door; then he stood with his forehead close to the panel and listened. "There's no one there," he whispered irresolutely.

"Just go in," said Pelle. "We can't stand here all day."

"Then you can go first, if you think you know better how to act!" said Lasse, offended.

Pelle quickly opened the door and stepped inside. There was no one in the office, but the door was open to the parlor, and they could hear the sound of Kongstrup's comfortable breathing. "Who's there?" he asked.

"It's Lasse and Pelle," replied Lasse in a voice that did not sound altogether brave.

"Will you come in here?"

Kongstrup was lying on the sofa reading an almanac, and on the table beside him stood a pile of old almanacs and a tray full of cookies.

He didn't raise his eyes from his book, not even when his hand moved routinely to the tray for something to put in his mouth. He lay nibbling and swallowing while he read; not a glance did he give them, not a question about what they wanted, or anything to get started. It was like being sent out to plow without knowing where. He must have been in the middle of something exciting.

"Well, what do you want?" asked Kongstrup at last in his lethargic voice.

"Well . . . well, you see, the master must excuse us for coming like this about something that doesn't concern the farm. But as matters now stand, we don't have anyone to turn to, and so I told the lad: 'The master won't be angry, I'm sure; many a time he's been kind to us poor souls' — and so on. Now it's true in this world that even if you're a poor wretch who's only fit to do others' dirty work, the Almighty has still given you a father's heart. And it hurts to see a father's sin tripping up his son."

Lasse came to a stop. He had thought it all out beforehand, and arranged it so that it would lead up to the matter itself in a shrewd, dignified way. But now it was all in a muddle like a slattern's handkerchief, and the master didn't look as if he had understood a single word. He lay there, taking a cookie now and then, and looking helplessly toward the door.

"And sometimes a man gets tired of being single," Lasse started in once again, but at once gave up trying to continue. No matter how the hell he started off, he went around and around the thing and couldn't get hold of it—and now Kongstrup began to read again. A tiny question from him might have led to the heart of it; but he just stuffed his mouth and began chewing vigorously.

Lasse was outwardly disheartened and inwardly angry, as he stood there preparing to leave. Pelle was staring at the paintings and the shiny old mahogany furniture, appraising each item.

Then energetic steps resounded through the rooms—you could follow their progress all the way from the kitchen. Kongstrup's eyes brightened, and Lasse straightened himself up.

"Are you two here?" said Mrs. Kongstrup in her confident manner that indicated so much solicitude. "But do sit down! Why didn't you offer them a seat, Father?"

Lasse and Pelle sat down, and the mistress seated herself beside her husband, with her arm leaning on his pillow. "How are you getting on, Kongstrup? Have you been resting?" she asked sympathetically, patting his shoulder. Kongstrup gave a little grunt—it could mean yes or no, or nothing at all.

"And what about you two? Do you need money?"

"No, it's the lad—he's to be dismissed from the confirmation class," said Lasse straight out. With the mistress you couldn't help being confident too.

"Are you to be dismissed?" she exclaimed, looking at Pelle familiarly. "What have you done?"

"Oh, I kicked the pastor's son."

"And what did you do that for?"

"Because he wouldn't fight, but threw himself on the ground."

Mrs. Kongstrup laughed and nudged her husband. "Yes, I see—but what had he done to you?"

"He said wicked things about Papa Lasse."

"Did he say really nasty things?"

Pelle looked at her hard—she meant to get to the bottom of it all. "I won't tell you!" he declared firmly.

"Well, all right then—but then we can't do anything about it either."

"I might as well tell you," Lasse interrupted. "He called me Madam Olsen's concubine—from the Bible story, I suppose."

Kongstrup tried to suppress a chuckle, as if someone had whispered a dirty joke in his ear, and he couldn't help himself. The mistress herself was serious enough.

"I don't think I understand," she said, laying her hand on her husband's arm to subdue him. "Lasse will have to explain."

"It's because I was sweethearts with Madam Olsen in the village, who everyone assumed was a widow—and then her husband came home the other day. And so they gave me that nickname, I hear."

Kongstrup began his suppressed laughter again, and Lasse blinked in distress at it.

"Help yourselves to a cookie!" said Mrs. Kongstrup in a loud voice, pushing the tray toward them. This silenced Kongstrup; he lay and watched their assault on the cookie tray with attentive eyes.

Mrs. Kongstrup sat tapping the table with her middle finger while they chewed. "So that good boy Pelle got angry and kicked him, did he?" she said suddenly. There was fire in her eyes.

"Yes, that's something he never should have done," replied Lasse plaintively.

Mrs. Kongstrup fixed her eyes on him.

"No, because poor birds only exist to be pecked at. Well, I prefer the bird that pecks back and defends its nest, no matter how poor it is. All right, we shall see. And this boy is going to be confirmed? Why, of course! To think that I should be so forgetful! Then we'll have to start thinking about his clothes."

"That's two troubles taken care of," said Lasse as they went back down to the stable. "And did you notice how nicely I let her know that you were going to be confirmed? It was almost as though she realized it for herself. Now you'll see, you'll be as fine as a shop-boy in your clothes. People like the master and mistress know what it takes, once they've opened their purse. Well, now they got the whole truth straight out, but damn it all—they're only human too. You just have to come right out with it." Lasse couldn't get over how well it had turned out.

Pelle let the old man brag. "Do you think I'll get leather shoes from them too?" he asked.

"Sure, of course you will. And I wouldn't be surprised if they gave a confirmation party for you too. I say *they,* but she's the one in charge of everything; we have to be thankful for that. Did you notice that she always said *we*—we shall, and so on? It's nice of her, because he just lies there stuffing himself and leaves everything to her. He sure has it made; I think she'd walk through fire to please him. But she's the one in command, by God! Well, I suppose we shouldn't speak ill of anyone; to you she's like your own mother."

Mrs. Kongstrup said nothing about the result of her drive over to see the pastor—it wasn't her way to talk about things afterwards. But Lasse and Pelle once more walked the earth with a feeling of security; when *she* took up a matter, it was as good as settled.

One morning later in the week, the tailor came limping in with his scissors, tape measure, and pressing-iron; Pelle had to go down to the servants' room and be measured in every direction as if he were a prize animal. Up to now he had always had his clothes sewn based on guesswork. It was something new to have itinerant craftsmen at Stone Farm; since Kongstrup had come to power, neither shoemaker nor tailor had ever set foot in the servants' room. This was a return to the good old farm customs, and placed Stone Farm once more on a footing with the other farms. The people enjoyed it, and as often as they could they went down to the servants' room for a change of air, and to listen to one of the tailor's yarns. "It's the mistress who's in charge now!" they said to each other; there was good peasant blood in her hands, and she was returning things to the good old ways. Pelle walked over to the servants' room like a gentleman; he was fitted several times a day.

He was fitted for two whole suits, one of which was for Rud, who was going to be confirmed too. It would probably be the last thing that Rud and his mother would get at the farm. Mrs. Kongstrup had won her point, and they were to be evicted from the cottage in May. They would never dare set foot on Stone Farm again. Mrs. Kongstrup herself saw to it that they received what they were entitled to, but she didn't give out money if she could help it.

Pelle and Rud didn't seek each other out anymore—they seldom went to confirmation classes together. It was Pelle who had drawn back, when he grew tired of being on the lookout for Rud's continual treacheries. Pelle had grown taller and stronger than Rud, and his nature— perhaps because of his physical superiority over others—had taken more open paths. In ability to master a task or learn it by heart, Rud was also the inferior; on the other hand, he could bewilder Pelle and the other boys if he started in with his practical understanding of human nature.

On the big day itself, Karl Johan drove Pelle and Lasse in the little one-horse carriage. "We're fine folk today!" said Lasse, beaming; he was quite flustered, even though he hadn't tasted any strong drink. There was a bottle of aquavit in the chest at home to treat the men with when the sacred ceremony was over; but Lasse was not a man to drink anything before he went to church. Pelle had not *touched* any food— that way God's Word would be most effective.

Pelle was radiant too, in spite of his hunger. He was dressed in brand-new twill—so new that it crackled every time he moved. On his feet he wore shoes with elastic sides, which had once belonged to Kongstrup himself. They were too big, but "a sausage that's too long can always be fixed," as Lasse said. He put in thick insoles and stuffed paper in the toes, and Pelle put on two pair of socks—then the shoes fit as if they had been cast for his feet. On his head he wore a blue cap that he had chosen himself down at the store. There was room to grow into it; it rested on his protruding ears, which for the occasion were blushing like two roses. Around the cap was a broad band, into which rakes, scythes, and flails were woven, interlaced with sheaves all the way around.

"It's a good thing you came," said Pelle as they drove up to the church and found themselves among so many people. Lasse had almost not come along, because the man who was going to look after the animals while he was away had to go off for the veterinary at the last minute. But Karna came and offered to water the animals and give them the midday feed, although neither could truthfully say that they had behaved as they should have toward her.

"Have you got that thing with you?" whispered Lasse when they were inside the church. Pelle felt in his pocket and nodded; there lay the little round piece of lignum vitæ that would carry him through the difficulties of the day. "Just you answer loud and straight out," whispered Lasse as he slipped into a pew in the back.

Pelle did answer straight out; his voice sounded wonderful in the spacious church, thought Lasse. And the pastor did absolutely nothing in revenge; he treated Pelle exactly as he did the others. At the most solemn part of the ceremony, Lasse thought of Karna, and how touching she was in her loyalty. He scolded himself under his breath and made a holy vow. She shouldn't have to sigh in vain any longer.

For a whole month Lasse's thoughts had been preoccupied with Karna, first favorably, then unfavorably. But at this solemn moment when Pelle was just taking the great step into the future and Lasse's soul was moved in so many ways, the thought of Karna's devotion broke over him as heavily as a song about unrequited love, which at last claims its due.

Lasse shook hands with Pelle. "Congratulations and God bless you!" he said in a trembling voice. The wish also included his own vow, and he had a hard time keeping silent about his decision, he was so moved. "Congratulations and God bless you!" was heard on all sides; Pelle went around shaking hands with his friends. Then they drove home.

"It all went so incredibly smoothly for you," said Lasse proudly, "and now you're a man, you know!"

"Yes, now you'll have to find a sweetheart!" said Karl Johan.

Pelle just laughed.

They had the afternoon off. First Pelle had to go up to his master and mistress to thank them for his clothes and receive their congratulations; Mrs. Kongstrup gave him red-currant wine and cake, and Kongstrup gave him a 2-krone piece.

Then they went up to Kalle's by the quarry. Pelle had to show off his new clothes and say goodbye to them; it was only a couple of weeks until May Day. Lasse was going to use the opportunity to obtain, in all secrecy, information about a house that was for sale on the heath.

XXIV

They still talked about it every day during the short time that was left. Lasse, who had always had the thought of leaving on his mind—and had only stayed on year after year for the boy's sake—was so sluggish, now that there was nothing to hold him back. He was unwilling to lose Pelle, and did everything he could to hold on to him; but nothing would induce him to go out into the world again.

"Stay here!" he said persuasively. "We'll talk to the mistress and she'll take you on at a proper wage. You're both strong and handy—and she's always looked on you with a kindly eye."

But Pelle didn't want to serve the landowner; there was no prestige or future in it. He wanted to be something great, but there was no chance of that out here in the country—here he would be following the rumps of the cows all his days. He wanted to go to town—maybe even farther, across the sea to the King's Copenhagen.

"You should come too!" he said. "Then we'll get rich even faster and be able to buy a big farm!"

"Yes, yes," said Lasse, slowly nodding his head, "that's fine for you to say. But things don't always work out the way the pastor preaches. We could be left penniless! What does anyone know about the future?"

"Oh, I'll manage," said Pelle, nodding confidently. "Don't you think I can try my hand at anything I like?"

"But I didn't give notice in time either," said Lasse as an excuse.

"Then run away!"

But Lasse would not do that.

"No, I'll stay and work toward getting something for myself around here," he said—a little evasively. "It would be nice for you too, to have a home that you could visit once in a while. And if things don't work out for you out there, it wouldn't be bad to have something to fall back on. You might get sick, or something else might happen—you can't always count on the world. Out there you've got to have calluses all over you."

Pelle didn't answer. The part about a home sounded nice enough; he understood quite well that it was Karna who was weighing down the other end of the balance. Well, she'd put all his clothes in order for his departure, and she'd always been a good soul—he didn't have anything against it!

It would be hard to live apart from Papa Lasse, but Pelle had to go. Away!—it was as if spring was shouting that word in his ears. Here he knew every rock in the landscape and every tree—yes, every twig on the trees as well; there was nothing more here that could fill his blue eyes and his big ears, and satisfy his soul.

The day before May Day they packed up Pelle's things. Lasse knelt before the green chest; every article was carefully folded and commented on before he placed it in the canvas bag that would serve Pelle as a suitcase.

"Now remember not to wear your socks too long before you mend them!" said Lasse, putting darning yarn on one side. "He who mends his things in time is spared half the work and all the shame."

"I won't forget," said Pelle quietly.

Lasse was weighing a folded shirt in his hand. "The one you've got on has just been washed," he said thoughtfully. "But I don't know—two shirts are probably not enough out in the world. Take one of mine; I can always manage to get another by the time I want a change. And remember never to wear it more than two weeks! You, young and healthy though you are, could easily get lice—and be jeered at by the whole town. Such a thing would not be tolerated in anyone who wants to make a reputation. At the worst you can do a little washing for yourself; you could go down to the beach in the evening, if nothing else!"

"Do they wear wooden shoes in town?" asked Pelle.

"Not people who want to amount to something! I think you'd better let me keep your wooden shoes, and you take my boots instead;

they always look nice on a man, even if they're old. You can wear them for your journey tomorrow, and save your good shoes."

The new clothes were placed in the top of the bag, wrapped up in an old shirt to keep them clean.

"Now I think we've got everything," said Lasse, with a searching glance at the green chest; there wasn't much left in it. "All right, then we'll tie it up in God's name, and pray that you may arrive safely — wherever you decide to go!" Lasse tied up the sack; he was not happy at all.

"You have to say a proper goodbye to everyone on the farm, so that they won't have anything to scratch my eyes out for afterwards," said Lasse after a moment. "And I'd like you to thank Karna nicely for putting everything in such good order. It isn't everyone who would have taken the trouble."

"Yes, I'll do that," said Pelle softly; his voice wasn't working quite right today.

Pelle was up and dressed at earliest daybreak; mist lay over the sea and augured well for the day. He went around well scrubbed and combed, looking at everything wide-eyed; his hands were in his pockets. The blue cotton clothes he had worn to his confirmation classes had been washed and freshly ironed; they still looked good on him. And the tabs of the old leather boots, which were a relic from Lasse's prime, stuck out almost as much as his ears.

He had said his "Goodbye and thank you for all your kindness!" to everybody on the farm — even Erik; and he had eaten a good meal of bacon. Now he was walking about the stable collecting himself: shaking the bull by the horns and letting the calves suck on his fingers — that was a sort of farewell too! The cows stuck their noses up close to him and took a long, comfortable breath as he passed by; the bull playfully tossed its head at him. And right on his heels came Lasse; he didn't say much, but he kept close to the boy.

It was so good to be here, and the feeling sank gently over Pelle every time a cow licked herself, or the warm vapor rose toward him from freshly fallen dung. Every sound was like a mother's caress, and every object was a familiar toy, with which the brightest world could be built. On the posts all around there were pictures that he had carved; Lasse had smeared cow dung over them so the master wouldn't come and say that they were destroying everything.

Pelle was not thinking, but went about in a dreamy state; it all sank so warmly and heavily through his child's mind. He took out his knife and grabbed hold of the bull's horn, as if he were going to carve something on it. "He won't let you do that," said Lasse, surprised. "Try one of the steers instead."

But Pelle put his knife back in his pocket; he hadn't intended to do anything. He strolled along the feed alley without aim or purpose. Lasse came over and took his hand.

"You'd better stay here a little longer," he said. "We're so comfortable here together."

But this put life into Pelle. He fixed his big, faithful eyes on his father, and then went down to their room.

Lasse followed him. "In God's name then, if it has to be," he said tonelessly, and took hold of the sack to help Pelle get it onto his back.

Pelle held out his hand. "Goodbye and thank you, Papa—for all your kindness," he said gently.

"Well, well; well, well," said Lasse, shaking his head—he couldn't manage anything else.

He went out with Pelle past the outbuildings and stopped there. Pelle walked on along the embankments with his sack on his back—up toward the highway. He turned around and nodded a few times; Lasse, overcome, stood gazing, with his hand shading his eyes—he had never looked so old.

Out in the fields they were driving the seed-harrow; Stone Farm was early with the planting this year. Kongstrup and his wife were strolling arm in arm beside a ditch. Every now and then they stopped and she pointed: they must have been talking about the crop. She leaned against him as they walked—she had really found peace in her love now.

Now Lasse turned and went in—how forlorn he looked! Pelle felt a quick desire to throw down the sack and run back and say something nice to him; it was an impulse that came and then blew away on the fresh morning breeze. His legs carried him forward, straight ahead, away, away! Up on a ridge the foreman was pacing off a field; Erik was walking right behind him, imitating him with foolish gestures.

On a level with the edge of the cliff, Pelle came to the wide highway. Here, he knew, Stone Farm and its lands would be lost to sight, and he put down his sack. Over there were the sand dunes by the sea, with every treetop visible; there was the pine tree that the yellowhammer always built its nest in. The creek was flowing milky white after the heavy thaw, and the meadow was starting to turn green. But the cairn was gone; decent people had removed it secretly when Niels Køller was drowned and the girl was expected home from prison.

And the farm stood out clearly in the morning light, with the high, white big house, the long rows of barns, and all the outbuildings. Every spot down there shone toward him so familiarly; the hardships he had endured were forgotten—or else they only enhanced the fond memories.

Pelle's childhood had been happy because of everything; mingled with weeping, it had been a song to life. Weeping, as well as joy, is heard as music; heard from a distance it becomes a song. And as Pelle gazed down upon the world of his childhood, only pleasant memories shimmered toward him through the bright air. Nothing else existed, or ever had.

He had seen enough of hardship and misfortune, but had survived it all; nothing had harmed him. With a child's voracity he had used it all to grow stronger. And now he stood here, healthy and strong—equipped with the Prophets, the Judges, the Apostles, the Ten Commandments, and a hundred and twenty hymns!—and turned the open, sweaty brow of a conqueror toward the world.

Before him lay the rich land, sloping toward the south and bounded by the sea. Far below stood two tall black chimneys against the background of the sea, and still farther to the south lay the town. Out from the town ran the paths of the sea to Sweden and to Copenhagen! This was the world—the great wide world itself!

Pelle became ravenously hungry at the sight of the great earth, and the first thing he did was to sit down on the crest of the hill with a view both backward and ahead, and eat all the food Karna had given him for the whole day. At least his stomach would have nothing to worry about!

He got up refreshed, put the sack on his back, and set off down to conquer the world, shouting a song at the top of his voice out into the bright day:

> A stranger I must wander
> Among the Englishmen;
> And with the folk in Africa
> My company will keep!
> And on this earth are also found
> The hardy Portuguese!
> And every kind of nation
> Under heaven's sky so blue.

TO THE READER

Author's Preface to the First Danish Edition, 1906

It would be futile to wander around looking for the literary father of this brave lad whom I am sending out into the world here, newly confirmed and full of appetite. For twelve years I have coddled him in my own way, and all of his joys and sorrows have resounded in myself since the time I could crawl—in my mind, in my guts, down my backbone. He is my own to the highest degree, and has every right—like the sons in the sagas when they left home—to demand a parting word from me. It will be easy enough for other people to notice all of his faults, but there is no one who knows him as well as I do.

Although he was not created with the wave of a hand, he still demands a lot of space—the account of Pelle the Conqueror's struggles and victories takes up four volumes. But that should not frighten off anyone in this country, where we are trained to handle the heftiest tomes right from the cradle.

And he ought to be accompanied by great throngs of people! *Pelle the Conqueror* is supposed to be a book about the proletariat—that is, about human beings themselves—who, naked and equipped only with good health and appetite, enlist in the service of life; about the bold stride of the worker across the earth on his endless, half-unconscious journey toward the light! No other social class has such a vast background for its path in life as does the peasantry, or such significant destinies—where the proletarian fights, it is always for fundamentals; *he* still remains a martyr to the most basic demands for justice.

Pelle will have his turn too. The second volume depicts his apprenticeship years in the little provincial town with its traditional artisan hierarchy; in the third volume he travels across the sea as a young journeyman—toward the King's Copenhagen—and becomes part of the rise of the workers; the last volume takes place in Copenhagen as it is today, thoroughly organized and controlled by the hands of the workers—*the people's Copenhagen*.

Fine fellow that he is, Pelle gets involved in all of it. And everything is intended to be echoed in him: in his footsteps resound the endless steps of the many who want to struggle forward; *his* sorrows and joys should serve as a foundation for their happiness in life.

Whether the book succeeds or not is up to the reader to judge. But to those who might be annoyed by a specific manner of publishing, I would say that the form of publication chosen here is the most natural, in the case of a work consisting of four thick, self-contained volumes — and the publishers deserve our thanks, because by printing the book in a relatively large edition at a very low price, they are making it possible for a young author to have such a lengthy work published at all.

The Author
Espergærde, February 28, 1906

AFTERWORD

Pelle the Conqueror is Martin Andersen Nexø's masterpiece, an auto-
biographical novel that traces the development of one boy growing up
during the turbulent changes of the late 19th century. It is also the story
of the development of the Danish workers' movement and the political
changes that were to determine the future of Denmark.

Martin Andersen Nexø (1869 – 1954) grew up in the slums of Copenhagen, the son of a stonemason and one of eleven children. Like Pelle,
he was born on June 26th and came to Bornholm with his family at the
age of eight. He too spent his childhood in poverty and was familiar
with the hard work of a cowherd, an apprentice shoemaker, and an
assistant stonemason. His descriptions of life on Stone Farm are taken
from his own experiences, and many of his Bornholm characters (particularly in Volume II) had their doubles in real life—much to the
chagrin of some of his acquaintances.

But *Pelle the Conqueror* goes beyond the scope of memoir and
autobiography. The narrative takes on an epic quality in its portrayal of
an entire class of people. It is the story of the rise of the proletariat from
a feudalistic agrarian society to a social-democratic industrial state.
Pelle's life mirrors the growth of the workers' movement as he becomes
more politically aware and finally takes an active role in his own destiny.

In 1894, Andersen Nexø was sent to Spain to convalesce from tuber-
culosis. There he encountered organized laborers who had a great
influence on his own political development. This same trip also convinced him to become a writer. In an article from 1934 Andersen Nexø
explains why:

> ... the sun overwhelmed me and I suffered at the thought of
> all those other people who were in as great a need as I was,
> but whom the sun could not reach to shine on, even though
> there was plenty of sun—and plenty of seats in the train too,
> plenty of everything! Involuntarily I came to people those
> empty seats, in the southern sun, in the trains, everywhere;
> and an entire society took possession of me and placed ever
> greater demands on me: life's downtrodden, *the passengers
> in the empty seats*. They were the ones who pressed the pen
> into my hand.

When *Pelle the Conqueror* was first published in 1906 – 1910, it did not sell well in Denmark. At that time, only the well-to-do could afford to buy books (13 Danish kroner for the four volumes was considered quite expensive at the time). And a lengthy story with a proletarian hero wasn't likely to have much appeal. In 1911, however, the book found its proper readership when *Pelle the Conqueror* was serialized in social democratic newspapers, both in Denmark and Germany. Since then, Andersen Nexø has become one of Denmark's most translated authors. *Pelle the Conqueror* exists in twenty-one languages, in numerous editions.

Unfortunately, Andersen Nexø's authorship is completely unknown to the English-speaking world today, largely because of the extremely poor English translations of his work. These old translations are riddled with errors and misinterpretations, and Andersen Nexø's wonderful, straightforward style has been completely lost. His earthy humor and robust sense of life are also missing, since the translations tended to omit any scenes or phrases that might offend a more prudish public. The 1913 translation of the present book, for example, omitted any references to sex (even barnyard procreation), bodily functions, body parts (the word "stomach" seemed to be particularly taboo), and anything else the translator deemed too immodest to put into print. Needless to say, this resulted in mysterious gaps in the story, as well as wreaking havoc with the author's style and intent.

Fjord Press is proud to inaugurate its Modern Classics series with this new, unabridged and unexpurgated translation of *Pelle the Conqueror, Volume I: Childhood,* which restores the author's original color and life to the text. And we hope you will look forward to reading the other three volumes about Pelle's life: *Volume II: Apprenticeship; Vol. III: The Great Struggle;* and *Volume IV: Daybreak*—all in new English translations.

Tiina Nunnally
Seattle, March 1989

Acknowledgments:
Omkring Pelle Erobreren, Ed. Børge Haumann (Copenhagen: Reitzel, 1975).
Litteraturhåndbogen (Copenhagen: Gyldendal, 1981).
A History of Scandinavian Literature, 1870–1980, by Sven H. Rossel (Minneapolis: University of Minnesota Press, 1982).

This book was typeset by Fjord Press Typography
in 10/12½ Stempel Garamond, a modern adaptation
by the Stempel foundry, Frankfurt,
of the classic French typeface
designed by Claude Garamond
in the 16th century.

Grateful acknowledgment is given to the following for the use of the
cover photograph by Rolf Konow from the film, *Pelle the Conqueror*

A FILM BY BILLE AUGUST

Miramax presents a Per Holst Production · A Bille August Film "Pelle the Conqueror"
Starring Max von Sydow · Pelle Hvenegaard ·Written and directed by Bille August
Based on the novel by Martin Andersen Nexø ·Director of photography Jørgen Persson
Production designer Anna Asp · Executive producer Per Holst

In cooperation with Svensk Filmindustri, the Danish Film Institute, the Swedish Film Institute,
the General Workers Union in Denmark, SID, and the Co-Production Fund
of Denmark's Radio/The Danish Film Institute

A Miramax Films Release © 1988 All Rights Reserved